BLESSINGS OF THE FATHER

Book Three

THE BOYS BREAK OUT!

Other Books By Mitch Reed

Blessings of the Father—Book One—Ties That Bind
Blessings of the Father—Book Two—LV is FAB
O.O.O. Obsessing On Obsession-the Documentary

Blessings Of The Father

Book Three

The Boys Break Out!

A Novel

Mitch Reed

iUniverse, Inc.
Bloomington

Blessings Of The Father—Book Three
The Boys Break Out!

This is a work of fiction. All of the characters, names, incidents, organizations, and dialogue in this novel are either the products of the author's imagination or are used fictitiously.

iUniverse books may be ordered through booksellers or by contacting:

iUniverse
1663 Liberty Drive
Bloomington, IN 47403
www.iuniverse.com
1-800-Authors (1-800-288-4677)

ISBN: 978-1-4401-6538-2 (sc)
ISBN: 978-1-4401-6539-9 (ebk)

Printed in the United States of America

iUniverse rev. date: 06/27/2013

DEDICATION

It's fitting that today is Mothers Day, May 10th, 2009. And since I have been blessed with such a wonderful Mother—as sainted as—any Jewish woman can imagine, I'd like to dedicate this volume to her.

Mom, I love you, and I thank you for making my time here—so exceptionally rich with life.

Happy Mother's Day, 2009

PUNCTUATION DISCLAIMER

Dear Reader:

At the risk of alienating you with my somewhat nonconformist grammatical and punctuation style, allow me to be upfront about it and explain. I believe that all languages are living, flowing, and yes—evolving. So too in my opinion—should the grammar and punctuation that supports and defines that language. I've simply taken that liberty and freedom upon myself in how I look at my grammar or punctuation. My use of both conforming and nonconforming grammar or punctuation is based on trying to convey a very comfortable or conversational style of writing . . . a genuine casualness hopefully comes through this way.

Our society today already openly embraces as well as utilizes a variety of nonconformist language shortcuts and systems to linguistically streamline, (shorthand) personalize, (texting abbreviations) or culturally focus (Ebonics). I believe this leaves both grammar and punctuation open to personalization too—so I've gone down my own road accordingly.

Grammatically speaking, I will always write my sentences and statements from the perspective of the naturalness and realism of the spoken, rather than the written word. This is number one~ as it supplants normal and conforming rules of grammar . . . why did I just use this mark: ~?

I've assigned enhanced meanings to certain punctuation marks I use in my books. I.E. I use ' . . .' to denote an afterthought to a preceding sentence or statement. This is opposed to where I use a dash — with or without an additional comma, for when the sentence needs a hard pause before continuing the same thought. I'll often use a comma alone for a short or soft pause, rather than just ending a complete thought. For the shortest or softest of pauses, I denote this by use of this mark: ~

My ultimate goal is to enhance the conversational style of my writing . . . not to insult anyone's knowledge of punctuation. I apologize now if it doesn't work for you . . . that's okay~ but for me—it does.

If you feel comfortable enough, try imagining reading my books as if someone is actually speaking the words audibly as you listen to the words being spoken . . . not merely reading them. You'll hopefully see where I was heading with this new casual style as a result.

Mitch Reed

PREAMBLE

"Marc, would you kill me if I confess something horrible to you?"

"I don't know Scoot; I guess it would depend on what you told me—along with the capitol crime laws of California. But on the whole, I don't care for the sound of this already."

"Okay—never mind then," he said.

"That's it . . . never mind? Do I look like an idiot Scoot—spill it Davis while you're still vertical. You know pal—death rarely comes when we're ready for it!"

"Alright Marc, it all started when I tracked down Stacy and gave her the tape of the boys from earlier today. She remembered the twins from our contest last year, along with my resignation naturally. I also suggested she check the news channels while watching the video. She agreed to that, but since she already remembered them from the contest, I'm pretty sure she would like them to do a crowd test for her."

"Fine, we'll have her get with Mom, when does she want to do it?"

"Bud, don't kill me but—tonight at 8 o'clock . . . here in the park."

"What! Are you going bloody crackers Scoot? I brought them here for some R&R for putting up with all the rehearsals and performing this afternoon. Now you want them to stop their fun and do some stupid test . . . tonight? What have you been smoking Scoot—but for God's sake, please tell me that was the last of it?"

"Marc, the crowd test wasn't my idea, so don't beat me up, but it's not any old test pal, believe me. In my opinion, it would be a critical benchmark for the twins to pass."

"What in the hell do you mean Scoot; what kind of benchmark?"

"Marc its simple, the boys have thus far performed either as amateurs or in an ideal and unusual situation, correct?"

"All right, I'll concede that fact, so what's your point Scoot?"

"Marc, we have totally unbiased and raw audiences here in the park, they're disinterested third parties if you will. If your boys can accomplish with our guests, what they did earlier this afternoon, we know we truly have something tangible. Stacy suggested the test I'm sure, strictly out of personal consideration for me, not to mention, our longstanding association. She's going way out on a limb doing this unauthorized, especially to help a soon-to-be-former Toonland producer, so just say the word buddy boy if you really don't want to consider it?"

"Damn it Scoot I hear you . . . why do you always have to complicate my decisions—with such sound logic?"

"Jesus, Marc, someone has to, what do you think about it now?"

"Honestly Scooter—I think—I had better call Mom first considering all of her bitching earlier!"

I picked my cell out of my pants' pocket to begin dialing home, as expected, Reg answered.

"Hi Reg, its Marc, everyone well?"

"Yes Marc, are you—and our fresh rising stars, having a good time then?"

"Yes, but damn Reg, that's a funny way of referring to the boys . . . still jazzed about the concert I see?"

"You know Marc, I'd love to garner credit for that quip, but I must defer to the news on the telly sir."

"Are you saying it's already been mentioned on the news Reg?"

"Oh yes Marc, and on all your stations. I'm afraid that poor Malcolm has been going bonkers keeping up with the VCR. I thought we finally had him trained . . . but alas, apparently not."

"Jesus, what was I thinking Reg? I never thought to prepare the TV's and VCR's to tape?"

"Malcolm's fine—now Marc. Of greater significance is what's being said by the press, it's very upbeat and positive."

"Great Reg, listen—is Mom free?"

"No Marc she's not, but by her own admission—she's—reasonably priced."

"Good show old bean, now may I speak to her?"

"Certainly Marc, let me fetch her."

"Careful Reg—don't throw her bone too far this time."

I thought for sure I would have Reg busting with my crack, but he was undaunted.

"Marc, might I be so bold as to suggest, that you leave the humor to the experts, while we leave you—to your soufflé."

"Oh Reg—that hurts, oh the pain . . ."

. . . "Save it for a rainy day Marcus, I've been down this road with you before, let me get Marilyn so I can end—my suffering". I swear to God; someone was rubbing off on him.

I was still in shock from his cracks moments later, when I finally had the 'reasonable' lady herself on the telephone.

"Hi dear, what's up?"

"Gee Mom, why don't you tell me? From what I hear from a certain valet, the boys are getting more airtime on the performance already?"

"Honestly son, I presumed that's why you were calling me?"

"No Mom, it wasn't my reason, but now that you mention it . . . look, never mind, here's the reason for my call. It seems that Scoot may be able to have the boys perform here tonight in Toonland. It's what they call a crowd test, and it would take place at around 8 o'clock if it materializes. Do I have your go-ahead to proceed with it, if the boys agree to it?"

"Marc, thank you. I appreciate your sensitivity in asking me."

"You know Mom, once you bark out the orders, I do usually listen."

"Yes son, whatever you and Scott decide, has my approval of course.

"Now let me fill you in—all of the local stations along with Fox and MSNBC nationally, have carried the grand opening today for the crusade. But they are all now spinning their focuses to include and promote the performance by the boys, it's been real gratifying Marc.

"They saw for themselves as they filmed the audience's reactions, along with more than a decent pick up of the music. Their stories were strong and flattering of the boys' talent, exceptionally so. One reporter suggested that they could stop selling the ice cream anytime they wanted. He suggested just putting them on a street corner with their keyboards and an empty ten-gallon hat to raise the money instead!"

"That's great Mom—and funny, but listen; did Dad figure the recorders out okay?" Mom started laughing at my question.

"Oh, I would say he did dear, your tutorial finally came back to him, but I don't know if poor Sofia will ever recover from it."

"Mom, what on earth did Dad do to poor Sofia?"

"Son it's not what he did per se, it's more what came out of his mouth—while he was doing it. He was trying to figure out all that hi-tech equipment of yours. And as usual, his mouth got away from him where unfortunately Sofia was the one to find it."

"Oh, say no more, I follow Mom. Listen I'm going to get back to Scoot, he's waving at a woman; it must be his old boss Stacy, the woman who's calling the shots this evening."

"Alright honey, let me know what happens, will you?"

"Of course Mom."

I hit the end button on my phone; Scoot seemed relieved that Mom had agreed in principle. I watched the mystery lady come up to us.

"Stacy, this is Marc Morgan, the twins' father."

"Hello Mr. Morgan, it's my pleasure to see you again."

"Again—Stacy, when did we meet?"

"I'm not sure we met per se, but I saw you and the boys the night of the contest."

"Oh yes, of course, so nice seeing you again too."

"Mr. Morgan, may I call you Marc?"

"Of course, I was going to suggest that myself, I hate sir names."

"Great, me too. Marc, at the same time I was watching Scott's tape, the boys were being featured on a piece on MSNBC. It appears they're getting some great responses from their performance for their charity effort earlier today."

"Yes, I heard it got some airtime on some stations from the boys' personal manager. Naturally that's wonderful to hear, as my foundation is the beneficiary of their charitable efforts," I added.

"Marc, given that, I want to give the boys a short twenty-to-thirty minute crowd test at the Futureworld Quad at eight o'clock tonight. If you give me the word, I'll call in some of our people to hear them."

"Scoot, you're the doctor, what say you?"

"Of course Marc, this is an incredible opportunity for them. Stacy please understand though, that I cannot speak for the boys' personal manager as far as anything beyond tonight's test. She likes to mull things over . . . she's likely to digest all of her options first. In short, there would not be an opportunity, I'm afraid, for any deep conversations or negotiations tonight."

"That's fine Scott, but if that's the case, let's not bring in our people, we can just film it instead."

"I'm okay with that, how about you Scoot?"

"Sure I agree, why disturb their weekend, and jade him or her into a negative mindset over a long drive on a day off—anyway?"

"Good point Scott, I never thought about that angle."

"See bud, that's why you're paying me the big bucks to handle the boys."

"Cute Scoot, but we also have to take into consideration that possibility with the twins themselves. I brought them here after all to relax and have fun.

I plan to respect their wishes on the subject. I would suggest we avoid getting too excited therefore until they've signed on to this little idea anyway."

"Marc I wouldn't be too worried about that, I spoke to them aboard Cedric. While I didn't have a clue about this naturally, I asked in general terms when they wanted to perform again. I wanted to gauge their responses to try to get an idea of their excitement level."

"What did they say Scoot?"

"Tre said the sooner the better, Tay was less anxious but wasn't negative on the idea by any means. He simply commented that he hadn't recovered yet from signing all of those autographs."

"The boys were approached for autographs Marc?"

"Yes Stacy, and far more than approached, I'd have to say they were mobbed!

And not just by the girls in attendance either. They must have signed somewhere near seven to eight hundred in all, wouldn't you agree Scooter?"

"Yes easily, I'd guess you're close with that number Marc, don't forget they were at it nearly an hour and a half."

"All right gentlemen—scratch my prior comment. I'm going to call in an executive, Saturday or not,—I want one here. You gentlemen should have mentioned this before; I'm surprised at you Scott—are you losing your instincts?"

"You know Stacy, I did say something to you, but it was when you grabbed that other phone call—remember? Perhaps you only heard my comment faintly?"

"Oh yes, I think I do remember something now, sorry Scott. But hey, let's not belabor it, at least I'm listening now, and this changes my entire perspective."

"How so Stacy, if you don't mind me asking?"

"No Marc, of course I don't mind. You see, initially your local crowd may have been simply motivated to show up from the press coverage for the fundraiser itself, as it's certainly for a good cause on a nice Saturday afternoon . . . get the picture? But people won't wait up to an hour or so, to have just any two eleven-year-olds sign an autograph, I'm certain of that. That audience knew better after hearing the boys perform—in a sense, they were foretelling the boys' future, don't you see? Candidly gentlemen and Scott correct me if you disagree—but you should never second guess an audience's reaction!"

"Yes Stacy, you're certainly right—I agree." Scott responded to his soon-to-be—former boss."

"So Marc, here's what we're going to do, first we'll ask your boys how they feel about doing this. And no pressure from you Scott Davis or you will have me to reckon with. You know, Marc is a pussycat compared to what I will do to you on your final way out the employee's gate.

"If the boys do agree, we don't change a thing to screw up their next couple of hours. What were your intended plans if any-for dinner Marc?"

"I made reservations to take them to 'the Door at Forty-Four'; Rudy promised them a crack on the harpsichord there. With these changes though, it might be smarter to stop in route—pick up something fast—you know . . . like a corn dog. We'll find a stand somewhere convenient to the Futureworld Quad. This will allow the boys their fun . . . besides—Scooter loves corn dogs. And after all, dinner at 'the Door at Forty-Four' takes two hours on a good night. I also have to fly us all home tonight."

"Marc, why rush home? Can't you all just spend the night at the resort as my guests? I can arrange a suite, clothing, and toiletries for all of you."

"I don't know Stacy; the boys have Sunday school tomorrow. And they have their friend with them who also attends the same school. I'm not sure his mother would be too happy letting him miss that?"

"Fair enough Marc, but why not call her to confirm that assumption?"

"Alright Stacy, I have her cell number, I'll call her. Damn, I'm already breaking one my own cardinal rules to allow this."

"That's mighty big of you bud. I know how much this one must hurt. But what the hell Marc, no one knew this was going to happen, did we? And we're merely considering this to extend the boys' good time and that's an admirable trade off as well. Besides, didn't Marilyn mention you were considering having your Dad tutor them instead?"

"You're right Scoot—on that basis, I'm okay with it if Carol agrees too."

While I attempted to find Carol's number, Scoot's cell rang as well. It was Beth . . . she and the girls were making their way to Mt. Splashdown, as Scoot announced their impending arrival.

Meanwhile, I found Carol's number and called it.

. . . "Carol, its Marc, has the coming out party begun yet?"

"No Marc not yet. Listen I caught the news, and my little ham along with the twins. Say, they are wonderful Marc, aren't they?"

"Yes and thanks, but that's more or less why I'm disturbing you."

"Oh Marc, you could never be a disturbance to any woman, at least not one with a bare ring finger."

"Cute Carol, but listen, how would you feel if your little ham missed Sunday school manana?"

"Is there a problem Marc—is he behaving?"

"Carol, he's been great, while having a ball—it's that something's come up with our plans. I may want to extend the trip into an overnight here, but only if you're okay with it."

"Oh sure, he gets to sleep in the same room with you, before I do—is that it?" Carol's momentary silence following her joke had me wondering if there wasn't a 'spot of truth' in her mock jealousy. But I had to say something.

"Honestly Carol, I have no comment to that one, I'm a proper gentleman after all."

"Fine Marc . . . avoid the subject, suit yourself, but tell him that I love him, and to try to mind his manners—not that he really has any! I was splitting over that one, I can assure you.

"When do you foresee getting back to Las Vegas Marc?"

"I'd be kidding you if I told you I knew for certain at the moment Carol. Right now, I'm not sure of any of this. We may yet still return tonight, although I doubt it now. Can I answer that question later tonight or should I just keep him either way until tomorrow afternoon?"

"Oh bless you Marc, I get my night out and my beauty sleep too—you've just been elevated to sainthood!" As I laughed.

"Good Carol, I'll call after twelve, or should I say later?"

"Twelve is fine, have a ball Marc, but thanks for everything."

"It's my pleasure Carol, talk to you tomorrow."

"Bye Marc." Carol hung up as I turned towards Scoot's probing expression.

"I guess this makes it official buddy boy?"

"Nope—not yet it doesn't, we still have two young rockers to ask, Scoot.

"Alright, well I guess we're about to find that out too, I just spied Larry I think—yeah, there they are bud."

"Hey guys, man that line still had some distance I guess?"

"Yes Dad, it was still a ways to go inside the mountain, but it was sure worth it . . . we're soaked too."

"Yes I can see that, but listen; do you two remember Stacy from the ToonCrooners contest?"

"Oh hello Miss, it's nice to see you again."

"Thank you young man—and what manners—now are you Tay or Tre?"

"Tre, Miss, and this is our best mate—Larry Levison."

"Well hello Larry, I guess you're planning on managing the boys'—right?"

"Look lady—I'm twelve . . . I still got my own life to mess up, you know?" Stacy was shocked with Larry's quick response I think.

"Oh Stacy, I apologize for being remiss, Larry is our resident stand up comedian. He has also offered to write their stage material too . . . he's brilliant."

"Marc please don't apologize to me—but I'd put him on the payroll immediately. I'm sure I'll have ample opportunity to get to know Larry—I'm so looking forward to it . . . actually."

"What's that suppose to mean lady, hey—are you sweet on Mr. M or something?"

"No Larry—I'm sweet on you—does that worry you?"

"Me—naw . . . but can you cook?"

"Why yes, Lawrence, I'm a fine cook."

"Oh, so it's Lawrence already? Well, what time's bedtime at your place then?"

"Oh I don't know, around eleven-thirty after the news, I suppose."

"Okay—I'm in."

We were all going crazy with our laughter, the twins especially.

Before our laughter had even ceased, Beth, Embeth, and Halley had joined us. With the way that family was hugging and kissing now, you would have thought they had been apart for a year—or more!

"Marc, how are you?"

"Great Beth, thanks for joining us—and hi girls."

"Hello Mr. Morgan."

"Now Embeth, I think we had better drop that formal Mr. Morgan stuff around here, why not call me Marc, or better yet—Uncle Marc?"

"Okay Uncle Marc, gee that does sounds good, doesn't it?"

"Yes sweetheart it does . . . and how are you this fine afternoon, Halley?"

"Oh I'm fine, how are you Uncle?"

"I'm great dear, now that's my idea of a question." I bent down to hug my new 'pretend' nieces as I received kisses to boot in return.

"Listen, would you three guys say hello to everyone?"

The boys and Larry got with the program quickly. After 'hello cousin' all around, including Larry insisting on the faux title, we sent the kids off for some ice cream.

Beth and Stacy were long-time friends since high school, so they were chatting away regarding Lawrence, Stacy's new beau. We listened and laughed as Beth was not making the connection yet.

When the kids returned, I grabbed the boys and Scoot to join me in a huddle of sorts.

"Guys, Scooter and I, have a situation we need to run by you."

"Is something wrong Daddy?"

"No son, nothing's wrong, it's very exciting honestly, but we don't know how you guys will feel about it? I want to go on record as being in favor of whatever you guys decide, it's up to you two. And Uncle Scooter won't talk you into something you don't want to do either."

"Jeeze HB, is there possibly something you want to get out to the guys and say—by maybe—next Tuesday?"

"Sorry Larry, I didn't mean to make you wait this long, but this does concern you as well."

"Well if I'm included too HB, get to the point for sure—hell I'm practically finished with puberty already!" God this kid was something else but my laughter showed it.

"Scoot, why don't you lay this out for our three amigos."

"Sure bud."

"Guys, what your Dad, and HB to you Larry may have eventually said by Tuesday next—was this. You two, have the opportunity to perform a twenty minute set here at 8 pm tonight on the Futureworld Quad. No one's going to force you boys to do this, if you prefer to go on the rides instead—or would rather not—tonight."

"Cool Uncle Scott, I've love to—how 'bout it Tay?"

"No problem here bro, I'm in, as long as there's no two hours of autographs afterwards, my hand's still aching from all the signing."

"Boys are you sure about this?"

"HB, cool it! My buds have spoken—we certainly don't need a whole new build up from you—again!"

"Oh forgive me Lar, I had no idea I was such a bore?"

"You're not a bore HB; you just talk too dang much without getting—anywhere . . . fast."

"My word, thank you Larry, I think?" God this kid was killing me.

"Now listen you three, I did promise you six good hours here which I meant. What with stealing away an hour for your preparations on top of playing, I'm rearranging things a bit. I cleared it with Carol that we are going to stay the night here—after all. Now was that succinct enough for you Lar?"

"Hell no HB, all you had to say was: boys we're spending the night! But not you—no way. With you, it's just not in the cards; with you it's—talk until someone shuts you up—what's wrong with you anyways?"

After I recovered, I continued.

"Gee Lar-man, maybe I should just hire you to write all my speeches then?"

"Hell's bells, HB—if you did—we'd all get to bed a whole lot earlier!"

That did it as we were all now rolling with hysterical laughter.

"All right guys, any objections to us spending the night—or Larry serving as speech and stage writer?"

"No."

"Okay Scoot, I guess it's now decided."

We all rejoined the ladies and girls. As the kids took in another two and a half hours of rides, Uncle Scoot and Stacy talked some. They covered the equipment needs while Stacy forwarded it on to her production techs.

Meanwhile Scoot sent Beth back home to pick up his set of Taylor's prerecorded synthesized instrument tracks. That alone would save nearly an hour with only minimal additional tracks to lay down as a result.

Time flew by, as I looked at my watch to see that we were now at six minutes to six. I suggested that the whole group join us at Forty-Four, if I was able to increase the party's size.

"Marc, you let me handle that and yes, I would love to join you all. I do have one condition though; I insist that Lawrence escorts me there of course?"

"Sure lady, are you kidding? At this point, as long as there's food at the end of the escortin', I'll put up with yah."

"Now Lawrence, wouldn't you prefer calling your lady by her given name of Stacy?" I chided.

"Now see HB, there you go again—why you couldn't have just said: Lar-man, call her Stacy?"

Meanwhile, Beth had now realized the connection of Larry's transformation to Stacy's—Lawrence.

"I'm sorry Lar; I'll try to do better next time alright?"

"Well see that you do! Stacy it would be my pleasure to escort you—see how it's done—HB?"

Larry extended his arm to Stacy in mock fashion as she took it, but wasn't able to stop from busting up either.

We got to, 'the door at Forty-Four' three minutes past six. Stacy approached Rudy at the podium. After a scant minute conversation, she returned to inform us that we would be seated imminently. Within seconds, we boarded their elevator up to the second floor then were escorted to a private dining room.

While we awaited our wait staff, Stacy excused herself to call her production office to conclude her arrangements. She returned in time to order, while I was hanging up on Mom filling her in on everything as well. I had also called Carol to confirm we were indeed spending the night.

Larry was super attentive to Stacy at our table, as he had been before in my own dining room. He had me in particular—impressed again now. Getting up to assist Stacy with her chair, along with standing when she left and subsequently returned. These were exceptional manners . . . evidential of great parenting at play here despite Larry's candid style of conversation. I would definitely make a point of bringing this all up to Carol tomorrow, as I'd already been remiss.

Larry was also giving the boys tips on working the audience; I found his comments intriguing, as his suggestions would have likely been my own . . . although—honestly shorter!

"Dad, will you ask Rudy if we can play the harpsichord, we'll be real careful with it—promise?"

"Stacy, do you think Rudy would oblige their request, he did promise he would consider it on our last visit?"

"Marc if he won't—I will. Besides, I for one would love to hear some of the classical roots of Tay 'n' Tre . . . the Morgan's while I wait to be served."

Stacy and I got up to escort the boys over to the priceless instrument that originally came from the Romanoff's palace in Russia. The placement of the harpsichord was ideal. Its sound carried throughout the entire maze of dining rooms without electronic amplification being necessary.

The boys sat quite gingerly on the bench for kids their age . . . here we witnessed great respect in play. They took a few moments, as they acclimated themselves. According to Trevor, they had only played on a harpsichord around a half dozen times in total.

Once they were set, they took turns with a marvelous assortment of classical movements. They played Mozart, Rachmaninov and Bach. As each piece was completed, polite applause followed coming from distant unseen diners. Most had no idea that they were listening to, two, eleven-year-old pishers taking turns at the ivories that much was certain.

All the same, over the ensuing minutes, a sizable group of on-lookers did start to amass around the harpsichord while they played. Most anyone who opted for the stairs for instance, stopped for a listen. Once seeing the two diminutive musicians sharing the keyboard yet playing so expertly, they became entranced naturally—so none of them moved further.

When the boys finished their performance to the generous applause of the restaurant, we went downstairs to thank Rudy personally. He was delighted, as he complimented them repeatedly on their wonderful playing and selections.

He refreshed his memory on their names again, along with some basic facts before we left to return to our impending dinner.

As we reached the mid-point of the staircase, we heard the restaurant's pre-recorded music track stop.

"Ladies and gentlemen, boys and girls, please join me in thanking our two talented harpsichordists this evening, Tay and Tre Morgan. And no, they are not with the London Philharmonic who entertained us earlier, these brothers join us this evening from Las Vegas, Nevada. And believe it or not folks; these twins are only eleven-years-old—thank you boys.

The restaurant reverberated now with thundering applause. As we reached the top of the second floor landing in the main dining room, guests naturally noticed us. They put two and two together quickly and stopped their conversations to give the boys a rousing ovation again. By the time we reached our private dining room, the applause was near deadening. Beth and the girls rewarded the boys with kisses, as Larry and Scoot congratulated them as well. Scoot also had a devious smile on his face now, which bothered me the moment I saw it.

"Scoot is there some reason why I shouldn't be alarmed with that smirk on your puss?"

"Yes bud—it's for a good reason, so—just relax."

"Fine, what is it?"

"You'll see, that's all."

"Moments later, we heard the piped music track stop as Rudy came on again.

"Ladies and gentlemen, but especially you boys and girls, I have been remiss. It seems that young Tre and Tay will be performing again this evening. They will offer a more contemporary selection of music at 8 pm at the Futureworld Quad."

"You know Scoot, you do have major cojonies, you know that don't you,—I thought we wanted a raw audience?"

"No sweat bud, but believe me, you'll be thanking me when it's standing room only later. And don't worry; this is a private dinner club, the audience will still be quite raw overall. Damn it man, relax will you?"

"Jesus Scoot, isn't this dinner thanks enough?" I was laughing at my friend now.

"I don't know bud; I guess we'll see about that, won't we?"

Owing to our upcoming performance, Rudy had arranged our meals expedited, so we were able to finish by 7:10. This had to have been record time for the place. At least during the time I worked there, it was.

As we exited the private dining room, the boys received more polite applause as one teen cutie even stopped Tre in his tracks to speak to him.

"I'll be seeing you at eight, so please look for me."

"Thank you, we will." Tre gave her a wink as we were leaving.

We boarded two large golf carts waiting for us at the entrance to the back lot, next to the exit. I got the opportunity to reminisce now with Scoot and Stacy, as I remembered the back lot route well. So well in fact, that Stacy asked how long I had been out of the organization. When I told her over a dozen years, she was impressed.

We arrived at an underground passageway that led to Futureworld's Quad stage. This quadrangle stage rises out and breaks through a futuristic sculpture like a giant transforming toy, as the performers begin their set. The boys were blown away by this fact when Stacy explained all the mechanics of it and how it worked.

We quickly walked down a long hall to a make up room. The boys received the full 'make-up' treatment while Stacy continued her instructions. When Taylor was satisfied she was finished with her instructions, my own little crusader spoke right on up himself.

"Say Stacy, may I ask you a question now?"

"Sure Taylor, go ahead."

"Are we possibly getting paid anything here tonight?"

Stacy honestly appeared shocked by my son's question, but eventually responded.

"Taylor, I hadn't thought about that, after all this was to be a crowd test—remember?"

"Hey Stacy, its okay if we weren't, I guess it doesn't matter."

"What doesn't matter Taylor?"

"Oh nothing, I was just going to ask you to give my half to Dad's foundation that's all. It's for charity you know."

"Oh?"

I couldn't believe it, but I caught a glance at Trevor as he looked totally ticked off.

"It's okay Stacy; you don't have to pay us anything. God Taylor, I can't believe you sometimes. Bloody hell bro, she's trying to help us out here."

"Yes boys I am, but you know, a wonderful gesture like that shouldn't go ignored either. Tell you what; I'll arrange our standard performance fee to be paid to the foundation, now does that seem fair?"

"Yes Miss, and thank you from both of us. I'm sorry Trev, you were right and I was wrong."

Meanwhile Taylor got up and gave Stacy a kiss on her cheek. Immediately, Stacy blushed—obviously touched by his gesture.

"Marc, what on earth did you feed these boys growing up?"

Stacy looked at me as she laughed, but in a way she was serious too.

"Don't give me credit Stacy, my late wife Miranda raised these two to have huge hearts—it shows, doesn't it?"

"It does . . . hell; I'll even kick in my ten percent too." Scoot interjected.

"Now—who said anything about ten percent for you Scott?" Stacy said it and was now busting up.

"Damn it, never mind then, I just thought it would be nice that's all."

Once the boys were finished with the make up artists, we went over to the stage itself. It had been set up according to Scoot's instructions to Stacy. He had also worked with the technical people, who naturally he knew quite well anyway.

The boys took their seats behind the keyboards, with Taylor taking the one that accompanied the adjoining synthesizer and computer. They adjusted these 'house' instruments now to their own liking.

Scoot did a check on the sound, but as he did, he went over the set with the boys as Taylor checked the synthesizer and computer out. He told us all that he was satisfied they would suffice for the majority of their set. He loaded Scoot's set of discs into the computer as he began laying down the limited additional tracks on the synthesizer that he wanted.

They would open with Pin Ball Wizard.

"Uncle Scott, do you think it would be alright if we didn't do Viva Las Vegas, but replaced it with something that really swings?"

"What are you two thinking about doing instead, after all—'Viva' has a great beat?"

"Have you ever heard of a song called 'The House of Blue Lights'?"

"No, I don't believe I have, what's so special about it?"

"We love it Uncle Scott, it's a mix of bogey-wogey, country swing, and a bit of Ragtime—its brill and wicked—the audience will love it. Both of us get to wail on the boards doing a whole mess of awesome bogey-wogey, which makes it real hot."

"Boys enough said, let me think a moment."

Scoot thought on it for a moment before agreeing. The final song would be the medley of Stardust and In the Still of the Night.

"Boys if we have enough time at the end of your set, your engineer will flash these two stage lights twice. This will let you know you may add an encore, all right?"

"Sure Stacy, but what should we sing if that happens?"

"Whatever you want Tre."

"Listen guys, are you ready?" Stacy asked.

"Right, all I have left to do is finish laying down these sound effects synthesizer tracts for Funeral." This came out of T-man as he slid back on a pair of cans (headphones) he'd been wearing.

"Do you want us to stay down here, or should we go up top, where we can see you from the crowd?"

"Upstairs Dad, we'll want to know how it looks from there. Besides, we've got our hands full, just getting ourselves psyched up before this bloody stage goes up."

"You got it Trev. Listen it goes without saying that we're all proud of both of you so—break a leg."

"Break a leg? What in bloody hell is that suppose to mean Dad?"

"It's a tradition in American theatre Tre, to avoid jinxing any performers. To wish someone 'to break a leg' therefore, is another way to wish them good luck . . . without saying it"

"Okay, I get it."

As the remainder of our group wished the boys well, Stacy wrote out a short introduction on the boys. She handed it to the announcer who was standing by her.

We went upstairs and found an employee holding two patio tables for us.

The terrace surrounding the quad on three sides was about a third to a half full at the most. At 7:55, Scoot pointed out he was sure that he recognized a few guests from Forty-Four arriving. It appeared that not many more of them would make it in time, but I didn't think that mattered anyway. I was interested in seeing a raw audience react without experience or impressions, as Scoot had promised.

Right at 8 pm, the lighting changed and the announcer began to boom out:

"Ladies and gentlemen, boys and girls, we're pleased to present two of the winners from last fall's ToonCrooners contest. Please join us in giving a warm Futureworld welcome to: Tay 'n' Tre . . . the Morgan's.

As I sat there listening to the announcer's introduction, I had to stop my thought processes for a moment to realize, that this man was speaking about my sons . . . not someone else's—these were my two little pishers.

These were my boys, beginning only the second, of what could become perhaps—thousands of performances in the years ahead of them. I had no way of knowing naturally at that moment, but I did know that I was excited, yet frightened for them at the same time. Yet most obviously, their lives would likely never be the same again—under any circumstances.

And now on with the next installment of our story; Blessings of the Father—Book Three—The Boys Break Out.

CHAPTER One

▼

THE WAKE UP CALL

"Ladies and gentlemen, boys and girls, we're pleased to present two of the winners from last fall's ToonCrooners contest. Please join us in giving a warm Toonland welcome to Tay 'n' Tre . . . the Morgan's."

Modest applause at this moment came from the approximate one-half capacity audience at Toonland.

With the announcer's intro done, I heard the stage's sound system crank on as the boys began playing their Scooter Davis arrangement of Pin Ball Wizard with Tre yelling in his adorable British accent, 1,2,3,4. This was followed by Taylor's convincing synthesized guitar track along with their strong keyboards, as the stage began transforming as it ascended to the Quad level. The polite audience was clapping, but certainly nothing earth shattering—gee—an honest reaction finally. Yet when the exposure of the stage was nearing all the way up, something weird and wonderful began to happen.

The audience now saw with their own eyes, that all of this impressive sound was coming out of two little pipsqueaks, with strictly their respective keyboards. At that point, there was an instant up tick in the applause, I would assume out of respect for the quality and tightness of their sound. The audience's reaction then sort of lit up the boys.

By the time that Taylor yelled out his 'How do you think he does it' line, the twins had the audience's sincere attention. At that moment, I was nudged by Scoot. I looked at him as his face had a smile as wide as the Mississippi at that moment—while he began pointing out towards the outfield.

I followed his finger as I saw why he was smiling now. Park guests were flocking to the Quad in actual hordes, which was starting to bulge to its limits. The boys' music was drawing them in—like flies to butter.

I had to laugh, as the scene reminded me of an old science fiction 'B' movie from the fifties. You know the type, an Ed Wood masterpiece, with throngs of zombies marching in lock-step procession in some weird trance with their arms all stuck out in front of them.

Coincidentally at that moment, Stacy's A&R executive from Los Angeles arrived, also reviewing this migration by the park's guests as well . . . hell, he'd been walking over to the Quad right in the middle of all of it. He sat next to Stacy, where he didn't even bother introducing himself over the music; he just watched as he listened intently instead.

As the boys closed the song, they played the final cords as they yelled out:

'How do you think he does it' in their stereo, as they then stomped on both keyboards to finish it off—it was a dramatic close.

The audience erupted now, as the boys received a good twenty seconds of strong applause. There was cat calling, whistling—you get the drift.

Stacy looked at me and nodded, as she introduced her 'suit' from Toon Media Records and Entertainment, Jared Morison. We shook hands, but Jared more or less continued to ignore me. I really didn't care if he ignored me . . . after all I was merely the father—so I was a certified nobody in the scheme of things anyway.

Morison remained focused on the boys' stage presence. Shit—he was using opera glasses just to watch their moves. He must have been satisfied by virtue of all the whispering he was now doing into Stacy's ear non-stop.

Meanwhile, the boys did an unusual twin bow, as Trevor next spoke to the enthusiastic audience.

"Hey there everyone, thank you. We're Tay and Tre; 'ow are you—that's Tay on my left, and we're the Morgan's. Right now, we want to play a favorite of ours from back home in England. Tay's going to handle the guitar lead and synthesized instruments, back up effects and harmony. I'll take lead on organ, piano, as well as lead vocal. Here's Sir Elton John's classic, Funeral for a Friend."

Taylor now piped up.

"Hey Tre, don't forget to tell everyone, that if we mess up—we'll just have to start the whole dang thing over."

This brought out some laughter from the audience, while I noticed Larry was beaming at that moment. Hum—was he rubbing off, or was that a set up he had coached them on?

The audience continued applauding, as the lighting and effects engineer began his magic with the mood ambiance for the upcoming tune. Obviously, he was familiar with this classic, or otherwise got an earful from Scoot earlier. He lit the stage with dark blues along with black shadows. This lent the perfect somber and eerie element to the Requiem portion of the tune, complete with fog now as if hovering over a graveyard.

The sound person was also on top of things. He made sure the volume pick up was higher than normal for the opening movement, creating additional drama. Meanwhile, with the fog spewing, the church bell gonging, along with the somber organ lead beginning, they ardently fashioned the desired effect. The audience seemed almost spellbound towards the stage with their attention—and silence. After all, the heavy organ lead nearly compelled the listener to do so.

As the heavy gothic dirge continued with the organ handing off lead to the piano, the audience sustained their entranced silence. The boys' proficiency on the keyboards was after all, remarkable for their years, let alone—twice their age. I would have to say honestly at that moment, that the audience recognized this fact as well.

Taylor's effects on the synthesizer in particular, were perhaps ninety-five percent of the fullness of Elton's original studio version. Not an easy feat for any eleven-year-old doing the song live. He even had the wind, church bell, and chimes down cold. His synthesized French horns and trumpets were awesome—but it was his electric guitar that blew the audience away . . . it was so right on.

I sat there literally dumbfounded myself—for the second time in the same day . . . in addition, I was loaded with Goosebumps up and down my arms, especially during the strong piano solos . . . this told me they had connected to the music beautifully.

Trevor's musical leads, first on the organ, then followed by hammering on that piano, were awesome in their own right. I noticed as I looked around the Quad, that some in the audience were shaking their heads in obvious amazement. At the transition into the vocals on the final portion of the piece, the boys hammered out the lyric. The lighting changed right on the mark, but this time, with fast moving spots in a full spectrum of colors that added an extra level of ambiance to the performance.

Trevor's big voice in his rich alto had near enough of both a guttural sound as well as British accent, to disguise his tender age. Taylor's harmonies, took me right back to that first time I drove them past that church choir school in England. He was angelic, yet strong and full.

By the beginning of the second verse of the lyrics, the audience was drumming on their tables, pounding on the floor, as they began singing right along with—'and love lies bleeding in my hands.'

Some people were trying to get up to dance, but there wasn't any room to do it any longer. This did not deter one couple though; they simply got up on their table to dance—until security stepped in. I looked over at Scoot, as he just kept right on a grinning. Actually, I thought for a moment that I saw dollar signs glowing in his eyes, he was so obvious.

At that moment too, I got an idea, as I took out my cell to phone home. Reg answered as I screamed into the phone to get the folks on. I heard them only slightly, but it was easier said than done anyway. So I just told them to listen, as the song was nearing its conclusion anyway. The audience was once again singing out the chorus as well.

The area outside of the Quad terrace was now quickly becoming an immense sea of people frozen in place, just standing still to listen after walking into the area. With all of the excitement, even people on rides or in lines, were craning their heads to see.

When the eleven-minute song ended, the inside terrace was on their feet as the entire audience went nuts with applause. I held the cell up so that Mom and Dad might hear all of the applause into my little phone.

When it all calmed down somewhat, I put the phone to my ear to ask them what they thought of the response.

"Marc, it sounds as though earlier today wasn't a fluke, was it?"

"No Mom, definitely not. You know, when you're right, you are so right, but what you can't see is even better. There are around two thousand people on their feet right now, giving your boys a standing ovation. I'm blown away here Mom; this is all too surreal honestly. I thought you guys would appreciate what the boys are doing, because right now—they own this stage. Damn—I wish the both of you were here right now, you can't believe how they're drawing them all in with their music . . . man it's a sight."

"I'm thrilled Marko, but you tell them that Gram and I are rooting for them."

"Okay Dad will do, I'll call you back later. Honestly Pop, I don't want to miss anything, if you follow me."

"Sure thing son . . . I don't blame you, but do call us back—alright?"

"Absolutely Dad, see ya."

When the boys stood to take their twin bow this time, people jumped right back up on their feet with another standing ovation. The boys smiled as they turned to give each other a high-five before returning to their keyboards.

This pleased the audience by their up tick of applause now—were they already becoming hooked, I had to wonder?

Immediately Trevor jumped on his microphone.

"Hey Tay—see, I told you we would make it through without messing it up and starting over. Now where's that fiver—pay up mate."

Taylor responded to his brother's demand.

"Later Tre, remember Dad's carrying my money, you know he doesn't trust me walking past the ice cream stand."

More laughter mixed with applause ensued, while there was another big grin from Larry. Taylor now jumped back in.

"Thanks everyone, we'll now play the song that convinced Mum, that all the bloody money she spent on our piano lessons—wasn't wasted. You know, she started us when we were five, we were really young . . ."

. . . "Yeah Tay—don't you remember—you'd try to play while still sucking your stupid thumb?" Trevor interrupted now.

The audience laughed hysterically at the crack, as did our group especially, but then there was Larry's reaction.

"Yeah!" He yelled out, before throwing me a wink to boot.

"Tre, are you ever going to let me talk?"

"Sure bro, sorry, knock yourself crackers."

"Anyway, before my 'big-mouthed' brother interrupted me, this next song is all about the music—bogey wogey music~that is. Our vocals are there too, but more or less they're just along for the ride as you'll see. Here's a brill tune, for all of you piano lovers out there—better grab hold of something, because here comes—The House of Blue Lights . . . 5, 6, 7, 8 . . ."

Immediately the boys dropped right into this toe-tapping, bogey-wogey, swinging song.

After the second verse, they proceeded to go into this incredible bogey wogey riff which was awesome, but they didn't stop there. Their riff quickly escalated into an all out duel between them . . . it was—indescribable.

There they were, wailing on their boards with each twin, out bogeying the other's—wogeying! The audience was once again going nuts, but this time like never before. Their competition was in fact—electrifying . . . it was truly extraordinary, as well as engaging to witness. Instantly, one felt privileged just to be there watching them—while listening even more so.

Taylor took lead vocal this time, nailing it solidly. Yet as he had said, the pianos themselves really took precedence. I, along with everyone with me, was simply dumbfounded.

The music, tempo, and the lyrics of this song, made it impossible for you to simply sit still—so no one did.

It appeared that very few in the audience knew the song prior to this magical performance, but by the time the boys finished it, including a reprise, the audience was in love with this tune . . . I don't think one could help it honestly.

Another standing ovation ensued lasting well over a half minute this time. And there were still screams, yells, you name it going on. Consequently, the boys jumped into yet another reprise, this time picking up at their bogey wogey duel. After that finished to the audience's yelling and screams, they also knew enough of the lyrics to join right in with the twins on the chorus this time around.

This time when they finished, the boys again took their 'patented' twin bow as the applause roared. They did these bows in perfect coordination, which is how I took to naming it the twin bow, earlier in our day. I was sure this was yet another part of their non-verbal communications; it was too perfect not to be. You see, the boys never had more than a fraction, if any, of their peripheral vision within range of the other. They were always at near sixty-degree angles opposing each other facing outwards towards their audience. Yet they moved as one person—it was amazing to watch actually.

Trevor now spoke.

"Thank you everyone, wasn't that one fun?"

The audience rewarded the comment with more applause.

"Now for our final song tonight . . .

. . . That was as far as Trev got out before receiving a loud group 'No' from the audience . . . you could tell they meant it too. Despite this, Trevor continued where he left off.

"Look mates, we're going to slow down with a unique medley of two ballads—Stardust and In the Still of the Night. We dedicate this song to our late Mum, and to our Dad, these are their favorite songs."

The boys performed the medley as they had that afternoon in Summerlin. Moreover, as before, it had the same effect on this audience. The boys' harmony was truly angelic. I swear I almost lost it—twice, I don't think the audience was far behind me either.

The audience's applause when they finished, told the story too. It was different from the prior songs. This time, their ovation kept growing as if they could not stop the momentum, even as some in the audience sat back down into their chairs, the applause itself continued unabated. I'm sure this was also influenced by Trevor's announcement before the song began, that it was to be their final offering for the evening . . . certainly that was taken more somberly by the audience no doubt. The applause continued right on through the boys getting up and doing yet another twin bow.

Taylor now grabbed the microphone off his keyboard. I knew where he was going already—as did Scoot by his acknowledging nod to me. Naturally we then started laughing before the poor kid even got a word out.

"Ladies and Gentlemen, I want to thank you on behalf of Tre and myself for your kind applause. I want you to know how we happened to be here tonight—you see Tre and I only began performing professionally earlier today.

Substantial applause interrupted Taylor from continuing after that confession.

"Right now, we're actually doing this to raise money for our Dad's charity foundation. By the way, Dad's over there at that table. Hey Dad, why not stand up and let the folks have a good look at you." Taylor was pointing me out and waving, so soon a spotlight found its way over too.

What was I suppose to do? I stood and waved to the boys, then sat back down. The audience gave me some polite applause, as Taylor continued heading towards his soapbox speech no doubt.

"Folks, you wouldn't know it to look at him, but Dad's actually a pretty famous bloke. You see, he started and runs all of the Verandas Restaurants in America."

I received more applause this time, not to mention a whole lot of small talk going on at the surrounding tables to ours.

"Dad's foundation needs to raise eight million dollars to build a residential center for folks with Cerebral Palsy. Some of you may have heard about our crusade, Tre's and mine. We came up with the idea of selling Dad's coffee and desserts alongside of Minis Ice Cream at all of his restaurants.

"So before we go tonight, we want to let all of you kind people know about our new Dessert Courts at Verandas. If you want some wonderful ice cream, coffee, or dessert . . . all for a great cause, you can just run into a Verandas from now on, to get it. Actually I guess, after next week should be fine.

"Remember, all the money we profit goes to Dad's foundation to help charities around the world, so thank you for having us tonight and good night and may God Bless."

The boys got another standing ovation as the stage began to transform and descend into the ground while they waved—apparently their set was long enough without an encore, Scoot and I were disappointed, but understood. Moments later though to everyone's surprise I believe—but especially mine, the stage started coming back up as the ovation increased even more.

"Thank you everyone on behalf of Tay and I—we love you. We've been told we may sing two more—so does anyone have a problem with that?"

Tremendous applause, along with yells of 'no' and laughter too, followed Trevor's question.

"What do you have in mind Tre?"

"Gee Tay, why don't we do two songs back to back by one of our faves—Air Supply?" Affirmative applause followed Trevor's comments.

"Wow Tay, the applause says it all, doesn't it bro?"

"Yeah Tre it does, so—congratulations on making that connection."

Taylor was rewarded with tremendous laughter now for his obvious crack at his brother's expense.

"Cool it Tay, don't start on me. Let's just sing these songs for all these nice folks."

"Fine bro, ladies and gentlemen, plus all you kids out there; here are two of our Air Supply favorites. Here are; Making Love Out of Nothing At All, followed by their excellent version of- Unchained Melody."

The boys jumped right into the first of the two Air Supply songs, Making Love Out of Nothing At All.

Now I was stunned somewhat, as the terrace audience literally stayed on their feet, choosing not to sit down when they certainly could have. I guess the people inside the Quad, were deferring their acknowledgement to the mass sea of people—outside the terrace who had no choice, but to stand, so they were lending their support I suppose.

However, what no one counted on, was Trevor. You see, my little pipsqueak was belting the lyric out as if a boy possessed. The crowd must have been shocked as many of them stopped their dancing on the outside of the terrace, to merely pay fuller attention to his vocal apparently. Then, as the song progressed, so did his intensity with his big voice on his vocal, along with his octave climbing too. He kept going right on up along with his energy and volume, it was unbelievable.

When the boys ended this song, I assumed they intended on going straight into Unchained Melody, but the audience's reaction and their deafening applause for Trevor's vocal certainly, simply made that impossible. Taylor very seamlessly conceded this applause break as he took the opportunity to pay deference to his brother:

"Hey everyone, please join me in showing my brother what a brill job he just did with his vocal. Ladies and gentlemen, and kids—my big bro, Tre Morgan on vocal."

Finally close to some forty seconds later, the audience quieted down sufficiently so the boys could continue. They then began Air Supply's excellent version of Unchained Melody.

The boys' harmonies were perfect and angelic, this time with Taylor on lead vocal. I also noticed that outside the terrace, there were at least three hundred couples slow dancing to this song.

As the song ended with Taylor's wonderful vocal singing the closing lyrics, the audience gave it all up.

They were screaming and applauding to a deafening level now. And they were sustaining it as the boys waved and bowed for several seconds. When the stage finally began to transform itself as it began lowering, I was personally convinced that my two sons had definitely passed 'this test' . . . but that was just me . . . then there was the audience's reaction—their screaming, cat calls and pleading began in earnest now.

The audience kept up their applause with a vengeance. Not only that, but their screams for 'more' alone, had to have really impressed Morrison, as I saw him take out his phone to call someone even as he continued to speak into Stacy's ear.

I had just turned to Scooter to ask what his impressions were of the actions by his soon-to-be former colleagues, when I heard a groundswell of screaming and applause coming from the audience all around me. This forced me to turn my attention back towards the stage . . . which was rising yet again! I was stunned, as this could only mean one thing—T-M was granting them a second encore! Moments later, I was already getting an earful from Scoot.

Scooter was kind enough to share with me in that split second, that in his seventeen years at T-M, he had only once before seen management order a second encore during a crowd test—that was on the occasion of their current number one selling recording star's first musical performance at the park, three years before. In short, Scooter advised me that the boys had no doubt just hit 'pay dirt' with the T-M management team sitting in front of him. He suspected it was Jared, but he couldn't rule out Stacy either.

Taylor and Trevor were both huddling together talking when the stage had finally raised enough to expose them. Given the smiles on their faces, it was clear that they realized too, that there was great significance to this second encore . . . Trevor now spoke.

"Thank you everyone, thank you. Tay and I are both crackers over all of this . . . thank you again. We'd like to offer one more for all of you, with all of our love . . . here's Tay."

"Thanks bro . . . and thank you Toonland, we'll never forget this so thanks again and like Tre said—we love you too."

As the stage lighting changed quickly now, casting deep shadows across the entire stage, the boys began playing the hauntingly beautiful opening lyric of Are You Lonesome Tonight. Their version of this beautiful song was not without its influences. There was not only Elvis in their vocals, but Jolson too in the melodies accompanying those vocals . . . the effect was outstanding.

Mass hysteria soon followed as they ended the song. After several bows joined with an equal number of thrown kisses and waves, the stage began transforming quickly now as it began to descend as the audience erupted forcefully.

They didn't stop until the announcer came on to thank everyone.

I was so proud of them, but just wanted to get right to them to express what I was feeling.

"Everyone, if you wouldn't mind, I ask that you excuse me, as I'd like to get downstairs to the guys."

"Yes Mr. Morgan, I would enjoy meeting your sons myself. Why don't we all go downstairs with you?"

Jared piped up immediately which surprised me, this guy hardly had said two words to me the entire time.

"That would be fine Jared, but please feel free to call me Marc."

Our group made our way across the Quad's terrace to the downstairs entrance. As we did, a few folks stopped me to congratulate me on the boys or otherwise compliment me on Verandas. I was as polite as possible for a father on a mission to get to his kids.

We made our way downstairs to the bunker's Green Room where we found Taylor and Trevor talking animatedly on the sofa, while totally covered in sweat—yet clearly very happy.

But the moment they saw Larry, they ran straight for him as they high-fived him repeatedly before their hugging took over. Taylor spoke first.

"God Lar-man, you were so right about thinking of funny things from when we were little. Did you hear them all laugh?"

"Dah, Tay. You would have to be deaf—not too." Larry responded.

"Yeah bro, but I think I got more laughs!" Now Trevor was laughing too.

"Who cares Tre, as long as they laughed—right?"

"You're right Tay—that was certainly the idea." Larry countered.

I broke up the little humor critique to introduce Jared to the twins at that moment.

"Guys, say hello to Mr. Morison from Toon Media Records and Entertainment."

"Hi sir, did you enjoy our set?"

"Yes I did, but which one are you; I'm honestly not able to see a single difference?"

"I'm sorry sir, I'm Trevor or Tre—this is my imposter; Taylor, also known as Tay." Jared seemed to laugh sincerely at Trevor's crack, but he also had cockiness to him, that grated on me somewhat.

"Hello sir."

"Hi boys, but please—call me Jared. Say, are you two always this polite—I'm not used to that?"

"I guess sir, but what did you think of our performance Mr. Morison?" Taylor now seemed to demand an answer to his question.

"Quite honestly boys—I refuse to buy your story. There is just no way you two turned pro only today—that simply can't be possible."

Jesus, how this guy had succeeded in ticking off Trevor already, was beyond me—but yet, he had—and that wasn't ever easy with Trevor . . . Taylor yes, but with Trev, no!

With a flushed face, taunt, defensive body language, along with the evil eye—Trevor, now more or less replied, yet bitingly so:

"Jared we did. And we get kind of upset when people don't believe us, because we don't lie sir. Ask our Dad if you can't accept the truth of what were saying."

"It's true Jared; the boys had their first professional engagement at three p.m. today—at my restaurant. If you don't want to believe us, that's your choice pal.

I thought to myself at that moment, that I could now understand Trevor's reaction . . . he was thinking about Concepcion, no doubt. Meanwhile, I did not care for this guy's cockiness at all.

Even if he was simply trying to flatter the boys, he was somewhat inappropriate with his comments. Nor did I appreciate him patronizing the boys in the slightest either.

Trevor's flash of anger didn't help naturally, although you could understand that part of the confrontation.

"Okay Marc, sorry—of course I believe the boys, I'm sorry for touching a raw nerve here . . . let me try again. Boys, all I am trying to convey, is that it's hard to recognize either of you as amateurs. Now having heard you, while watching your stage presence, along with witnessing the audience reaction to you and your music—it was all very impressive . . . as well as consistent of only seasoned, professional performers—now does that say it better?"

"Yes Jared . . . thank you for setting us straight." I said it in mock thanks although the Dufuss didn't get my sarcastic inflection, I'm sure.

"You see Jared; we're a tad sensitive to any accusations due to a wholly untrue press report that came out about us last week. It deeply upset all of us, so we're all just a little bit gun shy now, so sorry."

"No problem Marc, but please accept my apologies too. Now exactly who am I dealing with on our negotiations, you—or Davis over there, who looks like he's chomping on the bit to get started?"

"Neither Jared, all negotiations or decisions for the boys, go through their personal manager first—sadly; she couldn't be here." I said.

"Not here! Gee that's too bad, because I'm heavily impressed, authorized, and ready to sign them right now."

"Candidly Jared, knowing their manager—my Mother, she's not quite ready to commit or sign anything with anyone yet—so it's probably just as well . . . she's not here."

"Really, well why don't you let me speak to her on the telephone, you know, I'm a pretty persuasive guy. I'm sure I can sway her to dance and allow Davis to handle this with me?"

"Very well Jared, but good luck." I replied.

I had to laugh at what this asshole was thinking—he was going to out-skunk my Mother . . . of all people?

"Bud, why not get her on the telephone for me. Let me excuse myself to speak to her first . . . maybe I can soften her up?" Scooter said as he threw me a clandestine wink.

"Sure Scoot, I'll speak to her to give her the salient points before I turn it over to you—fair enough?"

"Perfecto, Marc."

I dialed the house on the cell, and ears must have been burning back at the Trail.

"Hello."

"Mom, since when do you answer the phone?"

Mom had answered the phone on the first ring, she never did that,—Reg typically answered.

"Since—the two lovebirds you refuse to talk about—disappeared into that stupid grotto of yours, over ten minutes ago!"

"Oh." I was laughing at her crack at my expense.

"So, how did it end up Markie, we're they a smash or what?"

"Yep Mom, they were—that's an unqualified 'yep' by the way. Those boys of yours sent that audience away—hooked."

"So are they still signing autographs then?"

"Not a one Mom, it's a different situation here."

"Oh yes, I guess that would make sense."

"Listen, Scoot needs to speak to you—got a minute?"

"Sure, put him on."

I handed Scoot the cell as he quickly walked down the hall to get out of Jared's earshot I'm sure.

While Jared waited for his cell phone audience, he was actively asking the boys all sorts of questions now. He didn't understand for one thing how they had an American father with their heavy accents. I kept my mouth shut, as they explained the family's unique story quite well, I might add.

Tay did a lot of the talking for the duo, but not exclusively. Trevor in fact did an excellent job explaining how it was that they were so proficient performing their tunes.

. . . "You see Jared, our Mum had a rule that she would never break. We were allowed to learn three 'rock' songs for every classical piece we learned to perfection at the same time. Natch, Mum made us practice all the pieces until they were all perfect, before we could move to new ones. We got to practice one hour on each of our rock songs after an hour on our classical piece. The classical music is always much more difficult to learn properly. The music and the proper techniques are much more challenging in classical music, so it just takes longer Jared. So natch, we'd get real good at the rock tunes long before the classical piece sounded acceptable to Mum and Clarice."

"Who's Clarice, Trevor?"

"She was our instructor for the piano Jared when we began studying. She lives in Australia now—I think."

"New Zealand, Tre, and God I swear." Taylor chimed in at his brother's error.

"Big deal Tay, right—it's bloody New Zealand, so it's the same stupid area isn't it, so toss off?"

"That's not the point Tre, is it?"

"Okay guys calm down, this isn't that important of an issue to start another fight over."

"Yes Dad."

At that moment, the sound of Scoot's footsteps and his distinctive laugh, made me turn around towards the hallway. My cell phone was in his hand—but the 'flip' was closed, which made me laugh naturally. It told me that Mom was already playing the fox, not that I was surprised in the least.

"Alright Davis—may I speak to her now?"

"Afraid not old man, she instructed me to direct you to send your proposal to her via the mails or fax. First, she's in absolutely no hurry on any of this, so she'll review it when she can . . . but after speaking to her, I don't believe you would want to rush her either—Morison."

"You're kidding me—right? This is Toon-Media calling . . . we don't call—twice Davis—you know that!"

"Sorry Jared . . . Mrs. Morgan follows her own agenda—yet she's tough besides, Marc told you as much already. You can count on some serious negotiations with her—if she'll negotiate at all. Even though I'm the boys' producer and business manager, as the boys' personal manager, she calls the shots on our interest level on recording deals naturally, so sorry pal."

I was doing my best not to laugh at the pompous jerk. He was cocky to be sure, along with being much too sure of himself in my opinion. I'm afraid that he had no idea of whom he was tangling with. A fifty-some-odd-year-old Jewish Grandma from New York was no pushover—especially one that was looking out for her boys . . . it was risky at best.

"Are you serious Davis—you're actually going to let their grandmother control the destiny of this extraordinary opportunity I'm offering the boys that you yourself, help manage?

"You know, I'm not talking just recording here Davis; I'm talking cross-promotion, a movie deal, and television. This is the big one Scott—the whole enchilada. You're not honestly going to tell me—as a T-M legend yourself, that you would allow her to blow this for your clients . . . are you?"

"Jared—it's simply not my call, besides which you know bub, you'll be saying all of this anyway, when you write her . . . now won't you pal?"

"I don't know—maybe—and then again—who knows? You know Scott, on principle, I may pass,—after all I don't need another prima Dona to deal with—do I?"

"Alright Jared, play it your way, but remember Toon Media isn't the only recording label out there. Nor are you the first to approach us, so your actions now—fail to consider if she's already in negotiations . . . don't they? Besides pal, she said on numerous occasions that your label seems far too specialized for her comfort level. So my friend, I certainly wouldn't expect her to just roll over and sign on the dotted line for you—or anyone else. You're going to have to sell her on T-M first, before you even attempt to convince her that she's wrong! I'm afraid that won't be an easy job either."

The Dufuss had already broken the first rule of negotiation—he led with his own ego! Naturally, following that mistake, Scoot just lured the bastard in, before pulling him into the net . . . but—would leave the gutting to my Mother of course. Here Morison kept right on talking, but already had been caught, fileted, and sautéed, as well as—pre-tenderized for parlaying into ultimate submission by my Mother—he just didn't know it yet!

"Fine Davis, you've made your point, so I'll humor the old woman. Marc what's your fax number or office address, please?"

I gave Jared my business card, while I looked him over with contempt—or pity . . . I couldn't be fully sure of which. He had grabbed onto Scoot's baiting his ego so fast, it was funny to see how naïve he actually was for such an experienced A&R guy. Then again, very few, if any performers, who seriously wanted to negotiate with the likes of Toon-Media—would ever dare lead with this kind of 'nonchalant' approach. Honestly, it was damn risky given their power and standing . . . so Jared's earlier comments were not lost on me either.

I had to hope that this wouldn't all blow up in Mom's face and therefore by extension, for the boys as well.

He looked at my card, as he then casually commented—I assumed to change the weight of the tension in the air now:

"I have to tell you Marc, I'm crazy about your one hundred percent Kona coffee, it's without a doubt, the best I've ever had. I drink the stuff at least three times a week."

"Thanks Jared—but I'll tell you what I'll do then. How 'bout I wager you ten pounds of my Kona, against your brilliant negotiation skills? If you're so convincing that you can get mom signed up, you get the coffee gratis. But if you don't, you donate to the boys' crusade, the equivalent of its retail cost of $27.80 per pound. That's two hundred and seventy eight bucks—in case you're without your calculator."

"You're on Marc." As Jared shook my hand he had a very cocky grin on his face.

He made small talk with Stacy for another minute or so, before saying his farewells to take his leave—oh, thank the Lord.

After he was gone from the green room, Stacy looked at Scoot who started smiling before eventually busting up.

"Damn, you're some diplomat Scott; you played him for the bloated egomaniacal fool that he is. I can see that you're wasting little time acclimating to your new position."

"Yeah I guess so, but hey Stace, don't give me all the credit—hand it over to Mrs. Morgan back in Vegas too—she's the real tough cookie. In addition, she does have a valid point here. Our label is overly focused on our soundtracks and the stars from our movies—we've never successfully promoted or launched budding rock artists directly—have we?"

"Maybe not . . . that's somewhat true I guess Scott, but look at everything else too that Jared mentioned . . . you have to look squarely at the larger picture here—which you already know."

"That's valid too Stacy, but you can be sure my Mother will certainly consider everything—just not before sweetening the pie some."

"I understand Marc, but remember this: Jared's the best at what he does, ego, or not. I will tell you, that he genuinely took to your boys right off . . . I couldn't shut him up during their performance. And that was despite how they reacted to him over that misunderstanding later on too, I can assure you.

"Honestly gentlemen, you couldn't ask for a better guy to go to corporate with your deal. The way he was speaking to me on the Quad's terrace, I can tell you—he was beyond merely impressed. Most of all, no other A&R

Executive in this company can build up an act better to corporate—than Jared. Believe me, I've seen him in action, he's incredible at what he does."

"Oh, we won't forget, but you know, to us, relationships mean much more than anything else. He just didn't earn high marks from any of us in that department, at least with his first impression. Right guys?"

"He got me mad at first Dad; I wasn't real keen on him, even after he apologized."

"How about you Taylor?"

"I second most of Tre's feeling Daddy, I didn't like him much."

"Dang—I'll third that. God—he's an a-hole. Oh sorry, I mean, I didn't— oh you know."

"Yeah Larry—we do know." As I laughed to lighten his burden at his mistake.

"Listen Stacy, nothing more is going to get accomplished here tonight on this subject I'm afraid. Why don't we all blow out of here so the kids can all have some fun?"

Five happy and screaming kids rewarded me.

"Fine Marc, I've had a full day myself, so I'm going to get home now. Boys, I can't begin to tell you how much you impressed me tonight. Whether we're fortunate enough to have you join us here or not, you two have a wonderful future in the business. My Teddy Toon hat's off to both of you."

"Thank you Stacy for everything, you're very nice and we had fun thanks to you."

"You are most welcome Taylor, but you keep your eye out for our check to the foundation, all right?"

"Yes Stacy, and thanks again for that."

The boys got up off the sofa as they encircled Stacy, giving her matching kisses on her cheeks which delighted her. She now turned her attention naturally—to her new beau, though.

Larry at that moment was staring at the ceiling just whistling, yet trying to act nonchalant.

"Lawrence, don't I get a kiss from you as well?"

"I don't suppose you'd settle for one after my Bar Mitzvah when I'll be legal—would you?"

"Now Lawrence—I'm surprised at you, are you going to make me wait that long?"

"Oh damn it—alright, but it better be quick and none of that tongue stuff neither."

"Okay I promise—love."

"Hey—none of that 'love lingo' either, Stacy, the next thing I'll hear is: What's your email address Lawrence?"

"Gee, Lawrence, since you brought it up—what is your email address?"

"Forget it Stacy, nice try—it's unlisted!

"Very well, I guess one little kiss on the cheek, is all I'm hoping for now Lawrence."

"Oh—all right."

Larry walked over as he attempted to kiss her left cheek, but Stacy turned to meet his lips on hers instead. Larry was floored as his eyes were bugged out totally. His eyes were also crossed now, as he tried to look at her before pulling away.

"Hey lady—you played that dirty."

"You know Lawrence; it seems I'm just putty in your big, strong hands, really I couldn't help myself, forgive me?"

"Yeah, yeah, yeah—now go on, get out of here before you want seconds— maybe you haven't heard—I'm closed for the night." We were all busting our guts now.

Stacy escorted us up top. Abruptly as she was leaving, she stopped as she ran over to Larry trying to box him into the corner for yet another kiss . . . he wasn't amused. He tried seriously now to dodge her as he succeeded to avoid her grabbing him once more. We were all laughing yet again. Lastly, she added a parting comment to me.

"Oh, I almost forgot, the suite's all set up with everything you could possibly require Marc. A DVD of their performance will be delivered first thing in the morning, it's the least that I can do. And believe me Marc, with that audience's reaction, it will be your calling card for them—anywhere, and I do mean—anywhere."

"Thanks Stacy, we appreciate it."

"My pleasure Marc, bye everyone. But let me add a special good night to my Lawrence, my one and only true love."

Larry was hiding behind the boys, fearing yet another lip lock attack, so he barely mumbled out any acknowledgment. As she was walking away, he asked the twins for covert surveillance.

"Let me know when you're sure she' gone."

"Yes Lar . . . she just went through an employee gate." Trevor answered.

"Thank God—dang can't she tell—I'm not interested?"

"I doubt it Lar." I answered in a laughing comment.

The boys began huddling with Embeth and Halley on attraction options, while the adults talked amongst us, still laughing over the great 'love affair'.

The kids decided on Wrong Way Murphy's Adventures . . . shock of shocks. Naturally I wasn't surprised at that one at all, so we began to make our way over to the Bayou Country section of The Louisiana Purchase. We got barely a hundred yards though, when—it happened. At the time, I merely heard the four words only; the screams were to come afterwards—naturally.

"Look—there they are!"

None of us realized, the significance of that statement at first, honestly we didn't. Yet a mere moment later, around thirty or so young girls, ranging from perhaps eight to maybe sixteen, were mobbing the boys. Armed with their cameras, autograph books and pieces of paper, the boys were surrounded and trapped. Within around three minutes hence, the crowd had doubled in size.

"Scoot, none of our kids will get a single ride in at this rate if we don't intervene. What do you suggest we do; you're the man with all the experience in this place, got any ideas?"

"It's a no-brainer bud, I'm way ahead of you, just give me another moment".

Scoot already had his cell out, as he punched in a code for the security office I assumed. He spoke to someone briefly before hanging up. Within maybe forty seconds, I saw first two, followed then by four more officers—walking quickly towards us.

"Thanks Scoot, now how about a VIP guide—do you think Hilary's still working this late?"

"It's possible, let me check." Moments later, he reported to me.

"Yes and no on that one Marc, she's already reassigned. They'll gladly send someone else instead if you want, but after all, with our security detail, it isn't really necessary?"

"Okay Scoot, I guess you're right, this will be fine I'm sure."

The boys had completed their fans' requests as the security men now took this opportunity to introduce themselves. We all listened attentively while they explained the ropes for our benefit.

The leader and spokesperson for their sextet was Irv. He was a retired military veteran, no doubt. You could pick this up from his manner of speech, not unlike my own Dad on occasion, as you will recall.

"Mr. Morgan, here's our protocol, the parameter may be compromised with bogeys at anytime, so HQ suggests, we retreat to the back lot area. Once we're there, we will acquire reinforcements, plus suitable ground transportation. After determining the optimal routes for our formation to follow to each area, we can then get you to any desired quadrant you and the children desire."

"Thank you Irv, the kids would appreciate getting to Wrong Way Murphy's." I said.

"Fine Mr. Morgan, let me call ahead to our forward position. After you're all through the back lot, we'll head straight there coming in through the east side of T.L.P."

"T.L.P. Irv?"

"The Louisiana Purchase bud." Scoot jumped in with.

"Oh yeah, how stupid of me, you'd think I never worked here before—in T.L.P. no less! How come we never called it that, back then Scoot?"

"I haven't a clue Marc; I guess it's the security department's jargon for it."

"Don't sweat it sir, we're used to you civilians."

"You see Marc, we're just civilians." Scoot jokingly got out.

I honestly had to hold it back big time with that crack, I'll tell you that. We headed to the back lot area closest to us, behind the Mars Attacks Again attraction in Futureworld. Irv had secured transport as promised in the form of two regulation-issue small surrey trams.

We loaded the 'troops' into these elongated golf carts, as we headed back to T.L.P., much the same route we took to get to Futureworld. We exited the back lot next to the Bahaman Buccaneer. Surrounded by our six 'horsemen', we walked down to Wrong Way Murphy's, where we all got into line with two from our detail too.

I was not about to allow my sons plus their three mates, to go alone on a ride now anyway, not after the mob we had dealt with earlier. I think Beth and Scoot understood why as well. After all, this was all new to me, so I was not quite prepared to face it yet. Reality was only beginning to set in—my twins already had some new fans from their performance here tonight! Despite this, someone yelling inside of me left me telling Irv to take us through the regular line.

As we 'waded' through the considerable line still in front of us, the boys, and girls were yapping away non-stop. Not about performing, or music—or anything else—but how they all loved this ride. And that little voice in me said this is why I was here at that moment. After it was over, believe it or not, I took real heart in what had just happened. It seemed to me that my sons could turn their professional personas on and off like a light switch. They weren't letting their newfound lives interfere or screw up their pre-existing and more private ones, which they obviously also cherished.

On stage, they seemed professionally mature and focused; off stage they were simply—them, acting as before. Yes, they were far more mature than last October when we met, but just the same, they carried themselves humbly . . . I liked that.

They made no effort to draw attention to either of them, or anything else really. Mostly—they were neither expanding their heads or their egos . . . so far. I was somewhat surprised, yet as I said, pleased. Had my mom got this through to them in one shot, that they got it already? I could not be sure, but all the same, I was impressed.

I didn't have to think on this too long, as I was about to witness my first 'test-case' situation. A girl of perhaps twelve to fourteen, two rows across from us, had just excitedly recognized them. She reached into her purse, frantically looking for paper and a pen apparently.

The young lady was also whispering into what I would presume was her brother's ear, by how much they looked alike. He was maybe a year or two older, as he now turned in our direction. Seeing the twins, he just smiled. She finally found some paper and a pen, handing both to her brother. He took them as he loudly cleared his throat to gain their attention.

"Hey dudes."

The twins turned to him, said hello and smiled back, but not saying anything further.

"Hey, would you mind giving my dopey sister here, your autographs? And dudes—your Funeral mix was like totally awesome."

"Right, and thanks, we're glad you liked it—so whose name do we put on this?"

Taylor asked as he accepted their pen and paper.

"How 'bout to Kelly and Kris, but both of our names start with K's?"

After Taylor signed it, he passed it to Trevor who did likewise, before passing it back to T-man.

"Cool, here you go and thanks."

Tay handed back the piece of paper purposely to the young lady. She blushed, exposing a mouth full of braces with her huge smile, as she said thank you silently with her lips.

"Hey thank you dudes . . . aah, like which one are you?"

"I'm Tay, nice to meet you Kris."

"Dude, I guess we both have the same problem, cuz I'm Kelly, Kris here is my sister."

Taylor laughed and replied.

"Cool, hi there Kris, sorry." Kris nodded.

Kelly on the other hand, kept up the dialogue.

"Hey, don't mention it and thanks dudes."

"Natch, it's our pleasure."

"Natch? What's that mean in American?"

"You know Kelly—in 'British'—that means 'naturally'. Whereby Taylor now laughed at his own crack at Kelly's expense.

"Oh yeah—natch! Say, do you guys got a CD out now Tay?"

"We're working on it, but you'll find it at our restaurants only."

"Oh yeah—Verandas, right?"

"Yep."

"Cool. Does your Dad own all of them for real?"

"Yep."

"Way cool dude—oh my gawd—you guys must be like super rich—right?"

"Nope, I don't think so."

"Dude, no way. I mean aren't there thousands of Verandas out there?"

"Nah, only three hundred and fifty."

"Still dude, aren't you all rolling in the dough?"

I decided to step in and intervene, why I hadn't before, I couldn't say at that moment. I guess my own curiosity over how Taylor would handle it, kept me listening.

"Kelly, I'm Marc Morgan, how do you do?"

"Ah, fine sir—am I getting too personal and stuff?"

"Kelly, yeah you are, but I understand, you're just curious is all."

"Cool, yeah that's it—curious."

"Kelly, its perfectly understandable, but talk about something else alright?"

"Sure thing Mr. Morgan, sorry again."

"No sweat kiddo."

"So Tay, where do I find the CD inside the restaurant?"

"First of all Kelly, it will depend on when we finish it, but they'll be on the kiosks where we sell our Minis from, after it comes out."

"No way dude, you guys sell Minis at Verandas? Kris are you listening to this?"

Kris nodded.

"Dude, they're like our favorite ice cream, we gotta drive all the way to University City to get them, are they in your restaurants already?"

"After next week Kelly, but at some of the units, you'll have to order them off the menu until the kiosks are finished."

"Way cool, well like hey, I don't want to be a skank, so it was nice rapping with you man, and thanks again . . . stay cool dude."

"Natch."

Kelly started a quiet conversation with his sister, while Tay rejoined his group as well. Moreover I was quite impressed with what I observed and heard. Little by little, other kids who had watched this exchange and seen the concert apparently came up to the boys to ask for autographs as well.

Each time, the boys accommodated them without complaint, while remaining as normal as before this very special day. With each kid that asked, I was that much more relieved with the exchanges going this well.

Finally, several minutes later, we entered our SUV for the ride, where we all had a wonderful 'serene' little drive—not!

We exited the attraction at its conclusion where we were surrounded by the remainder of our security team immediately. Irv was his usual self.

"Any problems to report, sir?"

"None Irv, let's move on to Ghostly's Mansion that's the next attraction the kids would like to visit."

"Very well sir, have everyone keep in this formation please."

"No problem Irv."

By this time, Larry was truly digging Irv. Larry told me, he loved military guys and even studied military history. He dug the nonchalant way that Irv handled everything. As we walked, Larry watched Irv's actions in surveying the quadrant, which duly impressed him.

After Ghostly's Mansion, we hit another six or so rides including the Calico Mining Railway Company twice, then once more at Mt. Splashdown, until the unthinkable—happened. I couldn't believe my ears as we were exiting that ride, right at eleven-forty.

"Dad, I can't speak for anybody else, but I'm whacked."

"Really Taylor, how does everyone else feel?"

"Yeah HB, me too . . . I need my beauty sleep." I knew exactly where Larry had picked up that line, instantly.

"Right, me three Dad, in fact I'm getting too tired to keep walking. Irv can we possibly ride out of here?"

"Sure thing soldier let me call in some ground transports." Irv got on his radio to arrange the tram carts at the nearest back lot exit.

When we got to the carts, Scoot and I decided to separate and meet at the airport at twelve noon. Everyone said good night, the boys and I received kisses from the ladies, which were returned before we began to part company.

Our group made it over to the Toonland Towers via the Transporter, with the boys now on their last legs. Luckily for them, we had no wait at registration. When we got up to our suite, I excused myself to visit the mini bar. On my return to the living room—all three amigos were dead to the world on the sofa and chairs . . . oh great—dead weight triplets!

One by one, I dragged them into their bedroom, helped them into bed before returning to my drink.

I grabbed my glass of the two doctors as I sipped my drink slowly, while I attempted to relax and reflect on the events of the day. Was it only this morning that our lives had last been typical . . . mundane . . . normal? Yes it was . . . but was I ever exhausted already.

Chapter Two

▼

Calling All Cars

My room alarm went off with an obnoxious buzz, right at nine. I felt every bone in my body aching. I could also feel something else though—the hot breath of someone sleeping next to me, with their breath hitting my shoulder blade. I was genuinely surprised to see it was Larry—and now alarmed as well . . . what was this all about? I woke him up gently.

"Hey buddy what gives, was there something wrong with your bed?"

"Nope. Look HB, don't tell anyone—but I got scared, so I thought I'd break you in, that's all."

"Break me in—Lar, what are we talking about here?"

"You know HB, that surro dad stuff you keep talking about."

"Oh that. Well that's surrogate—and yes, I think I understand now."

"You're not mad are you?"

"Heck Lar, I guess not. I mean—I don't think so. On the one hand, if I were your Dad, there wouldn't be a damn thing wrong with you being here . . . just ask the twins. But since I'm not, it might prove problematic if anyone got the wrong idea."

"I'm sorry HB; I didn't mean to make you mad."

"Lar, I promise you that I'm not mad, so relax. Hell, I just don't know how I should react honestly."

"Okay, that's good enough for me HB."

"Gee thanks Lar—I'm happy it's good enough for you, but I just hope your Mom feels the same way, after I mention it to her."

"Oh, don't worry about that HB; Mom will know it was just me getting scared. I always do it every time we stay at a hotel for the first night."

"Whoa—now that is a relief Lar, thank you for sharing that with me too."

"See I told you HB, there's nothing to worry about."

"Good—now get out of here . . . go wake up your best mates for me. I want to grab a nice hot bath for my achy bones."

"Sure thing HB—but thanks."

"For what Lar?"

"For taking away—my scared of course."

"Oh, you're most welcome Lar—sorry I slept through it."

"Don't worry, everyone does, you're no different, but you sure as heck snore something fierce HB."

"My Lar—thanks for sharing that."

Larry bounced out of bed, as I went to the john to draw the bath, while—draining other things.

I had a nice soak, but mindful of the time, got out to get dressed. I was surprised to see all three of the guys waiting for me in the living room. They were watching the TV in their matching 'billboards' of Toon Media apparel. The four of us now were a matched set with our Teddy Toon sweatshirts and pants. We looked like an ad for a frigging cloning clinic or something out of a movie scene. As we left the suite I worried we'd be laughed at by somebody walking the hallway . . . I felt that ridiculous.

We headed for breakfast in the lobby, which was quite nice and pleasant—you see I now had not two, but three—vacuum cleaners at the table for a change. At least Larry did his part by offering our entertainment during the meal.

Later, as we headed for the airport in a taxi, our cabbie will never forget Lawrence Levison, I can assure you of that.

"Hey guys, did your Dad tell you that he and I slept together last night?"

"So—he sleeps with Tay and me too."

"Oh yeah, I forgot about that."

"Are you kidding Lar, Dad loves sleeping with us?"

"You know guys; our driver, might get the wrong idea about this entire conversation, for his benefit, let's talk about something else, okay?"

"Why HB, I thought sleeping with you was cool, except for that one thing you kept doing all night—but we don't have to talk about that—do we?"

I could see the cabbie eyeing me in his mirror now, as I was starting to get seriously uncomfortable with this whole conversation and situation.

"Larry, enough!" I admonished him.

"Okay HB, but it's no big deal, I hear a lot of men do it . . . I've even heard some of my friends do it . . . but my Dad never has once." . . .

"I said—that's enough Larry."

"Okay, okay."

Fortunately, we arrived at Long Beach Airport but not a moment too soon, as far as I was concerned. This time when the cabbie began giving me another real weird look, I held up a very fair tip for the fare to just try to stop his glaring stares. That at least, did seem to perk him up somewhat though. Then again, maybe he just expected more when I directed him to the executive terminal, where moments later he was dropping us off alongside a private Lear Jet. Once we were safely alone inside the cabin, I pulled the Lar-man aside.

"Lar, can I suggest that in the future that you take into consideration what you are saying, before expressing it in front of a complete stranger."

"Gee HB, now you really sound like you're mad at me?"

"Larry, I'm not mad per se, but I am honestly concerned. Didn't you notice that the cabbie was staring at me like I was some kind of sicko? But why do you suppose he would do that Lar? Because he assumed I was sleeping in some fashion inappropriately with you boys? Worse, your words only reinforced that, while confusing him more so—Larry remember, people don't always understand the context that something is said. People can overreact or misconstrue words into inaccurate beliefs or meanings. Statements like: 'Except for that one thing you kept doing all night HB', certainly didn't help matters at all,—see my point Lar?"

"But HB, I was only talking about was your snoring, and that my Dad never snores."

"That's right Lar, and while you know that and so do I . . . does that cabbie know it from what you said—I don't think so? I think, he read something completely different into your remarks. Sadly Lar, there are a few sick people out there in today's world, that would take advantage of their own children, or kids in their care. Given that, what's that cabbie suppose to make out of our conversation Larry, that's my concern . . . understand?"

"Oh, I get it HB, dang I never thought of it like that, I was just kind of proud that I got to sleep with you—I guess the 'old me' is still there a little bit, you know—Larry the big mouth—Mr. Braggart."

"Okay, but don't sweat it Lar, realizing our own shortcomings is a clear sign of budding maturity as well as strong self-esteem and self-worth. I'm proud of you Larry for admitting your shortcomings . . . but something else is far more important to me and the twins."

"What's that HB?"

"I'm proud to know you Larry—you are a very special person . . . I'm so glad you've come into all of our lives."

"Jeeze HB, you're going to make me bawl with all that mush . . . can it, will ya?"

"Sure bud, but every word was true—you're aces Lar."

"Thanks HB; you're the best too—even when you're snoring!"

"Dang Lar-man—that hurts, oh the pain, oh the . . ."

. . . "Oh the pain of listening to all this crap, HB!"

"Yeah, yeah, yeah, Lar—give it a rest, I get your point."

I excused myself to check in with the tower, before loading our crap into the cargo hold, leaving it open for Scoot and family . . . but where was Scooter? I pulled out my cell to dial his home number in the phone's memory, but there was no answer. I called his cell next, which Beth surprisingly answered.

. . . "Morning Marc, did you sleep well?"

"Wonderful, but I'm sore this morning."

"Yes I know that feeling Marc—listen Scott can't talk at the moment as he's busy getting another speeding ticket—as we speak." I started laughing hysterically, although I wasn't one to talk with my own driving record.

"I'm pleased that you find this so amusing—Marcus?"

"Sorry Beth, but you know how we are at one another's expense?"

"Yes I do, but I'm afraid that this time—Scott's going to get the last laugh at your expense."

"He is—Beth? I don't see how that's possible really."

"No—well let me enlighten you then. Scott will be driving a company car from now on, correct?"

"Yes, I'm sure he mentioned the Jaguar will be in on Tuesday?"

"Ah ha, yes Scott mentioned that, and thanks again for that, by the way."

"My pleasure Beth—so where's the fire kiddo?"

"The fire—Marc, is right under his driving record. Since the company will be covering his insurance on the car, you may as well know right now Marc."

"Know what Beth?"

"Well Marcus, that our lovable Scott Davis—has a Masters Degree or PhD from every Driver's Traffic School in the entire State of California! Even with all of those many graduate degrees he's acquired to lessen his points on his record—it's still abysmal. Marcus, we have paid 'Stated Risk' on his policies, the entire time we've been married. So, as you can see for yourself, you really have nothing to laugh about yourself—do you Marc?"

"Now Beth honey, don't you worry your pretty little head about me. You see, our employee manual covers all of this quite explicitly."

"It does—you're kidding right?"

"No Beth, I'm not, why?"

"Oh, I'll tell you later, but be prepared for another laugh."

"Fair enough Beth, but listen, how much longer do you guess, Scoot will be groveling to the police officer?"

"Groveling? Are you kidding Marc, this officer knows Scott on a first name basis already!"

I was busting my guts right into my cell along with poor Beth's ear as well, no doubt.

"You can relax Marc; it appears that Mr. Earnhardt is free to go now."

"Good, so when will you be here?"

"That all depends. Assuming Scott can avoid another ticket before our intended arrival, give, or take, around eight minutes I would guess."

"Fair enough, we'll see you guys soon then, but tell Mr. Earnhardt to watch for the checkered flag."

"Alright Marc." As Beth hung up.

Meanwhile, I sat in the cockpit as I thought back on one of my very favorite gags. I realized it really would be perfect for the Scootmeister sometime. It would adequately test his mettle, while at the same time, his ability to keep cool under fire.

I went into the main cabin where the boys were all playing with the Playstation. Feeling domesticated, I put on a pot of the Blue Mountain Special Reserve to brew in my galley. If the coffee was done before the Davis' arrived, all the better, as I could have a cup before take-off.

It must have been fate working in my favor for when the Davis' finally arrived; I was swallowing the last of my second cup of Blue Mountain. I walked up to Scoot, threw my arm around his shoulder, as I gave my dear friend a nice morning hug. Actually, it was now 12:20, thereby making it an early afternoon hug.

"Buenos tardes bud how was your drive over—uneventful I hope?"

"Can it Morgan, I don't need the ticket rubbed in my face by your sorry ass, Robbie tells me your driving record is no prize either."

"My, someone certainly is testy this morning." I quipped sarcastically.

"Oh, and I suppose you wouldn't be?"

"Sure I would Scoot, but it wasn't me this time that got the ticket—was it?"

"Thanks bud, remind me to rub something into your face sometime."

"Hey bud, relax and don't sweat it Scoot. You're forgetting something which will undoubtedly make you feel a whole lot better—come next week in fact."

"I am, and what's that—oh great one?"

"Once you establish your Nevada residency next week, you'll get your new Nevada driver's license simultaneously. Those points of yours become history just like that—you'll start over with a clean slate here in the wonderful Silver State!"

"Damn, you know you're right, I hadn't thought about that."

"Well think on it, but don't think too long. By negotiation, our insurance carrier won't even consider your past record, but you must keep your Nevada record fewer than three points at all times, to wheel a company car without supplementing the cost. If you ever get to five points, we pull the car—no exceptions. It's our own, five points—and you walk for six months . . . policy!"

"Don't worry about me Marc; I'm turning over a new leaf behind the wheel, especially with the way I've seen them drive here in Vegas."

"Scooter, first off; from what Beth tells me, I wouldn't be pointing fingers at the way other people drive. Next, you'd better learn rule number one right now. True Las Vegan locals never say 'Vegas' it sounds so cheap and degrading—and somewhat 'touristy' coming out of a local. Polite locals say; Las Vegas, LV, or even Lost Wages, these are all acceptable choices—just never 'Vegas'."

"My—pardon my insult, oh great one, I'll be sure to remember that—when we get to—Vegas, but not before!"

"Suit yourself pal.

"But as far as turning over a new leaf with your driving record, this is certainly the opportune time pal. You know Scoot—if you're getting speeding tickets in your Malibu, heaven help you with a four hundred plus horsepower, supercharged V-8 in your new Jag. Honestly, you won't exactly be able to just casually throw caution to the wind anymore—will you?"

"What did you say Marc—did I just hear that right? Four hundred horsepower—and supercharged!"

"Yes Scooter, you heard right—did I stutter? I had to get you the damn R Model bud—just to find one in that stupid Indigo Blue you insisted on."

"Marc, what's an 'R' Model, and is it wise to give Scott a car with that much horsepower?

"Truthfully Beth—apparently it isn't wise, but like it or not, it was the 'R' Model or settling on another color. Beth, this model is Jaguar's race bred version of the S Type. Hell, I had no choice, but pardon my pun as well; as I didn't know any of this—for the record. My advice is that he better learn to drive this rocket of his much more conservatively or—he'll be walking soon enough anyway . . . believe me!"

"Oh, I guess I concede your point Marc. Scott, the ball's in your court honey, if you expect to keep this car for better than a week, you had better keep your nose clean this time."

"Can we all stop talking as if I'm some child here?

"Jesus—he got me the R Model—somebody pinch me." Scoot mumbled out after his question to us.

"Fine Scott, but don't give me any excuses."

"Suits me fine Beth, now lighten up on me, this is getting old."

The love fest continued between Scoot and Beth for a few minutes longer, much to the pleasure of the boys. They were enjoying the beating Scoot was taking at the hands of his lovely wife.

Meanwhile, as a multitasker, I gave Embeth and Halley a tour of everything on board the plane while their parents argued away. They had been oohing and aahing since boarding anyway. It was their first private jet after all. Eventually, I dragged them into the cockpit with me.

I first took the liberty to call the tower to commence my flight plan in six minutes, which would give me enough time to take a quick trip around the outside of my plane. I could kick some tires, check the oil . . . you get the drill.

The girls asked if they could stay in the cockpit while I did my inspection, which I of course said absolutely to. After checking outside the plane thoroughly, I returned to the cockpit where I got on the PA immediately.

"Ah, Ladies and Gentlemen, welcome aboard Miranda's Men #4-Cedric. Would our 'need for speed' flight attendant, Mr. Dale Earnhardt Davis, be kind enough to stop yelling at his wife long enough to close our hatch?

"My co-pilots, Embeth and Halley Davis, have informed me that we are now almost ready to—'kick this pig'. They'll be ready to depart as soon as they finish dressing their Barbies'." This elicited giggles from my able-bodied co-pilots, while abundant laughter came from the main cabin as well.

"Ladies and Gents, if you would take a look around the cabin now for any loose items, I would appreciate you placing them somewhere, because we're about to blow out of Dodge. My co-pilots have also advised me, that we may encounter some rough air on our short flight today. We therefore request, that there be no damn barfing all over my new leather, but rather aim carefully for your friendly little blue bag in front on you.

"By the way, would someone kindly tell Mrs. Davis to put away her chalkboard, Christ almighty Beth, isn't school is out of session now?" More laughing ensued all around.

"When we reach our cruising altitude of 31,000 feet this afternoon, our flight attendant . . . Scooter, will distribute the stale peanuts. He should also get his 'behind' up here with my cup of damn coffee . . . stat!" From the main cabin I heard Larry yell:

"Way to go HB, you sure told him."

I now continued my announcements to the main cabin.

"Now girls, if you would put down your Barbies' for a moment, I need you two to pull that long rope next to you to start our engines." You could now hear the girls giggling over the PA which satisfied Beth to no end by her sustained laughter.

So I started our engines now as I unconvincingly 'sputtered' into the PA.

"Ladies and Gentlemen, we are now ready to taxi—say, does anyone know the number for the cab company?"

I quickly instructed the girls on what not to touch, as the ground crew pulled our chocks as they pushed us back. I turned the Lear into the open tarmac, put on my aviators, and preceded towards our taxi. I told the girls what to expect, as they were inquisitive yet not nervous at all.

I had a textbook take off—well, I really did! Then, as we ascended through a thin cloud layer into unlimited visibility, the girls rewarded me with simultaneous 'wows'. An adult can always tell they scored huge on the kid meter, when the child responds with the stupendous, all meaning, and all knowing—'wow'. Look that up on the Web if you don't believe me.

We followed our flight plan perfectly, so that a mere thirty-two minutes later, we were touching down at home base. As our front wheel kissed the tarmac, I jumped on the PA yet again.

"Halley honey, the brakes girlfriend—hit the brakes!" I of course did this as I reversed my two fanjets. This was exaggerated enough, to give the impression that Halley had completed the maneuver herself.

"Damn, that's better." I bellowed over the PA.

We pulled into our hanger, where Wally stood waiting for me, with his hands resting on his hips looking seriously—pissed off . . . it then dawned me that I hadn't informed him of our delay. Why now, did I feel as if I was about to get grounded—by my own employee?

He came up and popped our hatch, but was all over me immediately.

"Boss you're late, what in the name of the Lord, happened?"

"Sorry Wall, couldn't help it, but where's the fire, it's Sunday for Christ's sake—remember?"

"Damn it boss, I never tell you how to crack those eggs, so don't ya tell me how to mind my girls. We need to service her for a 'special' this afternoon . . . so your little delay has put me way behind already."

"Oh, okay Wall, keep your shirt on,—please. Look, we'll be out of your hair in a minute, I promise."

"All right . . . but make it snappy damn it." He had barely muttered that last part out . . . but I heard it.

"Yes sir—Wall!"

We got ourselves out of Cedric, then immediately into Laverne, which I think was another wake up call for my new nieces.

"Boy, Uncle Marc, this is some car you've got here."

"Yeah Embeth, but we still haven't found the 'stiff' we're supposed to be carrying along for the ride." Larry chimed in.

"Okay Scoot, would you all prefer to go directly to your houseboat on Lake Mead now, or should we stop by my home first?"

"Whatever suits you Marc, we're in no hurry." Beth offered before Scoot could even open his mouth.

"You know Beth; believe it or not, the family hasn't seen my boat yet, so why don't we pick the folks and staff up, and then we can all go over to get you guys settled in. I've taken the liberty of having it pre-stocked for your stay . . . so I would appreciate checking their work personally. Besides, with this heat wave were having, maybe all the kids would enjoy taking a short cruise, how's that sound to all of you Davis'?"

"Wonderful idea Marc yes—lets." Followed out of Beth.

"Wow Dad, how come you haven't taken us there before now?"

"Trev my boy, you know, there's only just so much I'm able to get around to in less than a month's time son."

"Alright, but that sounds pretty weak Daddy."

"Well too bad Taylor, but thank you for your two cents worth."

"No problem Dadio."

"Oh, so now it's Dadio out of you too—Trevor alone wasn't enough?"

"When the spirit moves me, yeah. I hear you call gramps that, why shouldn't we call you that too, you are Daddy after all." Taylor responded somewhat like Larry would—you know . . . smugly.

"I see Tay, well when the spirit moves me; it's in my hand, usually across a nice fresh, British-American bum."

"Daddy, not in front of the girls, you're embarrassing us—besides I was joking."

"As was I honey—gotcha!"

"Oh, thank God."

"HB—am I going to the Lake with all of you too, or are you just ditching me?"

"My word Lar-man, what brought that on?"

"Sorry HB, but I was kind of worried I wouldn't get to go on a count of our little talk."

"No Lar, I told you already I wasn't angry . . . but it's not my decision in the first place—why not call your Mom on my cell to ask her yourself?" As I handed our comedic squirt the phone.

Moments later I made out Carol's voice on the speaker of the small phone.

"Hey Mom, how's Dad doing?"

"He's fine Larry, are you back in town now dear?"

"Yep, we're in Laverne, heading I think towards Spanish Trail."

"Laverne, dear?"

"Yeah Ma, didn't I tell you, HB's limo is named Laverne?"

"Really, no dear you didn't—but what exactly does Marc call you then, honey?"

"The 'pisk that roared' Mom, unless he calls me by my nickname which is: The Lar-man."

"When will I see you Larry, it's too darn quiet around here, are you heading home any time soon?"

"Not if I can help it."

"Larry! Would you care to try that one again, for a better fit please?"

"Sorry Mom, what I meant to say is I've been invited to HB's houseboat at the Lake. I'd really, really—really would like to go, please Mom?"

"Let me talk to your host dear." Larry handed me the phone.

"Carol."

"Marc, what's he talked you into now?"

"Nothing—I swear, it's just that we've been one happy group for the last twenty-four hours, so I think he wants to simply continue to hang out, that's all,—why don't you join us too?"

"Join you, no; I don't want to ruin his good time, even at my own expense."

"Now Carol, how many times do I have to tell you the kid's always welcome and so are you?"

"Fine, he can stay as long as you answer this first Marc—how did he behave yesterday? The truth Marcus—how was he? Remember, we're now speaking about Larry—so all normal parameters are naturally off the table." As she began laughing.

"Carol he behaved exceptionally well, honestly. But I must share with you, the three most significant highlights of his day from my perspective.

First, he was very attentive and well mannered to another of our female guests in our party. Literally Carol, I was blown away by his manners in particular. He was a consummate gentleman at the dinner table with her, so I must say that you and Rob can be truly proud of him.

"Secondly Carol, he was an enormous help in entertaining us, even as he came to the twins' rescue with their stage presence and comedy . . . so I'm putting him on the payroll by the way. That got us both laughing now.

"And Carol, lastly, he was concerned that I had become scared sleeping alone in our suite. So he gave up his own comfortable bed selflessly, while insisting on joining me in my bed, just to keep me safe . . . now, how's that for being well behaved, I ask you?"

"So, he got scared in the hotel, well, it figures. I should have forewarned you about that . . . sorry. Sometime I will have to share that story with you. But needless to say, if you're brave enough to put up with the pisher a little longer, you're welcome too."

"Thank you Carol—on behalf of all of us really, including the 'little pisher' himself, we thank you. You're indirectly responsible for providing our entertainment for the remainder of our day no doubt, so we appreciate that."

"When should I anticipate the little scamp home?"

"Oh I don't know, being a school night, what's good for you?"

"No later than ten, that will work for me Marc."

"No sweat Carol, should I put him back on?" Larry was shaking his head in the negative at my question already.

"That's not necessary—but tell him to stop shaking his head this very moment—it's rude . . . also warn him to behave, and lastly—that his father and I love him."

I couldn't help but laugh at her blind perceptiveness.

"You got it Carol . . . we'll see you by ten."

"Okay Marc, bye."

"See ya Carol."

I hung up as Larry let out a substantial sigh of relief while I found myself laughing just looking at him now. I was realizing just how well his mother had him pegged with her crack over him shaking his head.

"Larry, your mother says to behave. She also said that she and your father love you—oh and listen Mr. smarty pants—she immediately knew you were shaking your head not to have to speak to her."

"Yeah, yeah, yeah." That was all we got out of Larry with that comment.

Larry, along with both the boys and girls, passed around some high-fives, as we entered the Trail.

As we got inside the house, a fresh round of 'wows' escaped the girls' lips.

The girls were simply too cute. I was realizing how much I was enjoying them. Boys are wonderful, so don't get me wrong, but these two angels were whetting my appetite. If anything in my life was missing at that moment, it was a woman—one who could fill Miranda's boots, along with a little girl down the road, to love and fuss over as well.

After introductions from everyone offering his or her hellos to one another, Mom, of course, cornered me immediately.

"So Markie, how do you think I did with the putz from Toon Media Records?"

"Oh him—brilliant Mom, really. You should have seen the schmuck after Scoot told him you had declined his invitation to speak to him. His ego wouldn't let him believe it. After Scooter gave him the news, he first went nuts, before then trying to break him down instead. But I must say Mom; good old Scooter then worked him a little himself."

"Good, that's what we want, let him be on the defensive . . . the wanting it bad side. After all, it must be a rare occurrence at T-M. Mind you, there is a risk to this strategy Marc, but I believe this squarely puts us in the driver's seat. Do you think I'll hear from him anytime soon, did Scott sufficiently motivate him?"

"Oh, I'd say so Mom, you're approach was right on, as was Scoot's. I suspect there will be something on my desk before I even arrive at the office manana."

"Hey there Captain, how was the trip back?" At that moment, Dad had joined us in the kitchen.

"Great Dad, but I've missed you both." At that moment I realized I had been remiss, so I gave them hugs and kisses.

"See Marilyn, the boy did miss us."

"Of course he did Malcolm, well at least—his mother."

"Now Mom, play nice, you know I love you both the same."

"Sure you do Marc, but you still have to answer to me, now don't you?"

"Okay Ma, but don't blow a fuse."

We were still kibitzing when the boys came in to continue their walk through tour with Larry escorting the Davis ladies. The boys had completed giving the ladies an inside tour, so they were now heading for the 'main attraction of the lagoon!"

You could hear the girls' 'wows' all the way into the house even with the French door closed. Immediately, Tre popped his head inside, as he asked me to turn on 'the works,' which I did.

"Say son, I've been meaning to ask you, what's the 'juice' run for all that stuff anyway?"

"Dad, do you remember Clinton's stupid military policy; don't ask, don't tell?"

"Sure, I look back on that as the 'high point' of his Presidency naturally— why?"

"Dadio—don't ask, because I've now invoked the Clinton Doctrine, believe me Pop—you don't want me to tell you the number."

"That bad?"

"Well Pop, let's put it this way, but afterwards, the subject's closed forever. If I ran the works, as Tre called it, everyday, 24/7, for the year, here's where I'd be. I would be able to supply an entire small European Country for a week as an alternative. Does that satisfy your curiosity?"

"Jesus—I think I need to lie down, please tell me you're exaggerating."

"Yes Dadio, of course I am, but don't lie down anyway. We're all going out to the Lake, that is, if you'd both care to join us?"

"Yes dear, we would love too. I need to talk strategy with Scott about Jared. But besides that, I'm just curious enough about this little tug of yours, to want to see it at least once naturally."

"Okay, well then, why not go and change into some Lake appropriate clothing including deck shoes please, and we'll shove off shortly. Dad should we all pile in Laverne, or do you want to form a caravan with the company's Expedition? You know if Grace, Reg, and Sofia join us, we're thirteen. We'll all fit in, but it won't be completely comfortable."

"Fine, I'll take Beth and Scott along with Mom and you. That leaves all of the kids and staff to Laverne. I'm sure with Grace and crew along to chaperone the kids, they will all behave wonderfully."

"Yes, if they plan on surviving the trip over to the lake, I suppose they will. Good plan Dad."

"I thought as much son, that's why I suggested it."

"Okay, let's shoot for a departure in fifteen minutes all right?"

"Sure thing Captain, but I want the whole sorted story on their performance in the car. I'll also bring along the taped newscasts with me, that way you and Scott can watch them in the Expedition.

"That's an excellent idea Dad, why didn't I think of that myself?"

"Candidly son, perhaps being this close to the source of all ultimate wisdom—you were simply overwhelmed, is all?"

"Oh for Christ's sake Mal, you're throwing it a bit thick, don't you think?"

"Yes Marilyn—because I can!"

"Touché Dad."

"All right everyone—listen up, we'll meet on the drive in fifteen minutes, now go change."

Thirty-seven minutes later, we were on our way finally. Why is it that anytime Jews set a time to leave—they're always late? Really, I often ask myself these kinds of things. Is it any wonder why Moses and his tribes wandered that desert for forty stinking years—I ask you? You know, my Mother insists the only reason why Moses and company took so long is the fact that Moses—like any man—wouldn't stop to ask for directions!

This time though, the reason for our delay was legitimate. My driver Paul, not knowing our imminent plans, thanks to my screw up, had decided Laverne needed her weekly bath.

At any rate, we were now en route to the Lake, with our little caravan . . . including our clean limo. I was watching all of the newscasts with a lot of excitement. The folks were right about the 'performance spin' coming from the press. All the same, more than enough was covered on the crusade that prompted the performance in the first place. The word was going to continue to spread on that too, which was my main concern naturally.

Watching CCC's newscast, I had to laugh as their commentator couldn't have been more flattering—now! You see, Condescension Connors had not only groveled to speak apologetically on national TV last week, she was now—unemployed!

The word was our little shrimp had floundered before being swallowed whole by the sharks—all dressed in suits! Now one for the history books, she was certifiably un-hirable after such a debacle, at least locally. She had dropped off the radar already. All of her motives had been joyously exposed by her many detracting competitors, after Fox's expose, yet without as much as an ounce of pity either, from any of them. And good riddens to her I thought.

When we were through watching the tapes, Mom chided in with the best news relating to the airtime exposure.

"By the way dear, Robbie called yesterday to report tons of email for more information about the foundation's work on Verandas' website. Also, people volunteering to assist in construction of the facility, even donated building materials. And several requests for forming fan clubs and information about the boys, including all the major teen magazines."

"Damn Mom, that's awesome."

We all listened now as Scoot and Mom talked at length about Jared as we got ever closer to the lake. Later, when we were all alongside my massive fifty-two footer, Dad's candid words summed up his impression of it succinctly.

"Now this is living, but I don't see the Four Seasons Marquee anywhere son?"

"Can it Malcolm, don't embarrass the boy in front of his guests."

I jumped on the main deck to slide the gangway across the short distance to the pier so everyone could board. This time though, the 'wows' were cross-generational and greater in number, as I commenced a tour.

My boat was one of the few things I possessed besides electronics that I procured directly from the Orient. In this case—Taiwan. I had discovered through a fair amount of research, that in keeping up with the Italians, the

Taiwanese as well knew their stuff when it came to manufacturing boats. Not just regular yachts mind you, but domestic behemoths like mine—the proverbial combination yacht and home.

You see, I tried to order it to my exacting specifications, as I was full of ideas . . . I can still recall it like it was yesterday. Like a kid in the familiar candy store, I went through their catalogue almost driving my sales representative crazy with changes. It finally came to a head for him and me when I decided the whole experience was becoming way too draining on my limited time, so I pointed to a nice picture as I said to him: "You know what, I'll take this one—in teal—but super-size it with all-teak decks . . . Whew, thank God that was long over with."

It turned out to be a wonderful solution. My tug was striking, from the exterior with tinted swept-back windows running along mid ships of each level of the boat, to its rakish bow which conveyed 'yacht' more so, than houseboat.

There was bright teal and white-stripped canvas trim everywhere, from the railings to the canopy up top. That made it all stand out nicely, but the interior was in a class by itself.

You entered my 'tug's main cabin at either forward starboard, or stern. Four steps down, took you thirty-two inches below the main deck level. This provided a full seven and a half-foot ceiling on the main floor, and seven feet in the upper.

A two-thirds sized, open deck on top, included a canopied party area with misting system and fans. Add to that, a dance floor, a whirlpool big enough for twelve adults—and even karaoke. The adjacent winch was surrounded by six jet skis. Overhanging the stern was the water slide and springboard that both gave an exciting minimum fifteen-foot drop into the lake. The kids were all going nuts at that, while my folks were in shock—absolute shock I might add.

"Son, as I live and breathe, I don't believe I've ever seen something as nice as this."

"Thanks Dad, but you know, once you and mom make the move, you should take her out for an extended cruise yourselves. I'll send Randy my first mate along, to train you both."

"The hell with the move Marko—I'm free on Tuesday!" As we all laughed at Dad's crack.

I took the group on a tour of the berths which also impressed everyone.

My tug had four staterooms in all, plus a berth for the crew, and they were all spacious. Especially the captain's cabin naturally.

Mom was the first to comment.

"My word son, this is lovely, I wouldn't change a thing."

"Gee Mom—not even the linens once in a while?"

"Marc, dear?"

"Yes Mother—dear."

"Marc, did I ever tell you why we don't send donkeys to college?"

"Yes Mother, perhaps—a thousand times."

"Fine, then don't make me tell you again—smart ass."

Not desiring to be glutton for punishment nor insult, I ignored her comments by informing everyone of our itinerary.

"Okay everyone, here's the plan. We're going to take a short cruise out to one of my favorite spots that has a nice sandy beach. This way, any of us or the kids, have a nice place to play Robinson Crusoe. We'll anchor off shore there for the afternoon.

"Grace, if you and Sofia have inspected the galley, you already know that the three of us—will all fit in there! Not only that, but we can prepare one hell of a feast in no time flat."

"That's fine Marc, but we insist—we'll handle the food love, you have your guests to attend too after all. Don't worry about us we'll figure things out, as Sofia's showing us around." Grace said as she and Sofia continued to chuckle from my cracks.

"Thank you Gracie, that's most gracious of you both. Reg, if you would do the honors, the bar is located aft of the head in the main salon. I know I could go for a dose from the good doctors . . . I'm confident Dad wants his usual too. Now what can Reg get for you—Beth?"

"Wow, my first ever cocktail on a yacht, oh I don't know—how about an Absolute Martini shaken with Sour Apple Schnapps?"

"Yum, an Appletini, nice choice Beth—and Mom?"

"Well, since you're offering, do you have any of our Merlot on board dear?"

"Mom, do you think these little fish out in the water—poop in this here lake?"

"Thanks Marc."

"And Gilligan—what can we get you?" Turning to Scoot, I could see my crack had him somewhat miffed—like I cared, huh.

"Easy there Skipper, you don't want a mutiny on this cruise, do you?"

We were grinning stupidly at each other now, as Scoot gave me his order. Reg started to disappear to the Salon.

"Son, where's the engine room, I'm just dying to see your power?"

"Easy Dad, first, did you remember to bring along your heart meds?"

"Can it smart ass, you know my ticker's better than anyone's. Besides, right about now, I need a small testosterone rush, after all, at my age—I'm perpetually—a quart low."

We were all enjoying Dad's self-effacing crack, Mom included, who now couldn't resist the set up though, by adding one of her own:

"You mean, you wish—you were only a quart low, Mal?"

"Thank you dear, how kind of you to point that out for everyone's benefit. Come on son, lead me to those engines."

"Me too Marc, I want to tag along for the engine room tour myself."

"Sure thing Gilligan, let's go."

"You're pushing it—Morgan."

"Forgive me Scoot, I won't say another word." And I didn't.

"Good, see that you don't."

I now led our trio into the engine room at the stern of the lower level—all the while—humming the theme to Gilligan's Island. This peeved Scoot to no end, which of course fostered utter delight for the old man and me at the same time.

As I opened the door to the engine room, my two fellow males stood there silently. Likely they were both thunderstruck. Dad and Scooter were standing there salivating—like two ten-year-olds unwrapping their first Tonka Trucks . . . I knew all too well—what they were looking at . . . I'd been there myself.

There they were before us . . . my 'industrial-sized,' twin supercharged, Mercedes diesels. The engines were gleaming in their highly polished, all-aluminum glory, just longing for the push of a button to fire them to life. With each of the engines being the over-all size of an eighteen-wheeler's . . . they did tend to overwhelm the first-time visitor.

"Oh my God Scott, would you look at these monsters?

"You know son, are you sure you're not compensating for other, more personal 'power plants' of a more modest size? You know Marko, like—something out of—Bedrock—perhaps?"

Dad was hysterical—while I was beet red with his metaphoric reference to my penis . . . 'Freddie.'

I decided to do what I did best at times such as this—I ignored him totally.

"Yep, five hundred and eighty ponies a piece at twenty six hundred RPM. She'd cruise all day long at close to thirty knots."

"Damn, look at the size of the blowers, would you Scott?" Came out of Dad's mouth.

"Yeah Mal, they're something alright."

"Most impressive son, really."

"Thanks Pop, I'm so glad you approve of the family's—little tug."

"Some tug son, say, what did you christen her, I didn't notice?"

"Gentlemen I apologize. Say hello to 'What's Behind—Curtain Number two'."

Dad and Scoot loved the name from the 'Let's Make A Deal' television game show.

We headed back into the main salon to join the ladies, who were already enjoying their drinks. They had returned from the Captains cabin, where Beth had unpacked her luggage with Mom assisting in the girls' cabin.

"Ladies, are you ready to change into your suits for our cruise, we'll be shoving off in five shakes?"

"Yes dear, we're fine; you boys carry on . . . we know when to keep out of the professionals' way." My mom's sarcasm was priceless . . . as usual.

I gave my 'crew' their instructions as my two good doctors and I ascended to the fly bridge. I dropped my twin out-drives out of their safety no start positions to fire them up.

Dad and Scoot working as my crew, listened to all my sequenced instructions as I yelled them out . . . they did a fair job of mimicking the old Keystone Cops. Still, we were successful as we were free of the dock now. We were moving away at 'no-wake' forward right at three knots. At that moment, my gaggle of pint-sized crewmembers below the fly bridge joined me.

"Dadio, may we go in the whirlpool now, is it okay?"

"Sure Tre, the switches are on that panel over there, but it's already preheated."

I pointed the way to the controls for my son's benefit as the 'youngins' were quickly neck high in bubbling hot water. I now heard Larry's comment, which made me almost lose it on the spot.

"Okay you guys—now try to guess and tell me, when I let out a nice fart underwater."

"Larry!

I yelled through my mock shock.

"Are you forgetting you're in the company of two impressionable young ladies?"

"No HB, of course not—we've all already discussed it—think of it like a science experiment. You see, this is just a test . . ."

. . . "Of what Lar—your emergency broadcast system?"

I was rolling at my own crack, as were all the kids.

"Nah HB, but that was funny, actually, we want to try to hear a 'fart' underwater in this whirlpool when it's running . . . see—it's science."

"Okay, carry on then."

What else could I say to that? I was still thinking about it as I cleared the 'no-wake' marker.

I realized at that moment that my two 'macho' crewmembers were waiting. They naturally wanted a 'manly' demonstration of our power, so I decided to accommodate their unstated desire. I sounded my air horns; made sure I was unobstructed with traffic before opening my throttles three-quarters full, slowly. Impressively, the huge 52' footer responded with tons of torque. It was the equivalent of saying:

"Hey, who are you kidding boy—we live for this?"

We were cruising at a nice pace of 23 knots. Dad, Scoot, and the ladies came up topside where they each grabbed teak loungers under the canopy. They began a relaxed conversation of yesterday's events, each from their personal perspective.

My little hide-away beach had long since been programmed into my GPS. I just connected the dots to find it yet again . . . we arrived twenty-seven minutes later. As always, I had to approach this beach carefully, so as not to get beached. I got as close as I knew was safe, as I dropped my anchors, locking the tug in stationary place.

I shut down the diesels, as I then addressed the gaggle of youngsters specifically.

"Listen kids, despite the heat-wave we've had for all these weeks now, this lake is still going to be cold. You certainly can swim in it, but be prepared you're going to freeze for a moment or two. All of you brave enough to give it a try; I'm turning on the water for the slide—any volunteers?"

"Sure HB, I'll be the man."

"Oh no you won't Lar—I will?" Tre yelled out.

At that moment, I had two boys fighting each other for first position at the slide's ladder.

"You two knock it off now, there is to be no horseplay on this boat, ever!

Trevor, you will allow your best mate honors—right now!"

Boy, if only Tom Scott had been here, even he'd be impressed.

"Sorry Dad—go ahead Lar-man."

Tre now walked back to the tub where he got himself back in, looking dejected as ever I'd seen him.

"Thank you Tre, don't mind if I do." Larry baited back, but Trev was already defeated.

Larry then climbed the ladder. He waited for his 'associates' to goad him apparently to let go and fly. However, the minutes rolled by with nary a word out of the peanut gallery.

"Well; aren't you guys going to dare me?

He demanded more than asked after several minutes of being ignored.

"Damn, it sure is a big drop down this thing, I don't know if I've got the 'baitzm' for it?" He added when the kids seemed to continue ignoring him.

"What are baitzm; Lar?" Taylor asked innocently enough responding to Larry's taunts.

"These!"

Larry countered as he pointed to his crotch, while grabbing his testicles for affect.

"Hey guys, if you're not going to dare me—someone else can freeze their nuts off."

"Larry—watch it!"

"Yes Mrs. M, sorry ladies, my mistake—I should have said—testicles, right?"

"Honestly Larry, since you've asked, I would have preferred you'd said neither."

"Gee, Mrs. M, I gotta call them something you know, they're two-thirds of my 'meat and two veg', at least that's what Tre calls them."

"Thanks Lar, I so very much wanted to let Grammy and Dad know that, blimey—mate?"

"Sorry Tre, my screw up—Mrs. M., forget about what I said before."

"Thank you Larry, I'm relieved to hear that."

Then something weird happened:

All at once, little Halley jumped in to change the subject herself.

"Dang it Larry—go already." She yelled out loudly and authoritatively!"

Now apparently, poor old Larry wasn't prepared for the resumption of this topic at all, at least in his conscious mind. He was caught unawares on that conscious level you see, as his subconscious mind simply kicked in for him. He found himself—without thought or warning—following Halley's instruction to the letter—he had already let go!

As Larry did so, immediately you could tell—he had never intended to do so, yet it was hysterical too. There he was, still looking over his shoulder at us—but for once—not knowing what to say in his predicament.

His mouth was agape, with the right palm of his hand resting on his right cheek as he began to slide down. At that moment, he already knew that his goose was cooked.

Larry's body was going down for the count, closer and closer to that cold water—after an seventeen-foot drop! Yet in those final moments in mid-air, his lips finally expelled his most desperate of expletives—holy sh . . . oot!"

We didn't have a single person aboard who wasn't hysterical that witnessed it. That included all of us except Grace and Sofia who were otherwise occupied in the galley.

We all ran over to the rails, to await him surfacing below. When Larry resurfaced, he was yelling and giving himself kudos, knowing he had survived. And the water, while cold—wasn't too—cold, apparently.

"Okay Em, if he can do it—then so can I."

With that, little Halley climbed the steps, gave us all a big throwing kiss, as she let go. She chose to scream hysterically the whole way down while holding her nose. She came up laughing and happy, moments later too.

Now within another thirty-five seconds, they were all in. The twins took the slide while Embeth took the built in springboard, performing a marvelous swan dive. Well that took care of that, we were kid-free for the moment—oh happy frigging day!

The adults were all minutes into an enjoyable and light conversation over our cocktails, when Sofia emerged with trays of goodies. Meanwhile, all the kids had swum the short distance to the beach safely.

"Sofia, these look wonderful; muy bien!"

"Gracious Marko, de nada."

"Mucho gusto senorita." Dad chimed in.

"Oh, Senor Mal—gracious."

We all started ravaging the platters, with Dad of course in the lead. Apparently, Mom couldn't help herself now.

"Malcolm honey, keep that up, and you'll be getting a wee case of thee wind."

She had said it in her near perfect high-pitched impersonation of Lady Marisa's Scottish brogue. We were all on the floor busting—even Mom herself.

The kids were still playing on the beach, looking for treasures no doubt, along with the usual beach activities. Two hours later, we called them over to come aboard for dinner as we would head back to the marina afterwards. The kids all made it aboard safely, yet they were all shaking big time, once out of the water again.

They lay down on the deck across their towels to dry, before we could sit down to eat. Fifteen minutes later, they were good to go for dinner . . . but what a dinner it was. Gracie and Sofia had outdone themselves as the dinner was superb with a wonderful Lobster Newburg with all the trimmings.

After dinner, we were all sitting around the table talking and digesting. I then suggested playing the DVD of the boy's crowd test from the previous night.

Watching the film in the salon, it was amazing just taking into consideration how professionally done, T-M had produced it. Clearly the film made a singular impact on the viewer; no doubt . . . that was clearly the boys' passion for their music. Everyone agreed the boys had done an incredible job entertaining the Toonland guests.

"Boys, all I can say is, I wish Grammy and I had been there, you were fantastic."

"Thanks Gramps."

"You're welcome Taylor."

"So, men are you in the mood to give us a song to carry us over until your next performance?"

"Why sure Gramps, anytime for you." The twins got up, walked over to their Grandfather as they gave him hugs, while Dad of course, was in heaven.

"It's a shame we don't have an amplifier and microphones, isn't it Tre?"

"Yeah bro."

"Hold it a darn minute Sparky; we've got the karaoke system right by the dance floor. I'll go get it, or should we all just go up top?"

The unanimous decision was to go back up top. We made the journey to the upper deck on the spiral staircase then grabbed some seats as I dug the equipment out of the cabinet.

"So boys, what are we going to hear?"

"Something special Dad. If it's all the same to everybody, we would like to do a new song we've been working on for Gramps. We were going to surprise him with it anyway by next week. I guess this will be the surprise right now, okay Daddy?

"Sure T-man, I think we'd all love to hear Gramps' song, right Dad?"

"You're darn tooting son, go ahead boys, you've got my curiosity up. I can't even imagine what the song is." My father said just before Trevor commented to me.

"Dad, we'll use the microphone for the vocals, but we don't need anything else. This is something we've been practicing in our bedroom at night."

"Will this be your first time doing it all the way through Trev?" Dad asked now.

"No Gramps, but the first time in front of anybody else . . . you especially." Trevor corrected dad.

The boys had not even started, yet dad was already choking up with fresh tears. God, how he loved his boys, but after all, it was quite an honor they were presenting him.

"Cool guys. Whenever you're ready, we are too?" Embeth offered now.

The boys set up the karaoke amplifier and mic, while setting their volume with a test level check with Scoot.

"Gramps, Taylor and I, know you love this song by how many times we've heard you humming it. When we found the music for it, we knew we wanted to try to do it special for you, so this is for you a Capella, with all our love." The boys now ran over and gave their Gramps matching kisses on each cheek . . . Dad was certifiably a basket case now, meanwhile they have not uttered some much as a single note yet.

They got comfortable with the mic stand between them as they each had one hand securing it. Immediately, they closed their eyes to fully concentrate.

Even with tremendous musical talent and their 'twin' intuitiveness— singing a Capella is the most difficult of all vocal skills to master . . . along with being the most unforgiving too. In short, you are singing without the support of any instruments, live or recorded, and merely relying on oneself to hold the pitch perfectly while following the melody in your head. Beyond this, many would argue that amplifying this with a mic, leaves further room for mistakes to sound horrible as they are louder and clearer.

At the next moment, they began . . . it was wondrous, no—breathtaking actually. I let out a soft gasp, as my arms filled with Goosebumps instantly. They were doing a two-part, 'street corner' style of harmony within their do-wop, after Taylor carried the opening bars alone.

More than anything though, it had to be their passion in singing this song for their Gramps knowing how he loved it. I couldn't believe they were doing it this well. It was not only one of Dad's favorites, but one of mine as well. Everyone from Glenn Miller to Harry Connick Jr. had covered it over the years, but the Platters certainly made the tune their own, it was the classic hit, 'My Prayer.'

What I found astounding from a structural standpoint was they seemed to know how to pull this song off instinctively. The twins knew they had to carry their harmony to an exceptional level. With strictly two-part harmony to work with, that was the only way to nail the tune . . . that's exactly what they did.

Their timing and phrasing, as well as their perfect pitch, were all top notch. We were all just sitting there listening intently, silent . . . stunned. And we all gasped in unison—in shock really, when Taylor authoritatively, yet dramatically hit the final high crescendo on the words, My Prayer, as they finished.

I stood there with my mouth agape. I was speechless and unable to react; more so from the shudder that had run through my body during Taylor's final crescendo moments before.

Dad meanwhile was bawling like a baby, damn if he wasn't touched down to his core. My own frozen state was 'thawed' when I began hearing robust applause coming off the starboard side of 'Curtin'. We looked down to see a twenty-five foot Scarab with its passengers applauding enthusiastically; they assumed we had live professional entertainment aboard no doubt—which of course—we truly did. We all waved, as they pulled away.

"Oh my God boys; that was beyond awe-inspiring, it was heavenly. Truly I am so very touched by this expression of your love boys, all I can say is thank you both." Dad got out through his emotions finally.

He walked over and kissed both boys, then of course hugged them profusely.

"Your welcome Gramps, it sure is a beautiful song, isn't it?"

"Loverly boys, just loverly," Gracie added her two cents now.

"Thank you Grace, did you like it too, Grammy?"

"Oh yes Trevor, my God I loved it, are you kidding? In fact, I think that I would sing this one a Capella as you did it now, every time. It's so moving and dramatic. I can visualize the impact of you boys doing it on a black stage, in matching black outfits. I would place a single white spot over you two and flood you like an old-fashioned streetlamp. It will be overwhelming to anyone. And if you two want, why not pre-record full back up harmonies to go along with all that wonderful do-wop, and every audience will go crazy I'm sure."

"Bloody brill Grammy, that's a perfect way to carry it over!"

"I agree Marilyn." Scoot added.

"Good—then that's the way we'll set it up. I think it's strong enough as the ideal number to close any of their sets as well. You know, at first this song understates itself, but ends leaving the listener yearning for more—no; pleading for more—it's so dramatic. And yet it is so very tender, while haunting at the same time . . . it's perfect, I know it is! And what a beautiful way for the boys to honor Malcolm each time they perform it, don't you think Markie?"

"Yes Mom, I do, but to tell you the truth, I don't think the staging will matter one bit. I realize Dad and I are biased; after all we're both big fans of the song already. So I don't see how anyone can listen to it yet not be moved, even without all your techno gingerbread."

"Great, all that techno gingerbread as you call it honey, will add icing on the cake." My Mom admonished me in her tone somewhat with her answer, whereby I got the subliminal message too—don't challenge this!

Our conversations on this subject continued casually from this point on. We were making our way back to our mooring anyway, as we wrapped up our conversations.

When we had the 'tug' tied up and secure once more, the Morgan 'cavalcade' of members, started preparing for our ride home. We said quick good-byes to allow our guests to settle into their 'barracks' of sorts for their stay.

Our group departed, but on the way home, I asked Sofia to consider returning to the Davis' to prepare their meals and assist them. She agreed without hesitation. When I called Scooter to ask, he was thrilled for Sofia's help.

Paul stopped at Larry's first, but we were all so 'spent' and wiped out, that even the Lar-man was half-crashed. It gave Carol a nice laugh though, insisting that obviously we had all reached our 'Larry—limit' for once.

When we arrived home, we headed right for bed, except Sofia naturally. It had been a most remarkable and enjoyable weekend for all.

In the morning on the way to drop the boys off, I thought to call the school in advance. After last week's issues with the press, I wasn't taking any chances. Happily Mr. Riley told me we were in the clear. It appeared Mr. R had everything in hand, so we were to go through the rear receiving area again just as a precaution to prevent any surprises.

We got the boys into class, as I heard rousing applause as they walked into the room. I also heard Susan calming everyone down and restoring order, or at least trying too. I was glad now, that I had told the boys I would be picking them up. I hopped back into Laverne, and Paul had me at the office within a few minutes time.

Walking into the building, was my first real mistake of the day, it seems.

Robbie was bringing me a bag of Espresso Nuevo for my brewer when I saw the stack of messages and papers awaiting me, strewn across my entire desk. I saw perhaps fifty faxes alone, yet I was looking for only one in particular, but I did not see it, so I was somewhat pensive already.

Instantly, I was confused, worried, and guilty. Had we really pushed the stupid bastard too far—already?" Well I did not have time to fret over it now; I had some serious reading to do here.

Robbie plugged in the coffee brewer, ready for me to get it going, as he quipped in my direction.

"Out of the mouths of babes, right Marc?"

"Yes, you're right Robbie, but you should have seen the scene at Toonland Saturday night . . . remind me and I'll bring the DVD in for you to watch tomorrow."

"Toonland—I must be missing something, what happened there?"

"Rob, the boys did an impromptu short set for Toon Media's A& R people as a crowd test with a raw audience . . . they proceeded to bring down the house—honestly pal, it was electrifying."

"Wow, I guess my nephews are going to need a full-time staffer now—so I gladly volunteer boss . . . anything to get away from you."

"Now Robbie, that's nasty and nice of you bud, but I would be lost without you. Even with all your stupid jokes and insults, you know that—don't you?"

"Damn it Marc, I don't know whether to feel complimented, or dis'sed?"

"Trust me Robbie, I was complimenting you. But you may assist the boys from time to time I would imagine. That is, if you truthfully want the extra work?"

"Sure, I was serious."

"Okay, I'll keep it in mind bud."

"Good. Listen Marc, I was informed that a special package is on its way in. I was told that it went 'counter-to-counter' on the airlines. I didn't realize people still did that any more, did you? But apparently they still do. I understand it was couriered over here by messenger from McCarran."

"Really—who's it from, any idea?"

"Not a clue, but you should have it any minute; the mail room just advised me as they're delivering it personally."

Can it be I wondered to myself? Moments later, the mystery package arrived. Sure enough, the return address read Toon Media.

I tore it open, as I pulled out the many different enclosures. I gave it all a cursory read while my head just kept shaking. Robbie's curiosity was now getting the better of him naturally with all of my body language and sound affects . . . he never could stand waiting to find out things like this.

"Damn it boss, enlighten me already . . . will you?"

"Okay Bowser, stop begging for a bone—just relax. Why not get Marilyn on the phone at the house while I finish reading. Put her on speaker, that way you can share in all the juicy tidbits, fair enough?"

"Okay boss." Robbie eagerly followed my request, when moments later, I had the queen bee of negotiators on the phone.

"Mom, you had better jump in a cab to get down here—stat, you've got to read this stuff from Jared. You are the doctor Mom . . . and my hero—I salute you, oh great one."

"Is it that good, Markie?"

"Much better than good Mom, as I said, you're my hero. I'll bet the idiot worked the better part of his Sunday off on all of this stuff. He even sent it counter-to-counter air freight Ma, just to insure we would receive it all as original documents."

"Give me the nuts and bolts while I change Marc, I'm switching to speaker here too."

"Alright, but perhaps you should be changing in a seated position?"

"Don't dramatize Marc, cut to the damn chase . . . I want details."

"Okay, but don't say I didn't warn you."

"Spill it Marcus, you're trying my patience, I've already suffered through an entire afternoon of Larry's dissertation on his testicles, followed by a night of your father's wind section . . . have pity on me son." I laughed at her candid remarks.

"Yes Mom, but again, my condolences."

"Save it son—now spill it!"

"Sure. First, you're in the driver's seat with creative control of course, but hell, you've certainly earned that already. Step one on their agenda, is a screen test on the twins merely to confirm Jared's glowing praise of their stage presence. Assuming that goes well, you can sign a multi-media, multiple-year exclusive contract with flexibility for outside projects.

"Naturally, their package is comprehensive. It includes a TV series, four full-feature movies, as well as cable. Then there's total creative control for Scoot in the recording studio. And of course, perks up the ying-yang, along with the lion's share of any outside merchandising opportunities."

"Wow, now that is a mouthful Marc—have you reached Scott yet?"

"No, you were my first call—he's next, I'll call him on the boat once we hang up."

"Look Markie, I can take a meeting with both of you at eleven, will that work for you dear?"

"Fine, plenty of time Mom, let me go and call Gilligan to confirm his schedule."

"Marc, drop that stupid moniker will you?"

"Not while he's staying on my boat, I won't."

"Grow up son—while you still can, but I'll see you at eleven with bells on unless I hear different from you."

"See you then Mom . . . but by the way, that shot was real cute, thank you so much for busting my ego yet again." We were still laughing as we hung up our phones.

"Get Scoot on the houseboat please, Rob."

"Sure thing Marc." Halley answered the phone.

. . . "Hello, who is it please?"

"Hi Halley, its Uncle Marc, is Dad there?"

"Yes Uncle, but he's fishing right now—is it real important?"

"Yes it is sweetheart, so can you get him for me?"

"Okay, but only cause its real important—those were Daddy's orders, it may take a little while, can you wait?"

"That's all right dear, but go and get him for me, okay."

"Sure". She put the telephone down, as I indeed waited several minutes for Scooter to pick up.

"Bud what's up, I'm trying to catch my lunch, you know—Verandas style?"

"Better forget about lunch aboard 'Curtin' Scoot, I really need you here at eleven, for a meeting with Mom—may I send Paul for you?"

"Sure, send Paul, I'll leave the truck for Beth and the girls, was it his highness then?"

"Oh yeah, but wait till you see it my friend, you'll salivate, trust me."

"Really, well my hat's off to Marilyn, she's a born master you know."

"Yep." I answered.

"Listen bud, send Laverne now, by the time Paul arrives at the marina, I'll be ready for sure.

"By the way Marc, thank you for your hospitality and consideration with this incredible floating hotel you call the little tug. Beth and I had a wonderful night, if you catch my drift."

"Yes, but you can just keep your drift to yourself and Beth—I'm the cold shower guy these days—remember?"

"Honestly bud, you ought to do something about that. What about Larry's mom? I hear she's quite the looker and she comes with 'the little squirt' attached, besides that?"

"Yes, and she's way beyond a looker Scoot, she's a certifiable knock-out beauty, but I'm not sure about our characters jelling so well. I think we're too different in our philosophies, but who knows, we'll see? I do enjoy talking to her much of the time."

"Hey let me go Marc, I want to take a quick shower, see you soon."

"Alright Scoot but listen, you know that fish you're trying so desperately to catch—well it sucks big time for eating."

"Really? Well I guess thanks for the warning; I'll tell Sofia not to bother either then, right?"

"Do that bud, but trust me, Sofia's from Ensenada, she's used to 'fishy' fish, but most Americans are not."

"Okay I follow you, but I've got to run now bud." He hung up the phone now.

Robbie now buzzed me to pick up Desert Lincoln Mercury on line two.

"Mr. Morgan, its Victor Gomez, how are you today, sir?"

"Fine Victor, what's the status on my impending arrival?"

"Great news sir, your Navigator arrived an hour ago from our Special Effects vendor. I double-checked everything, with it all matching right down the list—so when would you like me to deliver it?"

"That would be much appreciated Victor . . . thank you for the personal service as I do have a full day, so when might you get her here?"

"How does within the next three hours sound, they're detailing her now . . . so naturally I won't rush that. You know sir; I must confess to you that you have created a magnificent vehicle with what you've custom ordered. You can't believe all the attention your truck is getting right now just sitting in our detail department."

"Perfect Victor, I can't wait to see her, let me transfer you to accounting so we can arrange the wire for the balance."

"Please don't go to the bother Mr. Morgan, after selling you four cars in the last several years all for cash, that's simply not necessary. The boss is more than happy to have me pick up the check when I arrive, it will save wiring fees on both sides too."

"Gee Victor, that's accommodating of your boss, thank him for me. What's the figure for the check, I'll get it cut now?"

"Sir, you lucked out somewhat, a major rebate hit last week, so even with your custom upgrades, your total has gone down." As I wrote down the figure that followed.

"You know Victor; you're all right, guy, so I'll look forward to seeing you along with the truck within the afternoon then."

"You can count on it sir."

"Thanks Victor." I hung up as I buzzed Robbie immediately.

"Guess what?"

"Oh—why don't you let me take a wild stab at it Marc? Your new Navigator is in, so you'll beat Scott by one whole day with his new car—am I warm yet?"

"You know Robbie, sometimes you take all the fun out of me messing with your brain."

"Too bad Marc . . . grow with love."

"Damn Robbie, spare me the new-age wisdom will you?"

"Good-bye Marc." As he hung up abruptly.

I buzzed him right back.

"Listen smarty pants, I wasn't quite through."

"Oh Jesus—sorry Marc, what else did you need?"

"I want our nicest coffee assortment basket brought in, along with say; one hundred dollars in gift certificates—stat!"

"Yes doctor, am I relinquished now?"

"Yes—nurse, you are."

This time, I was the one hanging up on him, but payback's a bitch, besides—he deserved it.

I used this time to review all of the faxes and messages . . . they were staggering. There were all kinds of offers—Letters of intent for recording contracts, requests from various teen rags, merchandising offers, and other information requests. There were requests for interviews too. Any opportunity you'd care to name . . . you'd eventually find it in that stack.

One fax in particular, did catch my eye though; as it was from one of the larger, but most respected teen magazines—hell they were in business when I was a teenager. They informed us that a story about the boys would go to press on Thursday. They planned to use the media kit photos, or we could call, whereby they would gladly send a photographer round. Along with that, they would send the article's author too, in case we wanted something added or corrected. Boy I thought—was that shrewd on their part or what? This outfit was assuring our cooperation along with a possible exclusive interview no less?

I thought that I would ponder this last fax, as we could all discuss it in our meeting as well.

Next, I dictated a suitable form letter to Robbie, for Mom's use in responding a polite no thanks to the various genuine opportunists. I would review the draft with Mom and Scoot for their input when the meeting started.

Once I was finished, I called Paul to check in with him on Scoot progress in getting here, I was told that they were in route with another seven minutes to travel. At ten-twenty, Scoot bounded through the door, followed by Mom right at ten forty.

"Should we start now, or do you need more time dear?"

"No Mom, I've got things under control at the moment. But we'll need to take a short break if my new truck arrives."

"Wow—congratulations dear. That's right, I almost forgot. My word, exactly what you need desperately—another car. Is this number forty-three—or four?"

Scoot was relishing Mom's berating efforts at my expense, while she gave me her smirk—I knew all too well.

"Thank you for your enthusiasm Mom, considering it got you and Dad my old '99."

"You're welcome dear . . . besides which, you already know we love our truck."

The meeting began in earnest with the first item on our agenda being, discussing and completing the form letter. This was then followed by the teen magazine feature.

Our feeling was that it would be in our best interests for the boys, as well as smart besides, to cooperate with the magazine. After some posturing on our few concerns, we agreed to their photographer and writer. Accordingly, I had Robbie see to it, by placing a telephone call to the publisher's office. They were delighted with our call but would call in the morning to set up a firm appointment for Tuesday.

Sidestepping the other record deals after a cursory review, we turned our attention to our main course naturally—the Toon Media offer.

Each of us went through everything in the sample contracts, reviewed their added opportunities, and then analyzed each one. After perusing everything sent, our trio concluded the meeting with a round robin, pro and con conversation on each of several major points.

Mom felt strongly that given the strategy we had used so successfully— so far, she desired to continue it, despite the risks. Eventually after much discussion, we all agreed for better or worse, to follow her lead and therefore remain non-committal at present.

To minimize the inherent risks of such a ballsy strategy, we would appear at least interested on some level. This would hopefully make Jared plotz as he would wonder what, if any, our actual level of interest was.

Mom now put it to both of us succinctly.

"Remember gentlemen, always keep them guessing some. While they are second-guessing, we'll all be planning our checkmate."

Mom dictated a brilliant letter off to Robbie who was grinning almost throughout the entirety of it, taking it down in shorthand.

I asked Robbie to read it back to verify it was correct, as well as free of any obvious mistakes or omissions. After the letter's opening pleasantries, he started a recitation of the body of the letter:

"Thank you for your interest Mr. Morison, as well as your most kind offer in pursuing an on-going relationship with Trevor and Taylor Morgan.

"We have reviewed your abundant materials, along with the various sample contracts carefully.

"As you can well imagine at the present time, we are reviewing several options presented for the boys' consideration from many diverse sources. Certainly, there is interest in what you purpose, yet we do not feel that we are in a position to proceed further, right at this time.

"Your desire therefore to set up a meeting as outlined in your letter of January 29th, 2000 is understandable; yet for the present, we feel we have an adequate understanding of what you are offering.

"If a face-to-face meeting is deemed more advantageous in further consideration of your kind offer, we will certainly contact you directly.

"Thank you again for the opportunity you gave the boys this last Saturday to perform for your guests and we look forward to further discussions with you and T-M.

"You may telephone us should you have any questions, but again; we greatly appreciate your offer and consideration."

Sincerely,

Mrs. Marilyn Morgan

Personal Manager;

Tay 'n' Tre . . . The Morgan's

When Robbie was finished reading, we discussed the chessboard move we were advancing. We all agreed the letter tempered the risk sufficiently, while hopefully motivating Morison, thereby baiting him for more unsolicited concessions just to gauge our interest level by sweetening the pot further. Given that we all knew that Morison's own ego-driven desire to prevail in this negotiation was overly ripe and thinly veiled, Mom reasoned that we should exploit that. It was the classic, 'take-away' approach, but we all felt it would continue to work to our advantage with his personality.

"Mom, let's have Robbie type this up so we can fax it over to his office . . . I'll wager you'll get a call from him before he take's lunch. Anyone care to wager a different outcome?"

"Not me Marc, you forget, I know this jerk too well. He lives to get that signature on the dotted line—just like a seasoned used car salesperson so I suspect he'll be groveling within an hour of receiving it." Scoot opined.

Mom now added:

"Well, I think we're all of the same mindset here Marc. Let's wait and see what happens. He might think he's dealing with neophytes and therefore decide to make us sweat for awhile himself, who knows?"

"Its possible Mom, but it would surprise me somewhat honestly too. He seems much like the type that carries his trump cards face up, but we'll see soon enough. But if he does try to play us, we won't flinch." I added.

"Yes dear, we shall all see how Mr. Jared Morison thinks."

The letter was finished within ten minutes, so Mom signed it as Robbie then faxed it immediately.

Well after we had adjourned our meeting, Mom returned to the house. Scoot meanwhile was being picked up by Natalie Garson on her way to the Lake where she was gathering up the remaining Davis' for a day of touring houses. These homes were from the many Scoot previewed during the week before, some of which Scooter was flipped out for.

Meanwhile I returned to my work.

Right at two hours of receiving my last telephone call from Victor Gomez, Robbie announced him. I greeted my sales representative warmly and offered him a chair as he sat down to relax somewhat.

"Here's the check Victor, all signed, sealed, and now delivered." Receiving my check, he handed me two sets of keys along with all of my pre-completed paperwork that I had signed and returned when I ordered the truck.

"Mr. Morgan, if you're ready to see your new vehicle, we can go any time you say?"

"I'm ready Victor, but please, first, accept this small gift as a token of my appreciation. I handed him the basket along with the envelope containing the certificates. He was genuinely overwhelmed. I then continued my comments.

"So Victor, shall we go say hello to my new off spring?"

I escorted Victor outside—where she sat upfront of the lot donning a giant bow as a personal thank you touch from Victor, beautifully justifying my own gift only moments earlier.

Hot diggidy damn, she was beautiful . . . no—stunning was more appropriate actually, just as I had visualized her countless times in my mind. Being that this was my second attempt to have this truck built this way; it was nice to realize now that my waiting was finally over.

The truck's special pearlescent brilliant tri-coat white paint was just what 'the doctor ordered'. The body itself was done at the factory beautifully—not totally at some paint shop. With the special monochromatic finish, everything painted on the truck was in the one brilliant pearlescent white color . . . it looked sensational.

It had chromed and custom, twenty-two inch wheels with lower profile tires. Add to that, a custom grill in the same beautiful wire mesh used in the high line Aston Martins and Jaguars. Hi-performance fog lamps and HID headlights, also replaced the factory-installed versions, with custom clear lenses gracing the taillights.

The factory air system suspension was tastefully lowered three inches. The factory running boards were gone, yet replaced instead with matching brilliant white Pearlescent aerodynamic body cladding with running boards integrated into them that further gave the truck a very tasteful lowered appearance. But most important to me though, were the dual Flowmaster mufflers that were installed identical to the Lightning pickup truck from Ford. They exited through the body cladding behind the running boards with huge 2.5 inch, dual chromed exhaust tips on each side—awesome.

Completing the package of course, were substantial engine upgrades from Ford's SVT hi-performance unit, which amounted to a modest bump to over five-hundred horsepower.

My beautiful new truck beckoned me closer as I unlocked the door, before sliding into the soft Palomino colored leather interior. I drooled over the custom matching birds-eye maple in its rich palomino color that trimmed the interior extensively.

When I put in the key to fire up those five-hundred ponies, whoa—was that truly a wonderful sound to behold all in all. The low, guttural tone of the

Flowmaster mufflers, coupled with a four-cam, thirty-two-valve V-8, made this truck sound truly harmonious. It sounded much closer to the Firebird W-6 or Mustang Cobra, than the luxury SUV that it was. Then I realized that my suspension system was automatically elevating and leveling the truck three inches higher to my amazement . . . God I love being surprised.

I couldn't resist, I just touched the gas slightly, as the harmonics of the rumble was like chamber music to my ears. To put it into words—I was thrilled—finally I had the truck of my dreams.

Victor now joined me inside as he began going over the assorted improvements and custom enhancements to my prior truck. Once we were finished, he thanked me again before leaving.

Naturally, I decided that I had to go out for lunch rather than our cafeteria in the basement. I was like a kid loose in the proverbial candy store as I was dying to test out my new hotrod Lincoln behemoth.

I called inside to Robbie on the Nav's built in satellite navigation and telephone system. I advised him of my impromptu plans, before asking if he cared to join me for lunch, which he seemed delighted to accept.

When he first came out of the doors, he panned the lot in a cursory fashion over to guest parking where he saw the truck. He was grinning from ear-to-ear by the time he got there. He seemed satisfied after completing a walk around the entire truck. Stepping inside, he looked around the cabin some, before commenting.

"Okay—let me just say this right away, to get it all out—what's with you, it's much less butch than the last one?"

"Is that your sole impression Robbie?"

"Not in the least Marc, it's stunning and drop dead gorgeous for an SUV and that's the truth of it. Use it well boss."

"Thanks Robbie. Now let's see what this baby will do on Sahara, shall we?"

"Isn't it identical to the last one in the giddy-up department?"

"Robbie old boy, I'll let you decide that for yourself. By the way, there's supposed to be a roll of toilet tissue in the console at all times . . . check and see, will ya!"

"Oh my, aren't we the prepared little boy scout this afternoon."

"Rob, what's that Boy Scout motto again; be prepared—so better buckle up?"

With that comment out, I dropped the shifter into 'drive' and peeled out of the lot. Like the first time I made love to Miranda, it was fast, furious,—but left a little rubber in its wake!

"Jesus Marc, what in God's name did you do to this thing, it's a friggin' rocket? Do they make steroids for trucks now?"

"No Robbie, it's just had some fine tuning from Ford SVT along with a performance shop is all."

"Christ . . . I'd say."

Robbie now grabbed his assist handle as he held on for dear life. I turned onto Sahara, where I found the road wide open, I floored the big Lincoln as I began singing that old fifties song . . . Hotrod Lincoln:

. . . "Son; you're going to drive me to drinking, if you don't stop driving, that—hot—rod—Lincoln."

The truck quickly shifted through the gears. It hunkered down the road to around 70 miles per, before I even felt any measurable drop of the power curve.

"Marc, welcome to your second childhood—good luck with our cops driving this thing."

"Thank you Robbie, I'll try to remember that." I pulled into the parking lot for Big Dog's on West Sahara, as Robbie blew out a breathe of relief as I killed the motor. He now quipped:

"And they say that unprotected sex—is dangerous."

I just had to laugh.

We got out of the truck where I continued to stare at it as we walked inside the joint for their signature Wisconsin Brats the restaurant was famous for. After being seated in a nice booth in the bar area, we eventually had a wonderful lunch after adequate cocktails.

We returned to the office via the Saint Cloud Stables, which were around the corner. I proudly showed Robbie the property. I don't think he was able to visualize it too well, but seemed interested all the same.

Immediately upon returning to the office, I checked my telephone messages for a call from Jared. Mom had requested this of me earlier. Upon seeing there wasn't a response from Morison's office, I decided not to sweat it. If Morison did intend on playing hardball with us, he picked a capable adversary in my Mother. And in the final analysis, he certainly deserved her too. Instantly I laughed profoundly, just thinking on that fact again, before returning to my day's agenda.

Robbie and I went over several items, including the internal cost for our foundation affair on the previous Saturday. After expropriating off a few expenses, I was satisfied and told Robbie to prepare a bill for the Foundation to reimburse us. You see, our coffers over there would be capable of reimbursing us—which I relished as it was a true 'first'.

Later while working through our usual issues along with the typical assortment of unforeseen problems of the day, Robbie put through a call from Mom.

"Well Markie, did he send anything over or call?"

"No, he didn't Mom . . . still think this strategy is best for this situation?"

"Yes I do Marc. Fine, did you get the new truck delivered yet?"

"Oh yeah, but Dad is going to be sooooooooo friggin jealous when he takes a ride—trust me."

"I doubt it Marc, your father loves his more than enough for one man, let alone a thousand. If it fit in our Queen bed at home, I'd be out on my ass—while she'd be in. Thank God it's at the winery now so he can't obsess over it constantly."

I laughed, but I knew my mom really was somewhat jealous of the attention that Dad paid to the truck. Rarely, did he do the same in consideration of her.

"Listen Mom, I'll be picking up the boys at school to bring them home. If either you or Grace needs Laverne for any reason, this is a good day for it?"

"I don't, but I'll check with Grace, thanks."

"Okay Mom, I'll see you at around 3:30 to 4:00—wait a minute, I have to speak to Susan Geary first, so I'm not really sure when we'll make it through the door actually."

"Okay son, but you drive carefully with my boys, no funny business. Dad warned me that this new Navigator is souped up, as you two call it. I don't want to see any injured twins . . . or you either for that matter. Do I make myself crystal clear, Marcus Earl Morgan?"

"Yes Mother, you do . . . May I grow up now please?"

"Not with that attitude, you may not!"

"Jesus Mom, cut me some slack, I'm thirty three years old!"

"Fine, see you at the house then, bye dear."

"Bye Mom."

I left my office right at three. I turned on the sound system which was a real wake up call in itself. The 'audiophile' system was 'aces' both from the sound quality standpoint as well as its sophistication, I was amazed actually.

When I arrived at the Meadows School, I parked in a different place than usual. This way, the boys would have a nice surprise when we left the building.

I went into the boys' classroom, where I found them talking to Mrs. G.

"Hey there guys, hi Mrs. G. How did it go?"

"Somewhat problematic Marc, but I won't say the boys contributed to it. For the record, they were wonderful throughout all of it. I'm very proud of them, so I've told them as much—you should feel proud too.

"My problem is with the girls in this classroom, in addition to a whole school full of new fans at recess and lunch. In fact, we were talking about all of it, when you came in. I'm at a loss to figure out what we should do."

"Gee Mrs. G, is it that serious?"

"Yes, if it continues unabated, it will be disruptive to everyone, but Marc—feel free to call me Susan here as well."

"Okay, but before you panic Susan, why don't we give it a few days to calm down?"

"Oh we will, but if it doesn't change Marc, I'm afraid we'll all have to discuss our options."

"What does that entail Susan—talk to me here?"

"Marc I don't want to alarm you, or the boys, but we hold to a strict standard of behavior at TMS. If that standard cannot be maintained, the school steps in to 'neutralize' the obstacle as best they can, by whatever means are open to them. On the one hand, that might mean very little, but as a worst-case scenario, it could also entail the administration asking you to enroll the boys elsewhere, next semester."

"Oh Lord, that's all we need Susan . . . the boys have been so happy here."

"Well, let's all stay calm. Maybe you're right; perhaps all of this craziness will dissipate within the next few days anyway. Why not call me on Friday or stop by, okay?"

"Sure thing Susan, boys, say so long to Mrs. G.—we have to get a move on, all right?"

"Yes Daddy, but I don't want to leave my school."

"I know Taylor, but let's not worry just yet—okay, remember what Mrs. G said? And boys, we always have some options ourselves, so I want you two to let this go for the time being . . . put it out of your mind . . . don't worry about it. No one is going to make you leave TMS without a fight from me—so relax."

"Yes sir."

I was surprised; but they seemed to take me at my word so they seemed calmer now. They really had more faith in me now, than I had myself, but I wasn't going to tell them that, I can assure you!

We walked out of the school quietly, eerily silent. We were within fifty feet of the Nav, when Trevor piped up.

"Hey Dad, where's Paul and Laverne?"

"I couldn't tell you Trev, I drove myself today."

"You did . . . cool—so where's the Bricklin?"

"In the garage back at the house—I drove my new truck, how do you like her?" As I pointed to my bright white beast.

"Bloody wicked Dad, she's awesome, dang—look at her Tay!"

"Whoa, Dad—she's bloody brill." Taylor added this to his brother's comment.

"Thanks guys, but just you wait until we drive her off."

"What do you mean Dad?"

"Oh; you'll see Taylor."

The boys of course, fought over the front seat. I therefore, cut that one off, right at the pass.

"Both of you get in the rear seats, now!"

"Yes sir." I got in a feeble response while I handed each 'bookend' a wireless headset.

"Here, put these on, then you hit that button there, so you two can listen to your own choice of music."

"Wow! This is too cool, Dad." The boys were holding their headsets while they studied the controls.

"Thank you Trev, I thought you'd enjoy it" As I fired up the engine.

"Dad, this one sounds a lot different from Gramps' doesn't it?"

"Yes Taylor—it should. But when I push down on the gas pedal when we're driving her in a minute, you'll understand why."

"Oh, is it faster?"

"I'll let you judge that for yourself Tay, remember your first ride in the Bricklin?"

"Oh my God, okay Daddy, let her rip."

We pulled out of the lot as I turned left onto Rampart Boulevard, heading south.

It was a 45-mile per hour zone. I decided I would get to forty-five miles per hour quick, once I was safely past the school zone. I put down the hammer, the rear end dropped into first as the Lincoln bolted . . . I do mean—bolted.

"Dad, bloody hell, God, she's as fast as the Bricklin!"

"Yes son, she is."

"Wow."

We got home in record time, even with picking up a new sticker for the truck at the main gate.

I had to laugh, as there in the driveway stood Dad now, on the front step as we drove in. It was obvious, Mom had tipped my hand. It was clear what he was planning—a thorough Malcolm Morgan 'military inspection' of the new beast!

We got out of the truck, as Dad got up to commence his 'eyeballing review' now. He circled the truck in its entirety, never saying so much as a single word. His first comment came at seeing the custom treatment of the exhaust. As he shook his head, the words escaped from his mouth.

"Damn that's nice, boy."

His next comment came while closely inspecting the front end, mainly the wire mesh custom grill. He then looked closely at the altered fog lights along with the Xenon headlights.

"Real nice son."

Finally in summation, he stood back far enough to take the whole vehicle in. He simply looked at me now as he remarked:

"You did good Marc; I don't think I've ever seen one prettier—well, maybe one."

The boys were enjoying their grandfather's inspection, but now piped up, suggesting that he look inside as well. Dad had almost forgotten about that, but following their lead, he opened the driver's door to step inside. He seemed duly impressed with the custom maple veneer on the console, dash, wheel, and so forth. He then took a good look at the leather before switching his attention to the upgraded sound system. He was about to exit when I walked up to hand him the keys.

"You've got your license right?

"Sure, right here in my pocket".

"How convenient—but you had better go alone—I'd hate to see a grown man cry in his son's presence."

"What makes you think I'll be crying?" Dad was protesting as he said it.

"Start her up Dad." He did as I suggested, as he gave the pedal a little push on the gas at the same time.

He instantly listened again to the low but rich exhaust note as I had done. Like me, he appeared to revel in the harmonics of its sound.

"Wow." That was all he could mumble out.

"Dad you're on your own, but remember a driving record is a terrible thing to waste?"

"Cute Marc."

"Gramps, we want to go with you, can we?"

"Okay boys—get your butts in here already."

The boys jumped into the rear captains, as Dad put the truck into reverse.

"See ya in a day or so Dad."

"Yeah, right son."

As they slowly made their way down the street, I went into the house to await Dad's field inspection report before realizing that I was a schmuck for not going along myself—I would miss the look on his face the first time he nailed the pedal, oh well.

"Marc, how was your day love?" I found my Gracie busy in her kitchen.

"I'm not sure yet Gracie, but what little delicacies do you have planned for our evening's meal . . . I smell something wonderful? You know, with your cohort in culinary passions relegated to the lake with the Davis', you're on your own for a change?"

"Believe me love—we'll survive. Oh, did I tell you, I'm spreading my horizons, I purchased this American favorites cookbook at Verandas today, so I thought we would all enjoy having a go at Veranda's Yankee Pot Roast tonight?"

"Really; gee that sounds wonderful. Say Grace; what do you know about the origins of that dish? Did you know it comes from the celebrations following the military victory over the British in our war of Independence?"

"No Marcus, I didn't—are you making this whole thing up just to get me miffed, because I really don't care?"

I laughed heartily, as I walked over to her at the island to give her a quick hug and peck on the cheek.

"I love you too Grace . . . but for the record, I did make the whole damn thing up. But don't let me catch you purchasing something in our units ever again. Hell, you're family Gracie; you don't pay for anything at Verandas . . . you got that?"

She smiled, but then pushed me away. She never did give me her answer.

"Let Reg mix you a drink Marc, you know he 'lives' to do that for you."

"All right Gracie, I'll do that."

I then went into the great room where I found Mom and Reg talking.

"Oh hello dear."

"Hi ya Ma—hi Reg."

"Hello Marc, can I fix you a drink?"

"Sure Reg, give me a round of Dad's poison of choice, will you."

"Right away Marc." He returned with a Cranberry and Vodka minutes later. "Here Marc, cheers."

"Cheers Reg, and thanks, no one can make it like you."

"Thank you Marc." As he left the room.

"Where are my boys?"

"With their grandfather, giving him driving tips on the new truck naturally."

"And you let him drive it, after I told you earlier he's been breaking wind all night and day?" Mom started to shake her head in disbelief.

"Damn, I forgot that, but I guess it's the price I have to pay to drive him nuts, Mom?"

"Trust me son, if he still has the wind, that truck of yours will smell something altogether different than 'nuts' I can assure you."

We were both busting over that one, before mom continued.

"But yes son, it will drive him nuts, so congratulations. You know Markie, there's a lot of my thinking in that brain of yours."

"Thank God for that Mom." I gave her a little peck on her cheek.

As we were getting round to the subject of Mom's adversary Jared, the boys came bounding through the door. Immediately they ran for their Grammy to give her their twin kisses.

"So did you two survive school alright?"

"Sort of Grammy, dang, didn't Dad already tell you things aren't so good?"

"No Trevor, your father did not—Marcus, what's this all about?"

"Sorry Mom, I wasn't holding out on you, I just hadn't got round to it is all."

"Fine . . . you can just get round to it pronto—spill it now!"

"The guys were great according to Susan, which is the most important thing to me at least. Nevertheless, the girls in their school, during lunch and recess are causing Susan along with the administration apparently—some concern. We're going to give it a few days to hopefully normalize, but I'm to call her Friday for an update."

"Yeah Dad, but tell her what Mrs. G said, if it doesn't calm down."

"What then Marc?"

"Later Mom—please?"

"Go ahead Daddy—tell her, we're not stupid g'nowhuta'meen?"

"All right Taylor, but neither of you are stupid, or anywhere close. I just didn't wish to upset you further."

"Thanks Dad, but we're already bloody nervous about it, so not talking about it won't help, will it? Don't you always tell us we can talk about anything, even the bad stuff?"

"Yes guys I did and you know what, you're right, which does make me wrong, so I apologize to you both.

"Mom, if it does not correct itself, the boys 'could' possibly be asked as merely one option; to change schools. There, I've said it now—is everyone satisfied at least with my admission?"

"Jesus Marc, isn't that a little extreme on the administration's part?"

"Maybe Mom, but it's far from a certainty—remember it's the worst-case scenario. Look, they have a strict philosophy about disruption issues, so it is only one of several possible solutions. Let's all just think positive that it's going to work out, shall we?"

"Okay Daddy, I'll try."

"Me too Dad." Trevor replied.

It was clear now that the two of them were putting up brave facades, even if I wasn't sure how they were really handling it now. Mom of course, believed in a more honest approach.

"Can it Marc, can't you see how upsetting this is to your sons—are you blind?"

"No Mom, I'm most concerned for the boys' feelings. I hope they both know that. I just refuse to think negatively about this, is all? I'm merely suggesting that both you and the boys keep the same positive approach to this situation that I am . . . see my point?"

"Okay son, I guess you're right—boys?"

"Yes Gram, we understand." Trevor agreed.

"Alright Grammy." This followed out of Taylor.

We now changed the subject.

"By the way boys, on the subject of what's new, here's something I think you'll both be pleased about."

"What Grammy?"

"Tomorrow after school Tre, you're both going to be photographed by Teen Pop Magazine; it's published just for teenagers. They're doing a full feature story on you two, so they'd like to speak to you and take some photos . . ."

. . . "Grammy, if that's going to make more problems at school, I don't want to do it—forget it!" Taylor said emotionally now, practically screaming it out, after having interrupted Mom.

"Me either Gram, it's not worth it."

Trevor's head had now dropped to half-mast to make a perfect matched set of bookends with his brother's.

My mother was a little shocked, as was I, but she was not going to leave them hanging either.

"Listen boys, come here, I want the two of you to sit next to me for a minute, will you?"

The twins immediately joined Mom on the sofa, as she wrapped her arms around both of her boys in a supportive cocoon of her love for them . . . this would surely prime their faucets. It was clear that their school surely came first to them along with their friendships inside it. They were profoundly upset over the matter. More than I had realized, even more than perhaps Mom had expected . . . so much for my 'let's think positive' pep talk.

I was now feeling extremely upset and angry at myself for somehow trying to sweep this whole thing under the rug. I wanted to ask them to forgive me, but also knew better than to interrupt Mom now. She would be just as capable, if not more so, in helping them get to their emotions.

"All right boys; let's just get this all out, shall we?"

The boys now opened their floodgates as they leaned into her embrace to surrender their emotions to their grandmother . . . they were bawling profusely.

Christ, I thought to myself, how in the hell did I not see this coming?

When their faucets had slowed to drips, Mom started her motor up. As she began, Dad walked in. He was about to speak when he froze from merely witnessing their distressed state of red, wet eyes.

"What gives—what's the problem son?" He whispered into my ear.

I whispered back a synopsis of the situation; whereby he nodded and then stood there transfixed like me, watching the master at work.

"Alright boys, Taylor you brought this up, so I want you to tell me your feelings about all of this first, and then Trevor will tell me, okay?"

She received weak nods of the heads.

"Okay Taylor, honey, tell Grammy how you're feeling?"

Taylor began, still not nearly composed enough to speak without the occasional crying shudder interfering with his sentences.

"Grammy, I love my school. I love all my friends and Mrs. G, I don't want to get kicked out—its not easy making new friends, so I don't want to have to do it again, bloody hell, I still miss my old ones. And it's all because we tried to do a good thing, but maybe going professional wasn't such a good thing to do after all; look at all the problems it's causing us in school?"

"Okay honey, I hear what you're saying but let's give Trevor an opportunity to say how he feels too. Then, I'll try to help both of you two understand things better, alright?"

"Okay, go ahead Trev." Taylor blubbered out.

Trevor then had his turn on the soapbox.

"Taylor's right Grammy, we don't want to leave our school, we love it there and everybody in it. How could this happen, it isn't bloody fair—it isn't?" As he cried some more onto his grandmother's shoulder.

Mom just held them both close, as they cried. She was no doubt stewing on their words and fears as she thought over her words for a minute or two. In between this, she was making eye contact with Dad and I, shaking her head from side to side.

Finally, she apparently knew what she would lead in with, so she spoke calmly to these two, most important boys in her life.

"Boys, I think you've both brought up some excellent points, I do, so let's address them, alright?"

The boys just looked up at her as they nodded their agreement.

"First, we don't have to worry just yet, because as of now, neither of you is leaving your school. Secondly, we always have the choice of stopping our own plans on getting you two a recording contract. Doing that, would allow things to slowly return to the way they were, before this all started in the first place—you boys would simply fade from all the limelight, so that eventually, things would return to normal for you both.

"If either of you wants to stop this right now, or ever decides that in the future, you know you always can. Either of you can come to any of us or just say so, do you understand that boys?"

"We can Grammy—for real?"

"Yes Trevor, your right to stop at any time will be spelled out in any contract we sign. You know, we're doing this, because you and Taylor said you really wanted to do it. If you've already changed your mind, we aren't going to carry on any longer."

"Grammy, I didn't know we could stop whenever we wanted to. I feel better about it now, but I don't want to quit. I love making the people happy with our music, besides I love to perform—how about you Tay?"

"Yeah Tre, I do too, but I won't lose my school or my friends, just to be some stupid bloody rocker. You know Tre; it's just not worth it. I want to make people happy, and I want to help people, but I shouldn't be punished for it—right?"

"No you shouldn't Taylor. I most certainly understand what you're saying, I really do." Mom responded back to him . . . to both of them really.

"Good, because it's how I really feel about all of this Gram. Sure, I want to sing and play, but I want to be me, just a regular kid—like Larry. If I can't have both, then I won't bother, sorry Trev—but I won't."

"So are you saying that you want to stop—now Taylor? If you do honey, just say the word right now, and it's finished. You know Taylor, Trevor can go out on his own after all, if he still wants too?"

"No, I won't let my brother down Grammy . . . we both want this. But if I can't stay in our school like any other kid, then I will stop if that happens . . . I swear it."

"That seems smart to me too, Taylor, how do you feel about what your brother said, Trevor?"

"I understand Grammy. I don't want to be out there without Tay, so if he's ever out—so am I."

"Trevor, I'll only stop if we can't stay in our school. I want to perform; I love it, especially how good I feel sharing happiness with all those people, but mostly doing it all with you bro. And it's just like Mummy said we could, but there has to be a way to fix this—right Daddy?"

Dad and I had been so far outside and removed from their conversation, we almost forgot we were in the room listening to it. Now I had to think on my feet about Taylor's question some before answering. Then remembering recent events, as well as, how they ultimately played out, I thought I had finally come up with my answer.

"You are absolutely right Taylor, but there is a way to fix this. I just can't believe it took me all this time to think of it."

"How Daddy?" Taylor asked.

"Yeah Dad, how?" Trevor added now.

"Boys, it's simple really. You guys remember our little rebuttal press release about CCC news and Concepcion Connors, don't you? Well, you two will write what we call an open letter instead, to all the kids in your school. That means it's just several copies of one letter for everyone to read—are you with me so far?"

"Yes Dad."

I might also emphasize that their response was said with a fair amount of hope and optimism in their voices now . . . thank the Lord.

"You'll explain in this letter, that you appreciate everything all the kids have done to support you and help you celebrate what's been happening so far. Nevertheless, if they really want to help you out, they should try to treat you both as if nothing has changed. Just say that you are both normal, regular guys, who—they shouldn't make any big deal over . . . either one of you.

"Remind them that you don't want to be treated any differently by any of them—or cause problems for the school. But I would say something else too—guys. I would remind all of these kids that your true, closest friends know who they are, because they aren't treating you a bit different from the way you were treated before."

"Marc, that's a brilliant idea truly."

"Thanks Mom, I thought so too, but what do you two think about it?"

I looked at my two sons deep in thought as I asked this question.

"Do you think it really could work Daddy?"

"Taylor, yes I do, but there is only one way to know for sure, don't you think?"

"Yes sir, Trev what do you think of Daddy's idea?"

"Tay, I say let's go write it. I think Dad's on to something here. I think we can make all the kids understand that while we appreciate all of their support, things aren't working out this way. And that we know are best mates are the ones who just let us be ourselves . . . which is true, Tay."

"What's true, Trev?"

"Think about it bro, what Dad said is spot on. Our best mates haven't treated us any different, have they? I mean look at all of them Tay. Blimey, they haven't changed one bit towards us—am I right or not?"

"Yeah Trev, you're right, and dang—thank God. I thought for a moment I'd really have to quit singing. This has to work bro, let's go write the letter like you said, even before our homework."

"Okay, let's do it, Dad, Grammy may we be excused?"

"Certainly boys, let us see it when you're finished with it though." My Mother said with a tremendous degree of relief.

"Sure thing Grammy—thanks. Dad, great idea, and hello Gramps." They now took off for their room in a sprint to compose their letter.

"Marc, I believe that if Miranda were here, she would be just as proud of you as I am. That was a brilliant little stroke of genius—more importantly . . . I believe it will work."

"I agree son, first class idea."

"Thanks guys, let's just hope it does work out the way we all believe it can."

"I think that this whole thing should be a wake up call and a good lesson for all of us. You two can't afford to take anything too lightly with them in the future, this was illuminating. Obviously the twins are still fragile, even though it's clear to all of us that they've matured tremendously as well. Dad said before continuing.

"Look, they're still grieving the losses of a wonderful, loving—Mummy, and their exceptional Grandfather, to begin with—and apparently, their old friends as well. This is quite clear by the concern they have concerning losing their new school friends over something this stupid too, don't you see? Jesus, how much do you want these two to handle in a year's time? I hope that you two have put this connection together, because I know it wasn't lost on me. My advice is, the more communication right now, the better."

"You're right Dad, but no, I did not miss that connection, nor did Mom I am sure. The thing is I think we need to speak to them in specifics about what this new professional life will likely mean. I want them to know how it will change things in general and specifically . . . we've obviously been remiss in that, I guess.

"Our talk in the car that first night, was not enough about specifics, it was just the warm and fuzzy parts. I would say we've done them a great disservice in not talking about more of the potential negatives too in our subsequent conversations—what say you Mom?"

"I can't argue with a word you or Dad has said. I'll certainly be more sensitive to it in the future as should all of us; I'll speak to Scott too. You know, when I'm working with them, I do point out the negatives, while I'm trying to reinforce good levels of humility too. Unfortunately, I haven't been able to cover everything already, naturally."

"Great, so let's get a little more out tonight when they present their letter, alright?"

"Definitely Marc, do you want to talk about it, or should I?"

"I'd say all three of us should Mom."

"I agree Marc."

"Thanks Dad. Say, it's nice to see you in one piece after your drive, but are you going to make me sweat? Admit it, my truck is nicer than yours—na, na, na, na, na? Thankfully I had laughed this last part out, so dad wouldn't think I was slipping into my second childhood. Oh my God—was Robbie right?

"Son, you realize if you get too cocky, I'll be forced to go out and do all these performance things myself. But I'll go a bit farther, say to around 550 horses, just to bring you down a notch or two. In other words Marko—don't push it, I don't take testosterone wars . . . or losing—lightly! That being said, your truck is unbelievable and beautiful. Marilyn honey, you absolutely must have a look."

"Jesus, enough about this damn truck already—fine Malcolm, I'll take a look at the stupid thing, satisfied? Come on you two, get off your asses and show it to me . . . my frigging God, two grown men, carrying on like teenagers over a ridiculous little thing like a truck . . . I swear."

"All right Mom, come on. Pops, I'd say your little speech took me down a notch or two already. I hope you know I was just joshing you?"

"Of course Marc."

I took Mom by the arm to show her the truck. I opened the front door of our house as we stepped outside, as Mom let out a slight sigh along with a complete change of demeanor overtaking her instantly—something was odd here.

"Oh my Lord, your truck is beautiful, I adore the color—oh my!"

Mom's new attitude and burst of excitement really surprised me—but honestly flabbergasted Dad.

"Give me the keys please son, I've got to—drive it."

"Drive it? You do—you're kidding right? The look she flashed me at that moment said otherwise.

"Okay, okay sorry, here's the keys—have fun, but you've never wanted to do this sort of thing before?"

Mom completely ignored me as she simply opened the door to get inside. She started the truck up . . . she winked at me as she tapped the gas.

"Sounds racy son."

"Thanks Mom—I think? Hey Ma, I'd take it easy on that first step of the gas, really . . . I would."

"Don't you worry about me son, I know how to handle a car; just ask your father." Dad was shaking his head now; mentally I think he was sitting

Shiva. To sit Shiva is the Jewish ritual of mourning the dead, but not happily like at a wake.

Mom took off out the drive and was gone seconds later after burning a little rubber with her exit. I looked at Dad now, desperately seeking comfort, consolation—anything. Yet he was in shock like me, as he just kept right on shaking his head. Finally he managed to speak.

"Well, I never!"

We just stood there waiting for her to return, both of us still in introspective thoughts, staring straight ahead like sentries dutifully standing guard on some foreign battlefield.

"Has she ever done something like this before Dad?"

"Never, what's with her anyway?"

"Couldn't tell you Dad, I was hoping you would know?"

"Maybe all the talk inside, got her curious?"

"That's possible Dad—I guess."

"How long has she been gone son?"

"Damn, it's been forty seconds already".

"Hum. Well you never can tell with Mom, sometimes she just has to show us that she's not so predictable."

"I don't know Dad . . . I guess that's possible."

"How long has it been now son?"

"Fifty five seconds now."

"Hum—think we should call the gate Marc?"

"What would that accomplish Dad?"

"I don't know, but maybe they can alert us when she returns?"

"I think we have to just wait this out Dad."

"Fine by me, but it's your truck not mine."

"I'm aware of that Dad—we're now at a minute, twenty by the way."

"Really, a minute, twenty you say?"

"Yep, a minute and twenty whole seconds."

"Hum, hey do you hear that, it could be your Mother, that's certainly a throaty exhaust?"

"Don't think so Pop, sounds too much like a hog."

"A hog?"

"Yep, a Harley Davidson, Dad."

"Oh, how long has it been now?"

"Minute, forty five."

"We should just go inside son."

"Dad you're right, we should."

Yet we both remained fixed like the sentries we were supposed to be.

"So what time is it now?"

"Minute, fifty two Dad, yep a minute fifty two."

"Nice weather we're having, don't you think?"

"Sure, nice weather Pop."

"Not a bit of a breeze, I like that."

"Me too Pop."

"So; how do you think the Dodgers stack up for April son?"

"Crappy, as usual Pop.

"And hell, I hear LaSorda is on another diet in the front office Dad, that won't help either."

"You don't say?"

"Yeah, I hear he wants to drop thirty pounds this time."

"Thirty pounds—wow that's a lot more to lose. Say, how long now son?"

"Just over three and ten Pop."

"Wow."

"Yep—wow."

"Think LaSorda can drop the thirty son?"

"Sure, if he 86's the linguine this time while drinking the Slim Fast® instead.

"Listen Pop, do you hear that one, now that one could be her?"

"Suppose so son."

"And it is Pop, it's her, look—see her?"

"Yes son, so what's the elapsed?" (Time)

"Three minutes, thirty eight Dad."

"Well—I never!"

Mom pulled into the drive, and then she killed the motor, but not without a little flick of the gas pedal first. She jumped out totally uplifted yet silent, handing me the keys as she blew right past us with her little smirk. She opened the front door of the house while we were just staring between her and the Nav.

"You've got a keeper there Marc, nice stereo and I love the pick up." As she went inside, closing the door behind her without further comment.

Dad and I whistled as we did a quick walk around the truck, trying to act like we weren't concerned. Satisfied the truck had survived unscathed; we went into the house ourselves.

We breezed through the foyer as we heard Mom in the kitchen laughing with Grace, although we hadn't heard a word—hum!

Dad and I walked into the kitchen, where we were greeted with instant silence now.

The two of them were smirking and hovering over Gracie's Yankee Pot Roast, which was smelling incredible and appeared ready.

"Grace, your roast smells divine, almost as good as—the smell of a new leather interior in a car." Mom said.

Grace just cavorted quietly while ignoring the comment altogether.

This give and take would have gone further I surmised, had we not heard two twins yelling.

"Dad—we're done, where are you? Grammy, Gramps, Grace, Reg—anybody?"

"In the kitchen guys." I yelled back.

At that moment, the intercom magically came alive.

"Roger, over and out." Then we heard the thunder of 'twin feet' running down the spiral staircase.

They ran into the kitchen nearly out of breath.

"Will you read it Dad, please?" Taylor was panting his question out.

"How about you read it to us, Taylor . . . or should I get Larry over here to do it, since he's our speechmaker and everything now?"

"Gee; could you?"

"Taylor, honey."

"Yes, Daddy."

"That—was a joke son!"

"Oh."

It went over Taylor's head for the moment, but not Trevor's, so he began laughing at his brother's expense now.

"Tre be cool bro, it's not funny to me."

"Sorry Tay, sorry."

Trevor then showed Taylor his utmost respect by going dead silent instantly. This had to be more of their non-verbal extra sensory bond between them, it was just too eerie.

"So, how about it Taylor, will you do me the honor of hearing you reading it to all of us?"

I thought to myself that my Jewish Guilt intertwined into my question to Taylor, was a nice touch. So, I was not surprised when his response was most endearing.

"Okay, but just because it's for you Daddy."

"Thank you son, for honoring me."

At that moment, we just looked at one another as he rushed me with a warm hug and kisses that seemed all too brief, as Taylor withdrew from the embrace.

"Is everyone listening?"

After affirmatives from everyone present, Taylor cleared his throat to begin. Taylor then read the letter which more or less followed all of our suggestions to it.

"So how did it sound Daddy?"

"Great Taylor . . . it's going to work, trust me boys. Son, it was perfect, really well done . . . I'm proud of both of you."

"I helped a lot writing it Dad."

"And it shows Trevor, it's great, don't you think so Mom, Dad—everyone?"

Everyone yelled out yes in agreement.

"Now, all you need to do is have Mr. Riley approve it, then we'll make the copies ahead of time. Assuming you have permission, you can hand them out at lunch I would think."

"Great Dad, we'll ask him tomorrow morning first thing."

"That's great Taylor, after dinner we'll run off the copies upstairs in the office, that way if Mr. Riley says yes, you're good to go at passing them out."

We all sat down as Grace called us to dinner.

I had to warn Gracie that she might very well be wrongly accused of being a native—American, her Yankee Pot Roast was that authentic and delicious, truly it was luscious.

After the wonderful meal, we settled into our normal evening activities. When it was nearing bedtime, we three older Morgans began a lengthy discussion with the younger two. We discussed most of the expected changes with their professional lives, and what it would or could mean.

Mom spent a considerable amount of time reiterating on why the boys should continue to keep their heads humble, so they would remain themselves as opposed to becoming snobs that few people would recognize . . . with even fewer liking what they saw with those changes.

Dad explained that in the long run, they would be happier doing so, while making more friends along the way. They seemed to understand the connection that snobs and brats don't typically make true friendships but more than likely, just flunkies or hangers-on, so they don't keep them for long.

After I reminded them of their own first impressions of their best mate Larry, it really seemed to click for them . . . they clearly got it now. Their ever-expanding maturity showed in their questions, answers and understanding. We three were all impressed honestly.

The conversation was not lost on deft ears, as the boys went to bed considerably calmer, as well as—enlightened. They now knew more of what to expect in the future possibly—but they were okay with it now too.

After they left for bed, we all talked further. We agreed we could not have asked for a better outcome, as the boys had left us all with huge smiles on their faces . . . they had even agreed excitedly to their Teen Pop interview opportunity now.

As the boys were once again bunking with me in my suite, I found myself staring at them sleeping in my bed. I couldn't help notice that they seemed to be sleeping contentedly, rather than troubled.

I then began thinking of Dad, who was still with us for another two days, but then I would have my solitude back again, while they would have their bedroom as well.

Dad at least, had returned last Friday with great news—he had already found a buyer for the winery, completely by accident during a scheduled tour of the winery. Seeing an excellent operation, along with a long-term food service contract, this buyer wasted scant time offering Dad an opening offer, nearly a half million above what the old man would have asked for at full price.

The deal would close right after the next harvest and bottling. They had already opened escrow with a $50,000 non-refundable deposit. I understood from Mom that when the check cleared, Dad had called her in tears.

Dad had always been an astute Real Estate Broker, so purchasing the winery years back was no different. He purchased it strictly as acreage during a depressed time for real estate values in the entire state. The prior owner had been behind in his payments, so he desperately needed an exit strategy. The folks stepped in with cash to bring the guy current after negotiating ideal purchase terms including assuming the man's loan.

After a lot of effort and hard work nonetheless, they turned the vast property into a thriving commercial vineyard, well before the real estate market itself, improved. When land values finally rebounded some time later, they had a property worth six times what it was purchased for . . . with the winery's business portion worth even more.

All told, they would clear around seven million, two hundred thousand, after the capital gains taxes and all costs were paid. Yet that didn't include twenty years of note income they would collect, along with their final harvest's inventory. These added another two and half million plus net—way to go Mom and Dad.

Naturally, I was thrilled for them. The winery may have been disappointing to them on some levels, but financially would not be included among them.

But enough thoughts about the winery, or the folks for one night, I thought to myself, I needed to hit the hay. So I stopped staring at my two tornados, as I joined them instead. My poor boys had not had the best of days. I snuck kisses as they snored softly, while I sang to them softly anyway. Tomorrow was another day . . . hopefully a better one for them. I could only hope and pray—and so I did.

My alarm, buzzing me at seven, reminded me instantly of why I hated mornings. I dragged myself into the bath suite, turned on the steam along with all eight of my showerheads, as I robotically followed my normal morning routine.

When I got out, the boys were just getting up to welcome their day. Trevor greeted me now by sitting up and running his hands over his face as he said good morning.

Taylor meanwhile, did a short—yet pronounced trumpet solo out of the horn section below his waist, I believe while still asleep. I think having shattered the sound barrier with his cornucopia of sound; he actually woke himself up—utilizing this method.

"Oh, thank you Taylor—Yankee Pot Roast indeed! But did I mention that you'll be bunking up with your Grandfather at all family camp outs in the future?"

"Oh Daddy, don't tell me you never do it?"

"Yes Taylor of course I—do it, we've all been known to do it—hell everyone loves—to do it. Yet we're usually too shy for an audience, as you should be—tune your trumpet privately in the future please . . . I've warned you about this before."

"Hey Dad, what can I say, I'm a musical kind of kid . . . but you gotta love me Daddy?"

"I sure do honey, but I'll love you just as much without the horn section, that's all."

"Okay Dad, I'll keep my toots to myself from now on, at least in here with you. Thank God Tre doesn't seem to mind them."

"Excuse me—did anyone ask me, I vote for Dad's plan too, thank you dear brother?"

"Alright you two, quit the kibitzing and start moving, come on or you'll be late."

"Okay Dad, we will. We'll see you in the kitchen."

I kissed them quickly, before making my way to the Euro-Morganland kitchen.

All the way there, I couldn't help feel something was different this morning, but at that moment, it seemed to elude me.

I found my foursome, all doing their thing; Dad had the paper, while Mom sipped on her coffee. My Gracie was at her post by the stove, while our dear Reginald, was just hanging in there, watering some of the potted plants we had all over the kitchen.

"Morning all—whoa! Jeeze is it my imagination—or is it cold as hell down here."

Bingo!

Hell, that's what's different this morning—dumbshit! I blasted out in my thoughts.

"Love, it's not your mind, it's the Lord's sense of humor. It seems that he's gone down a different road by ending the heat wave—look outside."

I peered outside, where I was shocked yet sad, to see it looking cold, drizzly, and gloomy. Moreover for some reason, I felt bad for Scooter and his group as their locale lent itself to the previous weather . . . not this crap. Christ; I had to hope that Scoot or Beth could figure out how to light the pilot for their furnace?

Then I had to hope it was not going to rain on his new S Type . . . or Jesus—on my Nav!

I got up to turn on the heat throughout the entire house. It seemed we were all a little down over the change in the weather. Later, we hardly got a word out of the twins at all; then again, you can't shovel it in—and chew— and still talk anyway, now can you? We all ate our breakfast in near silence.

CHAPTER Three

▼

ODE TO LAVERNE

As we sat there eating, I decided the risk of rain was just too great. Despite my original instructions, I called Paul to pick us up. After all, I couldn't let it rain on my new Navigator's—parade . . . could I?"

We left the homestead a little late because of these last minute changes, but I frankly didn't care. We all seemed introspective as we rode over to the Meadows School. I suggested we all speak to Mr. Riley in the office to discuss the boys' letter, which broke the otherwise silence . . . regrettably, their tardiness now necessitated we check in there anyway. Being tardy was seriously frowned upon at TMS, so it was a rare event school-wide. Hell, with the tuition a parent shelled out just to send their kid there—it wasn't any wonder besides.

As we walked into the attendance office, I spied Mr. Riley in his office through his window. I asked the secretary at the counter if he had a moment to speak to us.

She called him as we were subsequently invited to join him in his office.

"Morning, Mr. Riley."

"Always a pleasure Mr. Morgan—and young Morgans!"

"Morning Mr. R." Came from T-1.

"Good morning Mr. Riley." Originated from Taylor.

"So how may I be of assistance this damp and cold morning—burr?"

"The boys' have a request is all, so I thought I would lend a little moral support. Frankly Mr. R, I feel they're entitled to defend themselves, by way of contributing an alternative solution to all of this fuss their notoriety seems to be causing."

"That seems understandable to me Mr. Morgan, so what is your request boys?"

Taylor immediately took out the top copy from his sizable stack, handing it to Mr. Riley to read. After Mr. Riley read it, he put it down on his desk as he gave Taylor a small smile.

"Mr. R, we'd like your permission to pass these out at lunch by the tables?"

"Well boys, I don't have any objection to this request. I think it's a smart idea on both of your parts. However, with the rain today, lunch will be served in the cafeteria, so plan to pass them out in there . . . but not during class, understood?"

"Great, thanks Mr. R."

"You're welcome boys . . . certainly you have my support. Thank you as well for trying to help. As always Mr. Morgan, you can be proud of your sons."

"It was Dad's idea Mr. R, so he should get the credit anyways, not us."

"Thank you Trevor for your honesty, but somehow I suspected as much . . . you know you do have a pretty smart Father. Yet he's merely trying to help you two work through a few of these changes I would suppose. Some of them I'm sure, have been a little rough on you two, like that reporter—haven't they?"

I think the boys were just a little bit surprised at their Vice-Principal's candor and insight.

"Yes sir, maybe a little." Taylor replied as he wiped away a small tear.

"Now men, this is all to be expected so just take it one day at a time—try not to fret over it. This situation may take a little time to adjust—but it will, I'm sure, so don't worry boys."

"Sure Mr. R, we understand." Taylor validated.

"Boy, you said it Mr. R, we love our school, so we don't want anyone mad at us."

"Trevor, no one here is mad at either one of you, so don't worry, we've simply have a campus to run."

"Thanks Mr. R, that makes me feel a lot better, I mean coming from you."

"Good Trevor, but now—onto another subject, why are you two tardy this morning, this is certainly a regrettable first—there went your perfect records?"

"Gee Mr. R; you can give Dad credit for that one too. He didn't want his new truck to get all wet, so we had to call for Laverne to drive us over instead."

I had to laugh at Trevor's crack at my expense.

"Oh, I see. Well what did Laverne have to say about it, when you called her?"

"Laverne didn't say nothing Mr. R, dang; she never does—but Paul sure did. He was all nervous and said that Laverne would get there—a-sap, whatever that means?"

"Trevor, grammatically we would say 'anything' in this instance—not nothing . . . but Paul said that? Hum—so, who is Paul, Laverne's husband?"

"No—but Paul's pretty sure that Laverne's—his mother."

Taylor piped in before Trevor could answer, while I sat there silently busting now from their Vice-Principal's confusion, as Riley now inquired:

"Paul believes Laverne's to his mother, shouldn't Paul know—whether or not, Laverne's his mother . . . now boys, come on?"

This discourse had me really going, although my laughter was deviously silent naturally. This was all just too opportune for me as a practical joker, to step in and save Riley's ass. How easy it was for a child to confuse a totally sane and rational adult in a split second's time was beyond me, but this was becoming priceless.

I was beside myself—so Riley was on his own! I sat there instead; totally serious to see how far the whole farce would go. Aren't I a stinker?

Meanwhile, the madness soon continued, between Riley and Trevor.

"Gee, how should I know Mr. R, see Dad surprised Paul with Laverne last October before we moved here, so we don't know nothing about it . . . I mean anything, Mr. R?"

"Your Father gave Laverne to Paul?"

"Yep—because Paul really hated Mabel."

"Now who is Mabel, Trevor?"

"I don't know, because Paul had already dumped her before we moved to Las Vegas. All I know is Paul said she was worthless, but besides that, he said she was always giving him problems—I heard that he just dumped her on someone, I don't know the whole story, sorry Mr. R."

"Oh no, that doesn't sound nice Trevor, yet how does Laverne feel about all of this, I mean—about Mabel?"

"I don't know Mr. R. cuz I can't speak to Laverne about it . . . besides Paul doesn't allow us to say anything upsetting around her anyway . . . ever."

"Trevor, I can certainly understand Paul's concern, after all it's not nice to say upsetting things to anyone is it?"

"No sir, that's for sure, especially how Paul feels about Laverne—you never kid Paul about Laverne, believe me. He really takes care of her; just yesterday we had to wait for them because they weren't ready. Before all of us could leave for the lake, we all had to wait around for Laverne to finish her bath."

"Oh?"

"Yep, there was Paul, just washing her all over—and he really enjoys doing that to her too. That always makes him happy as he gets real excited whenever he washes her, doesn't he Tay?"

"Yeah bro, he goes kind of loopy."

"Trevor—oh my, now boys. Seriously, you're not trying to tell me that Paul gives Laverne her bath in front of both of you?"

"Sure he does Mr. R., why not—we're all family? Paul never likes Laverne when she's dirty. You should see him; he's always giving her some new perfume or something."

"Well Trevor, what does Laverne have to say about all of this?"

"About what Mr. R.?"

"The perfume and the bath of course?"

"Heck if I know Mr. R—I can't talk to cars—can you?"

That did it; as Riley sat there with a complete look of utter confusion on his face. Now, he was playing it all back in his mind it seems while mouthing words he remembered. I could not let him go on any longer . . . I had to come clean before the poor soul lost his sanity.

"I'm sorry Mr. Riley, but I couldn't help myself; I needed you to see my own problem first-hand. You see, how my afternoons go when I pick them up here and merely ask them how their day went."

Riley finally got it, as he began laughing so hard now, that his normally pale complexion was bright red from his fit.

He looked at me seriously.

"How do you sleep at night Mr. Morgan?" Riley continued his laughter.

"Typically confused—isn't that abundantly clear now Mr. Riley?" I replied.

And with that, we were both hysterical . . . and red.

It took Riley about two minutes more to regain his composure along with his administrative seriousness. Finally, he simply addressed the boys.

"I accept your excuse boys, so I suggest you two get to Mrs. G's classroom without further delay."

"Okay sir. Bye Dad."

"Bye T-man, so long T-1."

"See ya Dad."

The boys left as Mr. Riley handed them a hall pass while he walked me out to the lobby area.

"Mr. Morgan, I wouldn't worry too much about our problem, I think you've come up with a Cracker Jack solution. I'm confident with our student body it will work, but you'll certainly know by the end of the school day."

"That's a relief to hear Mr. Riley, you have no idea. You know, the boys had decided last night that attending this school took precedence over continuing their careers if push came to shove?"

"Really! My, I am impressed; it's most flattering to hear how much the boys love their school."

"Yes they do Mr. Riley."

We attempted to say good-bye, as we shared a few more parting laughs, before I eventually left for my office.

Another workday ensued with the usual problems—along with their required decisions to solve them. All day, I kept an eye out for anything from our adversary at Toon Media, but there was nothing, which continued to worry me.

The only 'T 'n' T' business during the whole day concerned Teen Pop Magazine. Since the boys had agreed to their interview, I had to confirm the appointment. I found them very cooperative on the phone . . . as well as appreciative of our outreach.

I then called Scooter into my office for an impromptu five-to-ten; he walked in floating on a cloud. I assumed he was still on his 'high' of finding the perfect house that the entire family flipped for. It was nearly right around the corner from my lot, being next door to the James Gang house, in fact.

Besides this great news, Scoot was anxiously awaiting his new baby's arrival all morning as well. Most people in similar circumstances would have been thrilled to talk at length on either of these two subjects . . . but apparently not Scoot. He floored me now with his choice for conversation starters.

"I'm convinced I have an awesome idea for a new Morison strategy, care to hear more?"

"Wow Scoot, pardon my blatant Teddy Toon reference, but—I can't 'bear' it any longer!"

"Good show bud. Look, I know everyone in his department pretty darn well obviously. There is only one woman in the whole place that honestly likes Jared—everyone else merely tolerates him apparently. I'm sure I can worm someone into being our little 'mole' around there. All I'll ask them to do is make some casual chit chat with him; to see if they can fish anything out of him . . . how's that sound?"

"Jesus Scoot—you don't have an ethical issue with that? You know pal, with your vacation time along with sick days; you're still on T-M's payroll."

"Not if you don't Marc? Hey, I'm not going after company secrets, or trying to steal some client, I'm merely confirming information that I suspect I already know."

"Fine; but can you keep it above board, or I won't be able to save your ass. Scoot, please know I'm being dead serious here, friendship or not—you've been through training. You know we have a zero-tolerance policy. You would therefore have to go down being the responsible party—do we understand one another?"

"All right bud, I comprende. Just leave it to me, I'll keep it on the level, I'm a Mason after all."

"Okay Scoot, yeah that's right, you are. Hey by the way, the magazine will be at the house at 3:45 for their photos and interview."

"Good. As we've discussed, I'll be there to lend Marilyn my support."

"Yes I know."

"Say, have you heard anything more on my car Marc?"

"What about your car, are you planning on buying a new one, I hadn't heard?"

"Funny Marcus, now tell me the truth."

"Fine. Yes Scoot, the car is in route near the dam as we speak according to the agency. It'll be in town before one o'clock, after which the dealer will inspect it, have it detailed . . . then call us. By the way, I'm personally going to be there to take you over to pick it up."

"Really, well bud, I'm touched big time—thanks."

"No sweat amigo, just don't make me regret my 'okay' for your little CIA action with our dufuss at T-M."

"Relax Marc, I've got it covered, don't you go nervous on me for Christ's sake."

"Fine, I'll call you when I hear on the S Type."

"Thanks." As he left my office, he walked out looking determined.

I immediately buzzed Robbie. Moments later, he flew in.

"Yes Marc?"

"Robbie, is everything ready for Scooter's Jag?"

"We're all set Marc; the agency is due to call at any minute."

"Great, thanks." And Robbie walked out now.

The agency did call me, right at 11:40 so I immediately called Beth at the boat.

"Hello?"

"Hi Embeth, Uncle Marc here, can I talk to your Mom?"

"Sure Uncle Marc, let me get her.

"Hi Marc, are we ready?"

"Yes Beth—all set. The car is in a little early, so if you guys are set, we're all ready on our end, for operation Scooter. I can leave now to pick you and the girls up . . . how's that sound?"

"Fabulous Marc, come get us."

"Great. So here's the plan. We'll return to the office where I'll call Scoot from the limo. As he steps inside, you can all surprise him, are we clear?"

"Got it, but I want to thank you again for including us at his presentation ceremony, its very nice of the company, Marc."

"Thanks Beth. Listen, I want all of you guys, to get in that beautiful new car, kidnap him, then take the rest of the afternoon off to take a nice long pleasure drive. However, at 3:45, Scoot needs to be at my house for Teen Pop, but you should all come—the boys will love seeing the girls."

"Sure Marc, that sounds great. Is there anyplace nearby you'd recommend to fill that timeframe where we can drive to for the scenery, or as a place of interest?"

"No, not really—wait a minute that's not true . . . you could take Charleston Boulevard all the way west. It will turn into Red Rock Canyon which is a nice place to test the new car out on the open back roads—just watch out for the wild burros. You could stop at Bonnie Springs for the girls as well, they have a petting zoo along with a western town with live entertainment."

"So all we have to do is drive west on Charleston?"

"Yep, you can't miss anything as Charleston becomes the road running through the whole canyon, while Bonnie Springs is clearly marked right along the way, so you can't miss it."

I then had Beth write down directions.

"Great, so I guess we'll see you soon, do you want us to meet you at the Marina office?"

"No, I'll walk down to you at the mooring."

"Okay, see you."

"Fine, bye." Beth hung up.

I leaned back in my desk chair, put my hands behind my head,—and thought about how much Scoot was going to enjoy his upcoming afternoon—so I smiled.

I followed our plan perfectly. The Davis ladies and I arrived back at the company lot right at twelve thirty. I picked up the car phone where I dialed Scoot in his office while relaxing inside Mr. Riley's favorite topic—Laverne. Naturally, Scooter answered pensively on the first ring.

"Scoot, are you ready to pick up your newborn?"

"Oh yeah pal, Daddy's on his way, where are you Marc?"

"Inside Laverne in the parking lot—care to join me?"

"You bet I do, I'll see you in two shakes." He hung up before I could even say so long.

I saw him bolt out of the front doors while he headed right towards us in a beeline.

"All right ladies, here he comes, get those kisses ready."

Moments later, he threw open the door to pop in, only to stop dead in his tracks when he saw his wife and girls.

"What's this all about?" As the girls yelled 'surprise Daddy' as Beth smiled proudly.

"Scoot, this is an important day in your new career here at Verandas. We look at these special events within our company, like any big happy family would. On important occasions like this, we often want the employee's real family to ride along with us whenever possible . . . forgive my pun."

"Damn old man—I am touched, thank you." Scoot then kissed Beth and his girls.

"You're most welcome bud. You'll come to find, that as your employer, we value you for more than just your accomplishments at work. We greatly value your excellence as a husband, father along with being an active participant within your community as well. We admire all of that in our employees—this is just a little demonstration of our sincerity."

"Dang it Morgan, you never cease to astonish me, I am really moved here man . . . thank you pal."

"Thanks Scoot, don't mention it. Oh, by the way, I have invited the ladies here to join us later at the house. After 'Teen Pop' leaves, I'm taking everyone to dinner."

"I am impressed Marc, damn, maybe I should be paying you to work here."

"Now Scoot, don't go soft on me."

We all laughed, as I directed Paul to Gaudin Jaguar on Sahara. Twenty minutes later, we arrived at the large agency in the heart of town. We stepped out of Laverne about the same time I spotted our sales executive, Mike Schiffman, walking over to greet all of us. We now proceeded to the agency's 'delivery' area. When we got there, Scoot froze in his steps-as his beautiful, new piece of sculpted British steel came into view. He was really choked up, but who could blame him—the car was stunning in its contrasts. He grabbed Beth's hand as he gave it a squeeze.

"Here it is sweetheart, welcome to the good life . . . at long last. You know Cuddles; you sure as hell paid your dues waiting for me for all these years . . . you deserve this too baby." He grabbed his wife into the most incredible kiss I had seen since my times with Mir.

Cuddles . . . I mean Beth, was crying softly from the tender words and kiss, no doubt.

"I take it the car meets with your approval Mr. Davis?" His sales executive asked.

"Mike, I think I could cry, right here on this spot . . . you haven't seen my Chevy, have you?" He and Mike laughed hysterically now.

Scoot was serious too . . . he was happy, I'm not kidding you, but you should have seen the girls' reactions.

As Scoot stopped to open the driver's door, Mike interrupted him.

"Now don't do that quite yet Mr. Davis, you see, we offer a complimentary series of photos of you along with your family of course, receiving your new touring sedan.

Mike handed Scoot the keys, as a photographer appeared. She came snapping away out of nowhere. Mike opened the door for first Beth, following that with the girls too. After the ladies were settled in, Mike went around to the driver's door as he opened it personally for Scoot, who was still gawking at the R model's signature alloy wheels, all chromed and beautiful. Scoot came out of his fog soon enough though, as he shook Mike's hand before stepping inside.

For nearly five minutes, he along with the other Davis' inside the car, just looked, touched, and admired as the shutter clatter continued. It was now my turn.

I approached his door where he fumbled to find the window switch to get it lowered. I leaned in to speak, as I reached into the pocket of my sports coat now. I took out a paper for my obvious speech:

"Scooter Davis . . . and family, it is my pleasure, to present to you all, your new company car . . . use it well. Here are your corporate gas cards, your company car user's guide, plus your proof of insurance. Enjoy the car bud, but always drive safely with those nieces of mine and Beth too."

"Thank you Marc—I'm speechless really. I don't know how to begin to repay your kindness, our friendship, or your trust in me."

"Don't sweat it bud, you've earned it all already, now get out of here. Take a nice drive, get to know the car, but we'll see all of you at the house by three forty five, okay?"

"You got it Marc."

Scoot shook my hand before opening the moon roof, putting up his window, as he then started the powerful V8 engine up. We were finally seeing the sun today so it was a nice touch with the moon roof, as they were off to a nice soft roll on the pavement.

After they had turned out of the agency, I thanked Mike again before retreating to Laverne.

Stepping inside, I told Paul he could head out as I noticed my old ham radio equipment of mine. I had him move it into Laverne from her trunk minutes before during the photographs.

Ham radio had been one of my favorite hobbies and pastimes since before learning to fly—they went hand-in-hand after all. Every now and then, I needed my fix on listening into the many bandwidths available from around the area.

All I had to do, was turn on the equipment as I raised the volume as well. My frequency had already been preset to my favorite . . . one of the Metro Police's traffic frequencies.

Just moments later as I listened, I heard the first conversation coming over my equipment.

"Control, this is unit one, I'm following a suspicious four-wheel in view heading west on Sahara, number three lane—appears to be distracted. Subject presently at 39 under 45, over."

"Roger, unit one, continue to shadow."

A few minutes elapsed before I heard more specifics, with chatter filling in the gaps.

"Control, unit one here, subject has just lane changed to number two lane, sans turn signal, acknowledge."

"Ten four unit one, take suitable action."

At that moment, I knew the statement meant only one thing; a car was being pulled over.

I immediately advised Paul to slow down some, so I could concentrate.

Then out of the corner of my eye it seems, I saw Scoot and clan in the Jag ahead of us on the right. There was a cop car behind them—Christ; that didn't take long I though to myself. To avoid any embarrassment by passing them, I yelled to Paul to pull over, which he did at the first available opening.

I watched Scoot talking animatedly with Beth, as the male officer approached.

Scoot lowered his window, as a conversation ensued that I certainly could not make out naturally.

You know to me, there's nothing more frustrating than when you can't hear a conversation you're dying to hear . . . am I right or what? So what could I do—I had to raise the volume on the receiver for the transmitter hidden under Scoot's seat . . . now everything came in clearly.

. . . "Sir, I am stopping you because you failed to use your turn signal for your lane change. May I see your license and proof of insurance please, as well? I can see the car's new, so I realize you have only temporary registration."

"Yes officer, you see, we just now drove it off the lot this very moment.

"Well, congratulations sir, it's a beaut."

"Thank you officer, so can't you give me a little break on the signal, heck I'm just getting acclimated in here?"

"No Mr. Davis, (the cop was looking at his license now) I would rather you learn a valuable lesson now. The lesson is on being trained to drive a new vehicle properly before you attempt to do so carelessly, like you have just now. That's better then having to respond to your family being injured from you making a fateful mistake causing an accident. Your driving sir, has appeared erratic and distracted for the last mile or so."

"Alright officer, I understand, it's just that I'm trying to keep my driving record clean here."

"I wouldn't worry too much about that sir; this will only cost you a single point on your record."

At that moment, I heard Beth's reaction to the officer's comment:

. . . "And—four to go Scott!"

Scoot ignored Beth entirely, but waited for an opportunity to keep up his sales pitch on the officer—which didn't take long as it turned out.

"Mr. Davis, I see this insurance certificate is in the name of Verandas Inc?"

"Yes officer, that's my employer."

"That's a fine outfit—they're a great place for food, the Missus, and I eat there nearly every Sunday for brunch-right after Church."

"Me too officer—so, can I arrange a nice private dining room for you and your wife this coming Sunday?"

"Mr. Davis, I hope you are not attempting to sway me from issuing this ticket with that invitation?"

"Oh no sir, I only meant that I would be most pleased to offer you a line pass as a valuable repeat guest. It's obvious you are one of our regulars, so we appreciate your patronage, that's all.

"Well, that won't be necessary Mr. Davis, but thanks all the same. I'll wait in line like everyone else thank you, but here sir, is your citation all ready for your John Hancock."

"Thank you officer, it won't happen again."

"See that it doesn't sir, you need to look after your lovely lady and those two beauties in back."

"Thank you officer, good bye."

I thought to myself, Gee Scoot, that was a smooth save at least—nice try.

I saw Scoot's window go up, as I heard Beth's comment that followed.

"Great work Scott, really—congratulations. It only took you what—exactly seven minutes to get pulled over for your first ticket in this car . . . however did you manage?"

"All right honey, enough with the cracks. Personally I think he was a little too obsessive over a stupid turn indicator—don't you think?"

"No honey . . . obviously he didn't think so, either?"

"Don't sweat it Cuddles, I'll go to traffic school, at least they don't know me here. Back in Orange when I walk in now, they all laugh and say—look who's back—hey, where are the donuts?"

"Honey—they'll be saying that here—soon enough Scott!" Scoot drove off again continuing west.

I was hoping that Beth would keep her conversation going, so that Scoot would lose his concentration. I did not have to worry as it turned out.

"Scott you're unbelievable, Marc gives you this beautiful car not ten minutes ago, and you're already at risk of losing it."

"Yeah Dad, Uncle Marc's not going to be happy with you."

"Thank you—Embeth—and Mommy, but why don't you let me handle Uncle Marc. When I tell him what this cop pulled me over for, he'll just laugh with me, I'm sure of it."

"Scott, I hope you're right, because Marc seemed serious to me about your driving. And look at your scorecard already; you couldn't make it through ten minutes, let alone one day."

"Cuddles you're overreacting. I've known Marc since we were eighteen for God's sake, he an understanding guy—trust me on this."

"I hope you're right Scott but he's still your boss—that makes it different, perhaps you should consider that fact as well?"

"Now you see Cuddles, that's where you're so off base. Marc and I each respect one another's talents. Sure, he's my boss now, but we don't play those stereotypical roles—we're more like a creative team, Jesus can't you see that yourself?

"On top of that, I'm part of his management team for the boys. And I know he trusts me as well as respects the job I'm trying to do with that too."

"Scott, I didn't say he doesn't respect you, I'm merely stating the obvious,—your relationship is different now. I've watched Marc closely honey, he's quite passionate with Verandas matters,—that passion could prove precarious to any employee which would also include you. Whether or not you and he are friends, I don't think you should lose sight of my observation.

"You know Scotty; there just might be other sides to Marc that you haven't seen yet. Please keep that fact in the back of your mind along with your empty beer cans and golf balls?"

"Cute Cuddles, that's just what the girls needed to hear their mother say about their father, now isn't it?"

"Sorry dear, I shouldn't have said that, you're right."

"Hell, it's okay, but just watch what you say, alright?"

"Sure Scotty."

"Control, this is unit three, I'm traveling westbound on Sahara, just east of Fort Apache. I have a four-wheel in the number one, heading likewise; subject is clocked at 47 over 45. Subject is also starting to 'ride the behind' of the four-wheel in front of him, over."

"Ten four, unit three, proceed."

"Damn it, I can't believe this crap Beth, what in hell is going on here? Christ, I'm getting pulled over again, I don't believe this,—how is this even possible honey?"

"Scott what were you doing now?"

"I swear Cuddles, I haven't a clue—but haven't you been right here with me—how was my driving to you? Look; the speedometer is still reading '44', so they must have some grace of three to five miles?"

"Just relax Scott, the limit's forty five. Your driving has been fine, it's must be something else. It certainly didn't seem like you were speeding, so that's a relief."

"It is . . . how? I mean thanks for the vote of confidence Cuddles, but let's just hope this cop thinks so too?"

From down the block, I could see Scott putting down his window as Paul parked Laverne.

"Afternoon officer, is something the matter?"

"Why yes sir, I didn't stop you for my health. May I please see your identification and insurance information?"

"Certainly, listen; I can't imagine what I did wrong?"

"Sir, you were clocked at between two and three miles per hour over our posted speed limit, plus you were following too closely."

"I was? I didn't think I was speeding, or following too closely—you mean tail gating right?"

"Exactly—and stop patronizing me Mr. Davis, this is a double violation."

"I'm sorry officer; I certainly wasn't purposely trying to patronize you, but are you really going to write me up for two miles over the limit—I just picked the car up?"

"I said two to three over—and yes Mr. Davis I am—along with following too closely as well. And if that doesn't satisfy you—bub, you just keep it up, as there will be more, I can assure you . . . I've seen your type before."

I could hear Beth now, starting to lose her own cool with this cop's quite cavalier attitude.

"Scott, I want you to get this officer's name, badge number, and his precinct, I don't like his attitude one bit. There was nothing out of line with your two questions."

"Okay Cuddles, but let's just take it easy for the time being, alright?"

As I listened to their conversation, I was impressed to say the least with Scoot's skills at tactfulness. I saw that Scoot was trying to keep things cool already . . . good.

"Scott, I don't care what this yahoo says, you were driving fine—so I will not stand for his insolence!"

I was thrilled that Beth was playing her supporting lead so well, without even realizing it. She was now adding to Scoot's problematic situation as well as increasing the stress level filling that car now. Still, Scooter endeavored to keep everyone cool.

"Honey please relax—alright? Let's say that I agree with you Beth—this guy has an attitude—but I do like my freedom more, so—just cool off—please."

"Fine, but I'm doing so in protest, this guy is definitely out of line."

"Mr. Davis, would you please step on the brake pedal for me three times, once you can see me in the rearview mirror of your vehicle."

"Why, is there a problem there too officer?"

"Sir, just do it please?" The officer said curtly as he moved to the rear of the Jag.

"Sure officer, anything to help out." A moment later, the cop returned from the trunk area.

"That's what I thought Mr. Davis; you've also got one of the lights burned out on the brakes. I'm going to write you for that as well." The officer said with an obvious smirk on his face, as if he were celebrating the brake light's failure.

At that moment, I could see Scoot finally lose his cool—badly!

"Sure officer . . . of course you will. Hell; you're already citing me for a whopping two to three stinking miles over the limit—oh my heavens, oh mercy me! And let's not forget, citing me for following a car too closely that I know I wasn't—sure, why the hell not?

"Listen my friend; I've just picked this car up from the agency not more than forty minutes ago. If you want to write a citation for a defective bulb, I suggest you cite them . . . not me! You're crucifying me here, so I'm advising you right now, I will not sign for an unjustified ticket! I refuse to accept that for a defective bulb on a car I just drove off the frigging lot!"

"Mr. Davis, step out of your car please."

"Certainly—after I see your identification please, officer. I find your actions deplorable. I certainly plan to speak to your superiors, you can count on it. You're not on a patrol sir—you're on a witch hunt!"

"Fine Mr. Davis, are you refusing to remove yourself from your vehicle?"

"Scott, you better get out of the car—this guy's a loose cannon, we can fight this later . . . but believe me—we will!"

"Quiet Cuddles, I'm handling this.

"Officer, I never said I wouldn't get out of my car, I insist however, that you present me with your identification—please!"

"Fine Mr. Davis, I'll have you look at my identification, while I complete your arrest—will that suffice"

"My arrest? Arrest me, for what?"

"For refusing to cooperate by signing the citation naturally. I have no choice sir; I'm compelled to arrest you. I must remand you immediately to the courthouse, that's the law in our county for refusing to sign a citation."

"Who's refusing to cooperate, I'll be glad to get out, but I want some ID from you first, officer. And if my two choices are arrest versus signing, I'll sign the stupid citation for you—and have the agency answer for it later."

"Certainly Mr. Davis . . . my, aren't we being cooperative now—here you are."

I could see Scott reviewing the Metro officer's credentials and badge, with a highly flushed face, but he had regained his tactical nature at least. Scoot was reading the information to Beth, who was taking the information down—as she was flushed as well—she was so peeved, I was shocked at this side of her.

Somehow this a-hole seemed to have the perfect name I thought, for a prick cop, as I heard Scoot reading it over to Beth.

"Are you satisfied now, Mr. Davis?"

"Yes, thank you, Officer Willis."

"Good, now if you'll kindly sign my citation, I'll be on my way. And you'll be on your way too, with your license, family—along with the three points on your record."

"Christ—three points?"

"Yes Mr. Davis, three points. You are charged two points for any speed violation, plus the one point for the tailgating; the brake light is strictly a functional violation. If you repair that, and then get it inspected at the DMV within ten days, there are no points charged. Isn't—that nice of us?" Willis added with a sarcastic smile.

"Oh yes officer, you are all—too kind."

A still-flushed Scoot, signed the ticket while giving the cop a look of both contempt, mixed in equal parts with a heavy dirty look.

The cop left on his motorcycle, as Scoot got back into the car, where the conversation was tense—at best.

"Is it me Cuddles, or was that whole episode—just too damn weird?"

"Scotty, I'm beginning to wonder if moving here is such a good idea, really I can't believe that officer?"

"That's my whole point Cuddles—I don't believe him!"

"What are you saying Scott, I'm not following you honey?"

"Honey, how many times have I told you about Marc's practical jokes, he's famous for them for Christ's sake? Baby, I really smell a rat here, a nice Jewish one, with a brilliant sense of humor . . . along with four jets."

"But Scotty, how could Marc control an entire police force—are you nuts?"

"I know you wouldn't think so Cuddles, but I'm beginning to have my doubts sweetheart. I'm convinced Marc has got a hand in this somehow! This is all beginning to smell just as fishy as those lousy carp at the lake. I've told you how Marc was infamous when we worked at Toonland, he's truly a gag genius—if anyone could pull this off—it would be him."

"Come on Scott, how could Marc get the City's entire police force involved in his prank—it just isn't possible dear. My God Scott, this isn't some two-cop town in the sticks—this is a major American City? Certainly their police department must have plenty of other pertinent matters to worry about, than a private citizen's 'gag' against an old friend . . . don't you think?"

I watched Scoot pull out into traffic in the Jag. He was so paranoid now, he was being overly cautious—he was making another blunder within minutes, without even realizing it.

"Control, unit eight here. I have a four-wheel in the number three lane westbound on Sahara. Subject is doing thirty two under a forty five, copy?"

"Copy unit eight, ten four, proceed."

So I guess it was not lost on the police either apparently, as evidenced by my scanner.

I think I saw the 'Crown Vic's' flashing red lights, even before Scoot did. From the Jag, I could hear Scoot's reaction—perhaps all of Las Vegas heard it actually.

"Shit! This is just not happening again—I frigging refuse!"

"Oh Scott, this is just unreal, but please watch your language in front of the girls. Do you think the police do this to simply go after people driving nice new cars? If that's the case Scotty, you give this stupid car back to Marc in the morning, or forget us moving here, I swear."

"I seriously doubt that honey, but something's going on here . . . I'm certain of it. If this isn't Marcus Morgan at work, I don't know who it is, but it's almost comical now, really . . . let's put Em behind the wheel next, and see what they do to her?"

"Now Scott, stop it."

The cop approached the window as Scoot put it down for the female officer. Scoot may have been slowly deflating the countless arteries that we're swollen around his neck and forehead, but nothing was going to help his coloring now—he was bright red!

"Hi sir, is there some reason why your speed is only thirty two in a forty five mile per hour zone without a traffic issue? Our minimum speed in a forty five is the lower of thirty five or whatever traffic will bear?"

"Wow Officer—what do you know a legitimate citation? Ma'am, I am impressed. Yet if I told you why I was only going thirty-two miles an hour, you would honestly never believe me."

"Really—well why not try me sir." As he handed over his license and registration.

"Alright officer, if you can believe this, I picked this car up at Gaudin not more than an hour ago. In that short span of time since leaving their lot, I've gone a grand total of eight lousy miles according to my odometer. In those same few miles however, I have been stopped by—not one, not two, but—three different police officers including you now. I've been cited for various supposed infractions, which I seriously believe were all unfounded and trumped up. Yours is the one exception Ma'am—but you know what; I plead not guilty—by reason of paranoia!" Scoot at least had her laughing.

"Really sir. Hasn't anyone ever told you that Gaudin is just across the street from our regional precinct center? And you know it doesn't help any that our mid-day shifts just began—you know sir, most locals usually know when to avoid this area."

"Oh my God, so that's it. You've got to be kidding me? Listen, are you guys having some kind of contest on how many tickets you can write on a single shift?"

"My word sir—of course not—that was last month. We were all trying to break our 1998 record."

"Oh."

"You know what sir, may I see the tickets please? Perhaps I can help you out before I have to write you up . . . okay?"

"Oh could you Officer—Simms, thank you. You know, that's the first nice thing I've got from any of your order today."

"It's my pleasure Mr. Davis; you just relax while I have a quick look okay?"

"Of course, be my guest."

It was at this moment, that I heard Beth interject.

"Honey, I don't get it, what do you think?"

"I can't say Cuddles; maybe she's got some pull or something?"

"Do you think?"

"Who knows, but at least she's trying to help us—that's certainly a refreshing first!" At that moment, Officer Simms returned to the Jag with the tickets in her palm.

"Mr. Davis, I've reviewed your citations. I'm so sorry to tell you, but without one in there for driving too slow already, I will still have to cite you, much as I honestly hate too."

At that moment, I saw Scoot throw up his hands, as he collapsed his torso over the steering wheel of the car in resigned disgust. He was shaking his head now, as was Beth, while Officer Simms went to her cruiser to complete her painful task . . . to write him up—yet again that day.

"Beth, I'll just bet you, that Marc picked this agency along with the delivery time to take full advantage of that shift change. He's had enough of his own tickets to know the score. He knew exactly what was likely to happen here, I know him too well Cuddles. I told you his gags were infamous, yet extremely creative—so do you believe me now Beth?"

"Yes Scott, you did mention his creativity honey, but I still say, don't be ridiculous—he can't control the police force . . . he just can't!"

"Fine, you don't want to believe your husband, suit yourself. But you have to admit that this whole thing is just too damn fishy?"

"I know Scott, but I also understand what this officer explained, so I do think it's possible—but it certainly isn't fair."

"Gee—thank you for that at least."

"And Scotty, I'm pretty sure Marc said something to me in passing that this was the only Jaguar dealership in town—if so, it's not like he had a choice of where to go to get you the car of your dreams."

"Fine Cuddles, but I'm sure that you're giving him way too much doubt on this . . . he certainly had to know about the shift change issue, hell probably every local does."

"Alright, maybe you're right on that point—what do I know, but what are you going to tell him about all of this?"

"The truth honey, what else can I do?"

"I guess nothing Scott, but at least you are doing the right thing by telling him."

At that moment I heard Halley.

"Daddy, if you want, why not let me tell Uncle Marc for you, he loves me you know?"

"Yes sweetheart he does, very much so. He loves both of you, but I'm the one who has to tell him sweetheart."

"Okay; but I hope we still get the new house?"

"Don't worry honey; if I have to take my own car to work—or the bus, I'm not going anywhere. I really love my new job baby, so don't you worry your little head, okay?"

"Sure Daddy."

At that moment, Officer Simms returned to the dejected occupants of the new Jag.

"Mr. Davis, I felt so bad for you, that I changed you're real infraction to an unsafe lane change. This citation will only cost you one point instead of the normal two . . . I wish I could do more sir."

"You know Officer, I do thank you for you're big heart. Can you imagine how I'm going to explain this? It's a company car after all, but I guess I can go to traffic school?"

"Now that's the spirit Mr. Davis—you're so right—you can! However though, only once each twelve months, so the rest of the points are there for three years . . . I'm afraid." With that final blow, Officer Simms handed Scoot his third ticket, as she waved good-bye to the girls in back before leaving.

From my vantage point, Scoot was laying his head on the steering wheel, pounding his fist into his head in near tears.

Beth tried her best to calm him back down.

"Scotty, look at the bright side—the Chevy's paid for. And you know what honey, if you want, we'll trade it in on our own new car, should Marc take this one away from you?"

I listened to Scoot's whimpering along with his under the breath cursing at himself. After several minutes of this, Scoot threw caution to the wind as he started the car and pulled into traffic again . . . undaunted . . . or was he?

"Honey, why don't we take that drive now, I'm sure that will cheer you up?"

"Sure Cuddles, but only if you drive the damn thing, because maybe it's me, maybe this car and me are jinxed? You know, maybe I was never meant to drive a fine car of this caliber . . . maybe God is punishing me for my old record?"

"Oh Scotty, don't be ridiculous."

"Gee honey, what else am I suppose to think, Jesus; three tickets in ten minutes driving time?"

"Okay, maybe you do have a point, pull into that 7/11 over there, and I'll give the car a go."

"Fine, but watch the gas pedal Beth, this car's a certifiable rocket."

"Don't worry Scott, I've noticed that already, but you know I drive conservatively."

"Yes I know that honey—and that's you, but—this car doesn't!"

"All right, I'll be careful."

I saw the Jag pull into the parking lot of the convenience market, where Beth and Scoot changed seats. You could see that Scoot was crushed, as well as ultimately defeated, emasculated . . . or deflated. Beth was going to be driving his dream machine.

Nevertheless, most importantly to me, he had passed one-half of his tests.

True, he had pushed the envelope a little with the second officer, but all the same, over all, he handled himself commendably. I was convinced he could withstand extreme, sustained, stress under fire now.

Now, if he would only come clean by the end of the day, he would pass the second 'honesty' test, too.

At that moment, I simply smiled as I picked up my cell phone. I dialed my friend and co-conspirator, Doug Williams. He answered on the second ring.

"Hello control?" I asked.

Doug instantly started losing it, but he got through it, as he responded— eventually. You see—poor Beth had no idea just how possible it was to hire your own police force as co-conspirators!

"Hey Marc, had enough . . . for once?"

"Yeah Doug, even I'm feeling sorry for him now."

"Good, listen Marc that was the easiest moonlight job we've had in months since the last time I guess. But I have to tell you, you've got more than a little bit of the devil in you buddy."

"Yeah Doug I suppose so, but I just want to see how long he takes to come clean now. If it's before the morning, I destroy the evidence and he gets his reward. If he doesn't, all the photographs taken at each citation will replace the real ones from the agency's delivery of the car. I'm just enough of a prick to pin them up on display outside his office walls tomorrow morning."

"Jesus, I'm just so glad I don't work for you Marc."

"Why's that Doug?"

"Because I don't think I could survive one of your gags without a coronary for dessert even though I run an entire precinct for Metro, that's why."

"Well Doug, I may be a stinker, but my bonuses always make up for it."

"Yes I know, Carrie's last one really made her flip out, we paid off our pool loan with it."

"Listen Doug, nice working with you again, is it like last time, I mail the PD a separate check for the vehicles?"

"Yes, it's still the same procedures. You know we're only supposed to offer this service for film and TV commercials, so keep this gag quiet, or it will be my ass on the line."

"Don't worry about me Doug; I know when to keep my mouth shut."

"Good, talk to you soon then."

"Bye Doug."

I hung up my cell, as I asked Paul to get us to the house. I had plenty of time, but I thought I would spend some time with the folks before getting the boys from school.

I got home to find Mom and Dad talking in the great room, while I could see Grace and Reg drinking tea in the kitchen as they casually held hands . . . until I walked by of course.

"Hey there gang, how's everyone?"

"Fine son, how was your day?" Reg and Gracie now came into the Great room to join us.

"All right, but the end of my afternoon especially—was a killer."

"How so Love?"

"Gracie, I pulled a Morgan classic on Scooter in his new car."

"Oh no Marc, please tell me that you didn't?"

"Alright Mom . . . I didn't, are you happy now? Yes Mom, I'm afraid I most sincerely did."

"Shame on you Marcus, you're no son of mine for the entire day!"

"Fine Ma, I won't hold my breath either . . . satisfied?"

"Which gag, love?"

"Oh thank you Gracie, I know who my real friends are. But nothing much Gracie, just the one I use on all my upper management to test their stamina under stress. I had the cops stop Scooter and cite him with three tickets and five points against his record, in less than ten minutes elapsed time."

The room was full of laughter from everyone . . . even Mom now. Perhaps I would get a reprieve out of her for my creativity alone?

"Bloody poor bastard." Came out of Reg.

This elicited even more laughter.

"You know guys; I must say that I'm indeed getting older, because this one just didn't give me the old zing. You know, like I used to get with you and me Gracie."

"Sure love, it only makes sense."

"How so Grace?"

"Love, you know I'll always give it right back to you, Scott probably won't. So there's no thrill of walking around the next corner, wondering what's waiting for you there."

"Yeah, maybe that could be it Gracie."

"Boy kiddo, you are now, and will always be—a practical joker. Face it son; it's in your genes despite your Mother's collybotching."

"Thanks Dad—I guess.

"But Dad, if Scooter comes clean before morning, I'm making it up to him, Beth, and the girls big time. If he doesn't, there will be a round two in the morning."

"What's round two, dear—pray tell?"

"Oh, I'll place the photos I arranged of the citations, on his office walls, blown up into posters of course.

"You know in the past, I've always sworn my VP's to secrecy that I've administered this stamina test to. But I'm getting tired of it, so it will end with Scoot, so he's getting this unique finishing touch if he doesn't come clean. Hell the whole office will know. But if he does come clean—the photos will also change to those taken at the agency when we picked up the car."

"Nice touch love, but only if he doesn't confess . . . did I get that right? You know Marc; this sort of reminds me of your newspaper gag on me."

"Yes Gracie, your right on both points."

We all sat around talking about that gag, as Gracie insisted on reliving it for the folks' benefit. That was followed by considerable debate along with some wagering, on whether or not Scoot would come clean about the tickets. This went on so long, that I hardly realized I had to run for the boys now.

I left the house in the Navigator, since the sun had managed to stay out, but it was cold again and gloomy. I arrived at the Meadows School a minute or two late, with the line of cars huge now.

The boys spotted my truck as they headed outside. I looked for their body language and expressions for clues of how their day went. I observed their small talk with several peers. I was delighted to see them all exchanging 'high-fives' with each other. Those exchanges convinced me that they might have had some success with their letter—thank the Lord for that.

When they got into the Nav, I immediately asked them the obvious.

"So did it work guys?"

They both wanted to talk at once, but realized through their non-verbal communication I assumed, that that would not work. Therefore, Trevor spoke first.

"Did it ever Dad, thanks—it was bloody brill. God I could just kiss you right here in front of all of our mates."

"Jeeze Trevor, I'll take that as your supreme compliment then."

"Yeah Dad you should, everyone really understood what the letter was saying. Lots of them came up to us to say they would be cool from now on, and sorry, and other stuff like that."

"Great T-1, that's a relief—so was the rest of your day better after that?"

"Oh yeah Daddy, not one problem—not even the girls in our class. And Mrs. G. thanked us in front of everybody Dad!" Taylor jumped in too.

"Really, well I'm sure she, more than anyone, appreciates what you guys have done."

"Yep, that's exactly what she told us Dad."

"Cool guys, I'm so happy to hear all of this."

"So is the photographer at the house yet?"

"Not when I left T-man."

"Oh, say can we wear our costumes from Saturday?"

"Sure Trev, if they're home from the laundry yet."

"Oh, well I didn't think about that Dad, what if they aren't?"

"Just pick out something else guys, but go casual, nothing fancy okay?"

"Sure Dad."

We drove back home in animated conversation as we pulled into the Trail right at three, twenty-five. As we approached the drive, I saw Beth getting out of the driver's side of the Jag. I just couldn't resist the opportunity as I yelled out loudly:

"What's the matter Scoot, don't you like the car, or are you just giving Beth—visitation?"

Beth immediately looked at me as she laughed awkwardly.

"Marc, we've never driven a more pleasurable car, or one that draws—so much attention."

"Good Beth, I'm glad you like it. So Scoot, did you open her up?"

"Nah bud, not really—never got the opportunity . . . I'll explain later."

"Okay, well use it well guys . . . I mean that."

"Thanks Marc . . . we're trying."

Scooter was so beaten at this point, as his weak answer reflected clearly now.

"Scoot, do you want to speak to the guys before Teen Pop gets here?"

The boys meanwhile were out of the truck and talking with the girls already.

"Yeah bud, that would be a good idea. Come on guys, why don't you take a little walk with your old Uncle Scott okay?"

"Sure Uncle Scott" as the boys went over to Scott. After hugs from the two boys, they walked slowly down the street talking.

I escorted Beth and the girls inside, where we would wait for their return along with the magazine entourage to arrive. The three ladies went into the kitchen to greet Grace, who had become special to all three already. Why was I not surprised, Gracie endeared herself to everyone, and it always seemed mutually returned.

The entourage from Teen Pop was cleared through our gate at exactly three, forty-one, making them right on time. Minutes later, the door chimes rang as Reg naturally went to greet them.

Walking into the foyer, I greeted our guests from the magazine.

"Hello, I'm Marc Morgan, the twins' father—and you are?"

"Hello Mr. Morgan, it's a pleasure to meet you, I'm Marna Baron from Teen Pop. I am authoring the feature on your sons, but allow me to introduce my long time photojournalist and good friend, Nancy Barasch."

"How do you do Mr. Morgan?"

Mom now joined us in the foyer.

"Hello Nancy, but please ladies, feel free to call me Marc."

"Certainly Marc."

"Ladies, allow me to introduce the boys' personal manager—my Mother, Marilyn . . . even though she's disowned me for the entire day, although that's a whole other story." All of us laughed now, breaking the ice nicely.

"Hello Marilyn, but just for the record, so am I correct in assuming your last name is Morgan?"

"Yes it is. It's my pleasure to meet you both, as well. Marna, where would you both like to set up your things?"

"Whatever works for you folks is fine by us—we're easy. Nancy wants to catch the boys in some of their normal daily activities as well as behind their keyboards later on, if that's workable?"

"Fine Marna, Marc converted his gym to a practice studio for the twins . . . so don't mind the mess, but would you two like to start there?"

"I think that would be great as a good use of this brief down time as well . . . I assume the boys are not yet home from school? . . ."

. . . "No they're home from school, but took a short walk, they'll be in any time". I responded.

We all walked down the hall to my old gym. With the high ceilings along with the mirrored walls, it was ideal for practicing stage presence, body language and blocking all while playing. The room's naturally good acoustics were an added plus.

But the room was also now loaded with the keyboards, microphones, headphones, amps, synthesizer, Klipsch® symphony speakers, along with sheet music strewn everywhere—making it look like a pre-teen—pigsty.

"Mercy sakes, I see the boys don't exactly want for a place to rehearse—or mess up, do they Marc?"

"No Marna they don't, but if you prefer, we can tidy this up a bit before we get started, it's only from the sheet music they constantly fight over?"

"Are you kidding Marc, we love it when our subjects are straightforward and honest . . . but this room is awesome as a studio either way."

"Yes it is Nancy."

"Might I add that you have an absolutely marvelous home Marc. I love how it's decorated."

"Thanks Marna, Marilyn's been responsible for the decorating—I just pay the bills."

"Since the boys aren't here at the moment, maybe we can sit down Marilyn, so you can give me your perspective on their phenomenon, being their grandmother as well as their personal manager . . . are you open to that?"

"I'd be happy to Marna, why don't we get comfy in the great room then, we can all stretch out in there . . . let's relax with some refreshments as well."

"Great and thank you."

We all headed into the great room where dad was watching the big screen. He got up to shut off the TV as he introduced himself to the ladies.

Afterwards, we all sat down while I called Reg in to take drink orders.

"So Marilyn, first off, what was it like discovering you had twin grandsons who possessed so much musical talent?"

"Honestly Marna, at the time the boys' mother, Miranda told me of the boys' talents, I hadn't yet witnessed it for myself. From that perspective, and having only met the boys for the first time, I had absolutely no idea of what to expect or just how talented that meant that they truly were.

"Naturally, I figured there also had to be some degree of parental bias, you know, the proud mother and that "yes and my kid is so talented" junk we've all heard over the years. Having been through a lot of that with Marc when he was performing, let's say I'm just a little doubtful of most parents' opinions when it comes to their own child's talent.

"When Miranda simply made me promise to have the boys do something with their musical talents, I truly didn't know what to expect.

"The first time I heard them reheating in the house, I honestly assumed someone had switched on the stereo system here in the great room . . . that's how professional it all sounded."

"As it turns out, helping Marc's foundation seems to have fostered along Miranda's request. It proved to be the catalyst for this whole thing getting started for the boys."

"So, when did you actually hear them the first time other than rehearsing, and what was your reaction then?"

"Other then doing some back up vocals on a tribute for their mother, it was at one of Marc's restaurants here in Las Vegas a couple of weeks ago actually. Honestly ladies, I was overwhelmed with their talent along with those big voices of theirs."

"Was this the concert they did for their crusade?"

"No, it was about a week before that; it was an impromptu performance that Trevor had asked Marc if he and his brother could do to entertain for Marc's guests."

"How were they received by that audience?"

"Fantastic Marna. It was after this performance that I shared with the boys and Marc, my conversation with Miranda. I guess as they say; the rest is history."

"By the way, do they have a favorite music genre?"

"Not exactly, you may be aware that they are classically trained first and foremost. Yet obviously, they're drawn to Rock music but more so, anything with heavy and unusual keyboard focus. Vocally, they're all over the map truly, yet I personally believe they lean towards ballads or softer rock."

"I've only heard one small sound byte where the recording was a bit muffled unfortunately. I was hoping you could get them to give Nancy and me a little sample today. We're both dying to hear what all the hoopla is about?"

"I'd suggest that you ask them that yourself, but the apple doesn't fall far from the tree. Their father here is the biggest ham this side of the Mississippi, so I doubt you'll have much trouble convincing them."

"Really? So how come Marc isn't up there with them then?"

"Marc, why don't you answer that for Marna?"

"Thank you for your lovely reference Mom. I'll be glad to answer that one—for my own protection.

I had everyone chuckling now.

"Marna, simply put, the boys, and I do sing regularly in their bedroom when they're getting ready to hit the hay—it's sort of a family tradition already. Nevertheless, that's enough of the Partridge family scenario for me . . . but I think for them as well.

"You know Marna; this is their dream, their lives—and careers. It's not a monetary issue for any of us; it's a labor of love, so that's all fine with me. Lastly, I can't exactly give up my day job, now can I?"

"I would suppose—but what do you mean, it's not a monetary issue—isn't it an issue for them at least? Aren't the boys excited by how their performing can financially set them that much better for life down the road?"

"Not really Marna—you see they've already decided that at least half of everything they'll eventually make will go straight to charity as it is."

"What? You've got to be kidding—my, that's most admirable if not down right unusual—was that your suggestion then?"

"Absolutely not Marna, Taylor was adamant about doing it while Trevor couldn't wait to agree with him. I did suggest some specific charities though, but that's all.

"Look Marna, these are simply two very socially-conscience boys, it's how they were reared,—that's all. You'll see it for yourselves I'm sure.

"For Taylor in fact, performing professionally, started out strictly with the goal of raising more money for their crusade."

"This is truly amazing Marc, can I assume the boys based their decision on knowing the family's financial standing then? I would hope that this isn't being too forward to ask?"

"No not at all . . . but the answer is going to surprise you Marna. You see the boys don't really have a full working knowledge of mine or their finances for that matter. Naturally they aren't totally oblivious either, but it's just one of those subjects we typically sidestep to avoid, pardon the pun—but at all costs."

"Really, I guess they're simply not your typical eleven-year-old kids then?"

"No, in this respect they're not, but it's greatly due to the cultural differences between living here now, as opposed to having been raised within the British class system previously. You see Marna, they already know they have money by their nobility alone—see what I mean?"

"Oh, I see your point."

At that moment, we heard the front door open and close, as the boys wasted little time tracking us down.

"Dad, where are you?"

"In the great room, T-1."

"What does T-1 stand for Marc?"

"Well, we all have our little nick names. T-1 is Trevor, as he is the oldest; his brother goes by T-man, which together makes them the T-men. I gave them those monikers, while they choose to refer to themselves as Tay and Tre."

"And what's their nick name for you, Marc?"

"You know Marna, if they have finalized one; they haven't shared that with me . . . no wait—that's not entirely true. I think I may be becoming—Dadio, like I call my own father."

At that moment, Scott, along with the boys entered the room quite dignified like.

The boys immediately walked over to the two female strangers and introductions were exchanged.

After everyone was seated, Marna began:

"I must tell you, that I have been most excited to meet you two since your Dad expressed his okay."

"Thank you Miss, it is a pleasure to meet you as well." Taylor offered now.

"Please boys, call us Marna and Nancy. We're thrilled to be your first magazine interview since going professional."

"Thanks Marna, it's great to have you both here today."

"My, you two are something else with those manners, aren't they Nance?"

"Yes Marna, but I would just love to get my hands on those adorable little cheeks of theirs too?"

"Which—cheeks would those be Nancy?" Trevor asked. Trev had shocked Scoot, Mom, Dad, and I right into laughter, while the ladies—now privy to the boys' classic British sense of humor, were hysterical too.

I could see that this was destined to be an enjoyable afternoon with Teen Pop. At that moment, Scott cleared his throat, as I immediately realized that no one had yet introduced him to the ladies.

"Oh Marna, Nancy, please forgive me, may I present Mr. Scott Davis.

Scott is the boys' business manager, as well as serves as their executive producer in the studio."

"Hello ladies, so nice to make your acquaintances."

"Same here, Scott." Marna offered.

"Well ladies, the boys are all yours for up to the next two hours, fair enough?"

"Most generous of you Marc, yes that would be great, but can't you stay with us?" Marna queried.

"No, Mom should be more than adequate, besides I think you'll get a far better interview keeping all of us out of your way—don't you think?"

"That is most considerate Marc . . . yes; you're probably right about that."

"Good, then it's all settled. Should you need us for any questions, we'll be here at the pool table shooting eight ball—fair enough?"

"Sure that's fine." She responded.

Apparently, Nancy then remembered something on her mind.

"Marc, might you have any photos of the boys growing up and perhaps a family portrait or two?"

"Sure Nancy, but can I email them to you, I don't want to lose my originals?"

"That's fine Marc, here's my card with my email address on it." Nancy handed me her card.

Mom suggested that they adjourn to the living room, while Dad, Scoot, and I stayed behind in the great room to play pool.

"Nice ladies, don't you think?"

"Yeah bud, I think this will go well for us."

"Me too Scoot."

"All right you two, who's going to challenge whom to a game here?" Dad asked.

At that moment, Grace, Reg, Beth and the girls, joined us in the great room from the kitchen where they had been talking.

"Scoot, do you want to take Dad on, or should I?"

"Maybe I had better Marc, I can't afford to have you too close to a weapon right now with what I'm about to tell you."

"Jesus Scoot, you're not quitting already, are you?"

"No! Nothing like that bud."

"Well that's certainly a relief—so what's going on bud?"

"Marc, you absolutely won't believe what I'm about to tell you."

"Damn Scooter, whatever you are so brilliantly avoiding here . . . sounds serious?"

"It is, in a way Marc."

"Alright then, let's have it."

"Sure—but first, I want to mention—I have witnesses."

"Witnesses! Jesus Scoot, you're really starting to scare me now. Say—this hasn't anything to do with Morison does it? I've already warned you about that."

"No Marc, not at all."

"Well, that's a relief too, so I don't get it then; where's the fire pal?"

"I'm getting to it buddy . . . look—it's like this, I got stopped by the cops and I was cited in the new car."

"Is that all, dang Scoot, I thought you had shot someone in self-defense the way you were talking. No big deal, go to traffic school and get rid of the points—how fast did they clock you?"

"Actually Marc, there's a little bit more to this story."

"Oh—what?"

"Well for starters, it wasn't one time; I was pulled over three times. In total, I got five points with three citations, all within a ten minute period of time."

In mock anger and shock, I walked over to Scoot as I began to stare him down, with my voice in a perfectly low ominous tone as I spoke:

"Do you mean to tell me, that in only ten minutes driving that stupid frigging car of yours, you managed to land three tickets?"

"Yes Marc—and five points, that's exactly what I said."

"Beth, I can't believe this—what do you have to say about all of this, Christ, you were with him for God's sake, I thought for sure that you would keep him mindful behind the wheel?"

"Marc, I don't know what to say, except having been there, he really got a bum rap. Honestly Marc, he was driving better than I have ever seen him. He was being so careful with the new car; I absolutely couldn't believe the tickets, one, and right after—the next."

"Girls, do you two agree with what your mother has just told me?"

"Yes Uncle Marc, Daddy was framed—I'm pretty sure that's the word?"

"Okay Embeth—yes, that's an acceptable word for this situation, you're absolutely correct that your father got framed—but—by me girls!"

"Damn it! Do you see Beth? Well I told you over and over, but you refused to believe it—impossible you said—well, do you believe me now for crying out loud?"

Beth turned to me as she was clearly peeved . . . staring me down herself—quite effectively I might add.

"Marc, do you mean to tell me as calm as a cucumber, that you did all of that to your own close friend?"

"No Beth, I actually did this—to my employee . . . an employee I might point out, that had to pass this important 'stress test'."

"You put your employees through hell, and you have the nerve to call it a simple little stress test?"

"Certainly Beth—how am I going to know if I can trust my key people to always be honest with me? More so, that they can handle stressful situations without losing their cool—I've done this to all of my senior people you know . . . for example every new VP for at least the last eight years."

"Yes, but Scott's not a Vice President Marc?"

"Well, he is—now—Beth, unless you have some objection on me promoting him and bumping his salary 24k?"

Both Scoot and Beth were standing there in silence with their mouths open and stunned. Finally, Scoot closed his, as he formed some words with it for good measure.

"Marc, I'm not even here a week—and I make VP, what gives?"

"Yes Scoot; you would have been a VP within a couple of months tops anyway. I told you that I don't like having any department without someone delineated at the top as a VP—didn't I?

"Honestly Scooter, I simply saw so much talent and ability from you this week alone, that I realized I had honestly erred in my judgment, that's all. In hindsight, I should have hired you on as a VP in the first place. So I decided that once you passed the prerequisite Marc Morgan, Classic stress test, you deserved the title. Congratulations bud—you're now Vice President Scooter . . . hereafter of Entertainment!"

I walked up to Scoot and threw him into an embrace as I shook his hand. He stood there still somewhat in shock as he just smiled and stared blankly. I then walked up to Beth, who still seemed more than a little bit peeved, as I quickly gave her a little kiss on the cheek.

"And congratulations to you too—Mrs.—Vice President of Entertainment."

"Okay Marc, I do get it—but I still don't like it. My God, he could have had a heart attack."

"And when he's at work in a demanding or stressful situation, he'll need his wits about him there as well, Beth.

"God Beth, don't you remember our situation in Texas three years ago when those two escaped wackos were holding everyone hostage for 17 hours at our Dallas unit . . . it made the national news? All the true sickos out there, demand we stay on our guard—and can keep our cool at all times Beth, that's the lesson I learned from that horrific day, trust me. It's the whole idea behind this exercise, without being half as stressful, believe me . . . been there, done that . . . and lived through that absolute hell Beth."

"Okay, yes I do remember seeing that on the news, well that does make some sense now, but I hope it was worth it?"

"Yes Beth it was, because I now know Scoot can handle his responsibilities, even under stressful conditions. But Beth, all of this also holds nice things in store for you as well."

"For me? Where do I come into it Marc, I don't understand at all?"

"Simple Beth, first, Scoot just got two grand more a month for passing the driver's test with his promotion . . . hell that will nearly pay your new house payment, won't it? Secondly, as the spouse of one of our VP's, you just landed your own company car, a Mustang Cobra in bright yellow with white leather, no doubt. That is, unless you still feel this whole thing was too harsh and decide to refuse it on principle?"

Beth started carrying on and having a good time now. Hell we were all laughing at her obvious happiness over this part of the news.

Scoot was finally out of his stupor as well, as he looked at me.

"Is this why Robbie kept giving me the run around on my business cards not being in yet?"

"Oh yeah."

I answered as I gave my bud another hug, while I then realized I'd been remised as I bent lower to the girls' eye level now.

"Now ladies, don't you think your good old Uncle Marc deserves to be forgiven now?"

"Sure Uncle Marc."

Halley gave me a big sloppy kiss followed by one from Embeth.

"Wow, two new cars in the same day!" Embeth candidly added.

Everyone was laughing with Embeth now, while both Beth and Scoot were back to their old selves' finally.

"You know Marc, I've never heard of a corporation giving the 'spouse' of an executive their own company car before. Not that I'm complaining mind you, but why would you do that, as well as go to the added expense?" Beth inquired.

"That's a brave question Beth, so it deserves a truthful response. You see kiddo, I do it for selfish, yet astute, reasons Beth. I only hire the best people at all levels, so every headhunter in the entire country knows that . . . word does get out, you know. Naturally, those same headhunters, along with all of our competitors, love to hire my top people away from me whenever they can. Honestly, I used to lose some very talented people this way, much too often for my liking. While that's challenging and expensive to our business, it also is disruptive and can greatly affect our morale. So a few years back, I thought of focusing on various retention strategies for each level of employee, instead.

"Since I began giving our executive spouses their own company vehicles as only one example, I haven't lost a single upper executive to anyone. Think about it Beth, how many talented executives are going to ignore replacing up to two vehicles when being competitively recruited? I also think it has fostered tremendous additional loyalty to our company as well."

"God Marc, you know, you really are incredibly smart and absolutely right—but now come clean about something else. How in God's good name did you pull that off with the police department . . . are you that powerful here?"

"No not at all. You see Beth, that's easier than you think . . . it's not even confidential . . . merely sensitive since Verandas cheats a little. If you will all promise it never leaves this room, I'll share it with you?"

"All right, I'm game, how about you honey?"

"Sure Beth, I've got to hear this, mostly because knowing what I know now, I want to pull a little payback on Officer Willis myself sometime!"

"Okay you two, it's quite simple. Our police have a special TV and Film department that coordinates our police officers to moonlight for 'policing' duties . . . even performing as extras on request . . . or acting like a real tough cop as Willis did so beautifully. Naturally it all must take place during their off time hours. This also includes using their vehicles if requested at extra charge, so the department benefits too. Primarily the officers are used for both traffic and crowd control on the location sites. As you may be aware, filming in Las Vegas is a frequent occurrence, so this has been a major revenue source for everyone concerned at Metro.

"So, now we come to how we cheat on the rules just a trifle. You see, under the guise of filming an actual Verandas TV commercial on location, Verandas has gotten away with this for years. Essentially, you, Scooter, all of the officers, and the girls were all filmed in a TV commercial legitimately for Verandas that will simply never be seen or aired on TV . . . that's it in a nut shell."

"That's amazing Marc, but there's just one more thing bud, I'm carrying three citations in my wallet as my contribution to filming this supposed commercial—so what's the deal with those?"

"Well pal—there is a big price to pay for this whole set up, I'm sorry to tell you . . . but none of it is yours Scoot—so got yah! Those citations aren't worth the paper they're written on—your slate is still clean bud. Your tickets are handwritten. Metro now uses electronic citations."

"Jesus, thank God for that."

"Yes Scoot, thank God indeed. By the way, I've reserved a track for you and I tomorrow morning at seven at the Las Vegas Motor Speedway. This way we can see what our two new rockets can really do without the fear of an actual citation." "Cool bud, I can't wait, but I've got a thought."

"Shoot—Scoot?"

"Why don't we wait a few weeks until Beth gets her Cobra—then we can all go, I think she'd enjoy the experience as well—wouldn't you honey?"

"Sure, after all Scott, I've never had that trill before—I might enjoy it."

"That's a great idea Scoot. Listen, since you're such a great sport Beth, why don't I see if we can arrange the car for tomorrow morning before I cancel the track time?"

"You can do that Marc?"

"Sure Beth, hell—let me have Robbie call Roland at Ford Country right now. If he's got a match, you can pick it up tonight after dinner."

"You're kidding me, that fast—just like that?"

"Certainly Beth, it's just a car."

"Okay, but we've never got a new car before today, so what we don't know, could fill a book".

"Don't sweat it Beth, they'll either have one there or at Gaudin Ford, I'd lay you even money."

I picked up my telephone to dial Robbie at the office.

"Marc's messenger boy, Robbie speaking."

"Cute Rob, obviously you checked your caller ID?"

"No Marc, I always answer the phone like this, why do you ask?"

"Can it Robbie, I know better, but so should you."

"Boy Marc, we are feisty today, aren't we?"

"No Robbie, but keep pushing the envelope . . . as we will be."

"So, what can I do for you boss?"

"Can you call Roland at Ford Country to see if he has a Canary Yellow Mustang Cobra Convertible in stock with white leather seats and soft top?"

"Cool. Obviously Scott passed his driver's test?"

"With flying colors—Roberto."

"Good for him . . . automatic or stick Marc?"

"Hold on Robbie, Beth do you want an automatic, or would you prefer a stick shift?"

"I don't know Marc, what do you want me to pick?"

"Beth, I want you to pick whichever you prefer."

"Go for the stick honey . . . be a trend setter."

"Gee, I haven't driven a stick since my '72 VW, are you sure Scotty?"

"Sure honey, it's like riding a bike, you never forget."

"But what about the traffic, with all that shifting that comes with it?"

"Actually Beth, plenty of people here drive sticks, the traffic here is nothing compared to Orange County, so it doesn't seem to bother most drivers here. My Bricklin has a stick that I drive around town all the time myself."

"Okay Marc, if you say so, the stick could be fun."

"Robbie, make it the manual tranny."

"Okay Marc, when do you want it if they have one?"

"Tonight of course, they can pick it up at 8:30 give or take. Also remind Roland that he sharpened his pencil for our fleet prices. As I recall, Mustangs are at $120 over invoice?"

"Okay Marc, but I'm not sure on your thinking."

"What do you mean Robbie?"

"I remember reading their rules before. I'm pretty sure the Cobra is a limited production vehicle, so those are excluded. I doubt a Cobra will be any where near $120 over invoice . . . still want it?"

"Oh whatever it is then, it's what our Mrs. Vice President of Entertainment wants."

"No problem."

"Alright, anything else we need to discuss Rob?"

"Yeah—when will the car ever be for me?"

"Now Robbie, let's not forget—'grow with love', shall we?"

"Okay Marc, I get it—but thanks for nothing. I'll call you back soon, bye Marc."

"So long Robbie." As I hung up while still laughing.

"Okay Beth, keep your fingers crossed—you're expecting."

"Don't worry Marc, I intend too."

The sound of the boys and our press friends coming out of the living room interrupted us now, so I called out to Mom.

"What's up Mom?"

"Oh nothing dear, Nancy's going to shoot the boys now, so we're starting in the studio. The boys are also going to play a tune or two, if you would all care to join us?"

"Okay Mom, I don't think any of us want to miss that, so call us when the shoot is finished."

"All right." As I heard her continue down the hall.

"Uncle Marc, can we watch the photos being taken?"

"I don't know Embeth; why not go ask Grandma Marilyn that?"

Embeth and Halley quickly got up to leave us, not to be seen again—for a while.

The remaining adults all chatted non-stop, while Scoot and Dad finally began their pool game in earnest.

Only minutes later, they completed the game when Dad sank the eight ball unintentionally. Apparently Dad must have been psychic, as Mom's voice was now heard on the intercom.

"Marc, the boys are going to play, so you might want to all get in here."

We went down to the studio where everyone but me had to stand in the hall naturally, as there wasn't enough room inside. The boys then proceeded to fire up their keyboards and amps.

Scoot performed a sound check, then adjusted the equipment accordingly while Nancy kept shooting her camera non-stop. Meanwhile the boys sought out requests from our Teen Pop guests. Marna shook her head as she continued writing feverishly into her journal, so Nancy jumped in while still shooting.

"Taylor, do you guys know anything from the Monkees?"

"Sure Nancy, what did you have in mind?"

"Can you do Daydream Believer?"

Taylor then smiled real wide as he responded.

"Wicked Nancy, that's like one of our total faves . . . its bloody brill."

"Great, because it's one of mine too; can you do that one then?"

"Sure Nancy, but I'm not sure you won't prefer the Monkees doing it."

"I'm confident you'll both do just fine . . . go for it."

"Alright Nancy, this is for you and Marna. We thank you both for making our day so special."

The two ladies were bowled over from the affection emanating out of the boys, with it being definitely mutual.

The boys went right into their piano introduction, doing the song 'solid'. Taylor was on the Davey Jones lead, as Nancy's camera flash was going off constantly. When they finished, the ladies led the applause, Nancy even catcall whistled which seemed a little too much for the small room's acoustics, but we understood her excitement.

"Sorry everyone, I just got a little carried away there, but that was so awesome guys."

"Thank you Nancy—so did you miss Davey Jones not doing that?"

"Not at all Tay, your version was wonderful, simply great."

"Thanks Nancy, I can tell you mean that."

"You bet I do, in fact, how about doing one more?"

"Sure, what would you like?"

"Well, your grandmother mentioned you have some new spectacular song to close your performances that you do a Capella—have I got that right?"

"Yes, but do you like do-wop?"

"Sure, how about you Marna?"

"Yeah Nance, naturally I like all kinds of Rock, but I especially love those smoky ballads from the fifties. You've got my curiosity up, what do you two have in mind?"

"Something right up your alley then, Marna."

"Oh really; holding out on me are you? All right boys—impress me."

"Okay Marna, just understand that we're going to record this with more back up vocals to add tons more do-wop. Today we just have a basic four-part harmony prerecorded, so it's really only partially the way it will sound finished."

"Come on already guys, I can't wait, what are you going to sing?" Marna was almost pleading now.

"Alright, do you happen to like the Platters Marna?"

"Like them Tre, my God—I worship them, are you kidding?"

"Cool, because we do too, so here's—My Prayer, just for you."

"Oh yeah, this is going to be so awesome a Capella, I love that tune—I just love it." Came out of a truly excited Marna now.

The boys did the song as before, but this time, there was even more feeling from the back up vocals they had prerecorded, in classic 50's style with lots of do-wop and harmonic emphasis. As before, their eyes remained closed, magically keeping both the rhythm and their perfect pitch right on the money.

When Taylor belted out his final crescendo, Marna literally grabbed Nancy's arm, and sighed loud enough for everyone to hear.

When the boys finished, Marna was clapping like an exuberant kid at their first circus experience. You could see clearly that she was genuinely moved; maybe even overwhelmed a bit at the way the boys had pulled this difficult song off. And having been in the industry fifteen years, she obviously did know her music . . . she was certainly no easy mark, after all.

"Oh my God—please tell me you're going to record that one first as a single?"

"Yes Marna, we plan to, but only if you promise to let us send you one of the first copies?"

"Oh, I think I can live with that Tre."

We all laughed heartily. Marna finally returned to being herself about five minutes later.

"Nance, why not get your outdoor shots out of the way now before you lose your ideal sun. We'll have just enough time to catch our cab to make our flight back to LA."

"Sure thing Marna, come on boys. Let's walk around your property, I want to scout out the best location spots—hey do you guys have a pool per chance?"

Both of the boys started laughing immediately.

"What's so funny guys?"

"Oh nothing Nancy." Taylor replied.

With that, the boys escorted Nancy along with the Davis sisters outside to the backyard. From the studio, one could still make out Nancy's reaction at seeing the lagoon, moments later.

"Oh my God—it's paradise!" We heard in the distance.

We chuckled as we waited patiently inside talking to Marna while Nancy did her thing outdoors with the boys.

"Marilyn, I can't begin to tell all of you, how much—the boys' version of that tune truly moved me, Christ—I think I'm still shaking.

"I simply can't get over the beauty or the power of their voices at their adolescent ages? I have heard countess people cover that song over the years naturally. I must tell you though, that the impact of their version doing it a Capella was simply breathtaking. I'm not exaggerating here folks—this was a telling experience, believe me. I'm so glad they performed that tune for me . . . it tells me so much about them."

"I'm so pleased you liked it Marna." I offered.

"Liked it? I'm way beyond liking it Marc . . . I'm in love with it, but so too, will the rest of their audience. Listen gang, I'm not only remaining unbiased, I certainly am not trying to patronize any of you, so listen up:

"Marc, Marilyn, I meet multitudes of hopefuls every week of the year . . . really nearly everyday. Most of these people have a pronounced tangible degree of talent, yet ultimately don't have the staying power or quite enough talent to sustain them . . . so they are therefore still doomed to fail or fade away, eventually. Mark my words well folks . . . your boys are going all the way to the top—the very top! We're talking super stardom here . . . trust me on this, as this industry I know well. A year from now, I'll be thrilled if they'll acknowledge me while walking down the red carpet at the Grammy Awards!"

"Really, are you absolutely sure of this Marna?"

"Yes Marilyn, I've been wrong twice in fifteen years . . . that's all. Your grandsons certainly will not be my third error, I can assure you. Their only Achilles heel is their anatomy. They're going to see their voices change eventually Scott, so you had better prepare for that now. I'll assume you know your stuff in the studio enough to prerecord adequate material to hold them over as they retrain their voices, because that's the only way these two could possibly misstep."

"Don't worry about me Marna, I've produced all my professional life, I'm prepared for everything. I also believe that I know how to perfectly capture them in the studio—so trust me. When I'm done with them, there will be no looking back. And just so you know, you're only mirroring my arguments to Marc from last October—when I kept saying yes, yes, yes, while he kept yelling—no, no, and hell no—if you can believe that crap?"

"Well Marc, get a life, because they are phenomenal. I for one want to make sure they get the very best from the beginning, but only the best. Simply said folks, they're that good and mega talented. Yet in spite of all of that; they're such adorable and sweet boys as well. Believe me folks—they are going to single-handedly, write the next chapter in the book on 'top-forty'."

"Thank you Marna, your encouragement means a lot to us, believe me."

"It's my pleasure Scott, in fact—let me do something else for them right now. I've never done anything like this before, so listen up. I want to offer them an awesome studio for their first sessions. You see, I have a dear friend in LA who owns one of the finest recording studios on the Coast, its Vinyl Spindletop Scott, are you familiar with it?"

"Yes of course, Marna, I've actually produced two albums there, it's a killer studio, with excellent acoustics, top shelf mixing board . . . yeah its great Marna.

"Marc, Marilyn, we owe this lady big time right now."

"I hear you Scooter, Marna, how can we ever thank you?"

"You can't Marc, so don't bother . . . hell, I should be thanking you for this opportunity of being their first interview . . . I think I feel sort of like how Sam Phillips must have felt that first moment when a young Elvis Presley stood in front of him.

"You see, for literally years now, my friend Kimberly over at Vinyl Spindletop has told me countless times, if I were ever to find someone truly spectacular and singular, I was to offer that artist her studio—immediately . . . gratis. But not until this very day, have I ever felt I had met her measurement . . . now I know I have. With your permission Scott, I would like to call her tomorrow on the boys' behalf.

"When I get finished raving about them to her, she'll throw in everything just for the 'cover' recognition when the CD goes triple platinum."

"Wonderful Marna, we can't begin to thank you enough."

"Oh, don't thank me Scott, just promise me, you'll put on your 'best' Quincy Jones hat, to produce the album of the year . . . Lord only knows, those two have what it takes to give it to you.

"They do Marna. While my production projects have all been exclusively for T-M, I can assure you that you have nothing to worry about."

"Good, so let me query your expertise on something I noticed then. You know Scott, I'm trying to figure out what exactly I heard that was so clearly different in the twins' vocals, was it something in their resonance, or their harmony?"

"Neither Marna, but you've got a great ear besides that . . . you see, as twins, they somehow naturally sing in a stereo of sorts beyond strictly harmonizing."

"Wow, I knew it sounded unique . . . fascinating."

As we were continuing small talk about recording studios, Nancy and the kids all returned.

"Marn, you have got to see their pool before we go, believe me, my pics won't do it justice."

"Nancy, are you okay? I've never seen you get 'hot' for a pool before—of all things."

"Just shut up and follow me."

I really had taken a liking to these two ladies, even without Marna's generosity, as they were extremely friendly . . . and we all know how I love the press already . . . not? My next question to them really shocked me more so than them I believe, when they returned to the kitchen.

"Well ladies, we hope you liked the lagoon, however we must be leaving for our dinner, so are we all wrapped up?"

"Yes Marc. Thanks so much for everything; we had a most delightful time getting to know all of you, but especially the boys and their music. I'm sure that I don't need to assure any of you that my feature will be most flattering after what we've seen and heard today.

"Thank you ladies, but let's get going as we have to get to dinner."

"Let us just call for a cab Marc, Nance can you hand me my cell, it's in my bag?"

"Yes Marn, here."

"I don't think you understand Marna, you and Nancy—are joining us for dinner—I must insist."

"Thank you Marc, but we can't miss our plane. I've got my deadline after all, so I can't risk waiting 'stand-by' on a later flight . . . not in Las Vegas of all places."

"Of course you can't Marna—that's why I plan on personally flying you both back to LA after dinner."

"You are—you do . . . can you do that?"

"Sure I can, why do you think I own a plane?"

"Oh, I didn't realize—all right, since you insist."

"Yes I do, you two are coming with us, end of discussion."

"You won't get an argument out of me Marc, except about the plane." Nancy offered now.

"What's your concern with that Nancy?" I asked.

"Oh you know Marc, I just don't care much for those little toy-prop planes. Honestly, it sort of makes me kind of nervous when you can hear—even your pilot throwing up!" We all laughed.

"I see Nancy, well, I don't blame you, but my plane is your choice of my four Lear jets! So don't worry, not one of them has any props—now does that make you feel less queasy about it?"

"Oh thank God, yes it does Marc, I love flying in a Lear . . . it's a real treat."

"Good, now let's blow out of this joint. Scoot you follow me in your Jag since I gave Paul the night off, alright?"

"Sure; now that I can drive it without some of that Jewish guilt of yours."

I laughed at Scoot's crack as we all headed out front on the drive.

At that moment, my cell rang—it was Robbie according to the number displayed.

"Hey there Marc, Roland's got a match. He's putting it on a seven-day, one-pay—whatever that is. He's having it detailed right now. The best fleet price he could do on a Cobra convertible was $1500 over invoice, I told him that was all right, given our discussion earlier. They can pick it up anytime between eight and ten when they close."

"Cool, thanks Robbie, good job as usual."

"Thanks Marc, you know I live for praise."

"Don't push it Robbie, you're sounding like one of those sappy Hollywood types at the Academy Awards."

"Thank you for that Marc, gee; that remark makes me feel so—superficial."

"As you should my friend." I laughed heartily into my telephone as I then said good night-before hanging up.

"Beth, you're expecting eminently; I think your water will be breaking at any time—how are your contractions now dear?"

"Oh Marc, you are the tease, are we picking it up tonight then?"

"Yes Beth, you'll leave after dinner to go straight to Henderson, you need to be there by ten."

"Wonderful Marc—thank you again."

"Beth, you deserve it after today, believe me."

"You know what Marc, you're right—I do, you little scoundrel." She laughed.

Being that Grace and Reg opted to stay home for the solitude and privacy offered at the Grotto so we were a comfortable sized group. We drove to our very first location on Flamingo Road, east of the strip in the heart of Restaurant Row. As the granddaddy of all our restaurants, this one has always held a soft spot in my heart.

Walking in, I can still remember countless nights serving as chief cook along with—bottle washer . . . waiter, performer, busboy . . . it's amazing how times change.

I had sent the kids on ahead to visit with Amelia while I located our manager Frank. Frank had the distinction of being both, our very first manager along with our very first employee—besides me, I guess.

"Marc! Always a pleasure to see you back home at old number one, so how are things at the office . . . tell me again how much you miss us?"

"Cute. The office is there Frank, but now I'm here, so let's forget about that, fair enough?"

"Sure thing boss, say did you happen to bring our two newest stars with you this evening?"

"Of course Frank, there in the parlor with our friends visiting with Amelia."

"Good, because after they've eaten, I would be delighted to have them sing for their supper . . . if my request isn't too bold? Hell, I hear they brought the house down in Summerlin—twice . . . now look at Summerlin's numbers—it isn't fair boss . . . my God man—where's your loyalty?" He said while laughing hysterically.

"Come on Frank, relax. It's a matter of Summerlin's location is so close to my house . . . I can't believe you sometimes Frank—so jealous . . . and at your age no less!"

"Fine. So when do I get to meet them, my kids want their autographs naturally?"

"Christ Frank, not yours too?"

"Absolutely boss, job or no job, my kids come first—you know that. I've been waiting days for this opportunity to ask you as a personal favor to my two and me."

"Okay Frank, but only because it's for Junior and Charlie. I'll bring them over before dinner, alright?"

"Sure Marc, and thanks."

"Don't mention it, now have you got the Forest all ready for us?"

"No Marc, I told Robbie to tell you I couldn't do that tonight—didn't he mention that?"

"No Frank, he didn't—I don't think?"

"I can't, it's booked . . . it's already occupied. Unless you wish to uproot and evict one of Hollywood's most popular power couples who are in town with their family?"

"Do I dare even ask who it is Frank?"

"Sure, dare all you want, but my lips are sealed . . . it certainly isn't . . . no I had better not." And then he went silent on me.

"Oh, I see Frank. Well I'll remember your refusal to tell me that when I'm signing your next Christmas bonus."

"Of course you will Marc . . . before you'll give it to me just like you always do . . . every year."

"Fine Frank, I can see I've played out my tune with you a little too often already, haven't I?"

"Now that's a smart lad Marc."

"All right, I know when I'm licked, so where are we sitting then?"

"Marc, I'd honestly like the boys to perform—I wasn't kidding. So I'd like to put you out on the terraces . . . I'm holding the ideal table by the stage. That way our kids can just pull them up for some tunes, if that isn't too brash of me to request? Hell I'm serious now—why should I let those neophytes in Summerlin get all the high numbers?"

"Now Frank—stop it. How many times do I have to tell you that you're not in a competition with Summerlin? After all, it all started right here with you and your crew—and no place else."

"Oh I don't know, about as many times as I ignore your assurances, I guess."

"Cute Frank. Look, I'll bring the boys by for the autographs, but if you really want them to sing, you'll have to ask them yourself . . . good luck."

"Fine—thanks for all of your help boss . . . but sure, I'm not bashful."

He now turned to assist some new guests arriving, before he again turned back towards me.

"Look boss, I've got paying customers, so go see about bringing the boys over here, alright?"

"No problem Frank, but don't pressure them to sing as were here on business too, are we clear on that?"

"Absolutely Marc, I'll only ask once . . . no means no."

"Thank you Frank, it's always a pleasure being here at number one with you of course."

"Sure boss, go ahead and tell that to whomever, because as for me, I'm not buying it now, or ever."

"I love you too, Frank."

"See ya Marc, but please enjoy your stay here at Verandas—sir."

Frank was still chuckling while he started assisting the guests behind me.

I retrieved the kids from the Parlor, as I brought them over to meet Frank along with securing the autographs. I made the introductions as Frank took right over, insisting they help him in greeting our guests.

Damn, that man would stop at no trick to get his numbers over the top. He was ruthless—and smart! He even had the boys handing out their own collateral piece for the Minis Desert Court.

The boys were having so much fun meeting and greeting our guests though that I had to pull them away so as not to ignore our guests indefinitely. They were not exactly happy about it either, until I reminded them of that fact . . . which did the trick.

While walking out to our table on the terrace to join our group, I noticed the immediate uptick in table-talk volume as the boys, Scoot and I, walked by. It didn't take a genius to surmise whom they were gawking at—honestly, it wasn't Scoot or I.

We sat down, with the boys insisting on bordering each of our guests. I thought this was sweet, if not ulterior in motive.

"Daddy, that bloke Frank asked us to sing with their singers, is that okay with you, we told him we would like to?"

"T-man, if you two are fine with it, so are we—just not all night long, don't forget that I have to fly the ladies back to Los Angeles after we leave here."

"Sure thing Dad—thanks."

"No problem T-1, did Frank mention what you two would be doing with the kids?"

"No, not exactly, he ran down their selections for this segment. We told him the ones we already knew, so he said to pay attention when the kids announced one of those. Frank says they'll pull us up at one of them."

"Great T-1, this will be quite a treat, hearing you two perform, twice in the same afternoon." I added.

Meanwhile, I could see that the wheels were apparently turning inside of Marna head too at that moment, by the thoughtful look on her face.

"Say guys, can I be as bold as to suggest that you try to slip in 'My Prayer' too? After all, you sing it a Capella, and I'm dying to hear how Verandas own singers will fall into the back up for you. Then you can see just how dramatic you can make it with 'live' back-up vocals harmonizing with you two, along with an idea I have for the finish.

"If I'm right on this boys, you're going to be shocked with how your audience responds to it . . . so do you trust me, because I have a killer idea?"

The boys nodded their agreement, so Marna went on to explain her idea which the boys were thrilled with . . . I think we all were.

"This is going to be so bloody brill Marna. Dad, I have to go talk to Frank about all of this so the singers know what we have in mind. I also think that Tay and I should go find some place to practice this a little—before we do it and screw it up, but that can wait until I speak to Frank. I'll be right back, promise."

"Okay Trev—just relax though son . . . meanwhile, what should I order for you?"

"You know what I like, so surprise me."

"Fine, but hurry back."

"Okay." Trevor then left to speak to Frank.

Our server Savannah came up moments later to greet us warmly.

"Mr. M.—gosh, it's always wonderful having you here at number one, it's been too long sir, how are you?"

"Fine Savannah, so how are your folks, is your Dad's back all healed up?"

"Yes Marc, he's feeling much better but thank you so much for inquiring. I'll be sure to tell both of them that you said hello, while asking about them."

"Thanks Savannah, please do."

"Now—wait a minute, this wouldn't be one half of that new singing sensation, would it?"

"Yes Savannah, this is my son Taylor, or more commonly known to his ever-growing list of fans, as Tay."

"Hello Miss, it's a pleasure to meet you."

"Same here Tay, it's my honor to meet you. But you know, I want to thank you and your brother as well, for seeing to it that we now carry my favorite ice cream."

"You're welcome Savannah; it is good, isn't it?"

"Yes, it's wonderful."

I now interrupted the love fest over the ice cream to introduce everyone else to our server.

I asked the ladies to order, as we went around the table. I ordered the baby backs for Trev, who was still gone, but I was not surprised when Taylor doubled that part of our order . . . twins are surprisingly predictable.

Savannah was busy ladling our soup for everyone, when Tre returned. I introduced them quickly as Savannah finished serving the soup.

We had a wonderful dinner—just ask dad, he not only enjoyed his, but also whatever the twins left behind . . . when they disappeared to practice in the kitchen somewhere. I swear nothing with meat was ever wasted around that man . . . or his protégés. Dad remained the 'poster' child for over-eaters anonymous. Surely one day, this was all going to catch up with him, but did he care? Not in the least.

Later, while we began to order our desserts, it appeared that the next entertainment segment was soon to begin, but that didn't break my old man's concentration on ordering his desserts—yes, that was the plural form of the word!

Mom was trying to hold it in, but you could see she was almost ready to lose it. Amazingly, she kept quiet as she stewed while staring at Dad the whole time in disgust. Dad was no dummy after all; he knew Mom would have to remain silent in front of the press. So he was milking this beautifully, for—all the desserts on his mind to order—which he purported—he planned to share with the twins . . . yeah, right.

I was still stewing on Dad's desserts when the twins returned from their practice . . . they're timing was impeccable, as two minutes later, the entertainment began.

Four songs into their set, the lead male vocalist, Ronnie, grabbed a microphone to speak to the audience.

"Ladies and Gentlemen, boys and girls; welcome to the very first Verandas in the entire world. Yes its true gang, our ghosts are so old here at this restaurant—that they're rumored to be alive—again!

"Tonight though, we have a very special surprise for all of you—young and old alike. You have no doubt seen them on the news recently, or in our papers concerning their crusade to raise millions of dollars for our own Verandas Foundation . . . but this evening, they've been most gracious to offer to join us up here on stage for a song or two. Please give a warm Verandas welcome, to the singing duo of Tay 'n' Tre . . . the Morgans."

Ronnie walked up to the boys as they rose to enthusiastic applause as the three walked up to the stage to join the rest of the singers.

I was very impressed to see how professional they were becoming. The boys waved around the terrace very animated while not forgetting to look straight into the cameras for our guests upstairs inside their private dining rooms too.

Joining the many wonderful voices of our singing wait staff, the boys did two songs with the group. Then afterwards, Ronnie brought over two cordless mics which he now handed to them. Naturally, we were all getting nervous already, wondering if Marna's great idea would produce the desired result, or not—a stunned audience. Fortunately, we wouldn't have long to find out.

Trevor now wasted no time; he spoke right up to the large audience in front of them and those he couldn't see upstairs.

"Hi everyone, thank you so much."

"Tay and I, would like to do a song that will be featured on our upcoming CD, to benefit the Verandas Foundation. As you may know, we plan on raising eight million dollars, so that Verandas can help to get a residential care facility built for CPF clients here in town.

"We are also very excited to tell you, that our fundraiser is now underway in over one hundred and thirty Verandas already across the country. At each one, we're selling Minis Ice Cream, plus your favorite Verandas desserts and coffee, with more to open each week . . . rumor has it that we've nearly raised a million pounds . . . I mean dollars, already! The audience seemed to enjoy his little monetary gaff.

"I'm happy to tell you that for the first time this evening, we will be able to perform this next song with live back up vocalists. You see, we sing this song a Capella, which we feel was the way it was really meant to be sung, but we'll let you decide that for yourselves. And tonight, we'll all get to enjoy it with the full back up vocals and harmonies—courtesy of our own wonderful Verandas Singers, aren't they fab everyone?"

"Ladies and gentleman, plus all you kids out there like us, here is, My Prayer . . . but please allow us, to dedicate this finale with love, to our Gramps, Mr. Malcolm Morgan—hi Gramps." This was greeted with strong applause . . . from the family's patriarch sitting at our table, naturally.

Both boys then waved to Dad as they then closed their eyes momentarily to begin their focus on their pitch. Thank God that they were getting comfortable enough with singing a Capella now, that they no longer seemed to need to keep their eyes closed for too long.

Our Verandas singers meanwhile, quickly jumped into their wonderful doo-wop chorus of sorts, but then abruptly stopped, as the spotlight now dropped over the boys, with the twins surrounded in otherwise darkness. It looked close to what Mom had envisioned, as it appeared to be a combination of a surreal and gothic ambiance.

Taylor now began to sing the opening lines, with Trevor and company harmonizing the back up vocals and doo-wop, beautifully all around him.

As I listened to the words with my own eyes closed, I could hear their letter-perfect enunciation and inflections.

. . . "When the twilight is gone . . ."

The song sounded so rich at this moment, I realized I was actually tearing up a little, along with being full of Goosebumps again . . . and we weren't even near to Marna's hopeful, dramatic finish.

But what a difference this live vocal accompaniment made in the way this powerful tune came across, especially when being sung a Capella with doo-wop to replace the absent instruments. Moments later, Marna's contrived drama began.

As the song was concluding with Taylor's crescendo beginning, each twin, with the precision of a Marine Corpsman presenting arms, brought his own palms together, stared upwards at the ceiling, then dropped to the knees as if in prayer . . . all done to perfection . . . simultaneously . . . just as Taylor belted out his crescendo singing the closing words of 'My Prayer'.

In a word, it had been—perfect. You know, some might think at first— how corny, or overstated . . . but Marna was certainly right. It made for a truly perfect finish to an already powerful and dramatic song . . . it stemmed from that perfect precise timing of all of the actions synced to the vocal . . . it was brilliant!

The audience was left sitting there—stunned into silence, just as she had predicted. For that split second or two, there was literally nothing from the audience at all as they stared at the twins in front of them, still on their knees and transfixed . . . mission accomplished.

Yet during that split second, one could visualize hearing a Termite in the walls of the restaurant—belching over chunks of the dry wall the little critter was eating . . . that's how silent they all were—for that one split moment in time!

Then, almost on cue, the stunned audience came out of their trance in mass, to give it all up . . . and I do mean—they really gave it—all up . . . they were going nuts now with thunderous applause . . . deadening applause, especially from the upstairs private dining rooms which naturally had a different, muffled character to it over the clapping on the terraces.

By the time the boys stood back up to do their twin bow, everyone, and I mean everyone, was standing, applauding, and screaming on their feet. Damn, my Mother had been worried about needing more drama added to their staging . . . Christ, was she ever getting a wake up call now with this audiences' reaction to that very concept, courtesy of Marna's idea.

I looked at Marna, who was in heaven all over again. Immediately, she tried to yell across to Scoot over the thundering ovation.

"Look—if you don't run with this one for your title track—you're nuts my friend!"

"Don't worry Marna; I'm way ahead of you." Scoot replied.

Marna winked at him as she continued to shake her head as she smiled, as the standing ovation continued for another near minute.

Taylor now addressed the audience.

"Thank you everyone, thank you. I guess I don't have to ask if you liked our final tune. But please, ladies and gentlemen, thank you—please sit down; I have something important I want to say to all of you here.

"On behalf of Tre and me, again thank you for your warm applause, we really appreciate that . . . along with you all being loyal Verandas guests . . . isn't that right Daddy?"

"You're darn tooting Tay." I yelled back to my head salesperson while most everyone was laughing at my candor.

"I would now like to ask for a favor though. Tre already told you about our crusade to raise this money, but I just want to tell you something else. Every dollar of profit that Dad makes on this fundraiser, goes to get that home built that much faster. So, if you enjoyed yourself tonight and our entertainment, won't you please come over in around ten minutes or so, when Tre and I will personally take over serving you your choice of flavors up at our Minis Dessert Court in the General Store. And if you want to say 'hi' or get an autograph with your dessert, that's fine too . . . thanks again everyone, and good night."

The room erupted again with strong applause as the boys walked back to our table.

"Gee guys, I think you need to say some thanks to Marna here, for her wonderful idea for the song's finish . . . that's definitely the way it should be done at all of your performances. And since our singers here, already seem to know it, what do you say we invite them to record the back up with you two?"

"Bloody brill, Uncle Scott." Taylor responded to his uncle as the twins now both thanked Marna profusely.

"Scott, that's an excellent idea, but why not use them for the entire album though? Why not make it a Verandas family affair if you will, it's all for our foundation after all?"

"Marilyn, the thought was running in my brain, just as it escaped your mouth, I swear. Marc how does that sound to you?"

"You know Scoot, that's not a half-bad idea coming from a man who can't avoid the cops, though I insist we pay our singers for their lost time . . . also, why not tie some form of employee contest to it as well . . . give every employee the opportunity to participate, not just our locals. And what the hell, I'll even add my throat if you want, but only for back up, fair enough?"

"Done Marc, now all we have to do—is see to the level of employee interest there is."

"That will be your first job tomorrow I guess, Mr. Vice President of Entertainment."

"Scott, I didn't realize you also worked for Verandas?"

"Yes, since last week Marna . . . but after surviving one of Marc's horrendous practical jokes earlier today, I actually earned my 'wings' as the VP of Entertainment for the company."

"My, that's wonderful—wow, congratulations, but are you trying to imply that Marc here likes to play pranks?"

"Yes Marna, most definitely he does." Scoot then went on to explain today's gag to the ladies.

Our entire group, including Marna and Nancy, were in hysterics, as Scoot ended that story before continuing.

"But I still remember the stunt he pulled at Toonland years ago, that nearly cost him his job there."

"Damn it Scoot, don't go there please—Jesus I've got my family here for Christ's sake."

"Bud, who started this whole thing—you, or me?"

"Okay, I'll concede that—I started it . . . fine . . . so did you hear me bitch with the gag you just reiterated for the entire restaurant? This is different though pal—just don't bring up the past—Christ."

"Why not Marc, you certainly know how to bring it up when it suits you?"

"Alright pal . . . fine, do whatever the heck you want—tell the stupid story then."

"Son, have we ever heard this story, or are we in for a wake-up call?"

"Let's just say the front desk just called your room Dad."

"Oh really, well this should be juicy then, right Marilyn?"

"Oh—I can't wait Mal."

Mom then gave Dad the evil look as she answered sarcastically seeing my obvious embarrassment growing.

"So go ahead Scott, dish us the dirt on old Marc here." Nancy chided in now.

"Okay, but first I have to give you some background, before I then lay out Marc's brilliant yet near fatal gag (to his career)."

"Honey, don't we have to pick up the car?"

"Oh—nice try Beth, but its pay back time now, remember, are you already forgetting your earlier day . . . dear?"

"Oh—yes . . . carry on Scotty."

Everyone was laughing with Beth on that one, I can assure you.

"Thank you sweetheart. At any rate, Marc and I both worked at Toonland, where we became fast friends while working there even though we worked in different departments. We actually met in the ToonCrooners, which was the employees' volunteer, performing chorale.

"By that time, Marc's reputation for gags, was already infamous within a select group of employees . . . I considered it an honor to be included within their company awhile after I met Marc. And we in the inner circle, kept his identity secret at all costs, believe me.

"His first gag I witnessed, before I even knew his secret identity. It was in a word—masterful. Had management ever gotten wise to him on that one, I can assure you Marc would have never survived working at Toonland long enough for us to have met—actually.

"You likely wouldn't know this, but T-land has a lot of employee activities and clubs arranged for off-time hours. One of their most popular is; the employee canoe races around Mystery Isle. Our little joker here gets an idea to intervene for one particular race . . . like I said before, it was masterful."

"Well, thank you for that bud . . . so get to it."

"You're welcome pal, because you deserve it for this one, just not the one I'm telling afterwards."

"Go on Scott, I can't stand the build up, get to it already." Dad added.

"The day of the big race finally came around—see Malcolm, I'm getting there. Out of sensitivity of the park's operating hours, the races were always held early in the morning, regardless of the weather . . . rain or shine in other words. They were always quite popular; with a sizable group of participants competing in each race with lots of team boosters from among other employees there too . . . dare I say to wager?

"On this particular race day morning, the weather absolutely stunk. It was so friggin' cold—that there were icicles hanging from the tree branches; with it threatening rain besides that . . . remember bud?"

"You're right on the money so far Scoot."

"Of course back then, I knew nothing about any of the plans until after Marc and I were friends, but as I recall from his explanation, it seems that boy-genius here, had slipped into the canoe storage area the night before, once the park closed. He had with him, two large bags full of goodies that he'd had stashed in his locker the whole day."

"What were the goodies, Uncle Scott?"

"I'll get to that Tay; just relax so I can tell the story, all right?"

"Sorry, okay go ahead."

"Thank you Tay, so where was I, oh yeah, I remember now? Marc's goodies consisted of a cordless drill, as well as, a handheld vacuum cleaner in addition to a rubber mallet that completed the first bag.

"One at a time, Marc removed the canoes from their storage racks. He drilled discreet holes in the bottom of each canoe right under their rearmost benches. Then he vacuumed up all the sawdust—like the good little perfectionist he was becoming in these gags . . . it was like watching an episode of Mission Impossible on the TV.

Marc knew with the obscure drilling locations he chose, along with the fact that the canoes were stored—right side up, that their crews were not likely to notice anything, as long as he didn't get sloppy, if you take my meaning.

"Marc then reached into his large second paper sack. From it he pulled out several matching and precise drain plugs which he immediately used to fill each of the holes in all the canoes with these plugs. Using his rubber mallet, he made sure; each plug was precisely installed to a marked line on each plug. Marc then slipped out of the storage yard to go home to await the morning's—upcoming dastardly deed.

"God Scott, this is an amazing story, but I'm somewhat confused, if he plugged the holes anyway, what was the big deal for crying out loud?"

"Marna, if you'd let me finish the story, you'd already know?"

"Sorry Scott."

"Don't sweat it. Anyway, the next morning, the teams were all boarding their canoes to proceed over to their starting line. Straight in a line, and right in front of where the Huck Finn moored, the pistol went off. All of the teams were off at a feverish pace as usual, despite the crappy weather and now foggy conditions.

"As they all rounded the bend for the home stretch, there they all were— neck and neck, which was also typical. Then it happened. Right there in all that fog and freezing cold water, the canoes—one by one—started sinking in the water—each with their crews all in a comical panic!"

Everyone at our table was busting up now, with the surrounding tables tuning in too while laughing at Scott's story.

"I don't get it Dad, what made the canoes sink, I thought they were plugged?"

Embeth was the first to voice what everyone assembled surely wanted to ask Scooter.

"They were sweetheart, it's really quite simple. Uncle Marc made his plugs out of salt sticks they make for horses to lick. These salt sticks are hard; almost like steel—until it gets wet, then it starts to dissolve slowly. Once it dissolves enough to lessen its hold of the hole in the canoe, it just drops out.

And being in the aft position, the canoes quickly sank in succession to the various lines marked on their plugs by Marc. This was augmented by the weight of the full crew of rowers as well!"

Our whole area of the terrace was hysterical laughing, while applauding too.

So what the hell I thought—why not be proud of it. I stood up as I bowed to my adoring audience to more applause.

"Oh my God Marc, that's brilliant. It must have been incredibly funny to watch?"

"Mom, priceless would have been a more apropos word, but yes, it was funny as all hell."

"He's not exaggerating Marilyn, the employee cheering sections were going nuts from the whole scene . . . some laughed themselves into tears. One guy I remember actually soiled himself, right there on the spot!"

My God—I could have done without that little tidbit—Larry!"

"Sorry Marilyn, but it really happened.

"So what's the other gag, because this one was certainly inspiring Scott?"

"I'm getting there Malcolm, God, cool your ponies will you, it's coming."

"Fine Scott, but get to it already, you know I'm not getting any younger."

Mom now jumped in:

"That's for sure Mal."

"Oh thank you Marilyn."

"Alright Mal, here we go. At T-land, we have this place for off-time employee recreation called the Toonland Recreation Quad or TRQ. It's a huge building in the back lot area. It has complete athletic facilities along with every other diversion you can think of . . . even a bowling alley. The point is—lots of employees at all levels, including management, used it regularly . . . think of it as an employee magnet.

"Well about a year or so after Marc's last really brilliant gag, he decided to have another go. He figured the coast was clear as they say, but besides that, the opportunity really presented itself this time, as you'll see.

"You see, the TRQ had a major pipe burst under their restrooms, so Marc seized on this mechanical issue—to plan an incredible gag. And he had accomplices this time too, yours truly included.

"Maintenance had to dig up the concrete floors, so they brought in those port-a-potty toilets early into the mess, for two or so weeks. Most employees didn't want to walk all the way to the locker rooms, so it was a considerate touch. These potties were placed under a covered patio separating a larger covered patio of tables and chairs that accommodated hundreds of employees right there.

"It seems Marc had been inspired by the LA Olympics the previous summer, so as they say—that served as his inspirational model. Marc was yearning for his own form of 'Olympic' competition, as it were.

"He decided that everyone would appreciate his Olympic spirit, if you take my meaning. So Marc hid wireless microphones inside the back of the men's port a potty's. With the skill of a sound technician, Marc spliced the microphones into the TRQ's public address system! Like the Olympics, Marc recognized that what he had in mind . . . needed to be judged.

"So Marc had moved a patio table directly parallel to the row of port-a-potty's, along with four chairs, to position behind the table. Then he, I, and his two other co-conspirators, took our seats in those chairs, behind the table.

"As each competitor went into their crapper, we four would make small talk like we weren't paying any attention whatsoever, nor there to judge anything, if you catch my drift.

"The moment the person was inside though, Marc hit the microphone for that potty so that the entire area began to get an earful. By the way, only sit down performances were judged in this event, rather than going tinkle—yes Marc insisted strictly on—number two's only . . . so if it was tinkle, he shut the mic off. Marc accurately surmised that tinkle, even when amplified, was just too mundane for anyone to get interested enough to judge . . . or score.

"So, each 'number two' performance was judged for clarity, speed of the performance's inception, originality of sound effects, creativity, and audible length. Any competitor who could impersonate a wind instrument—garnered double points automatically—after all, that level of talent was nearly—Godly!

"Then the competitor would ultimately finish, so he emerged, as the four judges would hold up their scorecards. This was for the benefit of the entire group of spectators to see and evaluate—and cheer hopefully."

At this point, almost anyone in earshot of Scoot was listening on pins and needles to his every word . . . some seemed spellbound. But he wasn't finished yet, so he continued onward.

"Now most of our competitors, were extremely good sports over this embarrassing little invasion of privacy. They would put two and two together, and then usually just ham it up afterwards for everyone's benefit.

"At any rate, some time later, a guy quickly walked into the competitors' area oblivious of anything going on. I might also point out, that by merely watching him walk; you knew he was on a time-sensitive mission of sorts.

"The guy entered his potty, as Marc quickly snapped on the mic . . . somehow he knew this one wasn't going to be . . . a tinkler. This was followed by the sounds of the guy unlatching his belt, pulling out a wax paper seat cover, cussing at the seat cover as he attempted to unfold it quickly, finally applying the seat cover, as he dropped his pants—with urgency.

"At the next possible moment, there was a loud explosion. In an honest effort to describe it dear reader, it literally seemed to lift the potty off its foundation; it was that profound of a biologic 'blast'.

"What came next was truly masterful. There was a cornucopia of 'horn' instruments breaking out of his sphincter, in near four-part harmony. I mean to tell you guys, it was a masterpiece of horn work. This competitor was his own entire wind section . . . he was off the charts! It was as if he had devoured a plate of beans the size of the Texas Panhandle. In a word, this dude was scoring 10's from all the judges . . . already!"

Scoot couldn't continue, until everyone around us calmed down somewhat. I myself was in tears of laughter, just remembering it again . . . but Scooter wasn't far behind me with his hysterics. Finally he regained his composure, right in keeping with the rest of us.

"So, this guy was still inside, going to town on the horn section, but destiny was about to present itself, friends.

"Outside the potty, our four judges, along with all the spectators assembled, were laughing wildly, naturally. Unfortunately, in our weakened and compromised state, one of the co-conspirators—a different sort of guy— named Vic, fell over onto the control panel for the microphones.

"Marc you see, was smart, he knew to keep the volume low enough that it wasn't obvious to the competitor occupying the 'recording' studio. From inside the potty, a competitor never had an idea of what was actually going on outside on that patio until afterwards.

"Regrettably, as our choir's most consistent 'klutz' . . . Vic Tremmers was not as cognizant as Marc . . . or as fast. While he only cranked it up for a split second or two before correcting it, that was long enough for the guy inside the crapper.

"Please pardon my words ladies and gents, but our competitor inside, naturally got 'wind' of what was at hand—as well as happening outside to his embarrassment!

"Suddenly and loudly, he yelled out an expletive that I won't bother sharing with any of you at this moment.

"In what had to be record time, he threw on his trousers, as he blew out of that potty faster than he went in—and the Dodgers can blow through an entire season. Mere moments later observing all of our signs and equipment, he was in our faces, with his being crimson red. In a word, he was pissed— pardon me ladies; he seemed somewhat—agitated."

"He proceeded to display his ID to all of us—the idiot was assistant head of park security! He instructed us to pick everything up. Off we walked behind him, carrying all of our crap, while receiving a well-earned standing ovation from the assembled spectators as we passed their very satisfied faces.

"By the time all the head honchos were done with us, it was a miracle we were still standing. To his credit—Vic tried to take the wrap for Marc.

"In their infinite wisdom, management decided that they would allow a total of three formal complaints to be filed against us within the following week. A fourth complaint, from any aggrieved party, would spell our terminations as a group. Meanwhile management planned to be proactive about it too.

"We were suspended for the week to allow the aggrieved to come forward anonymously. Before leaving on our suspensions, we were required to place our written formal apology into the employee newsletter as well.

"It was amazing, but a week later not a single person had come forward to complain, other than 'Horn Section' himself—but he was a given. To the contrary, we received over four hundred letters of support for our company spirit (I'll never figure that one out) and originality in concocting this gag.

"Not only were our jobs all still intact, we were heroes to our co-workers. And that, ladies and gentlemen, is my story of how Mr. Marcus Morgan and crew finally got theirs—well almost. Everyone was laughing yet again.

"Thank you, thank you." Scott said, as he stood and bowed to the large audience of listeners by this time.

By their numerous comments now, I deduced that this group all thought the gag was brilliantly played out.

"Well Marc, I take my hat off to you, that was some story—both of them actually."

"Thank you Dad, I'm glad you enjoyed them, but so you know, I recently hired Vic to look after our Belgians up in Logandale. And Scooter; good job, you were right on with your recollections."

"Marc, you are incurable, I'm convinced of it now."

"Thank you Beth—I think I'll choose to take that as a compliment even though—I certainly know better."

Everyone was laughing again, when the boys' commented that they had to go scoop the Minis, so they left to do that.

"Scoot, aren't you two ready to go get that beautiful new car of Beth's?"

"Sure we are, you don't mind us running out on you?"

"No, don't be ridiculous—get out of here already—I'll see you both at the track at seven in the morning."

I got a hug and kiss from Beth as well as from the girls on their way out.

The folks then made their own overtones about heading back to the Trail, so I ordered them a cab. Meanwhile, the ladies and I were deep in 'light' table talk while we awaited our twin Ice Cream scoopers. They had a sizable line to work through. It was during this separation from the boys, that Marna shared a few more of her professional observations regarding them.

To say the least, they were most flattering, and helpful, particularly about the business end of it and what pitfalls should be avoided at all costs.

When the boys were finished, I asked the ladies to indulge me in dropping them off at home first, so they could go to bed.

After we had accomplished the trip to the Trail, the boys said goodnight to the ladies but not without some serious hugs and kisses between the parties first.

I got the ladies out to McCarran and aboard Number One. We had an uneventful, but pleasant flight to Burbank Airport in the San Fernando Valley suburb.

When I made it back home, I got promptly into bed right at eleven, thirty-five . . . it had been a truly fulfilling, yet wonderful day.

CHAPTER FOUR

▼

THE BOYS ARE BACK IN TOWN

The bulk of our week turned out to be in a word, a whirlwind. The kids at the Meadows School had honored the spirit of the boys' letter. No one now was causing them any problems at school, so the twins were in heaven all week. I'm sure the administration was as well.

The boys were getting more invitations to parties etc, yet overall, they were being treated as regular guys again. It was as if the whole incident at Verandas hadn't started anything.

We still hadn't heard another word from Jared, which, while we thought that was disconcerting, we remained undaunted. And having been the party originating this strategy after all, we would have to wait for our opponent's next move anyway . . . or would we?

Nevertheless, it was not as if we were worried, we had at last count seven other bonafide offers from various labels on the table. They all wanted their letters of intent signed to lasso in the boys too—it's so good to be in the driver's seat.

After stringing along all of these firms on a weekly basis however for the better part of the month, we were forced to begin seriously entertaining all of their offers by placating the firms behind them. We simply couldn't put it off indefinitely . . . or they would lose interest possibly as well. Accordingly, we were beginning to lose patience in Jared to break our stalemate by caving in.

Christ; this dufuss was either shrewder than we ever imagined—or far more stupid than we even gave him sympathy for.

Mom decided that we would give up on Jared altogether, if there was no action by the time the boys' interview had been in the stores for a week . . . we thought this was smart . . . and fair to all parties.

Beth and her Bethettes had gone home on Friday, excited by having the offer accepted on their new home. The week before, they had accepted an offer on their California home, so finding a suitable replacement became more important.

Beth insisted on driving back to California, as she was so enthralled with her new car—too enthralled maybe. She got her own ticket just as she was heading across the border into California. Scoot of course, took the news in his usual calm manner. Upon hearing the news from the scene of the offense via cell phone, he was most philosophical.

"You were going—how frigging fast?" He barked into the phone to Beth, right in front of Robbie, who later relayed the story to—moi.

"Scott calm down, I wasn't going that fast, maybe twenty over."

"Twenty over—what was the limit Beth?"

"Oh, I don't know Scotty, maybe seventy, dear."

"So you're telling me, you were cited at ninety miles an hour with the girls in the car with you—and you're suggesting that 'I' calm down?"

"Well actually ninety two, but the officer's nice, so he's going to show it as eighty-five instead."

"Oh, good luck telling Marc honey, because he's never going to let you of all people, live this down Beth."

"Don't worry; I'll speak to Marc about it when we get back up there next weekend."

"Fine, but don't expect me to be able to keep it quiet between now and then?"

"Gee, thanks Scott, I knew it was too much for me to hope you could be compassionate about this?"

"Compassionate? I am being compassionate Cuddles, do you hear me yelling at you or making jokes now?"

"I guess not."

"See? I just know Marc's likely to hear about it from someone in the office. I think he should be told before that. Look, I'll break the ice for you, but you owe him a call—sooner than next week!"

"Okay honey, I guess you're right, I'll call him tonight,—I want to thank him again for our lovely visit anyway . . . not just for the Cobra, but the stay on the boat as well.

"Yes honey that's fine. Now listen Cuddles, don't expect me to go on out and get any tickets myself. Face it baby, you're going to be lonely in Traffic School. Those are the facts, cuz it ain't happening . . . but I will send over some donuts from Veranda's kitchen if that will help?"

"Very funny Scotty." But Beth was finally laughing some.

"Good, now drive careful baby—please, but give the girls my love too, will you?"

"Yes Scotty, I will—I love you honey."

"Right back at you sweetheart."

It's a good thing we have the above account of that phone call. You see, as I would later learn from Scoot himself, Robbie's version was; shall we say—slightly embellished.

Right at four-thirty, I was about to leave the office for the weekend. We were all going up to our log cabin on Mt. Charleston, as the boys had adamantly insisted. Now that they had been on the boat, they wanted to see our other home as well. Boy, did they ever hammer me about it; they wouldn't budge until I caved in and agreed to arrange the trip.

Nevertheless, two outside diversions occurred that forestalled my exit at that moment.

One of our secretaries brought in the newest edition of Teen Pop she had picked up earlier at the market apparently. There were my two matching bookends, plastered all over their cover, but did they ever look endearing. I had to admit, Nancy was one heck of a photographer. More importantly though; Robbie put through a call from England of all places.

"Mr. Morgan, my name is Miss Soames. I am the private, personal secretary for Duchess Constance Wadsworth Kenneyson; may I put my Lady on the telephone for you sir?"

I recognized the name of course. It was the mother of Trevor's closest mate; Toby, back in the UK so I was justifiably surprised by the call—as well as instantly wondering—should I be concerned too?

"Why yes, of course." I said, with a very short silence on the line that followed.

"Mr. Morgan, I'm Constance Kenneyson, how do you do sir?"

"I am well my Lady, how may I be of service to you?"

"Mr. Morgan, I am calling to tell you regrettably, that my son Tobias has been in quite a serious accident. He was struck by a fellow skier yesterday in Switzerland, and is currently in serious condition—he is unconscious at the moment sir."

"Oh my Lady, I am so very sorry to hear all of this, Toby, oh, forgive me; Tobias, is such a wonderful lad. Naturally, I will pray for his speedy recovery, and I speak for my entire family when I tell you that I'm confident—we will all pray."

"Thank you Mr. Morgan, by the by, Toby is perfectly acceptable. I know you are aware that the boys talk daily by email, so I thought I should warn you. You see, I wanted you to be aware of this situation when Trevor doesn't hear back from my son."

I could hear the tears through the telephone line as she detailed all of Toby's injuries . . . hell, they were substantial. I now knew what it meant to be a parent, as I felt beside myself with pain for everyone concerned, but especially for she and her husband, Toby—and of course- Trevor!

"I understand my Lady, is there any way I can be of help to you or Toby?"

"No, I'm afraid not sir. It is almost one a.m. here, and I have just opened Toby's computer and found Trevor's email. I just thought I owed you the courtesy of this call, especially knowing all of Toby's mates here have now already heard of his plight.

"You know Mr. Morgan, my son has been absolutely miserable since the twins moved to the States. He misses Trevor terribly—along with Taylor too. You know, it's so sad but Toby has been calling out to Trevor in his coma—yet even with his calls going unanswered, it gives us hope that the coma is not too deep, so we continue to pray that he will be waking up soon.

"His Lordship and I are as distraught as you can well imagine, it's such a shock seeing your baby laying there helpless surrounded by machines. We are both so unprepared for this. While we've been assured repeatedly that he'll make a complete recovery, until he actually wakes up, we simply haven't been able to sleep ourselves. We are in such a state of fright at the moment; I'm really at a loss."

"I certainly can understand my Lady, but don't you fret, God will watch over Toby, I am sure of it."

"Thank you Mr. Morgan, good day to you sir."

"And to you, dear Lady. We will all pray for a speedy recovery for Toby."

"Thank you sir, good bye."

She hung up, while I was reeling in utter disbelief. I was shocked, sad, and struck by an incredibly weird irony—I had planned to spend this very weekend—skiing at Lee Canyon on Mt. Charleston with my own sons along with our entire family."

I finally cleared my shock and thoughts long enough, to look once again at the magazine lying before me on my desk.

While the nature of the call I just completed, made it impossible for me to focus totally, I did feel compelled to read on. Naturally, I was continually torn between my thoughts of Toby as opposed to my attention to this magazine article.

I couldn't help feel proud, looking at my two budding rockers with the magazine's cover crazy caption:

"Tomorrow's Super stars—the T-men Twins—who are they?"

So I opened the magazine to begin to read Marna's feature story . . . I was immediately impressed with the numerous photos bordering the double page article.

Reading Marna's story, I couldn't help wonder, why I had not already offered her the position as the boys' publicist. She was certainly touting their talents, while praising their sweet dispositions like any talented publicist would. While she clearly spoke through her heart about the twins, all the same, there was a no-nonsense honesty in her writing style.

After completing the feature, I realized that the 'bar' had yet again been raised on the boys' potential for both exposure and success. I also could not help laughing, thinking about poor old Morison—what if it was part of his job to have to read this stuff?

I then turned my one hundred percent attention back to young Tobias Kenneyson, and what I should do about him. I was still thinking about that subject while driving home, as well as during some inquiring calls I had placed.

Most present in my thoughts was Lady Kenneyson's comment about Toby calling out to Trevor. Dang it, could Toby responding to Trevor's conversation and physical contact, be enough to wake the stubborn kid up? I wondered. By the time I had passed the gate at the Trail, I was committed to what I knew I felt compelled to do. My only concern was what to say to Trevor . . . and when?

Upon entering the garage, I had to slam on my brakes, as Trevor came running out of the interior door. He was running towards me, while crying in overload. I knew he was already wise to what was happening across the pond. So much for when, I thought!

He was near convulsive in his crying jag, as he apparently had been at it for a while. One look at the redness of his eyes alone, told me that. Climbing over the doorsill of the Bricklin's gull wing, I was nearly at eye level with him as I grabbed hold of him as I began hugging him while rubbing his back.

"Daddy, there's been an accident, Toby's hurt real bad, he could die Daddy".

He was overwrought and somewhat numb to reality, nearly running into the gull wing with his forehead. I knew the moment I'd heard the 'single' word 'Daddy' coming out of him—and not Taylor, that he was simply not himself.

"It's alright son, you just let it all out, go ahead now—let it all go. I know all about it honey, I just got off the phone with his mother. Sweetheart I have promising news—it's not that bad, he isn't going to die, so don't worry so much. He'll pull through just fine; it's just that he's in a coma right now which is always scary for everyone. He's also got a real bad bump on his head, lacerations on his face on top of a badly fractured leg too."

"What's a coma mean Daddy, can't he stay up?"

"No honey, he can't even wake up just yet, but he has been talking some, which is always an encouraging sign son, really. In fact, he even asked for you when he was talking in his coma." That news seemed to upset Trevor even more now.

"I gotta help him Daddy, he's my best mate, I never should have left him—please, please Daddy, we have to do something."

"I know you want to help sweetheart, I really do."

Trevor's words were coming through in spasmodic sentences as I continued my efforts to comfort him—clearly I was losing at that moment.

"Listen Trev, I know what we're going to do about this, but we can't do anything until tomorrow I'm sorry to say. In the meantime though, I don't want any arguments or complaints about it, all right?"

"Alright Daddy, but what are we going to do?"

"First son, we're going to go up to our cabin for tonight, because we won't have Cedric or Uncle Bill back in town until tomorrow afternoon. But then, you and I are going to go see Toby straight away, that's what you want—isn't it?"

Trevor could not even speak after hearing my comments, he just bawled as I had never seen him do so before. And yet, he squeezed me so tight, I thought he was mistaking my midsection for an overripe tomato. Finally he spoke faintly.

"Oh Daddy; thank you, thank you, thank you."

Moreover, this was not enough thanks in his opinion apparently, oh no. He then started kissing my shirt over my midsection in between more hugs and thank you's.

"It's all right son, I really do understand how you feel. It wouldn't be any different if this happened to your Uncles Bill, Scott, or Robbie—I would want to do the same thing myself . . . so were going to, end of story."

He was so spent from his crying and still distraught over Toby, he now did something surely by instinct, but he had never done it before with me. He held up his arms for me to carry him, along with a true pleading in his eyes . . . I was honestly flabbergasted by his silent request.

At first I was so shocked, I hesitated, but then I thought to myself, that it made perfect sense. And more so, I was going to get back a little of what I had lost to our strange circumstances, all those years before. It was a profound joy I had been deprived after all. Sadly I had never experienced this while he or his brother were babies, or toddlers obviously, as well as during their younger childhood years either.

So I tenderly picked him up, as he rested his head on my shoulder and started kissing my face. He really was outside his normal personality at that moment. I think this trauma had somehow actually regressed him some . . . I couldn't be sure, but I would be mindful of it.

Honestly for me though, it was a priceless moment that I don't think I'll ever quite forget. I could hear my thoughts—praying to freeze time. Here I was, carrying my eleven-year-old son in my arms, but for me, he might as well have been a baby again, because that closeness and that tenderness was a priceless feeling to me in that instant.

Yet my son himself must have thought about these same compelling feelings along with the physical closeness we were sharing at that moment too.

"Daddy, you know, I don't think I ever realized how much I've missed you for all those years—until just now . . . I love you Daddy."

It was so sweet, that right there, I was toast; I now had to fight back my own faucets . . . unsuccessfully.

"I love you too my precious one." I somehow got out—but don't ask me how.

We went inside the house now where we were immediately surrounded with the entire clan.

"Son, I suppose Trevor told you everything? He kicked us all out of the garage while he waited for you. We didn't know what was up until eventually detective Taylor here back-tracked things where he found the news on Trevor's computer."

"Yes Dad, but I had heard from Toby's Mum—so I was able to give Trev some much more encouraging news myself—he's going to be fine everyone."

"Thank God Markie, but we must all pray for him."

"Yes Mom, I agree."

"Listen I don't want to appear insensitive, but did you happen to see Teen Pop yet?" Mom decided to try to change the subject.

"Yes Mom, wasn't it wonderful?"

"Yes honey it was, yet I can imagine how it will change things come Monday morning. I guess it's a good thing we're stringing out all of the offers still, don't you think son?"

"Yes I do Mom, but I was also speculating that something in the article might finally light a fire under Morison too?"

"No doubt honey, of course it will. I'm sure he'll be ready to cave, or at least grovel some now—joining in with the others . . . but he's only got a week to do it . . . starting right now." As we both laughed.

"I guess we'll just have to wait and see. In the mean time, we're leaving in 'twenty' for the cabin, is everything set for the trip?"

"Yes son, I've got the Expedition loaded to the gills with all sorts of crap from food to board games . . . everyone's packed and ready, including you according to Reg."

"Good, but listen, tomorrow afternoon, Trev and I will take leave of all you guys at around one. This is an extremely important situation to Trevor, so we're going to go see Toby personally."

At that moment, my appendage rewarded me with yet another wet one on the cheek."

"We understand Marc . . . hell knowing you, we more or less assumed you'd do something like this."

"Good, then hopefully no one here is going to be upset with me about bailing on the trip, after tonight?"

"Well Daddy, I am. If Tre's going, I want to go; you know Toby's my friend too, right?"

"Taylor I understand, but are you sure you want to miss all of that white powder waiting for you on the mountain tomorrow?"

"White powder can wait Daddy, Tre I can't ever replace. Toby's my brother's old best mate, I owe it to both of them Daddy. I need to be there . . . and with Tre especially if it isn't real good when we get there . . . he'll need me Daddy."

Trevor looked at his brother as he started bawling some more at his incredibly sweet and heartfelt words . . . we were all touched really.

"Okay, who am I to argue with that, I guess that settles it then, I better get the passports, hadn't I?"

"You're darn right Daddy." Taylor added.

With everyone in tow, we loaded into the SUVs to head for parts north. We got on the 95 expressway to commence the thirty-eight mile drive to the wintry paradise within our—daily paradise.

We made wonderful time up the mountain, reaching my second home only thirty-six minutes after departing the Trail. We were at 9,500 feet, but you could feel it in the chill of the thirty-one wonderful degrees outside!

There was a nice amount of snow on the ground from the recent weather of this last week. Beyond the boys' bitching, the climate change was my motivation in picking this weekend to come up in the first place.

Mom and Dad were thrilled with the surroundings of pines along with the brisk cold air. The family of deer marching by didn't hurt either. Then of course, their first good look at my mountain retreat as it came into full view down the cleared path.

"My good Lord, would you look at this place Marilyn?"

"I'm looking Mal, I still have eyes you know, it's my ears I would like to stow for the moment. It's so nippy up here, but my, it is beautiful. Imagine all of this just a half hour away from downtown Las Vegas, go figure?"

"Yeah Mom, most tourists are amazed when they hear about this place, or Red Rock, or the Valley of Fire. They think we're all just about the slot machines, with a dam and lake near by."

"You know son, let them just keep thinking that way. I'm in no hurry to share any of this with anyone else . . . present company accepted of course."

"Thanks Dad, I'm so glad to be included." We were busting now.

Honestly daily life in LV for locals wasn't the shows, gaming, and 'chilled' towels at poolside, we all read about . . . far from it truthfully. People worked hard and long hours here . . . making their regular lives thrive here, just like everyone else around the country does in their own towns or cities.

The perks that one hears about from returning tourists, are just that; the perks—for the tourists. Yet as cities go to live in, LV was still at the top of the list in my opinion. After all, weren't we the fastest growing city in the country for over five years for some reason?

Our family and staff made our way slowly through the snow to the porch of the giant modified A-frame log home—all five thousand feet of it. It was built with giant vista windows at each end of the A frame, two surrounding decks encompassed both the A frame and the giant wings on each side of it, complete with a redwood hot tub, and a large basement garage replete with snowmobiles and toboggans.

As its centerpiece feature in the A Frame, there was a massive elliptical stone fireplace, visual indoors or out. It stood dramatically right in the center of the home's interior, from floor to ceiling through both floors. From the cabin's rear deck, you were rewarded with an unobstructed, three hundred and twenty-degree view of the entire mountain range. And in wintertime like now, it was in three words—breathtaking and surreal.

I was glad I had sent one of our maintenance people up to open the house earlier that afternoon. This way as we entered, the toasty great room invited you in with a fire still going in the fireplace. The scent of the mountains filled the room along with the music from the surround sound which was on, as were the many lights. Add to this, the aroma of fresh pinecones, hot apple cider simmering on the stove, with fresh cut flowers everywhere. It just made it all seem almost magical to everyone.

"Gee son, all we need are some chestnuts, Nat Cole at the piano and we've got Christmas all over again?"

"Well said Pop, hey—care to don your Santa suit for us? Grace, you're awful quiet, is there a problem?"

"Oh no love, absolutely not a thing I just had a thought that this home would be perfect for some young couple to honeymoon in, that's all. It's so breathtaking what with that view out the rear windows and this fireplace."

"Reg, are you taking notes old man?"

"Mom—zip it, for crying out loud!"

Both of them immediately flushed as they laughed at Mom's crack.

I immediately changed the subject—naturally.

"Gracie, if you and Sofia need help with the food, I know of three volunteers willing to assist you. That is, as long as it means they eat that much sooner?"

Dad immediately cleared his throat, which was not lost on Mom.

"Markie, would you be referring to your Father along with the boys?"

"Mom, whatever gave you that idea, I meant myself of course."

Nevertheless, my smirk said it all.

"I can help too, come on,—let's get it over with men."

Dad chuckled, but led the way to the call of his stomach, waiting in the trucks.

"Dad, your house is so cool, how come you don't come up here more often?"

"You know T-1, first of all, it's not my house—it's—our home. Secondly, that's a simple question to answer, as you are one of the two reasons—I haven't been here lately!"

"Are you saying we're the reason you don't come here a lot?" This was now Taylor asking.

"Hell yes T-man, that's exactly what I'm saying. I have a different life now boys, with new responsibilities and priorities. But more importantly, with a revised sense of what's most important to me. Sometimes, that puts wonderful things like this home from my old life, way down the list of what's 'important' . . . now.

"You have to realize boys that my many prior trips here, were always trying to fill the void of what was missing in my life . . . namely—your Mother's presence. Something I must say, you and Trev have beautifully filled to overflowing—God how I love you two."

"Oh, I do get it, but still, this is really so beautiful and peaceful here. Hey Dad; which life do you like better, your old one—or this new one with us?"

"You know T-1, it is beautiful here, but I would give it all up forever, if I had to make the choice: Me going back to living in this paradise—alone, versus being with you two in a hobble somewhere else—wins any day.

"But by the way, there's a beautiful and peaceful place waiting for all of us on the island of Maui in Hawaii. Trust me boys, it truly is paradise there, you're both going to love it."

"You mean we have a home in Hawaii too Dad?"

"In a manner of speaking Trev—yes . . . you see the company owns it. We use it as a corporate retreat, test kitchen, and as a Bed and Breakfast open to the public. But since I own the company, I'd say it's more or less ours too."

"Dang—cool, so when can we go there Dad?"

"When I say so Trev, so no harping about it, or I'll put it off that much longer."

"Are there Verandas in Hawaii too, Dad?"

"Yep T-man, there are . . . we even have one of them—built into a tree!"

"No way Dad."

"Yes son—way!"

"Bloody hell, I'm miffed we aren't there now—it's sort of like—this is so beautiful . . . but I want to go there." Trevor candidly remarked.

"Welcome to America boys, you ain't seen anything yet believe me."

"We'll take your word for it Dad, but when are we going to see all of this stuff?"

"Tre; are you already forgetting what I just said to you about harping?"

"No Dad—sorry, but I only said it cuz you brought up all the places to see in the States."

"Oh yeah, I guess I did do that, didn't I? Nevertheless guys, you know between your Grandparents and I, along with those four 'girls' of Wally's, I wouldn't worry too much. I have a pretty fair idea it won't be too long, is that soon enough to satisfy you?"

"Yeah, I guess that works Dad."

"Thank you Trev."

After we had everything settled in the kitchen, Gracie and Sofia were going full-steam in their dinner preparations. We all meanwhile, sat around as we noshed on snacks while talking back and forth about the wonderful article Marna had written. Even Reg who was occupied setting our table joined in with us . . . but now seemed to be waiting for something in anticipation—then it hit me.

"Reg, how about a round of Dad's poison for the old man and me?"

"Straight away Marc, but where is the 'spirits' cabinet, I haven't come across it yet?" I quickly grabbed the remote off of the tabletop next to me and handed it to Reg.

"Reg, I'm not surprised you haven't, but if you will push the remote in the upper right corner—you'll get your answer."

Reg did as I suggested as his mouth now dropped open . . . along with everyone else's too. You see, over in the corner of this huge open room stood a nine-foot high, hand-carved grizzly bear standing on its hind hocks. When Reg pushed the remote, the bear growled loudly as it then began separating it's upper paws, while opening up it's stomach to expose a beautifully detailed small bar inside.

"Your bar's in the bear, son?"

"Why yes Dad—of course, this is the mountains . . . you can't have just any old bar, after all. Here you have to be a little creative with how everything looks—it all has to have a 'mountain' feel about it."

"Oh I see, well I can only imagine who your crapper must take after then."

We were all busting up with Dad's comment, but it was most particularly— not lost on Mom.

"Mal, I'm surprised at you, don't you remember that gag gift Marc gave you for your fiftieth birthday? Come on Malcolm—think back. Remember that sculpture Marc had commissioned of you—as Rodin's 'the thinker'?

"Sure, how could I ever forget that gag—why do you ask?"

"Well Malcolm—have you seen it lately?"

That was all it took, to have a house full of Morgans, along with their extended staff family, rolling on the carpet. Mom was especially laughing at her crack, God, how she loved to 'rub' him the wrong way at times.

"Grammy; is Gramps really the loo, cuz I haven't been yet?"

"My dear Taylor, if he isn't—it's fitting that he would be!"

"Thank you Marilyn—you're so full of, shi . . . love."

"Yes Mal, it's full alright, but I'm not sure its love?"

We were all still busting, while Dad painfully realized he wasn't saying another word for a spell, if you catch my drift.

"Seriously Mom, I thought Marna's story was nicely outlined and presented?"

I was sincerely trying to help Dad out at this juncture by steering back onto the subject of the article.

"I agree Markie, but what did you two think about it?"

Mom was addressing her question directly to the 'subject matter' of the article.

"I knew it would be good, cuz I think Marna fancies us." Trevor said.

"Definitely bro, but you fancied her right back . . . bloody hell, she was so brill too."

"Tay, I liked how she got to know all about us and what we liked, and didn't. It was also cool how she talked about our friends from what we waffled on to her. That reminds me, we forgot to call Lar-man to tell him he's in there too."

"Yeah, well, we'll never hear the end of that Trev, believe me. When Larry reads all the stuff we said about him bro, he'll go bonkers—just you watch."

"So you guys are satisfied then?"

"Yeah Dad, it was real cool, don't you think so?"

"Yes Trev, I thought it was good for many reasons, while on many different levels. Not that I'm trying to confuse you two, but . . ."

. . . "But—where's Larry when we need him Tre, cuz there goes Dad again?"

Taylor immediately interrupted my commentary before I could finish my remarks.

The room was laughing yet again, this time at my expense however.

"Okay Taylor, can it—yes I liked it a lot, there; are you satisfied?"

"Yeah Daddy, but keep it up."

"Thank you—'Lar'."

At that moment, the phone rang, so I jumped in and answered it wondering who was calling. I suspected it would either be Robbie or Scooter. As it turned out, it was neither, which is why I never should assume—and you know that saying already . . . I'm sure.

"Marc, hi, it's Beth Davis."

"Beth; how are you, did you make it home without any further problems?"

"So you heard?"

"Yep, but not from Scoot though—apparently he felt no need to gloat. I heard it from Robbie naturally."

"Robbie, my word, I guess Scotty's right—talk certainly comes cheap around that office of yours . . . doesn't it?"

"Yep, especially at other people's expense I'm afraid."

"So, are you totally disappointed in me?"

"Honesty Beth, yes I am a little—I would never allow myself to get 'clocked' at anything below three figures! You had damn well try harder next time; after all you did have the fastest straightaway time at the track."

"Marc, you are a dear for being so understanding."

"Honestly Beth, it's naïve to think someone driving a four-banger for three years wouldn't want to celebrate a little. When you get into a Pony car with four hundred ponies, you're going to take them out for a little run once in a while."

"Yes, and more like a stampede in my little Honey Bee, but thanks, I really appreciate you not killing me."

"In your what? My God, now I've heard everything, but let's save the slaughtering for Scoot because I hear he's jealous. Word has it; you've had yours up to ninety two off the track, while he's not been over sixty on the street yet."

Beth was chuckling, as was I, but we continued our conversation between laughs.

"Listen, did you hear we got the loan already for the new house?"

"Yes and congrats by the way . . . it's all official I guess; we'll be neighbors and everything . . . hell, we already met your neighbors, the Jones'. I know the boys can't wait to have the girls only around the corner from them, but you had better be careful."

"Of what Marc?"

"Beth, trust me. It's likely that some real ponies might just waltz their way into my nieces' lives—and real soon!"

"Oh Marc—you wouldn't?"

"Beth honey; I would, I could—and I will—as soon as those stables are built, so consider yourself forewarned. In fact, why not start them on dressage as soon as you guys make the move, if you want . . . I'll arrange it with Kathy at the stables."

"Marc, please don't, that's too much,—Scott and I simply can not accept something that extravagant from you as a gift for the girls."

"Yes you can Beth. As I see it, you and your old man have no choice—so, I love that. Let's review, shall we? First, Scoot gets a Jag, followed by you landing the Cobra . . . that's a hundred grand in sheet metal all in the same week Beth! In all of this—where do my nieces fit in . . . I ask you? Hell, I want to see those two beauties sitting high and proud in their English saddles and togs, looking even prettier doing their dressage, which will please all of us I'm sure."

"All right Marc, you do make a fair point, so we'll have to discuss this at greater length later, as the two Equestrians just emerged from their bath."

"Fine, but don't say that good old 'Uncle Marc' didn't warn you ahead of time."

"Marcus Morgan, you are too dear for words."

"Oh no I'm not—throw some at me."

"Now you're just being silly Marc."

"Yep—and loving it!"

"Listen, I'm being paged; as I'm sure you can hear, to finish Nancy Drew so I'm going to run".

"Cool, go run, but good luck getting the words out while you try to breathe at the same time?"

"Good night Marc."

"Night Beth, and kiss those nieces of mine for me."

"Sure and thanks again, you know for the not clobbering me thing.

"Don't mention it, night—Cuddles."

"Cuddles?" Marc Morgan, you come clean, right this minute."

"Never!"

"Good night."

"See ya, Beth."

She hung up in mock anger. Although how much was mock, and how much was not, could likely fill a chapter, so we aren't going there.

We were called to dinner during my conversation with Beth, so I quickly got to the table—naturally I had too. After all in my absence, Dad could merge it all onto his plate . . . honestly, I made it there barely in time.

We had a wonderful dinner of arroz con pollo; served somewhat British style in a milder suiza sauce, it was delicious either way. After dinner, we all relaxed.

Taylor was casually playing on the baby grand, while Trevor sat on the sofa with his laptop, complaining about the slow dial up. From his many emails, he became more worried over Toby again.

Mom, Dad, Reg and I, decided to play bridge, which was also not without its share of complaining. Before we all knew it though, everyone was ready for the sack.

Everyone had slept well according to the reports the following morning as we played in the snow. We stayed outdoors in various pursuits until the boys and I had to prepare to leave.

I think Gracie was still off riding somewhere on her snowmobile, she was having such a ball with the damn thing.

Right before one, the boys and I began our way down the mountain to McCarran.

We arrived at the airport just as Bill was completing his final external inspection on Cedric as we walked over to him.

"Hi Uncle Bill." My close friend heard from his matching nephews.

"Hey there buds, how are my two singing sensation Nephews this fine Saturday?"

"Alright Uncle Bill, but did you hear about my friend's accident, that's why we're going back home?"

"Yes I did Trevor . . . I'm so sorry, but don't you worry, we'll get you there as fast as possible."

"Okay Uncle Bill, and thanks—say where's Suzie, I don't see her . . . isn't she coming along to bug Dad?"

"No, she's still off on personal leave, but then I thought you guys would be the first to know that. I'm told that she plans on moving right in with Grace the moment she gets back."

"So is her father any better?"

"Yes, he had the hip replacement surgery last week. I understand Suzie's just staying on long enough for him to be able to get around. I'm sure he's counting the days."

The boys totally missed the real meaning behind Bill's crack.

"Oh, well that sure is nice of her to stay with him like that for all that time?"

"Yes it is Taylor, but Suzie's all right, deep down—it's just her surface that bites."

I rejoined our threesome once I had called in our flight plan and reviewed it with Wally. I was still in shock over Wally's tizzy fit when I insisted my Navigator be kept parked inside the hanger. You would have thought I asked him for his first-born, for God's sake.

Our in-flight food service showed up, but our 'rent-a-stew' was not there yet . . . I was beginning to wonder if he or she would ever show. Fortunately—I did not have to wonder that much longer. I finally saw him coming over to the hanger from the parking area.

"Mr. Morgan, I'm Joe from the registry, sorry I'm a little late. You know kids sir, mine weren't very cooperative letting me leave the house this afternoon, as I was a last-minute replacement at the registry, so the kids were disappointed that I had to cancel plans with them to be with you."

"That's all right Joe, this is our first officer, Bill Sklar, he'll be flying right seat, while speaking of kids; here are my two, say hello to . . ."

. . . "Tay and Tre Morgan, oh my God, I had no idea I would be serving celebrities."

The boys were laughing, but also were a little taken aback by Joe's apparent adulation.

"Hi Joe, I'm Taylor—he's Trevor."

"Well it's a pleasure to be flying with you two. My kids are going to be so jealous; I should call them right now while I prepare the cabin. I can rub it in how they made me late getting to you, that ought to teach them a real good lesson on arguing with me, don't you think?"

"Sure Joe whatever you say, but please don't punish them on our account. You know, we already make enough trouble for the two of us with Dad." Trevor offered in response.

"So let's get aboard, shall we."

Bill and I opened our flight plan twelve minutes late; therefore we were already getting into a big hurry to get airborne when Joe announced that the cabin was ready for departure.

Bill decided we were going to put the 604 through her paces to pick up time. We would maximize the degree of our accent as my boys weren't ever squeamish over that anyway, but then, we would hold the maximum long-range speed of Mach .078, at give or take 578 nautical miles per hour on average. With the cooperation of the tower, we had requested our cruising altitudes to be a minimum of 41,000 feet, which is sparse territory anyway.

After we finally got underway, I gave Bill the airplane, while I went back into the cabin to find the boys deep in conversation with Joe—they were hanging on to his every word . . . while summarily ignoring everything else, so eventually, I returned to the cockpit.

"Everyone okay?"

"Yep, the guys have made a new friend back there."

"Oh, say that Joe seems like a competent attendant, don't you think?"

"Yeah, but he was thorough as hell, checking everything out equipment wise too."

"Good, cuz you can never have too many barf bags." Bill quipped.

"Ain't that the truth Bill, you can't, can you?"

"So what's up with my nephews, I'm still in shock at what came out of those two you know?"

"Yeah, I find it hard to believe myself sometimes, where do you suppose they get all that talent from?"

"That's an easy one pal, why Miranda of course, Marc."

"Yep, that's it all right—asshole!"

"Okay, so there's a little of you in there too, but when did you ever sing that well?"

"That well—Bill? Oh you're pushing for it now Sklar, I'm telling you that."

"Alright, so you have a fair voice Marc, I'll admit it."

"Yep, it's fair alright, as in—pretty fair incredible." I replied to my friend and co-pilot.

"My, you seem unusually full of yourself today old man, what gives?" He asked.

"Oh, I don't know Billy; it's just one of those days when you do a lot of nothin'—but thinking and lamenting, I guess."

"Jesus Marc, what do you—of all people, have to lament over? Seriously, you have the perfect life, a pair of exceptional sons, a breathtaking home, forty some-odd exquisite cars, four awesome jets—and of course—the perfect best friend."

"Wow! I guess if you put it that way, then why am I lamenting right now?"

"Hum; let's see, because maybe you're certifiably nuts?"

"Oh that was choice Bill, care for another go?"

"Damn it Marc, then what's bothering you that you're having all this obvious regret?"

"Choices Bill—just my life's choices."

"Oh . . . care to continue, then?"

"Bill, you see it's like this, here is the great life I supposedly have—right? Well, how do I really know that it couldn't have turned out even better? Let's just suppose I hadn't left Miranda back in England in the first place—what if I had stuck it out instead?"

"Oh now I get it, you're in one of your wonderful self-pity moods, aren't you?"

"No Bill; not at all, it's a philosophical question is all, honestly. You know whenever you watch a movie about time travel; they will always make the point about a parallel future, once you change something from the past? How if you change one iota from back then, you start a whole new parallel future from that point forward?"

"Yeah, so what?"

"Hell, I don't know, I just wonder what that life would have been like now. Or how my life might have been different . . . as I said—had I only stayed in England with Miranda by my side?"

"Okay buddy, where's this all coming from?"

"Bill I'll tell you, yesterday when I arrived home from the office, Trevor nearly stampeded me, he was so upset over Toby. The long of the short of it is, after I calmed him down by suggesting this trip, he was overwhelmed; I think he actually regressed a little. We were about to make our way into the house, when he stopped me—yet he was silent. Bill, I swear, he just held his arms up like a baby so I would pick him up to carry him inside.

"At first I was a bit shocked, after all he's eleven for Christ's sake, but I did it anyway. There I was, standing there, more or less cradling my son. I was hugging him in my arms, but Bill; it felt so frigging wonderful, honestly—I'd never had that wonderful feeling before, holding my own child like that. I was simply loving and caressing him, despite his age and size. He was at once, just my own little boy held preciously to my heart. As far as I'm concerned, that feeling was truly priceless Bill; I just can't explain it any more succinctly than that.

"At that moment Bill, I realized what I had potentially lost in taking that fateful trip home to the States—yet so had he."

"He said as much?"

"He sure did, right after I had my own thoughts about it enter my mind. So you see, philosophically, I have to wonder which one of my two choices truly would have produced the richer and more fulfilling life, Bill."

"Damn Marc, you do make a good point from that perspective, but how the hell should I know, this is too heavy for me. But I sure like listening to you talk about all of those wonderful sentiments, makes me realize you're indeed blessed."

"Stop going corny on me Bill, I'm serious here . . . that's what's really bugging me at this moment."

"Okay Aristotle, I'll tell you, my advice to you is simple. Accept your present reality from the choices you could have made, while you continue to make the most of it."

"Bill, I just spilled my friggin deepest and most personal regret with you, yet that's all I get—accept my present reality?"

"Absolutely Marc, that's it, like it or not, this is your life's path—you're on it right now. Make the most of it—like you've been doing darn friggin well for twelve years. Don't think about the 'what if's', leave the damn philosophy lesson to those left-wingers in Berkeley. You're far too grounded of a person to go off the deep end now Marc—you know I'm right, pal.

"And one more thing my friend, but remember it well; you really got the best of those choices already. Sure, you left Miranda behind, but you would not have had her in a pleasant situation—had you stayed. You know that, while she knew it too . . . that's why she misled you to do what was necessary to spare you the truth. She rightly kept you focused on Verandas instead . . . where you could make a personal difference . . . see?

"Marc, she would still be gone, down either road you traveled . . . her farce that she so brilliantly perpetrated on you merely kept you where you belonged . . . while thereby making you the success she knew you could be. Lastly Marc, neither of your choices came with providence if you stop to think about it, so all things considered . . . this was your best choice, and the one you chose.

"And you did come out of those two choices with wonderful sons, who are incredibly bright, sweet, loving boys. Forget their talent, erase their great save for the foundation, they are still your true Godsends. And they friggin worship the toilet paper you wipe your backside with—now how damn blessed—can one man be, my friend?

"So like I said before Marc, you really got the better of the two choices, case closed. Alright counselor, I rest my friggin case so argue your way out of this one—Perry Frigging Mason."

"Jesus; you know what Bill—I do believe you're right."

"Just a second, I need to get out my camera so I can capture this moment for all mankind. Marc Morgan telling Bill Sklar he's right? My God; take the controls—I've got the shakes big time—Christ almighty."

I was laughing at my friend, but I was still in agreement with his logic, so I was relieved the remainder of our entire flight.

When we arrived at Gatwick, we quickly made it through customs right at 9:45 Sunday morning. It was weird, I could swear that the customs officer recognized the twins, this was weird, but the mystery went no further as we didn't hang around long enough to find out.

What we did do was to fetch a cab over to our Corporate Suite at the Mayfair, as Bill and I, while exhausted—were busy calculating. After reviewing our calculations, we were impressed as hell with our new baby's performance numbers for the flight over.

While Joe had his own room, Bill agreed to bunk with us, as he himself suggested it.

After freshening up, the boys and I made our way to the hospital to visit Toby. Meanwhile Joe and Bill caught some much-needed sleep. I also called Uncle Teddy to tell him we were unexpectedly in London so we would stop over after some sleep.

We got to the hospital right at 11:50. Trevor was both anxious as well as scared as hell, all in the same 'frame' of mind. He would drag my arm awhile, hurrying me along, before stopping to slow down. Taylor, on the other hand, was just excited to be back in England—it clearly showed in his attitude and comments.

We entered the children's hospital, which was huge . . . this necessitated that we ask for directions only seconds later for Toby's room. We eventually reached the nurse's station for Toby's room on the fourth floor. We were politely stopped by a nurse at the entrance to the ward.

"Might I be of service sir?"

"Thank you, yes ma'am, we are looking for Toby Kenneyson's room please?"

"We do have a Tobias Kenneyson sir, but are you related? Only his immediate family is permitted to visit, at least until he regains consciousness?"

"No ma'am, we are not related; my sons are mates of his. We have just flown here from the United States however to see him, so I certainly hope some consideration can be made?"

"Oh I do understand sir—so yes, most certainly, we will do our best to accommodate you and your sons. If you'll wait a moment, I first must clear this though with our head administrator."

"Thank you ma'am that is most kind of you." The nurse then left us.

"Dad, they have to let us see him, don't they?"

"Technically no Trev—they do not, but relax. I've never seen a hospital that wasn't compassionate or accommodating in this sort of situation, I'm sure it will all work out. Son believe me, I'm confident Toby's only a few moments away from you visiting him."

At that moment, our helpful nurse returned. Her look though, already told me everything I needed to know—I was not going to be happy. She herself looked somewhat upset and confused.

"Sir, regrettably, my administrator can not clear you to visit just yet, he wants to first speak to his Lordship and Lady personally, as they are not here at the hospital at the moment. Please understand sir, but apparently due to the importance of the boy's father being in the House of Lords, the rules are set in stone, it is immediate family only—sorry, I honestly didn't expect this resistance from our administrator."

"I understand, but thank you for all of your personal kindness dear lady. Would it be possible for you to ask the administrator if I might have a word with him personally, then? You know, perhaps we can be of some help ourselves."

I took this opportunity to explain that with Toby in a coma, we were here because he had been calling out to Trevor.

"I see. Certainly sir, let me call him for you."

I now listened as our very helpful nurse called her administrator on the telephone. Anyone within earshot of that phone could easily make out the terseness and lack of civility in the man's voice, even through the telephone's limited volume. In essence, he was unmoved, unsympathetic, and certainly not concerned with our wishes—only following his rules along with strict adherence to following his day's schedule.

In curt and uncompromising terms, he told the nurse how much of a waste of time this was, since he had already been interrupted enough by such an unimportant event, in his—otherwise, much too important schedule—or however they stinking say it. His workday was far too full—especially for some 'pushy, self-serving American'—then he abruptly hung up.

After the nurse heard the telephone bluntly hang up, she turned to me shocked, and I think further embarrassed. Again she had a sad expression on her face.

"I'm sorry sir, on behalf of the hospital, I . . ."

. . . "You have nothing to be apologizing to me for ma'am. You have been most kind and courteous . . . none of this reflects upon you at all. But I feel compelled to ask you, if that person on the telephone, is the hospital's highest authority currently available to me?"

"I'm afraid—he is love, although I often wonder how some people ever get as highly placed as they do?"

"Touché ma'am, I see your point as I certainly agree."

Meanwhile though, I now had another problem. My son, who either from jet lag, sleep depravation over worry, or otherwise, was becoming a certifiable basket case right there in front of all of us.

"But Daddy, you promised, it would only be a few minutes—now we'll never get him to wake up."

Trevor now began bawling while Taylor attempted to console him. All in all, things couldn't possibly get much worse—nor could they.

"Now love don't you fret, we'll figure something out. The nurse said to Trevor.

"You know sir; I must ask you something I find odd?"

"Certainly ma'am, what is it?"

"Why do your sons look so familiar to me, have we all met before?"

"I am so sorry Madam, forgive my rudeness, I am Marc Morgan and these are my sons Trevor and Taylor. Boys; do you know this kind lady who's been so helpful to us?"

"No, I don't believe so Daddy, but maybe she saw us on the telly about the crusade?"

"My word that's it! You're the twins that sing that have gone to America to help your Dad with his charity work. And CCC did that nasty story on your late Mum that they later had to apologize for? Yes I remember it all now; wasn't Lord Richards from Guildford—your Grandfather? My heavens, they are the grandsons of a very fine man indeed. May God watch over his blessed soul too?"

"Yes ma'am, you are so right of course, thank you for that wonderful tribute to my late father-in-law. He was indeed a very fine gentleman, who we all miss deeply. And these are those boys, I had no idea their efforts had reached Britain?"

"Actually sir, I only heard about your sons because of that nasty CCC woman's bloody story . . . but wait a minute—that means you're the poor sod that never knew about his . . ."

. . . "Sons' births. Yes ma'am, that's me."

"Oh love, please forgive me, I never should have said . . ."

. . . "Nonsense, don't give it a second thought, but just so you know, my wife had very good reasons for what she did." I said defiantly and proudly to this lovely stranger who was quickly becoming my closest friend with her kindness and graciousness.

"Yes I know."

"You do?"

"Yes sir, certainly I do."

"Forgive me Madam, but how exactly do you know that?"

"From the other investigative report I saw a week or so later on TV."

"Really, I wasn't aware there was anything further reported about it?"

"Yes sir, there was, it was reported on Sky News."

"Really."

"Yes Mr. Morgan I remember it well. More importantly though, it clearly vindicated your wife's actions sir."

"I'm thrilled to hear that ma'am, but I must tell you, I'm a bit shocked too. Back in the States, we all had to wait for Fox News' report to clarify things."

"Yes, I saw that too, but that came afterwards sir. The Sky News report was much different. Sky focused their investigation on how those CCC reporters' twisted words took so many issues out of context. Sky's report, grew out of complaints from some of the people with clout, that CCC had interviewed. When these noble people interviewed saw how the intent of their words were so misconstrued, they were furious. They found a sympathetic ear at Sky News apparently—at least that's the story as I understand it.

"I would have to say that Sky's report was more on how some news agencies at times misreport the news intentionally, by manipulating what is said in interviews, or by asking double-sided questions. Sky then cited your wife's story as a most recent example of this. In order to prove the validity of their argument, the Sky reporter investigated what truly was said in these interviews, along with how it was all meant to be taken. Sky re-interviewed all the same people essentially. This thoroughly debunked the CCC story in the process."

"Amazing, I had no idea. By the way, I haven't caught your name ma'am?"

"I'm sorry Mr. Morgan, I am nurse Frances."

"It's a pleasure meeting you Frances, but thank you again for enlightening me on all of these facts."

"It's my pleasure, really sir."

While Taylor was listening to all of this, his brother was still in the middle of his meltdown, so I tried my best now to console him myself.

"You know Trev; I can't force that administrator to cooperate with us, so we will just have to take this situation to the next logical step."

"How?"

"We have to try to reach the Kenneysons ourselves."

"Oh, well I still remember their telephone number, does that help?"

"Sure it does son, let me have it please."

As Trevor gave me the number, I put it into my cell phone's directory as I then dialed the number.

After three rings, I heard what could only be a British Butler's voice answer the phone.

"Good afternoon, thank you for calling Chatsworth Manor, this is Winthrop speaking, how may I assist you?"

"Good afternoon Winthrop, my name is Marcus Morgan. I was hoping that I might be able to speak to Lady Kenneyson, or her secretary Ms. Soames, I believe?"

"I am so sorry sir, but Lady Kenneyson is likely still at Church with his Lordship and much of our staff sir including Ms. Soames. Perhaps you haven't heard sir, but their son Tobias, has been seriously injured in an accident."

"Yes, I have heard Winthrop; I am at the hospital right now, along with my sons Trevor and Taylor—we've just arrived from Las Vegas to visit him. Regrettably, we've reached an impasse of sorts here at the hospital."

"Oh my, the twins are there with you sir?"

"Yes Winthrop, they would both very much like to see their mate, so they are quite unhappy at the moment."

"I understand sir; might I have your telephone number? Perhaps I can be of some assistance."

"Thank you Winthrop, yes it's . . ."

. . . "Very well sir, please allow me a few minutes to see what I can arrange."

"Thank you Winthrop, good bye. We hung up as I returned my attention to the boys.

"Guys, let's give Winthrop a few minutes to see what he can do."

"Okay Dad, but I hope he . . ."

Trevor had stopped in mid sentence, but now I think I understood why. At that moment, a distinguished, yet obviously exhausted couple had just come around the corner. Trevor and then Taylor were off in a flash running in their direction. When the boys were directly in front of his Lordship and Duchess, they froze momentarily. Lady Kenneyson then embraced both of them tightly, as the boys were priming their faucets.

"I simply cannot believe you boys are here, how wonderful it is to see you both, even under these horrific circumstances."

"Thank you my Lady, but can we see Toby please, I have to know he's going to be all right?"

"Certainly Trevor, my both of you look well, and filling out too, look how tall you're both becoming—don't you agree dear?"

"Yes Constance, they're looking quite, how have the two of you been?"

"Fine your Lordship, at least until we heard about Toby."

"Is that your father over there?"

"Yes your Lordship, but you'll have to forgive him for looking so haggard. You see your Lordship, he flew us all night to get here this soon, as we weren't able to leave right away."

"He personally flew you here himself?"

"Yes your Lordship, it was his idea, he knows how much Toby means to me."

"Well, I most certainly want to meet your father Trevor. Any man that would show that much compassion for his son's feelings is someone I most deeply respect and admire. Not to mention, bringing such an honor to Toby in the process. Will you be so kind as to make the introductions boys?"

"We would be honored your Lord and Lady." Taylor finally piped up.

The boys and the Kenneysons made their way over to me as I concluded speaking to Frances on this latest development solving our crisis. Once they were in front of me, I turned and smiled at the strangers I was about to meet.

"Daddy, may I have the honor of presenting his Lordship and Lady Kenneyson of Sussex. Your Lordship and Lady, may we present our father, Mr. Marcus Morgan of Las Vegas, Nevada."

I kissed the Lady's hand before then shaking his Lordship's hand as Lady Kenneyson began speaking.

"Mr. Morgan, I am absolutely so deeply touched by your gesture of bringing the boys over like this."

The Lady's eyes were full of tears now.

"Your Lady, after our conversation, I just thought that perhaps Trevor might help Toby break out of his coma, by being here and speaking to him. Who knows what might happen . . . besides, it certainly can't hurt?"

This elicited an immediate response from his Lordship who still seemed somewhat in shock over my actions.

. . . "And so, you just stopped everything happening in your life, to pick up and fly half way around the globe to be here . . . for our mutual sons. My word man—thank you that is all I can say without losing my emotions. You are truly most kind and exceptional of character no less."

"Think nothing of it your Lordship; but your words touch me deeply. As for the boys, they know well the value of their friendships here in England. And sadly, they have known losses on a personal level in this last year themselves. I want them to realize that we all share their pain as well, so I am humbled therefore, to bring them here today to be with Toby."

"Remarkable, simply remarkable, well then, I think we should all go see to Toby—shall we?"

"Yes your Lordship please." Escaped from Trevor.

We walked down endless halls before finally coming to Toby's room after taking a 'maze' of twists and turns. We walked in to find Toby with a humongous welt on his face but that wasn't the worst of it. His leg was a total mess, with it laying in a sling brace to support the multiple compound fractures to his femur.

Simply said, the boys were not used to seeing someone so injured, so it frightened them terribly. I was ticked off at myself for not warning them more beforehand, as this was a truly disturbing scene. In essence, other than the serious concussion issue, the kid looked a lot worse than his actual other injuries, so both Trevor and Taylor immediately began crying. I had to bend down to comfort and compose them. Once I had done so, I whispered some suggestions into Trevor's ear.

"Okay Trev, it'll be all right so don't worry honey, now here's what I want you to do. Go up to Toby's bed, then I want you to grab hold of his hand gently like you were shaking it. Just hold on to it lightly while you rub his arm a little too, if you want. Then begin to talk to him about anything on your mind—maybe remind him of your best memories together . . . the things you two mates have done together over the years. Don't worry son if he doesn't answer, as that doesn't matter . . . can you do this for me?"

"Yes Daddy, but I'm scared—he looks so bloody bad. I don't want to hurt him more."

"Don't worry honey—you won't. Besides Trev, like I said, it looks worse than it actually is, so don't fret."

"Okay, but I hope you're right."

"I am, trust me son."

Trevor slowly approached Toby's bed as I slid a chair over for him to sit on. Trevor followed my advice to the letter as all of us looked on. He was now clasping Toby's right hand like a handshake while rubbing Toby's lower arm with his other hand. You had to give Trevor credit as he was following my instructions perfectly. Then he began to speak to his best mate, a boy he had known and loved like a brother from the time these two were toddlers. The two boys had been mostly inseparable until this last January of course.

"Tobe—it's Trev, mate, can you hear me? There was nothing from Toby.

"Taylor and I are here with you Tobe, aren't we Tay?"

"Yeah Trev—hi there mate."

Trevor then proceeded with a non-stop, one-sided conversation with Toby, often laughing over the memories with Taylor joining in as well. All toll; this went on for around an hour and twenty or so minutes. As before though, there were no responses from Toby whatsoever.

I had to admit that I was disappointed myself, having read a fair amount about comas over the years. I could see by this time, that apparently Toby wasn't going to wake up for us. And seeing the apparent frustration in my own sons, I suggested we take a short break to let Toby continue to rest. I could also see the obvious grief on the faces of his Lordship and Lady. What with their obvious hopes of their son perhaps finally waking up, being dashed for the time being.

Thinking on my feet, I thought of some reverse psychology that I believed, could at least give us a gauge of Toby's attentiveness.

"Boys, it seems that Toby doesn't want to wake up at the moment to say hello to either of you. Even though you've come from so far away in America, to be with him."

I wondered if Jewish guilt inflected in my terse words could still work its magic on a gentile boy . . . in a coma. I had spoken them intentionally loud and honestly—quite obnoxiously, in keeping with this new strategy of mine.

"We have to be going boys; we can't wait forever, so give Toby a hug while you say your good-byes for now. Hopefully, we can see him one more time before we leave London to head back home."

The boys were both giving me dirty looks at my choice of words in front of their badly injured mate. Yet they also knew better than to argue with me, so they did as I instructed. First Taylor leaned over and hugged him while saying so long, then Trevor who was crying big time now, hugged him several times. Then he actually kissed Toby on the hand while still holding it all this time from before.

As Trevor now attempted to free his hand though, he couldn't—Trevor now realized that Toby alone—wasn't releasing his half of it, if you will. This instantly gave me hope as I saw what was happening . . . it perked all of us right up obviously.

"Dad—he must be able to hear me so he knows we're leaving now, and he doesn't want me to go. My God Daddy, he's really squeezing me tight now, bloody hell . . . oh my God, he's telling me I'm right by squeezing my hand harder Daddy, I'm sure of it."

Silently, I nodded to Trevor before giving him the thumb's up along with a wink.

Again speaking loudly and rudely, I said to Trevor.

"Tell him you have to leave Trev, ask him to let go of your hand so we can get going—unless he is ready to wake up this moment to tell you himself—not to leave."

Trevor had his own light go on in understanding my strategy finally. He wasn't about to give up now either, so he nodded over to me while throwing me a wink this time.

"Tobe, I have to leave mate, I really got to go. Dad says I can only stay if you'll open your eyes to tell me, yourself."

Trevor was proud of his own strategy, as he turned to me for an affirmation that he was on target, right as I began my next little spiel.

"Come on Trevor, we have to leave now—we must get going!" I yelled this comment out authoritatively and pretty loudly too, followed by a wink back at Trev as he nodded.

"Sorry mate but I really have to go, dang it Tobe—you gotta let go of my hand now."

"No!"

This came loudly yet almost indiscernibly out of Toby's swollen and mangled mouth, as we all jumped . . . we were so shocked. The Kenneysons of course, jumped up to run over to the side of their son's bed to lend their support too. His Lordship in particular seized the moment:

"Son, you must let go of Trevor's hand, he has to get back to the States . . . you can't hold him here like this forever. He's making it very easy on you—if you want him to stay longer, you must open your eyes to tell him so yourself—do you hear me Tobias?"

"No."

Again Toby forcefully said it; although it was clear his throat must have been dry as well. Now his mother took the lead:

"Toby, its Mummy, you must let go of Trevor's hand, he must leave now unless you open your eyes. Please open them for him precious, just one time so we know you hear us."

We all stared hopefully at Toby's eyes now. In mass, our mouths dropped open as Toby popped them open in a blank stare. Then he closed them again as our hearts sank—but then he opened them again. He truthfully seemed more animated somewhat, although I wasn't sure be was back—quite yet.

Then, after a moment or two, he slowly looked down at his own hand connected to Trevor's, before he then looked up at his best mate sitting next to him. Toby started crying seeing Trevor holding his hand which started the rest of us off likewise as well. It was an emotional moment for all of us, but certainly for his parents.

"Don't go Trev, don't leave me again mate—God Mummy, I need some water."

At that moment, we were all bawling so hard, I hardly even noticed the look on Trevor's face. Have you ever seen a boy capable of bawling his eyes out, yet all the while, simultaneously smiling a big toothy grin too? That was Trevor now, while we could all understand why too . . . and he still had Toby's hand deeply clutching his.

It was Trevor's unwavering love and persistence for Toby that had brought forth this small miracle, as much as anything else.

"Mummy, Father, where am I—what are we all doing here? Mr. Morgan—Trev, Taylor—how are you . . . bloody hell?"

"You had a bad accident mate, you've been asleep in a coma, but you're going to be just fine now, right Tay?"

"Right bro—how are you feeling mate?"

"Like I'm in a bloody fog Taylor, but can someone please give me some water? Oh my God—I'm bloody naked! Nobody look at me—Mummy—how could you let them do this to me?"

"Dearest, your leg has a broken femur in three places, I'm afraid there's no other way for you to be, I've already asked about it, believe me."

Toby was desperately looking for anything to cover himself, finally settling for his pillow to cover what he could. Taylor meanwhile, handed Toby a cup of water which he drank it down in two gulps.

"But Mummy everyone can just look at—all of me, even my bloody willy . . . and why is this hose connected to it for . . . it hurts?"

"Don't fret over it love; I'm pretty sure they may be able to remove it now that you're awake. Meanwhile, it's only been your father and I, until the Morgans arrived earlier this afternoon, so other than your doctors and nurses and us, we haven't allowed anyone else to visit you for this exact reason, so let it be for now."

"Now don't you worry Toby, as of late, I've seen lots of willies. Your mates don't care who sees theirs it seems, so just relax alright?"

"Okay, but no more free shows, there must be some way to stay covered up; this pillow will slide off the minute I go to sleep?"

"I'm sorry dearest, so why don't you just try to not think about it—be of good cheer now that you're awake?"

"Oh Mummy, get real—what a bloody Nora . . . why not put me back into the damn coma—bloody hell!" Toby lamented.

Well, at least the kid hadn't lost his sense of humor.

Now that Toby was in fact conscious, it dawned on his Lordship to advise the nurse to get the doctor. When he hung up the phone, he heard more from Toby.

"Father, just what happened to me at St. Moritz?"

"Son, according to the gent who ran into you, he lost control beginning his run—and he slid right into you. He pushed both of you into a large tree I'm afraid. By the way, most of these lovely flowers are from him, he feels so awful Toby."

"Bloody hell—I would hope so Father—my God, I could have been killed!"

"Yes son that's true, and as it is, your doctor said that you had a severe sub-cranial hematoma that had to be relieved, but God watched over you, as now you're back with us thanks to Trevor here."

Toby now realized Trevor's role as he looked at his hand still grasping his friend's. Without so much as a further word, the tears began anew between the two boys with that acknowledgement, actually from all of us again—it was a truly emotionally charged hospital room. After we had all composed ourselves, Toby got a brainstorm:

"Can I go home now, since I'm awake Father?"

"Son, do you honestly think you're going anywhere with that leg looking like it is . . . with your face not looking much better? Son, you might as well know right now, the doctors have told us your leg will require two or more surgeries to fix."

"Right, bloody hell—does it ever hurt too, oh my God—Mummy it hurts so badly."

"I know love, I'll ask the nurse to give you something to relieve the pain now that you're awake,—Edward call her dear."

His Lordship hit the nurse's call button to advise the desk of Toby's pain. It seemed Toby was becoming more aware of his situation as the minutes elapsed in his newfound consciousness.

It appeared that Toby must have stopped to concentrate and assess what he was feeling from around his entire body, as he next grabbed for his swollen face. Naturally, being a good-looking boy, he was in a panic as he began screaming out:

"Oh my God, my face—my bloody face, oh no. What does it look like Father, I'm afraid to know?"

"Son, your face will be fine, the doctors have already assured us of that, so don't worry."

"It doesn't feel that way Father."

"No son it wouldn't . . . let me warn you Tobias, it will give you a fright when you first look. You might not believe this son, but it already looks so much better than it did only two days ago."

At that moment, a nurse came in with some pain medication for Toby's IV line. After that was in, he quickly became somewhat loopy—yet delightful to listen to, actually he was hilariously funny.

We spent another hysterical hour visiting with Toby's altered state while I watched my two beginning to yawn incessantly. I finally told the Kenneysons' that some sleep was in order for the three of us.

I promised that we would return for evening visiting hours, after seeing Uncle Teddy for a while. After considerable pleading and complaining, the boys finally saw that I was not relenting. Giving in to their fatigue, they acquiesced as we said our fair wells for the time being before departing Toby's room.

Walking past the nurse's station a short minute later, I wanted to thank Frances once more for all of her support, but another nurse currently sat in her place, so I decided I would simply leave a message for her.

I thought it somewhat odd when the nurse looked at me a little weird when she saw the twins.

"Hello ma'am, might I leave a message for Frances with you?"

"Ah, I don't think so sir, as I understand it, I'm afraid that Frances has been discharged sir."

Smelling an immediate 'rat', as I stood there dead exhausted, while shocked . . . I lost it there on the spot as I responded:

"What!" I yelled it out quite loudly, I can assure you.

"I'm sorry sir, I probably should not have said anything, but Frances was called to a meeting into our administrator's office, where the next thing I knew, she came back in tears as she cleared out her drawers."

"That's it, I've heard enough. Miss, what is Frances' last name, along with this administrator of yours?"

"Mr. Ross Richman is our head administrator sir while Frances' last name is Culpepper."

"Could you call him so I may ask if I may come by to see him?"

"Certainly sir, but if you don't mind, may I just get him on the line, and not mention Frances' discharge?"

"Yes of course, forgive my lapse of sensitivity; I'll handle this in my own way—so could you simply direct me to his office?"

"Thank you sir, I appreciate this."

"Think nothing of it, ma'am."

As I took down her instructions, I sent the boys back to Toby's room requesting they return with his Lordship if possible. Minutes later, they returned along with his Lordship who looked somewhat confused.

I quickly filled his Lordship in on the entire earlier event.

"So what do you suggest we do, Mr. Morgan?"

"I'm going to propose that we pay this 'gentleman' a brief visit, if you would care to join me?"

"Why certainly Mr. Morgan, I would be most beholden to join you."

"All right boys, let's go".

We made our way down to the first floor as we followed the instructions I took down, until we were outside of the administrator's office, standing before his secretary's desk.

"Gentlemen, how may I help you?" I now spoke:

"Could you please ask Mr. Richman, if we might have a moment of his valuable time?" I had said it with so much sarcasm that his Lordship gave me a somewhat shocked look.

"Certainly, please excuse me for a moment, might I have your name sir?"

"Of course, please tell him my name is Marcus Morgan from Las Vegas, Nevada."

"Fine sir, I will be right back." The boys sat down on the sofa.

"Thank you ma'am, you are most kind." As she disappeared, I turned towards his Lordship.

"If you are a betting man your Lordship, I will wager you a ten pound note that he will refuse to see us without an appointment or will be otherwise unavailable."

"We'll see Mr. Morgan, are you offering any particular odds of that?" As we both laughed.

Meanwhile, our friendly secretary returned."

"I'm so sorry Mr. Morgan, but Mr. Richman regrets he is leaving for an outside appointment shortly. He therefore requests that you make a formal appointment—say for next week?" At that moment, both the secretary and I witnessed his Lordship flush crimson—right in front of us.

"Miss, what is your name please?"

"I am Miss Finch, sir."

"Thank you Miss Finch and I am Lord Edward Kenneyson—would you kindly tell Mr. Richman, that I am accompanying Mr. Morgan in this request of his."

"Most certainly, your Lordship."

"Thank you Ms. Finch."

As she disappeared through the door a second time, I noticed that both of my boys were already sleeping on the office's sofa, obviously riveted to this entire exchange. Meanwhile, his Lordship and I could make out some muffled conversation coming from Richman's inner office.

Seconds later, Miss Finch returned looking somewhat sheepish.

"I'm sorry gentlemen, but it appears that Mr. Richman has already left his office while we were speaking before, I'm so sorry.

I think she was honestly startled when his Lordship walked right past her now as he brazenly opened the inner office door to confirm the facts. Sure enough, a slight man with his back to us was just leaving the office out of a rear door. Without hesitation, Edward said nothing as he closed the door quietly, turning back to the secretary. She was definitely flustered now, but did try to sidestep the matter.

"May I get out Mr. Richman's schedule and put you in for an appointment next week?"

"No Miss Finch that will likely not be necessary, as he will have no appointments next week if I have my say, but thank you." He said this, while directing me to the doors as he rousted the boys.

Once out in the hallway, I noticed he had gone from a softer shade of red, back to the bright crimson from minutes before.

"I'm sorry for bringing you into this fray of a mess your Lordship."

"Honestly Mr. Morgan, don't be. But I will need the nurse's name again, what was it?"

"Culpepper sir, Frances Culpepper."

"Fine. Consider the matter concluded for the time being."

"Might I inquire as to what you plan to do, your Lordship?"

"Certainly you may, I plan to have Miss Culpepper reinstated while I place Mr. Richman into a minimal state of suspension, if not unemployment, thank you."

"Are you sure you want to do this?"

"Yes Mr. Morgan, most assuredly I do sir."

"Thank you for your assistance your Lordship."

"You are most welcome, Mr. Morgan. Now you men get some rest and we'll see you later this evening, alright?"

"Yes your Lordship, thank you again." As we parted company to leave. I had to wonder just how much pull, one Lord had—to be so certain that Richman would be suspended (or worse) and poor Frances—might be back at work?

We returned to our suite, set the alarm for four pee, before we bedded down for a few zees'. When we woke, we showered, dressed, and then picked up our rental car, as we drove out to Surrey towards Uncle Teddy's farm.

We had a heartfelt reunion along with a wonderful visit. Teddy surprised the boys by inviting all of their close friends over for the occasion, so the boys were sincerely shocked by their Great Uncle's unselfish actions. Later, after so much food I thought I would burst, we left Uncle Teddy and all of the twins' mates.

Before heading back to London though, we took a quick drive up to the manor to see all the construction going on. The conversion into the Research Center and hospital was moving full steam ahead. We also stopped at the cemetery where we paid our respects tearfully to our own dear Lord and Lady.

Arriving in London just before seven, we made our way slowly through traffic over to the hospital. We knew Toby was anxiously awaiting our return and with limited time ourselves, the traffic exacerbated us.

When we arrived again at Toby's room, we had to give the kid a lot of credit, because he was resourceful. He had fashioned a makeshift tent of sorts over his bed using hospital sheets with the assistance of his nurse. It was in fact, able to conceal his 'natural' state underneath. We were impressed; but of course, it looked absolutely ridiculous as you walked into the room, but who cared about that anyway.

I was immediately addressed by his Lordship.

"Mr. Morgan, here are my results to share with you and the boys.

"I called two dear MP friends of mine in the (House of) Commons that are both senior members on the Health Committee. As you know, our health delivery system is under government control fully, so this wasn't a tough assignment. It appears that Mr. Richman's professional past was checkered with numerous complaints already, so my efforts were actually quickly celebrated and rewarded.

"Both of these MP's were quite familiar with Mr. Richman's history— and his management style."

"That's wonderful to know that we will not have to lose any sleep from guilt over his potential demise, your Lordship."

"Yes, he was truly a scoundrel apparently. And your Ms. Culpepper knew in an instant that you must have intervened on her behalf, so you are to be commended on both accounts according to my friends."

"I am relieved your Lordship, but I can not thank you or your colleagues enough."

"Think nothing of it, my good man; you've done the National Health Service a great favor by opening your mouth to this injustice."

Meanwhile, Toby and the twins began another two-hour visit.

When we were told directly by his nurse that we had overstayed our welcome at eight-thirty, Toby's nurse, while sympathetic, was a true ball buster about the rules all the same.

I knew this was going to be a difficult goodbye for Trevor. So, Taylor and I said our goodbyes, as we left the two boys for a few minutes of private farewells. We gave Trevor five minutes alone with Toby, as our hosts followed us right along into the hallway.

"Mr. Morgan, we can't thank you and the boys enough for coming over on behalf of Toby. We are simply thankful for the blessing of having you all here, along with your extraordinary efforts to help Toby wake up."

"And I thank you your Lordship, but really it was our pleasure and our honor—right T-man?"

"Yes Daddy. Your Lordship, my Lady, thank you for your kindness in allowing us to visit with Toby."

"No Taylor, thank you for helping Toby wake up."

"Okay, I guess that too."

When Trevor emerged from Toby's room, he was crying again, but at least this time, his worst fears were assuaged.

We wished our hosts well as we left to return to our hotel.

Returning to our hotel room, we found Joe and Bill deeply involved in a game of Gin Rummy. I ordered up some room service, then suggested once we had eaten, that we take another nap. We would be leaving in a few hours and I knew rest was in order . . . especially for me. After eating some minutes later, I got no complaint from the twins as we went off to our bedroom for that purpose.

Fast—turnaround, trans-Atlantic flights are always horrendous on your body. You are out of sorts with everything, as it was with us. By the time we had arrived back at McCarran Monday morning, we were exhausted beyond anything I could remember. Worst of all, we had to try to return to our normal schedules, as it was already past 7 am locally—oh my God!

I was in no condition to go into the office, while the boys appeared in worse condition to return to school, so I said the heck with it as I suggested a two-hour nap.

At nine-forty, I got the boys awake as we started our day officially. Twice later on though, the twins fell back asleep watching television. I was not much better, falling to sleep right in the middle of replying to an email. There I was, resting my head on my palms, which was supported on my desk by my elbows.

I heard the sound of returning 'snowbirds' come through the door at just about three pm, waking me up—yet again.

We all had a warm reunion, while we exchanged full reports from each 'camp's' adventure. We were having a nice conversation on Toby's improvements, when the phone rang. Reg answered it and then called out for Mom.

When Reg returned, he informed me that it was Scoot on the phone with Mom. According to Reg, Mr. Davis sounded 'anxious'. I excused myself from the family as I headed for the kitchen so that I could ease drop while Mom took the call. As I walked in, Mom pointed to a chair for me to sit down, while she pushed the speakerphone on as she continued with Scoot.

"Like I said Scott, let's allow him to sweat a little longer, that's all I'm suggesting."

"Alright Marilyn, but I don't think we want to totally alienate him either. My 'fly' in his office tells me he already believes we have no real interest with their offer. I would hate for him to totally give up and move on."

"So what do you suggest we do then Scott?"

"I don't know Marilyn, maybe a short letter stating that it's perhaps time for all of us to sit down to go over the specifics of their offer . . . or maybe we mention that we've accumulated a few questions too. Just suggest to him that we feel the face-to-face would be in order now.

"Look Marilyn, the bottom line is, apparently he's too stupid to realize he has been played all this time. He seriously thinks he's out of the running already, so obviously, we played our part too well. Maybe that's no longer to our advantage Marilyn, if you follow my logic?"

"Yes Scott, of course I do. Your position makes sense, so that's what we'll do then. First though, let's really confuse him, we'll ask for some nonchalant additional information on a few issues in an initial letter. This will make him realize that we're not nearly as disinterested as he suspects, so that should rekindle his hopes sufficiently. We'll hold the suggestion of the face-to-face for a second letter though, for after he responds to our questions. Remember our mantra Scott: Always keep them guessing."

"Yes Marilyn, that sounds even better. While I'm still at the office, I'll write it up. As soon as it's finished, I'll email it to Marc's computer—will that work for you?"

"Perfectly Scott, just call me here when I can expect it."

"All right, I'll call you as soon as I have it sent."

I was convinced as ever, that this poor schmuck would never know what hit him as I told my mother as much. With my Mother's skills at negotiation, Jared had already lost . . . he just didn't know it yet.

Over dinner, Mom, Dad, and I reviewed Scoot's letter to Jared. It was short and direct . . . while it asked an assortment of questions we already knew the answers to. It would leave Jared with two impressions: First; we were still interested. Secondly, it gave the appearance that perhaps we weren't as astute as he may have originally given us credit for!

Mom thought the approach was workable. In all, she made a couple of minor changes, before emailing it back to Robbie for a final copy to be prepared and faxed to Jared in the morning.

The boys meanwhile, were ready for bed right after dinner concluded at seven—thirty, the food apparently doing them in nicely. I suggested they take a nice long soak in my tub first, before then hitting the hay as it would get them closer to their normal bedtime.

I reminded the twins to give their grandfather lots of kisses as he was leaving early in the morning. For once, the boys were too exhausted to argue, so they comically accused him of desertion.

The following morning, we faxed the letter off to Jared at around nine, thirty-five. At ten-ten, he had already responded back. Apparently for Morison, appearing too anxious wasn't a concern—the poor fool.

I called mom with that news as Scoot had already reviewed it before leaving my office.

Mom was on the phone in an instant.

"Should I read you his answers Mom?"

Mom was laughing hysterically, but eventually composed herself.

"What for Marc, we already know the answers—but a good morning to you too."

"Sorry Mom, how are you this morning?"

"Good dear, I got Daddy off as well as can be expected. God, he really hated that we left so early. Not getting that one additional kiss out of the boys totally depressed him, but that's how it goes sometimes."

"Yep, I certainly know how he feels myself."

"So Mom, do I spill it, or are we going to continue our little chit-chat?"

"Sure, but like I said, we can already accurately guess his answers, so what else if anything, did he have to say?"

"Not much, but he did allude to some additional negotiating room on some issues. I thought that was stupid of him, given how intentionally naïve we sought to portray ourselves this time around."

"Well Markie, to quote our dear friend, Forrest Gump—stupid is, as stupid does?"

"Yeah Mom, but not only that—I'm guessing his box of chocolates is perhaps a few pieces—short. You know Ma; he's not the sharpest knife in the drawer, is he?"

Mom was laughing hysterically at my crack, when Robbie popped in my office to tell me Scoot needed another five-to-ten—immediately. There was some new startling information concerning the boys and Morison, apparently from a urgent telephone call Scoot had just received.

I shared the comment with Mom of course, so she suggested getting Scott in immediately while putting her on speaker. I relayed this suggestion to Robbie, who then ran off to call Scoot in for the meeting.

Moments later, Scooter was sitting opposite me, beaming from ear to ear—Christ, this had to be good.

I explained to him that Mom was on speaker, as well as what had already transpired between us. My two geniuses exchanged morning pleasantries before Scoot explained his cryptic message.

"Listen to this Mar, my little fly inside Jared's department called me not two minutes ago, laughing his ass off over poor little Jared."

"What specifically about Scott?"

"Yeah Scoot, what gives?"

"As I understand it from our friend the fly, Jared's boss is furious and on the warpath—I'm afraid Jared's got himself into serious trouble now.

Donovan Sage is the Executive VP for the entire subsidiary. She apparently was introduced to the boys' talents only today, having seen the Teen Pop spread. While casually walking around the office discussing the spread with the suits within her department, she was shocked to learn, that some of those among her inner staff were absolutely sure that the twins had already performed at the park. Then somehow, the video of the boys' performance then magically materialized for her to watch. According to what is filtering back to me, she watched the video several times as for one thing, she's like this major Elton fan. When she heard the boys' version of Funeral for a Friend for the first time, she apparently went absolutely crazy for it—then flew into a rage that they weren't already signed to an exclusive contract already."

"How do you suppose she got the video, Scoot?"

"Naturally I'm guessing it was Stacy, Marc, but who knows. Obviously, we'll thank the Good Samaritan when we find out. Clearly, someone made those staffers inside of Donovan's office aware that the boys had performed here before, that wasn't luck or coincidence . . . maybe Stacy circulated the video beforehand?"

"So, then what happened Scott?" Mom inquired.

"Marilyn, its like this. Eventually, Donnie was armed with enough of the facts that it all led to our boy Jared. So she called Morison on the carpet for not having the boys signed. She is furious and is giving him only another two weeks, to put the ink to the deal. Additionally, she told him that the boys had better not sign elsewhere in the meantime. Apparently if that happens, she told him he was as good as fired on the spot."

"So, the word is—he's got a do or die situation here. He is desperate to make any deal with us now. That would explain his fast response to our letter and his unsolicited carrot of additional flexibility being available."

"Gee Scoot; ain't this a kick in the head—we got the bastard right where we want him? I have a fair idea of exactly how we can test the accuracy of this information as well. I think that's important to do—besides; we'll really see him grovel and cave, if it's true.

"You see, if the information proves accurate, we can just string him out to within a few days of his deadline. He'll be so desperate by then, we can write our own deal for the boys."

"How do you suggest we do that son?"

"Gee Mom, is your name Scoot?"

"Can it son, I'm in no mood for your cracks, spill it—now!"

"Fine, fine, okay it's like this. We'll wait until this afternoon to send him back a thank you letter for his timely response . . . let's not appear as anxious as he is, right? Next, following your plan Mom, we tell him it's time for a face to face . . . but" . . .

. . . "But what Marc?" Apparently my Mother was short on patience today as she interrupted me.

. . . "But here's the rub—Mom, we'll insist that meeting can't be held until early next month, which is still three weeks away. If he squawks and goes nuts over that timeframe, we know the information is accurate. Given his circumstances, he'd never risk alienating us further over the timing of an initial meeting, unless it truly was, a do or die for him—already—and past his deadline from his boss."

"Brilliant bud, so who's going to write this letter then?"

"Why don't you handle it Scott, your last one was fine after all?" Mom interjected.

"All right Marilyn, I'll get right on it. Hey guys; should we throw him a curve ball too, to see how much he panics as well?"

"Such as what, Scoot?"

"Hell, I don't rightly know at the moment bud, but let's think about it some." Scott offered.

"What we could do boys, is drop an innuendo that even Mr. Dullest Knife in the drawer, can't miss the significance of. How about dropping the implication of a looming deal well into prior negotiation with a competitor?"

"Jesus Mom, you're absolutely brutal . . . let's go for it."

"That's my boy, so Scott what do you think?"

"I'm right there with Marc—Mom!"

"Okay, so how do you two think we should word it?"

"Simple Marilyn, we just pick out one of his better terms in his deal which we'll then tout back to him . . . but then, we drop the bombshell. We allude to a phantom competitor who we're in heavy talks with. We'll say something like; they won't even entertain that particular term in their deal. Then our closing comment becomes his Achilles Heel. We'll simply close with: We'd have walked ages ago if the rest of their deal wasn't so exceptional.

"This will send him the message he's a distant second already, while losing more ground by the minute . . . he's bound to totally cave. If I know this guy at all . . . and I do, he'll just start groveling, pleading for that face-to-face meeting sooner than next month."

"Perfect Scoot, get working on it. Can you have it finished before lunch?"

"For sure bud, no problemo."

"Good. Mom, any other words of wisdom you'd care to impart?"

"Yes. Scott, pour it on a little thick for this particular letter, maybe even patronize him a little, but so subtle the putz will never see it coming."

"Alright Marilyn, I can do that."

Scoot then left to 'create' his masterpiece.

Mom and I finished our conversation then hung up.

I started writing out terms of my own for the boys' contract. I was convinced we were in the driver's seat now, but more so, could ultimately demand just about anything we wanted. Jared would be too fearful to balk at much of anything. We therefore could have any item we demanded, at least considered.

I was well into my list, when Robbie buzzed me that I had a call from my architect, Milton. I picked up the call.

"Milt, what's happening, you almost through with my plans?"

"Yes Marc, they're done and through plan check with the city, and the compound will be dazzling, but I'm exhausted. Hell, I didn't even play one round of golf during the whole design process—shame on you Marc! I want you to give the plans your final okay, before they're off to Herb in Scottsdale for the model."

"Okay, send them over so I can drool some, did you get my plans for the lagoon all right?"

"Oh—don't you mean for your 'mini water park'? Yeah I got them, but hell, I'm sure glad I'm not writing that check."

I was laughing at Milt's crack, which set him off as well.

"Listen Milt, I don't tell you how to design your houses, so don't you tell me how to design my pool buddy boy." I laughed, just in case he took me seriously.

"Marc, the hell you don't tell me how to design a house. I suppose it was my idea to have subterranean parking—for fifty cars as part of your foundation?"

"Okay, so maybe I did contribute—a little."

"Did you just use the word contribute, Marc . . . contribute you say?"

"Yep—why?"

"Oh, it's just that I look at something that's contributed, as more of an idea or suggestion—than a demand." He was laughing again.

"Alright already, you made your frigging point, so how do the plans look Milt?"

"Marc, like I said before, the home will be dazzling, I think you'll be more than pleased with it. And hell; you should be, because it's going to cost you $1.7 mil, just to build the son of a bitch. And just a reminder, the outside security contractor isn't in that estimate that we spoke about last week!"

"You know Milt; you're still not scaring me, throwing out those figures."

"Fine, but my construction cost breakdown only estimated a budget of one hundred, twenty-five 'k' for the lagoon initially—so good luck with that."

"Jesus Milt, don't you worry your little old head over my lagoon. That's my signature element in the estate, so whatever it costs—it costs. And don't forget, my home in the Trail is worth somewhere between two and a half million to two million, eight hundred, so what's the big deal anyway?"

"Fine, but listen, you still have to decide on the colors of your faux stone work for the lagoon so I can instruct Herb?"

"I'm going to go with the rose, slate, and gray tones, Milt."

"Fine . . . that will look nice with the general scheme of the house."

"Yes . . . gee, I guess I should be glad you agree with my contribution on the faux stone."

"All right Marc, I think we've covered enough for now. I'll have the plans over in around a half hour, any questions just call me."

"Sure thing Milt and thanks."

I hung up the phone as I returned to my dream terms for the boys until Robbie buzzed me to say Scoot was ready anytime I was prepared to see him. I told Robbie to tell him now was fine. Minutes later, Scoot arrived at my office door where I pointed him to a chair which seated him opposite of me.

"Jesus Scoot, you know, that was like so fast, are you sure you covered everything we spoke about?"

"Reasonably sure bud, go ahead—read it, then you can tell me."

I read the letter; and was more than satisfied with it, so I got Mom on speakerphone at home.

"Mom, boy wonder is already finished with his narrative—care to take a listen?"

"My God—already?"

"Yep, it's pretty darn fair too."

"My letter—only earns 'fair' Marc, what am I suppose to make out of that crack?"

"Sorry Scooter, your letter is excellent, but let's allow Mom to be the final judge, all right?"

"Sure Marc, sorry for overreacting."

"De nada amigo."

So I cleared my throat just as I began reading the letter for Mom's benefit.

Dear Jared:

Thank you so much for your expedient response to our letter of this morning. How a busy executive such as yourself can find the time to react so quickly, is very impressive. I wish that all the companies would react as fast.

I believe your answers to my questions warrant further consideration that only a face-to-face meeting can appropriately address.

I will be most interested to learn more about your merchandising terms. The other label we are most serious with, doesn't offer anything close to what your offer presents for our side. But of course, the rest of their package is excellent; otherwise I wouldn't be speaking with them nearly non-stop.

I suggest that we get together tentatively any time after the first week in April, to discuss these possibilities further. This should give me sufficient time to conclude my ongoing conversations with the other label—one-way or the other.

Please call me at your convenience after April 3rd, to set up our appointment.

Again, thank you for getting back to me so fast with your answers.

Sincerely

Mrs. Marilyn Morgan

Personal Manager;

Tay 'n' Tre . . . The Morgans

After I finished reading the letter, Mom asked me to read it through another time. After the second run through, she was ready to respond to it.

"Scott, it's near perfect. I especially liked the 'busy executive' reference, as well as addressing him as Jared . . . you get an 'A' for patronizing young man. Personally, I don't know if I would have gone quite as heavy on the competitor comments, but that's me. But I'm not sure you haven't got the better way with that, so I say we send it, as is."

"Me too Mom, I wouldn't change anything, myself." I added.

"Cool Marilyn, I'm going to email it over to you. You can print it out, sign it, and then fax it back over."

"Fine Scott, I'd like to read it again before it goes out anyway. After I fax it over to his office, I'll drive into the office personally. If I know this idiot, he will be on the phone to me from this point forward."

"Thanks Marilyn, that sounds great."

"All right, I'll be right over, meanwhile you boys can think of our telephone strategy with him."

"Okay Mom, we'll be thinking about it, see you in a bit." I had Robbie email the letter to the house before Scoot and I ran out for lunch.

Scoot and I had a lengthy discussion as Mom had suggested. In the expanse of time it took us to eat and come to some conclusions, Morison had already called—twice!

Reading Jared's messages, as I stared at them in my hand, I again had to take my hat off to my mother. She had this dufuss pegged—I could only imagine, how the telephone conversation itself, was likely to go.

When Mom arrived, we showed her the messages as we enlightened her on our own ideas for the telephone negotiations to follow. Mom was busy taking notes, it was clear she wasn't going to leave anything to chance. Around fifteen minutes later, it appeared Mom was ready.

"All right Marc, let's make the call, I'm ready."

I had Robbie place the call—moments later, he buzzed through that Mr. Morison was on line two.

Following our protocol, we were on speaker while Mom would do the warm up strictly by herself. Mom nodded her head as I pushed the button.

"Hello Mr. Morison, this is Marilyn Morgan calling. I'm here with my son Marc, and our business manager Scott Davis, both of whom I believe you already know."

"Yes Mrs. Morgan, it's a pleasure to 'finally' be able to speak to you though, but please call me Jared. May I call you Marilyn? Hello Marc and Scott . . . I'll assume you're on speaker so everyone can hear?"

"Yes they are Jared. I'm assuming your two telephone messages concern preplanning by calling to book our appointment for April, or was it another question?" Mom asked.

"Yes—I mean no—I meant to say that yes, I'm calling to confirm an appointment. But no, I don't have another question, sorry for the confusion."

"That's all right Jared, don't give it another thought. So what date looks good for you after that first week in April?"

"Actually Marilyn, I was hoping to move that date up, say to sometime this week?"

"Now Jared, I'm shocked—you just finished telling me you didn't have another question. Apparently your idea of what defines a question—and mine, have two different meanings?"

God, Mom was playing him like a fiddle already.

"But to answer 'that question' Jared—that's simply impossible, I'm totally booked. You know Jared, between my appointment schedule, and this other record label, I simply can't meet with you now, I'm so sorry though . . ."

. . . "Marilyn, Marc, and Scott; may I cut right to my point?" We all chuckled silently at Jared's expected interruption.

"Sure Jared, go ahead."

Mom responded, clearly knowing where he would lead. As we had all suspected, Jared was going right for the jugular with all of his cards exposed on the table. I had to give Scoot's 'fly' major kudos, apparently he was totally accurate. Jared's groveling appeared to be about to commence—big time.

"Marilyn, gentlemen; it's like this. We have been searching, to find a wholesome and talented kid suitable for multiple mediums for some time now, as well rounded as Tay or Tre. Naturally, we would have been happy enough with one—let alone two. And we would have been more than satisfied if the kid was half as good looking as your two are, honestly.

"The long of the short of it is I'm already authorized to cut the deal of the century for the twins, pure and simple. If you'd only give me a few hours of your time, before you continue on with that other label, I'm sure that I could easily demonstrate why we are your number one option to consider?"

"I see Jared—but I don't know. I have so many reservations concerning Toon Media's ability to handle the boys recording career, to begin with. After all Jared, look at your roster of artists for God's sake—you're so specialized".

"Marilyn, our roster is specialized I'll admit that, but I'll still put our stars up to anyone else's."

"You will Jared? So, are you including Dodger Duck, Jumbo, Bettie Swoons, and Teddy Toon himself in those 'stars' then? Because last I checked, Madonna wasn't signed with you, or anyone else of major musical significance, for that matter.

"Our research indicates that the boys need a major 'bread and butter' label behind them promoting their music feverishly—preferably a 'hungry' label trying to breakout or rebuild their talent roster. Pretty much like the one we are negotiating with at the moment, so you know!"

"Marilyn, gentlemen, I understand you all have concerns, I really do. But each of those concerns can be addressed and more importantly . . . resolved directly in negotiations. If something doesn't look right or work for you, just say so and it becomes open for discussion in negotiation. But gang; please don't sell us out short, until you hear us say no to something of importance to you. Do this right the first time, and then you'll never have to go through it again, now doesn't that just make sense?"

"And no disrespect intended Marilyn, but if that label's hungry—where will they be in five or ten years? That label could be on top of the industry—but it could also be out of business and long gone in far less than five years. You know, we've been around the block—we're financially sound . . . for today, as well as tomorrow."

"Yes Jared, certainly your point's well taken, but your label simply lacks a lot of experience and connections in this genre. Don't you agree with me on this Marc?"

"Yeah Mom, I most certainly do. After all, we could easily start our own label for the boys; after all we have no shortage of money ourselves Jared. Our issues are unique; it's more the skill-set we lack. We need the experienced professionals, plus connections, and the right skilled technicians that are a little harder to just up and acquire—the boys deserve the best support we can get them after all.

"What we want if you will Jared—is the right label partner for the twins. Honestly we don't want your company's reputation, as fine as it is in many other areas, to in anyway hurt the boys' chances . . . that's are key concern. They'll need to get air play and immediate promotion, as well as, support and publicity out the ying-yang, that's what we're looking for—nothing else will suffice."

"Marc you're raising some excellent points, but again consider what we are offering, we're not merely talking recording. Even if that is your focus for the moment, it's merely one of many components within our entire spectrum.

"With our various divisions and multi-media posture, there simply can't be a better place for the boys to launch. Right here at Toon Media is the ideal place as overall, we will be your best possible partner, offering the brightest future for your sons . . . just give me the chance to prove it to you all!"

"Jared, Scott here, how are you doing buddy?"

"Fine Scott, but I was hoping you could help me out here. Can you explain to both Marilyn and Marc how we work, because I don't seem to be making much headway? Can you explain the dynamics to them of how it all comes together here? Let them understand that with us, recording is merely one integral piece of an entire and larger synergistic pie."

"I already have Jared. They already know what Toon Media excels at and can provide. Here's where you're missing the boat yourself, old man. Marilyn and Marc are not sure they want everything else you guys are offering the boys!

"Jared, as unbelievable as it may seem, some parents actually do not want the whole shebang overnight! It's called concerned parenting. Honestly Jared, Marilyn wants them to have recording as a primary focus to begin with. She would in fact prefer the rest of it to be as limited and unobtrusive as possible. Now does that help you to understand their situation a little better too?"

"Oh sure—yes of course—wow, now at least I understand the issue Scott, so thanks for clearing that up. I was not aware of anything like that as their reason for resisting our offer. Clearly, in our industry it's a rare phenomenon yet I am extremely impressed with their motives.

"Nevertheless, Marilyn and Marc, you two have to get 'a little real' yourselves. No matter with whom you ultimately sign the twins with, while I am still hoping it's us, the boys' lives are never going to be the same as they were before. Believe me, I know this.

"My friends, as this all unfolds—especially with recording, the results are certainly going to have the typical snowball effect. You'll end up crossing into all of our other media anyway, so why not start out with the best company to do that through, from the get go. Toon Media knows cross-marketing and multimedia better than anybody, hell I don't have to tell you that."

"You know Marilyn, Jared does make an excellent point—it will happen anyway—hell you can't stop a runaway train . . . can you? At least at Toon

Media it's a coordinated effort out of the box with all the various opportunities 'in-house'."

"Scott's right Marilyn, and honestly, we won't need twelve hundred reps running around getting the boys constant air time. We can more than make up for that with what we do over-all, which gets them that airplay—anyway.

"And hell; if you want your own label doing their promotion and the like . . . with twelve hundred reps, no problem—you now got it. We can even do it as a JV and split all the costs and profits. Just sit down with me now, rather than later, that's all I'm asking of you."

At our end of this conversation, we all nodded to acknowledge he was making perfect sense in his logic. In short, we were warming up to his request, since it was all contrived on our part anyway.

"My, you've all given me a lot of food for thought to mull over and chew here. I'll tell you what Jared, I'll move the appointment up for you, but it still can't be for another week." Mom offered.

"That's fair enough Marilyn. I sincerely thank you for allowing me to put forward my position. May I ask you an honest question however, because your answer will weigh heavily on our next step?"

"Yes, of course Jared." Mom answered.

"If I can essentially negotiate everything you all want from corporate, can we possibly sign a letter of intent at least? I'm speaking as a conclusion to our meeting and strictly with the boys' consent of course."

"Well Jared, I can't and won't promise that, but I will say this. If our concerns for the boys can be addressed and assured, things should go fine. If your pencil is sharp enough and creative besides, then yes it's possible—it's just not probable. Take it or leave it, that's all I'm prepared to assure you of at this moment."

"That seems fair to me Marilyn, so I thank you for going that far. As far as sharpening my pencil, I will ask you to do likewise on top of keeping an open mind too. We do have big plans for the twins, some of which your gut reaction might be to avoid for now or altogether, so I need to know when we cross that line, because I can't read your minds. Given what you've shared, it would be perfectly understandable that we will cross that line Marilyn, so don't worry about hurting our feelings, it's precisely for this reason that you will have the final say so, on most everything concerning the boys.

"Next, bring me your own laundry list, a wish list if you will—anything you want to call it. Hell, fax it to me anytime, today, tomorrow, whenever—let me know what you are looking for—up front. Give me the ammunition if you will, to do my job with corporate—now. As they say in our business, once the ink is drying on the dotted line, everything else is a 'could have been'. So tell me upfront, and I'll do my best to satisfy all of you—and the boys of course. Now does that seem fair to you Marilyn—and gentlemen?"

"Yes Jared it does, but let me warn you, I'm no push over—I'm one tough old broad."

Jared, Scooter, and I were all laughing at this honest self-assessment.

"You know Marilyn—I do indeed believe what you're telling me, but I welcome the challenge. You will find that as a negotiator, I believe in the 'win-win' strategy. I want the boys to win, T-M to succeed, and you and I to be able to remain friends in the process. Therefore, let's bring it on, and get this show on the road—by cutting the deal of the century. Hell we're wasting time folks—I'd like to see the boys at number one on the charts by summer's end, wouldn't you?"

"My Jared, I think I'm going to enjoy this negotiation with you."

"Good Marilyn, because I've got a real killer Tango to sweep you right off your feet—so shall we dance?"

"Yes Jared, I do believe we shall, so here's the situation from my end. I can give you up to four hours, one week from tomorrow, but that is the absolute best I can offer. I will also go one-step farther though, to show our good faith. I will not meet again with your competitor, until after our meeting; does that make you feel a little better?"

"I appreciate that Marilyn; more than you'll ever know. Now listen, I was serious with the wish list too, so get it to me soon so I can give you some preliminary answers that much sooner. After all, why shouldn't we work out as many of the smaller issues as possible, before we sit down?"

"Jared, its Marc—are you suggesting we actively negotiate before sitting down face to face?"

"Hi Marc, I guess I would say—yes. I'm suggesting we get past those elements of what you guys want, that we naturally won't have a problem agreeing to now. Believe me, anything T-M doesn't want to agree to out of the box, you'll still have to negotiate directly with me on. It's simply that if we know what you want up front, we can agree to those items not at issue right away. We save our meeting for the major obstacles if any, we're truly at odds over, doesn't that just make sense?"

"Fine, I can see the logic to that—okay."

"Good, now all we have to decide is, where our dance is going to take place—in your ballroom or mine?"

"Well Jared, I would naturally assume you want the boys present?"

"Yes Marilyn, of course—this is their future, not ours. I for one, insist that they're with us. So what would be easiest on them?"

"That's most considerate of you Jared, how about 3:30 then, here at the house? This way the boys won't miss school. We'll also plan on having you stay for dinner too."

"Sounds perfect to me, and I do thank you for your gracious invitation—may I bring some wine along to go with our meal Marilyn?"

"As long as it says Morgan Winery on the label you can."

"You're kidding me, you're not—that Morgan, are you Marilyn?"

"Yes Jared, I am that—Morgan."

"Wow, I had no idea; I mean I obviously know a bit about Marc—hell who doesn't. But I didn't realize you were the Morgans in the wine business—hell, your 1996 Cab Sauvignon Special Reserve is superb. Wait a minute Marilyn; I guess you already know that, don't you?"

Jared was laughing at his own stupid remark now as we joined in . . . it was funny.

"Yes Jared, I'll admit I knew that, but it still doesn't lessen the kindness of your compliment by any means."

"You're most welcome Marilyn, but all kidding aside, if you're Morgan Winery, why the hell am I bringing the wine—how about I bring dessert?"

He was laughing again.

"Jared, you make an excellent point—skip the wine . . . you're welcome to bring anything you'd like for dessert."

"Okay Marilyn, I will, but I always come with lots of goodies too, it's sort of inclusive with the employment here. I can assure you the boys will be pleased too."

"I'm sure that they will . . . just bring that razor sharp pencil and an appetite."

"Good, I will, so when do you think you could have your first list over to me?"

"I'm not sure Jared, perhaps tomorrow, how does that sound?"

"Splendid—that should be fine. Listen, it's been a real pleasure sincerely talking to all of you. I look forward to our meeting, but could you also extend my greetings to the boys. You know, they quickly get right into your heart, talent or no talent.

"You know Marilyn, just the other day I was speaking to Stacy when she told me about Taylor asking to be paid—and why. I was just so blown away by that, you have no idea. With their hearts that big, I want to see these boys succeed—no matter whom they sign with—and I mean that Marilyn."

"Thank you Jared, that is most kind of you to say. I will be sure to share that with them."

"Good bye all."

"Good bye Jared." We cut off the speakerphone as we stared at each other somewhat in a fog of sorts as we all tried to sort things out I suppose.

"My God, Mom is it possible, or did we not give Jared enough credit for being a decent human being, underneath that huge ego of his?"

"Please Marc; the guilt is already tearing me apart right through the kishkies . . . please don't add to it honey."

"Okay Scott, forget our sentimentality, what's your spin—you know him best after all?"

"My take is simple Marilyn; I think he now sincerely respects your motivations and desires for the boys. His comments as well, were plainly sincere and genuine; I have absolutely no doubt of that. And yes, none of us were prepared to think of him too kindly. I feel a little angry with myself as well . . . but not—too much.

"Naturally, he knows he has to make a deal with us to save his butt at this juncture. He certainly realizes that the first impression he left on at least you and the boys, was not particularly favorable. I wouldn't have expected him to act like the ass that he can be at times anyway.

"However, with that being said—this is a whole and new other side of Jared Morison I can assure you . . . one I've honestly never seen before. You can tell he sincerely wants to be instrumental in the boys' career and success. Essentially—he wants to help them and I believe, he feels he can make the personal difference to accomplish that. But since we're being completely honest here guys, let me add that I believe he is equipped to make that difference Marilyn."

"Jesus Scoot, he really got to you, didn't he?"

"Honestly Marc, yeah, he did. You have to understand something else about Morison that I can share with you having interacted with this guy for over my entire seventeen years—he has no shortage of talent bud. He's quite astute around that place, so he truly does know his stuff . . . all in all, we could do a whole hell of a lot worse Marko, with that being the truth of it."

"Interesting, so what do you make out of the 'list' request?"

"That's easy. One, he wants to know what you want, so he can gauge the difficulties of what he has to get out of management. Secondly, he wants ammunition to use with management . . . anything he can pick up, so that they will be prepared to compromise where necessary. Third, he definitely wants an 'end' play. You know, like if I can get you this, that, and the other, do we have a deal—already?"

"So boys, do we start getting serious with him now, or do we play him a little longer?"

"Mom, that's up to you, but as for me, I think its time to let this thing run its course with them. Scoot what are your feelings?"

"I think the sooner we get this show on the road, the sooner we sleep nights again . . . that's my two cents amigo."

"Well said Scott—alright men, I think we're of one mind then. Tomorrow, we commence Jared—phase two."

Scooter and I were laughing at Mom's comment, even as she continued.

"Boys we've just completed the easy part, now we have to actually develop a list, to share with him what we expect, what we need, and what we would like . . . so who wants to go first?"

"Marilyn, speaking for myself and the boys; I think we should follow through with Jared's own suggestion to the letter on a new label for them. Let's form a Joint Venture with T-M to create it. One far enough removed from Toon Media Entertainment and Records that it is taken seriously, right out of the box . . . but with the legitimate purpose of growing a new recording label, not just an extension of the boys' efforts . . . hell, I'd like to invest in it too if you have no objections. So, if we can sign other artists down the road that would be great as the more, the merrier!

"On a more personal note though, this is where me serving as their Executive Producer in the studio also hits pay dirt. In reality, we now have total 'creative control' of content, musicians, writers—there will be no missteps in other words! Lastly, like Jared himself said, they'll need their own promotional team, publicist, reps—the works, so we want the control there too . . . the JV is how we get it."

Mom then jumped in with her ideas.

"Okay Scott, that's a very good start, but as for me, I want much more. Nevertheless, we have already played our hand with Jared purposely in one direction. I don't want this list to appear like a contradiction in terms of what we've laid out to him already. I will therefore leave myself some wiggle room for additional points to be discussed in person, rather than the list. Nevertheless, in as much as the list is concerned, I will demand some things.

"I don't want the cumulative amount of time the boys work to exceed about thirty weeks each year. I want them to have their private lives too, away from all of this crap. I also want them to have two tutors at T-M's expense, one for their regular studies, plus one for their Hebrew.

"I want us to have some creative control in other mediums as well as the recording studio and label. It would also be ideal to have Toon Media pay our percentages from their end, so that it saves the boys' money.

"I also want them kicking in a little to the boys' foundations independent of other considerations, once those are established. They're already excellent corporate citizens, so this shouldn't be a hard sell.

"The rest of what they've already offered us, I don't really think we have to quibble over, as it's all excellent. One exception however, is residual income royalties—they need to be increased, at least on a sliding scale. I also think T-M should capitalize the new record label JV up front, with us repaying our contribution strictly out of our share of net profits or a period certain.

"Lastly, I insist on control over the merchandising offers. I don't want their faces plastered on just any stupid thing they can come up with.

"Well, I think that covers my issues, what about you Marc?"

"Gee Mom; I can't think of anything minor you two haven't already covered—and quite well I might add. There's one major aspect though, that must not be overlooked. Speaking for myself, it pains me to even bring it up."

"What's that Marc?"

"Mom, I know you won't want to hear this, but it must be said. We must all come to terms with it sooner or later, so now's about as good of time as any."

"Jesus bud, what are you talking about?"

"Scoot, Mom, the boys must have some form of personal, full-time security thanks to all of this, along with my financial standing—they're simply overloaded with security risks . . . ask any expert on the subject.

"Once they are out in the public's eye, every nut, wacko, and kook, is going to be thinking sick ideas. Also, I'd say that the sons of a multimillionaire alone make for a desirable target to a whole other group of sickos. As such, I don't plan on waiting for the last moment, or going down that road ever—so now is the time to be proactive and prepared—follow me?"

"Marc dear, I absolutely never thought about that, what was I thinking, or not thinking, as the case may be?"

"Don't beat yourself up Ma, it's simply not something that's on most people's minds in the beginning, but it certainly must be a priority for us."

"Yes bud, I do have to agree with you, sad as it is. So what do we do about it?"

"First Scoot, we only hire the best—the very best. Second, T-M picks up most, if not all—of the tab. Listen, I've given this a lot of thought. While I don't like it, it's necessary. I went so far as to include security in the plans for the new house anyway. Actually I have to credit Milton my architect; he put the whole issue of security in general, in my mind in the first place.

"Jesus Marc, all of this security talk is really depressing me amigo."

"I know Scoot, but ask yourself how much you love Embeth, Halley, and Beth—then answer this question—is it worth it?"

"Yeah, I guess I see your point. So are you going to have guards on site then, at your new compound?"

"Scoot, does Beth get speeding tickets in her Cobra whiles she's driving towards LA?"

"All right, you two knock it off already—this whole conversation is upsetting me as well."

"Sorry mom, but it's absolutely necessary."

"I'm sure you're right honey, I do understand your concern, so I agree . . . just don't go paranoid on me."

"Don't worry Mom, I won't, but you can never be too careful."

"True son, you can't. Okay boys, I think we're through for now; I'll fax these items to Jared in the morning. I've written them down, so we'll just see how he reacts to this first list."

"Good Mom, now let's get going, I need to grab the boys from school in ten minutes. Jesus where did this day go? Mom, if you don't need the Expedition any longer, you can just leave it here and go with me?"

"Sure, that would be fine Marc—as long as I get to drive your Navigator?"

"Christ Mom—I've created a monster! You know Ma, you're incorrigible, but yes—you can drive it, just keep it under eighty . . . will you?"

"Don't worry Marc, I won't embarrass you."

We drove over to the Meadows School where we arrived around a minute or so before the bell.

We saw the boys eventually, and they seemed particularly delighted that their Grammy was driving my truck for some odd reason. When the boys got inside, it was non-stop talking. Finally, they stopped long enough to allow me to interject myself into a change of conversation.

"So, how was the day fellas?"

"Great Dad."

"Is that all you can say about it Taylor?"

"Yes Grammy, it was great from start to finish."

"Trev, do you wish to add to your brother's lengthy comments?"

"Nah, he said it all Dad."

"Fine, excuse us for asking."

"Grammy; how come you're driving?"

"Because I enjoy driving Daddy's truck Taylor."

"Oh."

"So listen guys, there's some news on the horizon that concerns you, would you like to discuss it with us?"

"Well how can we discuss it Dad, if you don't tell us what it's all about?"

"That's true Trev, forgive me."

"It's alright Dad, we understand it's sometimes hard for old folks to remember things like that."

"Old—folks, Trev?"

"Yeah Dad, you know, people as old as you."

"Oh thank you for that son; you've simply made my whole day."

Both mom and the twins were cracking up now.

"You know Daddy; you are going to be thirty-three next week—aren't you?"

"Oh, so that's what this is all about . . . yes T-man—but I'd hardly call that old—just ask Grammy."

"And what is that—suppose to mean Marcus?"

"Nothing at all Ma, it's just you certainly can explain to the boys that thirty-three isn't old, now can't you?"

"You know Marc, you're right—but you're not too old for me to take a bar of soap to that mouth of yours either."

"You tell him Grammy."

"Alright you two, that will be enough."

"Gee Dad, we were only kidding around—can't you ever take a joke—in your old age?"

"Son, when you're my age, you'll realize that another birthday is anything but a joke, I can assure you."

"Okay Dad, we understand—it's a sensitive subject, right?"

"That's right T-man, so try to remember that, will you?"

"Sure Dad, by the by, am I speaking loud enough so you can hear me okay?"

"Cute Taylor—real cute."

We continued our drive home, when the boys finally realized I had never shared my news with them.

"Say Dad, so what was it that you wanted to tell us before?"

"You know Trevor—dang, I'm just so old, what with my ever-expanding dementia setting in, I can't say I remember anymore. Oh well, I guess it wasn't that important anyway."

"Dad!"

"Yes Trevor?"

"Come on; give it up—what's the news?"

"Gee, let's see, I know it had something to do with the both of you, that much I'm certain. Hum, let me think. Ah—no, that wasn't it. Maybe it had something to do with your careers? Wait a minute; I think something might be coming through my senility even at my advanced old age here. Yep, here it comes, almost there . . . damn—I lost it! Jeeze, I'm real sorry guys, but I guess you'll just have to find someone else to ask. I'm simply too old to remember apparently . . . forgive me?"

"Dad! God Tay, sometimes he makes me so dang mad the way he waffles on."

"Yeah Trev, he can be a real poop sometimes, you're right."

"Markie, I think I can recall what it was, so should I tell the boys then?"

"Why certainly Mother, if they'll let you out of the 'home' long enough yourself?"

"Thank you Marcus—that was so very rich. Boys, what your father can't seem to remember, is that next Wednesday, we're having a guest for dinner at the house. It's with the gentleman from Toon Media you guys met during your test there, you remember . . . Jared?"

"Oh yeah, how could we ever forget him, so that's it. Hey Tay, I guess this means that they liked us though?"

"Don't know, but I thought that was clear by what Stacy said to us Trev."

"Yeah, I guess you're right bro."

"Of course I am Trevor, I'm not only the smarter of us two, but I'm the sensitive one . . . remember?" Taylor announced to his brother.

"Yeah bro—right!" Trevor responded back quite lividly.

"Listen Dad, for your birthday, Tay and I want to take you for dinner at the Summerlin restaurant, okay?"

"Gee, I don't know T-1; maybe we had better call my doctor first. We need to find out if it's safe for me to be out in the cold night air and all."

"Daddy we get the bloody point, so give it a rest, will you please?" Mom and I were laughing big time at this crack.

"So what's this dinner with Jared all about Dad?"

"Dinner, Trev—what dinner is that honey?"

"Dad!"

"Okay, rest your horses. The meeting T-1, is to see what else Toon Media has to offer you two. I don't want you two to get too excited yet, because nothing is signed, but it's an exceptional package already."

"Like what Daddy? Aren't all the record companies about the same in what they offer blokes like us?"

"Yes son—all the record companies are, but not Toon Media, T-man. They want to give you guys the 'Full Monty' with your own weekly show on the telly for starters. And there would be full feature movies too, plus recording naturally."

"Oh my God, bloody hell—us on the telly with our own show?"

"Yep, plus the movies, sport."

"Wow, now that's what I call an offer, what do you think Tre?"

"Dang, sign me up Tay, that's what I say . . . blimey us on the screen at the Cinema."

"So should we assume you guys are interested then?"

"Have you gone crackers Dad—yes, we're interested."

CHAPTER Five

▼

SIGN ON THE DOTTED LINE, SON . . .

The time for our meeting with Jared, passed about as fast as it takes a bottle of Heinz Ketchup to make that first plop—to drip out onto your burger. Everyone, and I mean everyone, was on edge as that Wednesday afternoon appointment neared. We had an active week along with an enjoyable weekend, but nothing seemed to make Wednesday get there any faster.

Mom and Scoot had sent three lists back and forth between themselves and Jared. To his credit, Jared never flinched at anything. He agreed to most everything on the lists up to that point. This included confirming a new recording label . . . he agreed it was a necessity. He also okayed the security measures, along with a secure, secluded home in the Hollywood Hills for when the boys were working in LA, or desired at any other time. They also offered the use of the founders' apartment inside Toonland on Americana Avenue whenever available. The boys would enjoy a horde of staff, handling everything from their publicity to administrative duties, the tutors, almost everything.

At this point, the meeting was soon to be about the weather, because there wasn't going to be much of anything left for the parties to discuss . . . or so I thought at the time.

The boys-to their credit, tried to act as if nothing special was going on either. They kept up with their homework, rehearsed a lot, and had friends over. Of course that included Larry, who was selling his autograph inside the boys' issue of Teen Pop, for a cool five bucks a pop at his school.

Our clan also had a wonderful time at the twins encounter ice cream social, with a visit to our friends' house, the Scotts afterwards.

As for me, I chose to do something novel—I got back to running my business! When Wednesday finally showed itself, we were all anxious, but the boys were almost afraid to leave the house for school, just in case Jared showed up early. When I picked them up right at 3:10, they apparently planned to remain silent the whole ride home if I didn't intervene . . . so I did.

"So are you two ready, you're awfully quiet back there?"

"Don't know Dad, we're nervous, what if something goes wrong?"

"T-man, I can assure you, we're all far too along for anything major to go wrong at this point. Trust me son, so far—so good."

"Okay Dad, but if your wrong, your birthday dinner is canceled for Friday."

"Fine son, I haven't heard back from my doctor yet anyway."

"Dad stop it, this is no time for jokes."

"Yes T-1, I'll try to remember that."

"Thank you Dad."

"My, aren't we all just a little bit testy today?"

"Dad cool it, we're nervous."

"Hey guys just relax . . . look, there is really nothing to be nervous about, either we strike the deal with them, or we don't. There are other major opportunities on the table boys, believe me, we're not exactly in a bad situation here."

"Yeah, but not one like this Dad. Bloody hell, what did Grammy say they wanted us to do in that show for the telly?"

"Trev, you two play singing brothers, who perform regularly at Toonland, but during your off-time, you also just happen to be great amateur sleuths, you know, detectives?"

"So what exactly do we do as detectives, Dad?"

"Taylor, I'm going to go way out on a limb here son. I'll guess that you two have to solve some mystery or maybe even a crime during each episode."

"Wow, that sounds so cool, but we don't know anything about solving mysteries or crimes—were only eleven Dad?"

"Trust me Trev; I know you're eleven—but anything's possible in twenty-two minutes on network TV, believe me son!"

"All right Dad, if you say so, but I'm not sure about any of this."

"Don't sweat it Trev, everything will be spelled out to you two when the time comes, fair enough?"

"Yeah, I guess so."

We pulled into our driveway where a regulation-issue rental car was parked next to our house—Jared was already there apparently!

The three of us walked into the house quickly, to find Mom speaking to Scoot and Jared in the foyer. Apparently, by the pleasantries being exchanged at that moment, Jared had only arrived moments earlier himself.

Both Mom and Scooter had spent so much time on the telephone with Jared over the previous week; that they were pretty much convinced of his sincerity now, so the greetings going on in front of us, were genuinely warm.

We all quickly finished our greetings to one another, as Jared handed the boys two identical giant bags. He wasn't kidding when he said that there would be 'goodies'. The boys were excited, yet a little leery of some relative stranger bringing gifts for no reason. They politely thanked him, sat the bags down, and summarily ignored them; after all, they had bigger concerns now. I think Jared was a little taken aback, but he kept his thoughts to himself—smart man. Walking into the great room, Reg offered drinks all around. Mom had two bottles of her Special Reserve Cab already corked and breathing—naturally Jared couldn't refuse her offer. I purposely abstained for the moment, by requesting cranberry juice . . . Scoot did the same. Mom went for broke with the Cabernet, but only half a glass.

Jared took a moment to look around at the portion of the house within his view including a panorama of the lagoon outdoors.

"Wow Marc, I'd say you certainly aren't missing living in Southern California, are you?"

"No Jared, I love living in Las Vegas for many reasons, most of all—I love the weather. After that, I'd say the friendliness and community pride of its people. After all, they've been extremely good to me Jared."

"Yes, but it must have been tough competing with all the hotels in your business' infancy?"

"Brutal Jared—I mean really brutal. We were giving out two-for-one coupons, doing live remotes on radio, you name it—but nothing helped much.

"Then a funny, yet fateful thing happened. One of our smallest community papers with a well-respected food critic, had dinner at our restaurant one evening. Fortunately for me, he brought his grandchildren along, having heard about our theme. When he wasn't able to get his grandkids to budge in leaving the place after nearly three hours, he figured I had something, so he wrote as much. His observations, along with glowing praise for the quality of the food, entertainment value, and service, did the trick. Within a month, our reservations were six weeks out on the weekends . . . the rest is history, literally."

"Now you see Marc, thank you; you're doing a nice job of supporting my next point that I would like to put forward" . . .

. . . "That would be what, Jared?"

"Marilyn, its simple really, Marc benefited from being promoted, in his case by a respected food critic. In the case of the boys, we would like to take that effort to an unheard of level.

"Look folks, we all know how talented they are, and let's face it, they're darn handsome too. Honestly, they don't really need that much of a push. Yet that fact won't stop us from promoting the heck out of them across the full spectrum . . . and I do mean that."

"What does that entail exactly, why don't you run it down for the boys Jared?" I asked.

"Sure Marc I'd be glad too, boys it means it comes through all the elements of our organization, all of our networks and companies. Let me give you an example.

"We are going to have you do some concerts in both California and Asheville, then eventually—all of our parks worldwide. This lays the groundwork for what you do on the TV series as well, so there are two levels alone. Next, let's discuss our promotion team at your new record label. They will be promoting your music full time to the various radio stations and DJ's with one special single cut. We're going to offer that one cut as merely a 'tease' to pique everyone's interest, while building some additional excitement. Scott has requested this promotion be to the top 40 stations—not the under eighteen formats.

"And simultaneous to this, boys, we'll be promoting you with a special DVD introduction to the trade and press.

"Naturally, this will take place while you're still in the studio with Scott recording the remainder of your first CD. Please don't confuse our CD for your father's foundation's effort; they are two distinctly different projects boys.

"Next, our broadcast network will promote your TV series, while cable will do in-depth features on your music. Finally, our publicity department in Los Angeles will be arranging a major media blitz tying it all together.

"We call this a synergistic approach friends. With it, I can assure all of you that within eight weeks of inking our final agreement, you will all be impressed. There will be less than one in five homes in this country that 'haven't' heard of you two!"

"My God Jared, this is all a little overwhelming, must we put on such a push? I'd like the boys to grow into all of this like we discussed, not have it forced-fed down their throats."

"Marilyn, remember you're in the driver's seat, you'll be the one driving this humongous effort, so don't sweat it. I'm merely explaining to the boys what's available . . . I'm certainly not dictating terms. And I must say, that those concerns have really made me respect all of you so much more, along with the boys' motives of course."

"Thank you Jared, that's most kind of you to say. The rest of your answer also makes me feel much better too. As long as this 'Marilyn rules' philosophy prevails down your organizational chart with the people below you, I'll relax some too?"

"Don't worry Marilyn, it does, as I've already seen to that, believe me."

"Good, why don't we start with the issues we have left on the table, then we'll all see if this marriage makes sense?"

"That's music to my ears Marilyn, so are you ready for our tango then?"

"Yes Jared, but perhaps I'd better find my long stem rose first. I know you'll likely want to rip it from my teeth later on."

"Now Marilyn I'm surprised at you, I thought we were friends now?"

"Oh—we are Jared. I just want to remind you again, that I'm still one tough old lady looking out for my boys. You know, my sweetness will wither faster than wine to vinegar, at the first hint of something that even smells like a skunk heading our way."

"Fine—I can respect that Marilyn, I believe you'll find me most sensitive to your concerns . . . so let's turn on the music, shall we?"

"Sure".

We moved over to the game table, where all of us sat down around the boys. I was glad to see that Jared not only encouraged their participation, he insisted on it. He went so far as to suggest that the boys take notes too, or to stop any of us anytime something was confusing or otherwise concerned them.

Jared was making some serious brownie points with me on this score alone at that moment—likely with Mom and Scoot too! It wasn't patronizing, Jared was trying to educate them, or maybe mentor would be a better word . . . walking them through the steps. Only once Jared believed the boys to be fully engaged and aware, did he commence.

"Okay gang, here's the situation as I see it. There really aren't many issues laying any distance between us, but a few. I'm going to be honest enough to admit to you all that we need to listen to each other. Each side of any issue must be discussed openly, to see where some common ground can be found. From my experience, that's the only way we'll come to any agreement on them, does that seem fair?"

We all agreed with Jared's observation.

"Great; because first on the list is a biggie! You have requested a total annual schedule of no more than thirty weeks—the studio feels they need forty. Let me give you their 'spin' on the issue first . . . then you give me yours.

"The studio recognizes the need for the boys to have a life outside of entertainment, and for normal healthy development. After all, we are a family-oriented network that has always demonstrated strong family values.

"The studio sees the forty-week schedule as providing one full month off for the boys within every four months. They believe that to be quite reasonable, as they guarantee to keep to that schedule.

"Their rationale on forty is simply that thirty weeks doesn't allow us to produce product for all our media. We were hoping to keep all of the twins' options open to pursue, so this is our position for your consideration. Who wants to respond to this point first?"

"I will Jared, as their father I'm quite sensitive about this issue. It falls on me to make sure they get to enjoy their normal childhood activities . . . actually, I insist on that. We will not allow their friendships, sports, and outside interests to suffer because of any of this. That's not to say that there won't be some adjustments, of course there will. Missing birthday parties or sleepovers will have to be tolerated, but can be lessened by taking that friend along for a weekend concert instead.

"I do concede your point however, of always producing quality work, which is important to us too after all. Therefore, if everyone in our group agrees, I'm open to a compromise of thirty-six weeks. Boys—what say you?"

"Trev, what do you think bro?"

"Don't know Tay, I really can't see it making that much of a difference—heck we practice nearly everyday, anyway. What's it matter if we're playing for an audience somewhere . . . it's more fun than practicing anyways? But I do think it would be more fun for us to have two full months off during the summer. I want lots of time to be with our mates while they're on break too. I think we would like this way better than Jared's."

"Yeah, I like that idea Trev, you're right, that would be more fun. Could we do it this way instead Jared?"

"Sure guys, I don't see why not. Summer is always a bit long on down time in TV and film, so I think that should work. Marilyn, you're certainly part of this decision as well, so where do you sit?"

"Thank you Jared for including me. I'll be most happy to offer my opinion to you. I'll agree to the compromise against my better judgment, because the boys are fine with it."

"While were at it though, I think we should ask Scott his opinion. After all, as a working producer for years, he knows how tiring this all is on two growing kids—Scott?"

"Thanks Marilyn . . . you're right though, I do know how tiring this work is. The good news is I believe they can handle thirty-six weeks just fine. Even with their Bar Mitzvah next year, I think they're troopers. But I do have a concern, one that I'm not sure any of us have considered, you included Jared."

"What's that Scott?"

"Honestly Jared, are you sure you can shoot any film in a one hundred and twenty day window anymore? I mean I realize the boys just changed the breaks, but can it be done under either schedule, I know that my expertise are parades and stage shows, but come on, is it possible in today's higher tech world?"

"Yes Scott, I'm convinced it can. Besides, with what the boys' have just changed, affords us a longer production window when we need it. It just has to conclude with their normal break. By the way folks, T-M is speaking of five-day workweeks naturally. We're trying real hard to keep the boys from getting exhausted or tired, ourselves. Likewise, we don't want it affecting their relationships with friends and family or their schooling.

"I'm also able to say that their workday would never run over six hours on any given project. That leaves another four hours for strictly their schooling, with teachers of your choosing at studio expense as we started discussing last week."

"So Jared, are you confirming that assuming my husband was willing to do their Hebrew lessons with them, he could be compensated like a tutor or instructor?"

"Certainly Marilyn, at our daily rate of $240 per day plus his meals. But if he also chooses to act as their on-set chaperone simultaneously, that's another $160 per day."

"Alright, that's good to know. It gives Dad some other options outside of mucking stalls all day."

"So gang, have we come to a compromise on this issue?"

We all agreed to the compromise, as Jared moved on to his next issue. Using the same discussion format, each issue went around for discussion, and then each issue concluded with successful compromises. Less than an hour later, Tay 'n' Tre Morgan, through their representatives, officially agreed to sign a letter of intent to form a Joint Venture with Toon Media for the new label, along with a multi-media deal with the studios. Everyone was excited right on down to Sofia now.

Jared took out the letter of intent to begin filling in the blanks on the sections that we had just negotiated. Afterwards, he signed his name before handing it off to Mom, which was a nice touch to respect her position as manager.

Mom read it thoroughly, noting the section that spelled out the agreement was contingent upon our attorney's review or revision. Satisfied with everything there, she signed her name. She then passed it on to the boys, who gave it the once over before signing it. From them, it went to me next, before finally going to Scoot. We both signed it below the boys' signatures and next to Mom's. Within five minutes, it was officially executed . . . just like that.

"Gang, I just want to add, I can't remember a more enjoyable negotiation with anyone . . . I mean that sincerely."

"Thank you Jared, while we certainly haven't done this before, we feel this was most enjoyable and amicable as well. Your comment of a win-win was certainly accurate. I personally want to thank you for all of your courtesies and sensitivity to the twins."

"Thank you Marilyn, I consider that a major compliment—so I mean every word of this—I dig your spunk."

"Thank you Jared, now that I really know you, I think you're pretty darn spunky yourself." Mom's crack wasn't lost on any of us, it was perfect and instantly acted as an agent to eliminate our pent up stress and anxiety over this now-concluded negotiation.

"Mom, Jared, enough with the mutual love fest, let's crack open a bottle of Champagne to toast this great Mitzvah."

"Hey I know that word Marc, it means a great celebratory event."

At that moment I was on a natural high as I affirmed Jared's comment.

We eventually returned to the great room to relax over our drinks. Meanwhile I had Reg crack open a bottle of Cristal as well as some sparkling cider for the boys, so that we could all toast. Jared asked to make the toast, which we happily acquiesced to his request.

Mom asked Jared to wait while she got Dad on the phone to give him the news. Once she returned to the room, Jared spoke.

"Friends, here's to the beginning of a long and mutually satisfying relationship between our two families—Trevor and Taylor and family, along with the Toon-Media organization—may it be long and fruitful for all."

We all raised our glasses to drink. Our negotiations had concluded so quickly that dinner wasn't even ready yet, so we had some nice casual conversation as we waited.

Jared and the twins were hitting it off well now, so they were having a ball with him. At Jared's prodding, they finally broke down to begin rummaging through their bags of T-M goodies.

"So guys have you and Scott come up with your first hit tune yet? You know that little teaser I mentioned before, as the special single to pique everyone's interest?"

"Yes they have Jared. I believe everyone's going to go nuts over it, if I do say so myself."

"That's great Scott, can you enlighten me, or is it still a trade secret at this point?"

"Not at all Jared, we'd be delighted to share it with you, it's 'My Prayer'."

"Hey that is a great tune for this situation. I seem to recall that the Platters were the last group to have a mega hit with that one . . . right?"

"Yes Jared, but lots of artists have covered it successfully over the last sixty years. The boys though, do it quite uniquely.

"Great. I remember the tune well, so hopefully you'll honor me with your version in the near future guys?"

"Sure Jared anytime—now's okay too."

"Boys, I'd love to hear it now, but I didn't mean to imply you needed to do it today. We're celebrating; I don't want you to go through all the bother now—so just relax; we're about to eat dinner anyway."

"We don't mind Jared; we just finished recording our backgrounds Monday, so we'd like everyone's opinion on that anyway."

"Alright boys—I'm honored then, but tell me, what makes your version so unique Taylor?"

"Well Jared, we sing it entirely a Capella, just like a street corner group would. The Platters do the introduction a Capella, but then switch to instrument tracks."

"Wow—entirely a Capella, now that I cannot wait to hear . . . but isn't it hard to do an entire song like that, without a music tract to follow?"

"Sure Jared, it is. We have to close our eyes to stay on key, what with the harmony, but it's wonderful. It's such an awesome ballad Jared, that we love doing it especially because it's our Gramps' favorite song too."

"Jared, if you'd like, since we have a few minutes before dinner, why don't I go to ready the studio so you can give us your expert opinion. We feel it's your one cut 'teaser,' but more so, a great closer for the boys' performances—Marilyn has it staged incredibly."

"Listen Scott, if no one really minds going through all this bother, I honestly would be thrilled to hear it."

"Okay Uncle Scott, please set it up and we'll be there in a minute." Trevor added.

Scoot left while we talked a little more, but mere minutes later he returned to tell us he had everything ready.

We made our way into the boys' rehearsal studio, where Jared too, got a laugh over the mess. The boys meanwhile, took their place behind their mics, as Scoot kicked on the sound system for the backup vocals.

Once all the doo-wop had kicked in, the boys immediately closed their eyes to begin joining in.

Using our singers from unit #1, turned out to be a simply marvelous solution, as they really put their all into it.

Jared stood there transfixed, with his arms crossed while listening intently to the combined live and recorded vocal tracks. Every once in a while, he would just shake his head in sort of disbelief I think. I assumed over the fact that he was really listening to two eleven-year-old vocalists, but maybe it was something else.

When the tune was over, Jared along with the rest of us, clapped enthusiastically. You could tell Jared was choosing his words before speaking this time around.

"Guys, I simply don't know what to say to you both. I'm being sincere when I say this: That was simply perfect—but beautiful too. Honestly, I can't find better words to convey the song's power or its emotion in the way you guys do it. That is most definitely your first hit. Perhaps it should be your cover tract as well. Scott, you're absolutely right on for choosing it."

"Thanks Jared, I thought so too, the moment I heard them do it the first time."

Scoot then went on to explain how they surprised Dad with it while on the lake.

"Wow guys, that's quite some surprise. Congratulations though, because My Prayer will definitely be your first million seller on the pop charts. Mark my words; I'm never wrong with a prediction on a tune . . . you're looking at triple platinum on that track."

"Do you really think so Jared?"

"Yes Trevor, of course. I'm absolutely sure of my prediction proving itself true."

"God, wouldn't that be wicked Tay?"

"Yeah bro . . . wicked."

We now all went into dinner in the dining room where we had a wonderful meal, and great conversation all around. By the time we walked Jared to the door, we had all made a lasting friendship with our former 'poster boy' adversary.

Mom asked him to wait at the door for a moment, before returning seconds later with Reg in tow. He was carrying a case of her 1996 Special Reserve Cab. Having Reg hand the sizable case over to him, she quipped to her new friend.

"Now Jared, you know what this costs, so I expect some of it to survive your plane trip home?"

We laughed as Jared surprised us by simply kissing mom on the cheek without as much as a word. He then mouthed to her 'thanks Marilyn' without speaking.

Now it was my turn.

"Jared don't forget you've now won our little wager, so ten pounds of our pure Kona coffee will be delivered to your office on Friday morning, I hope you enjoy it my friend."

"Marc, that's most considerate of you to remember our wager, I'll truly look forward to that package arriving too. And along with enjoying this truly superb Cabernet from Marilyn and your Father, please thank him for me, will you?"

"I'll be delighted Jared, have a safe trip home."

"Thank you all again, and welcome boys, to the finest family in entertainment."

After Jared left, our entire group screamed, yelled, kissed, and hugged each other for around a minute. Mom immediately called back home to Dad again, while the boys called Larry along with some of their other friends. I had quite a list myself, while of course, Scoot called Beth. There was not an unused phone, computer, or cell in the house at that moment.

The boys emailed every one of their mates back home. Trevor sent a lengthy one to Toby who was still staffing his tent, but apparently was also having another surgery in the morning, our time.

Before we all knew it, it was nine o'clock, so I sent the boys up for their evening soak, followed by bed. When they were through with their bath, I went in to sing a couple of songs with them. This was amazingly something we all never seemed to tire of, but first, we talked at length.

"Guys, I'm just so proud of you, of how you handled yourselves tonight, really I am. You have both grown up so much in these last few months. And see, I told you this would work out—didn't I? I guess the only real surprise was how much we all enjoyed Jared's company—wasn't it?"

"Yeah Dad, God, I really liked him tonight I can tell he only wants the best for us too. But Daddy, we know that you feel the same way. You were really good tonight—for an old man, I mean."

"Gee, thank you T-man, I so appreciate that."

"Yeah Dad, we can't thank you enough for supporting us in this whole thing. We'll always try to make you and Mummy proud of us, okay?"

"Don't worry Trev, speaking for Mummy and me; no parents could ever be prouder of their sons honestly. I bet Mummy, Grandfather, and Grandmother are having a major party up in heaven right now, want to bet?"

"I hope so, but we're going to have our own real party Friday night for you, so don't feel left out."

"Oh believe me boys, I won't. This will be the first birthday party that's being thrown by my own sons; so it's a most precious gift indeed, boys."

"We understand Dad, but we can't wait for our birthday either, because it'll be our first from you too."

"Yes I know Taylor—believe me, I can't wait either."

"Listen Dad, just so you're not upset Friday, we have a few surprises for you. If you don't like any of them, we apologize now."

"Oh honey, don't worry, I'm sure whatever you two have cooked up will be fine, so don't fret over it. I'm a big boy, so I know anything you two do, will be in fun or out of your love for me."

"Cool Dad, that's what we were hoping you'd say."

We sang our tunes together, before I left them to dream pleasant thoughts about their futures.

The following two days leading up to my birthday, were hectic for my sons. Whatever they had cooked up, it apparently was involved enough that clandestine conversations ensued from Thursday morning on through Friday. Between the boys, Mom, Grace, and Sofia, there was no shortage of secret conversations going on at any time . . . day or night! Reg apparently was assigned to keep me occupied or otherwise unawares. Mind you, it wasn't a surprise party, so I never did figure out why they were all so hush, hush. But I was not going to spoil all their fun planning it anyway. I was so enjoying watching them having their fun plotting away.

Friday evening was upon us. We all loaded into Laverne for the ride over to our Flamingo unit, which the boys had decided to switch to for some reason. When we arrived there, my first pleasure of the evening awaited me—naturally it was Dad. He was all smiles and gave me a warm hug and kiss, which I returned happily.

Next I was greeted by everyone close to me personally and professionally, before then freezing in mid step. Walking over to me now, was my dearest and oldest friend, Gary Stein from LA, along with his wife Debbie and son Jeremy. We had a wonderfully warm reunion. The boys and Jeremy instantly became fast friends as they all shared a love of soccer for one thing.

When we were escorted onto the terrace, all of our corporate employees along with their spouses, stood up to warmly greet me with applause.

Of course, the party would not be complete without Larry, who was also there—with Carol, who looked stunning. At that moment, I heard a microphone test, where I turned to see Robbie ready to address the crowd.

"Good evening everyone, for those of you that do not know me, I'm Robbie O'Hara, Marc's personal assistant—and man servant. I'm actually the man behind the curtain, responsible for running Verandas on a daily basis . . . despite what Marc says."

This was greeted by loud laughter from my employees.

"Tonight dear friends, we honor what some have come to call—the world's oldest 'little practical joker'—a true master we're told. A man who's never lost sight of his inner child, because that kid—is a real pain in everyone's ass!" The audience howled as more laughter ensued.

"Now for those of you unfamiliar with Marc's propensity towards pulling gags, tonight you will meet—the very few survivors. They will all share their close calls because Marcus Morgan—this is your night . . . as the world's best practical joker!" As everyone applauded.

From some area out of view, I immediately heard Gracie's voice over a microphone.

"When I first met Marcus back in England, I thought to myself, what a dear sweet young man. A good heart, wonderful manners—blimey . . . what was I thinking?

"Marc, I am sure you will recall the first 'gag' you pulled on me. You remember don't you love? You switched the contents of my baking powder and baking soda canisters in my kitchen. Thanks to you; I had a loaf of bread completely fill the oven—before it blew up!" Everyone was laughing at the hysterical story.

"Yes Marc, it's the other woman in your life, here's your closest soul mate in practical joke making, your cook and compadre, Mrs. Grace Jones." Gracie came out to give me a big kiss, while she also got a nice hand from the audience now."

The roast on my gags continued with all my victims reliving their own harrowing tales, right on down the line. Suzie shared her story of the Parachute gag. The boys told of the food fight, while displaying Reg's photos of me—those especially, depicting me in a bad light, all blown up. Scoot and Beth concluded the roast from the week before in the Jaguar. By the time Robbie finished the skit, there wasn't a person in the room left that had not been cracking up. Particularly with the last segment coming from Scoot with yet another retelling of the canoe race and port-a-potty stories.

"Now Marc, come on up here. All of your friends here at the 'receiving' end of your gags, would like to present you with a—hum, gift. It's a special token of their appreciation."

Everyone gave me an ovation as I walked up from the dais to Robbie at the rostrum. He brought out a large gift-wrapped box as I made jokes with the assembled group of co-workers, family, and friends. Finally free of the wrapping paper, I opened the box where I looked upon my gift—as I laughed myself to tears. It was a sculpture of my face protruding out of a donkey's ass whereby everyone went nuts . . . sadly, the resemblance was remarkable!

"Thank you everyone. I cannot begin to tell you, how touched I am with all of you being here to honor me like this. And most importantly for this, ah—unbelievable gift. I'm sure that I will treasure it always. Matter of fact, I'm thinking of—burying it for safekeeping tonight in my backyard—under the foundation at a minimum."

"Marc, I'm going to turn the microphone over to two special young gentlemen now . . . but for any of you that perhaps haven't heard the fantastic news yet out of their proud papa; please welcome the two newest recording stars at Toon Media Records and Entertainment under their own new recording label! Here are my nephews to say a few words, Tre, Tay, please come up here." They quickly walked up to excited applause.

Trevor grabbed the mic from Robbie as he greeted our guests.

"Thank you Uncle Robbie, you did such a great job, don't you think so everyone?"

Everyone applauded Robbie as he sat back down in his seat.

"Ladies and Gentlemen, and all our friends here, Tay, and I would like to thank you all for being here. You being here helps us show Dad, how much we all love him, even when he can be a real pain in the bloody old bum!"

"Tre, don't say that about Dad today . . . not on his birthday bro, God, don't you know that's not nice? You should wait until tomorrow for that . . . today you just gotta lie!"

Larry of course, smirked and grunted at the crack.

"Sorry Tay, oh yeah I forgot. Well anyway, we have a couple of gifts for you Dad—good ones too. There would have been one more, but that didn't work out, so this first one, we thought was perfect for you since you're so ol . . . mature, now. See how its done Tre?" As the audience laughed, Trevor nodded to his brother . . . quite comically.

Meanwhile, through the continuing howls, Taylor now handed me a large wrapped box.

"Go ahead Dad, try to open it . . . show us all how strong you still are." Trevor yelled out now, as Taylor threw him a mock dirty look. Everyone busted up again.

"Watch it boys, I'm very sensitive in my old age, besides, I don't know how much more I can take of this in one night?" At least I was getting a chuckle or two with that.

I began opening the box. My laughter commenced about three-fourths the way through the wrapping paper. It was one of those tennis ball-footed walkers that some older folks use. When I opened up the legs it was the typical walker except this one had some interesting accessories. There was a bicycle headlight and flashing taillights, along with a bumper sticker that read: WARNING: I brake at all Verandas. This was going to look great in my office's decor; it was truly 'me'. The audience went nuts as I held it up so everyone could get a good look at it.

"Boys, I get the real impression that someday, I just might be surpassed in the gag department by you two?"

"Why Dad—whatever do you mean?" Came out of Trevor with an added giggle. Taylor then spoke.

"Daddy, this next gift is kind of serious, so please open this one next."

Taylor then handed me another flat wrapped package, which my intuition told me it was likely a picture frame. I tore off the wrapping to find a beautiful new professional oil enhanced photograph of the boys in their Sunday best, posed next to the lagoon.

As their proud father, I continued to stare at it before finally realizing that no one else could see it. So I turned it out to face the room, where everyone gave affirmative nods, oohs, aahs . . . and the like. I put the photo down as I grabbed the boys into a deep twin-hug, to the accompaniment of our guests' applause. Trevor now spoke:

"Grammy, Gramps, it's time for you two to come up here."

My parents got up, and walked up to us with a nice round of applause from our guests. Once there, Dad went behind the table, where he brought out yet another flat wrapped package, but this one was huge. It looked to be about three, by five, feet.

"Son; this one is from the entire family including Sofia, Grace, and Reg."

Dad then handed me the gift. As I unwrapped it, I all but totally lost it. It was a magnificent oil portrait of Miranda and me. While it had to have been done from a photograph, I don't believe I'd ever seen the photograph itself. I did recognize our attire however; I remembered the affair it was from instantly.

Miranda had thrown one of her many galas for her foundations' benefit. Miranda had this particular gown designed in Paris. It was truly stunning, so it instantly became my favorite gown of hers. Looking at the portrait now, it captured all her beauty and our deep love for one another in our pose. I was overwhelmed, so I couldn't say too much at that moment. I barely got out:

"I will treasure this always, thank you all, from the bottom of my heart."

I then held it up for everyone on the terrace to see, as everyone applauded while I attempted to compose myself.

We then had a marvelous dinner, while our wait staff entertained us, along with a quartet of meandering violinists. The beautiful flowers and centerpieces adorning the tented in terrace made a wonderful setting to accompany the dinner.

Then all at once, the room went dark as I heard our many singers crooning out happy birthday while a large cake was wheeled over to my table.

Everyone was singing and then the whole terrace of guests it seemed came up to congratulate me when it ended. Most of them peeked at the cake as well as the portraits—and the gag gifts.

The evening flew by, so before we knew it, we were making our way back home to the Trail.

Once home, I thanked everyone for all of their efforts . . . especially the boys, with plenty of kisses exchanged all around. I now excitedly got out my toolbox to hang both of my beautiful new portraits in my master suite. The boys' oil I hung next to my bed so that it should be the first thing I saw each morning upon waking. The big oil painting was far more challenging . . . I needed a huge space. Eventually I realized the logical spot was above the fireplace in my sitting area, so I moved the artwork already there, to hang this new treasured gift in its place.

As I finished hanging the portrait of Miranda and me, I soon found myself sitting on my sofa admiring her beautiful gown yet again. Jesus, she looked so damn beautiful that night, she just overwhelmed me with her beauty . . . and everyone else for that matter.

At that very moment, I now heard a very familiar voice coming from over my left shoulder:

"Your old lady was a bit of all right in that gown—wasn't she?"

At first, I couldn't believe what I was hearing at that moment, so I simply followed the sound to its source, over at the foot of my bed, almost dead-on center . . . pardon my pun.

Sitting there in the very same gown was Miranda! She appeared three dimensional, yet glowing in a warm lustrous light. She looked to be around twenty-four or five years of age . . . but damn if she didn't look more beautiful now. I couldn't help myself; I quickly walked over to sit down next to her. I then put out my left hand towards her cheek, but all I felt was a sort of cool energy force, almost somewhat like wind against my fingertips . . . but not!

"Hello love, and happy birthday . . . what do you think of your present?"

Naturally I wanted to kiss her, but already knew that wasn't going to feel any more real than my fingertips had. So instead, I spoke excitedly:

"Baby, I can't believe this, how is this happening—but thank you?"

"Honey, we don't have a lot of time here, it might surprise you to know that what I'm doing right now, requires a lot of energy to be expended for me to be sitting next to you like this."

"I understand babe, so how are you doing?"

"Love, I'm wonderful, but naturally I miss the closeness of you and the boys, so today was something special. We can both thank Mummy and Daddy for their contributions too."

"Sure baby, please thank them for me, will you?"

"Of course I will Marc, but I want to tell you something else, far more important to me at the moment."

"What honey . . . what's wrong?"

"No love, nothing is wrong. I just wanted you to know that you are doing such an incredible job with the boys that we're all so very proud of you . . . so I just wanted to thank you of course."

"Please baby, these two will practically raise themselves . . . honestly they're growing up so damn fast already. They are my greatest joy honey, so as I've said before, I have you to thank for them everyday, truly I do baby."

"Thank you sweetheart, but look, things are looking pretty interesting for their future, so stay on your toes love."

"Alright, I can do that, anything else you care to share with me?"

"Cute Marcus, I can see your old curiosity is still ever-present."

"Honestly honey—can you blame me? I mean, I'm sitting here talking to a dead lady . . . but one—who never look prettier, I might add."

"Okay Marcus, look my time's nearly up, so please think about these two things before I leave you my love. First, keep your eyes on the boys over the ensuing months, nothing necessarily critical to worry about here, just be mindful. Remember, not everyone out there has innocent intentions concerning our sons. Secondly, keep your own eyes open to new relationships, as you need to find love again yourself . . . really sweetheart . . . it's time".

"Okay baby, I'll try, but look I'm still in love with you."

"Yes sweetheart of course you are, but I'm dead Marc, and you won't be with me again for over sixty years, so I truly want you to move on. One of the greatest lessons you learn here, is that we don't have just one soul mate love—we have many. So you can love me, but continue to look for her . . . understand?"

"That makes sense babe, so I'll try, if that's what you really want, alright?"

"Yes love . . . that's what I want for you. Look sweetheart, I have to fly now so please tell Grace hello for me. I realize you're still careful with the boys, but do let them know always, how proud I am of them and love them . . . alright?"

She began fading now, but somehow, I was resigned to it even though I felt differently naturally . . . damn this was so weird.

"Sure baby", Was all I could get out now, before she quickly disappeared.

Afterwards, I sat there reliving the entire event several times in my mind, being mindful of not only her serious concerns, but all of the other little sound bytes too, it was all so unbelievable really. I knew in an instant that her reference to multiple soul mates was to assuage my fear that somehow I would have to choose only one—someday, which I had shared with her on her deathbed. And of course, she went out of her way to make a point that I would live at least another sixty years, thereby assuaging my own issues of mortality as a single parent, raising two young sons alone, who were still traumatized over two very close deaths in their recent pasts.

The rest of my weekend was by comparison to Miranda's visit—reasonably uneventful. I shared the whole conversation with Gracie of course, but she thought it was all so very special of a birthday present . . . and I had to agree . . . thank you again baby.

Larry of course was with us, having deserted his mother to stay with the boys. Susan Geary had been kind enough to drop off Becky on Saturday. Becky simply reveled in the attention the boys showered upon her each time she came over . . . she ate it up. She also helped the boys with picking out possible songs for their CD, well into the afternoon.

The four friends went back into the boys' studio where they continued their search for songs that they liked.

When Rick Geary picked Becky up at six, none of them were too happy, but there wasn't any wiggle room. The boys then presented her with a wonderful autographed framed picture which they had made for her, so we couldn't get her to stop crying for any length of time, the rest of the time she was with us. Only after she left, did I then notice some very moist eyes on both of my boys' faces.

Meanwhile, apparently Larry wanted to sleep over again, as he gingerly approached Mom directly to ask her, knowing she was the easier 'touch' on this subject . . . but I overheard all of it anyway.

"Grammy, may I please sleep over again?"

"Yeah Grammy can he?" The boys added.

"Fine boys, you may all have a ball as far as I'm concerned, because your Father will be watching you three, not me!"

"How come Grammy, where are you going?"

"Gramps and I are going to the Strip tonight to see Johnny Mathis, that's where."

"Oh, well have fun" came out of Taylor.

So the trio of boys had a calm Saturday evening with TV along with the Playstation but turned in at midnight . . . per my threats!

Sunday morning flew by, with all the boys first in Sunday school, but then at Larry's for the day. This was a nice change, yet reminiscent too—it was quiet at Euro-Morganland for a change.

When the boys were ready to come home at six—not, I picked them up where they wasted little time in beginning to work me over. In a weaken state of mind, I agreed to fast food for dinner—oh why did I ever agree to do that?

Chapter Six

▼

It's—Showtime!

The following week flew by for me at the office, but I was on vacation compared to the twins. The boys went through all of their school week, followed by rehearsals, recording instrument and vocal tracks into Taylor's new keyboard . . . then more practice right up to bedtime . . . they had to be exhausted, but they were also becoming super excited once our attorney had reviewed the letter of intent with only minor changes.

These changes concerned the income allocated to the boys' new foundations for proper tax treatment. In their final decision, they chose to put sixty percent of their earnings into their foundations. They were keeping forty percent for themselves, when I shared with them that they would personally never want for money.

I saw no reason to take it farther by telling them that their wealth topped ninety million dollars each. It was all in US dollars now, but more importantly; had amassed some steady growth already.

Once these contractual changes were made, Jared had the contract approved by Toon Media management before the final contract was prepared as well as reviewed by all the lawyers . . . I even had Eric look at it, just to be sure no one missed anything.

To commemorate the occasion of the signing, we were all invited down to Toonland, where it would be photographed and preserved for all time on video. Teddy Toon was to sign for the studio ceremoniously, with his gal; Bettie Swoons as witness. I thought that the entire idea, while farcical, was a cute touch. The guys especially liked the idea when I told them.

Mom insisted that Dad be there of course, so we flew him back into McCarran. Our entourage beyond the usual suspects included Bill, Larry, and the entire Davis clan along with Austin Scott. Austin had begged Taylor to go along, so I agreed.

With our largest plane Cedric, on a QA trip, Bill and I each flew one of our matching Lear 60's, which was appropriate enough anyway.

The boys would be performing four shows over the weekend. They had plenty of great material ready according to Mom so we were all excited by the time Friday rolled around.

As we were all loading onto our jets, Larry was continuing his training with the boys. Embeth and Halley were now requisitioned to serve as judges of how the material played over.

The adults flew with Bill, while I of course had the kids. With Austin in right seat, the whole flight consisted of Austin telling me how mad his Dad was going to be. There was Austin riding shot gun, laughing about Tom stuck at home riding around in a crowded van. He had fun though; he was such a great kid, so we had a blast in the cockpit. When I gave him the controls, he wanted to stop to call his father to make him jealous. He was disappointed that I wouldn't allow that, but he was a great sport to have along for the ride.

We landed our twin Lears at Long Beach Airport, but I had forgotten that Jared had arranged publicity with Stacy. As such, we were now directed to where we were to meet with a huge entourage of T-M management and staff including Teddy and Bettie. There was a small band playing, along with select press invited as well.

When the boys' departed the plane, we heard the sound of camera shutters clicking away. Teddy and Bettie walked up to hand each twin a golden key to Toonland while the photographers clicked away some more as everyone smiled. A short welcome followed with the Toon Media film crew there—catching everything including a very animated conversation with the boys giving Stacy kisses as they all hugged while talking away.

"So boys, are you glad to be back here at Toonland, but as family this time?"

"Yes Stacy, we can't wait, we even brought Larry back too so you wouldn't be lonely. But we also brought along our other mate Austin, in case Larry wears you out with his mouth."

"That's wonderful to hear boys, how considerate of you to think of me so thoughtfully . . . so where is 'my' Lawrence—I don't see him?"

"You're welcome Stacy, but I'm pretty sure Larry's hiding somewhere." Trevor replied.

Larry was conspicuously obscured somewhere—silently, apparently determined to keep his distance from Stacy's clutches . . . but where was he?

So as the boys introduced Austin to Stacy, we all began to make our way over to a large shuttle. Somehow, Larry was already ducked down in the last row of seats . . . what a macho man!

When we arrived at the Toonland Towers, we checked into our two, three-bedroom suites. Bill planned to leave for Laguna Nigel to visit old friends after that evening's performance, but on his return, he would bunk with me, along with the four boys. Mom and Dad, along with Grace and Reg, had their own three-bedroom suite, so we were all comfortable.

God bless Sofia. She selflessly opted to stay home as Suzie was moving into the guesthouse at that moment. She decided to help Suzie, so that Grace and Reg would make the trip. She knew Grace wanted to stay home, but the boys wouldn't have that, so she acquiesced, realizing the importance of it all, too.

As we were getting our own selves settled in, Stacy went over the performance agenda for the weekend. The boys would have their first performance right after ceremoniously signing a mock up of their exclusive contract with T-M. Tonight's festivities would begin at six pee on the Future World Quad, which was only an hour and forty minutes away. Saturday would incorporate two performances, the first at two, with another at eight. Sunday would be their last performance, again at two. We were free to leave anytime after that.

There would be a fair number of the press at their signing naturally, plus at their first Saturday performance. The entire staff of the boys' new recording label; 'Tornado,' would also be attending naturally. Other recording industry insiders and shakers would be there as well, particularly songwriters invited by the label. In short, it was going to be a circus of the first magnitude.

The entire afternoon performance on Saturday, would be filmed for the T-M Channel for music videos, as well as, in-depth introductory specials.

To say that the boys were excited—would be an understatement. With more new costuming supplied by Mom, along with the all-new instrument tracks prerecorded under Scoot's supervision, they were—ready! And according to the twins, they had dozens of good jokes from Larry to use, along with a few surprises as well. We knew better than to question what these revelations might be, beyond a quick warning to Larry that everything had to be in good taste.

Our entourage left the Towers right at 5 pm, to head over to Future World via the Transporter. We then went underground into the Quad, where the boys were taken right into a make up room. Afterwards, the boys and Scoot did all their sound checks before firing up the keyboards.

Taylor's new synthesizer was a highly evolved instrument over its predecessor, so it necessitated either transferring the existing tracks, or recording new ones. Taylor being the perfectionist that he was, spent much of the prior week recording, as he chose the latter with Scoot's help. That being the case, their tracts for each instrument or effect were now laid down individually, along with all their various back up vocals and harmonies. As a result, Scooter believed their sound was going to be far fuller than ever before—purer too.

Poor Taylor had already spent the entire week prior to this last one, getting himself acclimated on this new miracle of music and science, before ever recording a single note of music. This new Korg was far more computer than just instrument, it was all too daunting a task to my way of thinking, but Taylor seemed jazzed by the challenges it presented as he mastered it from a technical point of view . . . I was impressed with his talents as well as his prowess.

Meanwhile, Scoot had spent several hours on the phone with both lighting and sound techs the previous Wednesday. Those affects were going to be ideal for all the songs the boys would be doing in their fifty-minute sets. We were especially interested to see how well, My Prayer's and Still of the Night's lighting would go over. Mom was still shooting for a convincing street corner feel. Scooter assured both Mom and I that we would be thrilled . . . after all, we did trust him implicitly now as well.

It was now ten before six, as Teddy and Bettie just walked into the green room where we were all congregating. The kids of course, found this a big thrill, despite their 'too cool for that' ages.

Stacy advised us that Teddy and Bettie's voices would be voice-overs during the presentation, so she then explained what Teddy would say. While the boys just needed to follow Teddy's instructions over the PA system, they immediately convened a last minute meeting with Larry. Apparently they wanted some help on how to stage their responses to Teddy and Bettie.

Stacy joined in to help but was convinced everything would work out fine by their conclusion.

We now had two minutes left to give the guys our last minute hugs, break a leg's, love, and support.

"You two are going to go out there and make me so proud of you, I won't know what to do next!"

"Thanks Uncle Scott, we're ready and dying to get out there, don't know, but this is what we really love to do." Trevor offered.

"Don't worry Uncle Scott, that audience won't know what hit them . . . or the record people or press neither—like Grammy said last week—we're taking no prisoners.

This came from Taylor, before he asked:

"Daddy, did you remember the camera?"

"Yes T-man, I have it right here in my pocket with fresh batteries."

"Cool, take lots of pics okay; we'd like to know after, how we looked from out there in the audience."

"Don't worry T-man, I will, but remember there will be a film crew tomorrow as well. So are you two ready to blow their socks off again in this joint?"

"You know it Dad. Mummy will hear it all the way up in heaven too, we'll see to that."

"Good, now listen, you guys have lots of fun out there. Remember we're all proud of you two, right Mom, right Dad?"

"Yes we are boys; you two go out there and bag you some bear."

"What's that mean Gramps?"

"Trevor, that's another way of saying what Grammy says about prisoners—knock 'em dead."

"Oh . . . okay, we can do that, but according to Larry—we're not responsible for that."

We were all having a much-needed laugh for relief at that moment, with Trevor's remark perfectly fitting the bill, as I now commented.

"That's right boys you're not, but when you do knock 'em dead, believe me that audience will never forget you. But more importantly, nor the great time they had listening to you both, so go do it."

"Oh, we get it Dad, but don't worry, we'll bloody hell try."

"That's the spirit T-men, now we're going up top to our tables, so you two look for us. We'll be screaming and clapping the loudest, okay?"

"Okay Daddy, we will."

Our entourage gave the boys hugs along with assorted kisses, as we left the boys sitting on their stage. A stage we all hoped and prayed—they would shortly own!

We got topside to our reserved tables, where we found that the Quad was packed. Some people were just taking a meal break no doubt, without a care as to who would be entertaining them shortly. Other guests apparently read the promotional material handed out with their admission tickets that included lots of photos and excerpts from the Teen Pop article, so they made an informed decision . . . while still others knew exactly why they were there; as it was their job to sit there for one reason or another.

Within a couple of minutes, we were all holding our breath when the announcer came on.

"Ladies and gentlemen, boys and girls; Toonland is pleased to welcome, Teddy Toon and Bettie Swoons, for a very special presentation." There was an abundance of applause as the stage began to transform to the theme of Teddy's theme music.

"Hey Gang, it's me Teddy Toon, nice to see you all. And this cute little lady next to me is my long time gal—Bettie."

"Oh Teddy, you're so romantic." Bettie answered with a theatrical 'romantic' flair. The king of teddy bears then continued.

"We're here to share the story with you of two young men . . . these twin brothers standing behind us in fact. They're Tay 'n' Tre Morgan from Las Vegas—but they originally hail from outside London, England.

"This last fall, at the ripe old age of eleven, these two Brits entered our contest; Sing with the ToonCrooners. You know Bettie—they were brave to do that, don't you think?"

"Yes Teddy they were, but now that I've looked them over, top to bottom, they're pretty darn cute too. Land sakes—I'm getting pretty tired of waiting on you—Theodore!"

"Whoa there—girlfriend, let's remember who you've been dating without a ring for the last seventy-four years! Now let me get back to my story, we can fight about this later.

"You know folks; these two boys sung their hearts out that night, so it's not surprising that they were among the winners of that contest. Since then, they've returned to perform here at Toonland to a very appreciative audience, in fact Bettie—they brought the house down.

"Most recently, many of you have no doubt heard about their crusade to raise eight million dollars to build a state of the art residential center in Las Vegas for Cerebral Palsy clients, or read about them in Teen Pop magazine.

"Tonight though, marks their first full performance as the newest members of our big entertainment family. So it's only fitting, that they sign their employment contract right here on this stage, because we do need witnesses.

There was a nice round of applause and some laughter.

"So, Betty and I are proud to be here along with all of you, as we officially welcome Tay 'n' Tre into the Toonland family. Isn't that right Bettie?"

"Yes Teddy, but my, oh my—they really are cute!"

"Now Bettie, that's the second time you've mentioned that?"

"Is it Teddy, gee, I must be under their spell—already?"

"Bettie snap out of it then—you came here with me remember?"

"Yes Teddy . . . but I'm pretty sure—I don't have to leave that way . . . do I?"

"Bettie! Look, I'm sure there are plenty of ladies that would love to share a dance with Tay 'n' Tre.

"Yes Teddy, and—count me among them!"

"Listen Bettie, like I said, you don't have to worry about the boys."

"No I don't Teddy—but you do!"

"Why Bettie, after all these years, am I seriously being replaced?"

"Well Teddy, can you sing as well as them?"

"You know gang; I think we had better get going signing these contracts . . . for my own protection! The audience was howling now.

"Boys, on behalf of everyone at Toonland—especially Bettie apparently, we wish to welcome you both to the family. Now if you will sign this, you'll both officially become our newest members of America's leading entertainment family."

Teddy handed the pen to Trevor, as he bent down to sign it as several cameras were clicking away. Trevor then handed the pen to Taylor who then did likewise, but you could see his hand shaking a little as he did. When the signatures were on the ceremonious contract, the applause increased into a nice hearty round.

The boys kissed Bettie to keep up the tension, even as they shook Teddy's hand now. Teddy mockingly kept peering over Bettie's shoulder to keep a mindful eye for a little levity too. Teddy then spoke again.

"Ladies and gentleman, boys and girls, please welcome our newest Toonland stars; Tay 'n' Tre . . . The Morgans." The applause was growing now as Trevor spoke first.

"Thank you Teddy, and thank 'you' Bettie . . . call me."

Trevor purposely gave her a wink before then immediately walking up to her as she and Teddy were walking off stage now. He handed her a piece of paper in view of the audience. Everyone laughed, realizing this was supposed to be a little love note or Trevor's phone number. This brought out an immediate reaction from Taylor now.

"Tre, have you gone crackers? That's the boss' girl?"

"Gee Tay; someone's got to show me around this huge place after the show."

"Really. Well, I'd suggest you find Dopey the Dog then Tre!" This elicited some laughs from the audience.

"Listen baby brother, you let me worry about Teddy, I know how to treat a lady after all, don't forget, I'm older than you."

"Oh yeah Tre . . . but you learned so much more in those—four fleeting minutes, didn't you?

"Besides Tre, you're only older because Mum couldn't wait to get rid of you with all your kicking and complaining in there."

"Maybe so Tay, but at least I had the good sense to cry when the doctor spanked me bum . . . all you did, according to Mum—was giggle?"

"Yeah bro—but who do you suppose I was laughing at—Tre?"

"Listen bro, we can argue this all night. I'd like to sing something for all of these nice people, so what do you say?"

"I'd say—you're finally learning when to close that 'trap' of yours Tre."

I looked over at Larry who was genuinely pleased with himself at the moment.

"Fine Tay, have it your way mate, let's both stop talking and start singing, shall we?" This brought out warm applause from the audience.

"Suits me fine Tre, I'm not the one with the bloody problem keeping my mouth closed—right folks?" The audience greeted the comment with more laughter.

Trevor then said his own peace.

"Ladies and Gentleman and kids, on behalf of my baby brother and myself" . . .

. . . "It's a stinking four minutes folks!"

Taylor interrupted as he yelled above Trevor's comments, much to the delight of the audience.

"As I was saying before I was so rudely interrupted, here's a little tune called the House of Blue Lights."

At that moment, the stage area became bathed in blue flashing and moving lights.

The boys nailed the song as they had the last time they performed it here. As before, the audience went nuts with the duel that grew out of the bogey wogey riff between them. The audience began singing right along with the final verse and chorus. The audience rewarded the twins with a spirited ovation when it was over. The boys yelled out 'one more time' as they jumped into a reprise delighting the audience. When they finished, Taylor then went for a comment.

"Thank you everyone, we're so glad you liked that, it's one of our favorites, even if Tre sings it 'flat'!"

"Flat? Flat, Tay—I never!" . . .

. . . "Yeah Tre, never; as in—you're 'never' going to admit to doing it flat every time we perform it."

"All right mister smarty pants, we'll just see who goes flat—but who doesn't, on this next tune, cuz this one's going to be a Capella. Listen everybody; you make sure to be listening real good to Tay on this song so you can hear him do it, all right?"

"Okay folks—you just do that, we'll see about this! Oh . . . here's 'In the Still of the Night'." Taylor shot back to his brother.

At that moment, a projected silhouette image of roof joists covered the stage while a streetlight appeared between the two boys. Two small white spots, one over each twin, completed the illusion.

At that moment, the boys closed their eyes, covered an ear, and then began snapping their fingers while beginning their do-wop of 'shuby doo's' and 'shu wop's' in beautiful harmony. It was sans any instruments, but with prerecorded four-part harmony they had produced in their studio with a little tenor and baritone help from two of #1's singers, along with Scoot's excellent production.

I immediately heard whispers, as guests began shushing one another so they could listen to the beautiful 'do-wop' rhythm and captivating harmonies coming out of my two little pishers with their big voices. I think some people were actually stunned hearing this beautiful music out of two eleven-and-a-half-year-olds.

Taylor harmonized to Trevor's first verse, before they reversed themselves throughout all the remaining verses, until they approached the end of the song in a beautiful harmonic chord of their voices. They closed with a final verse of strictly 'shuby doo's with some 'scatting' thrown in too.

When they finished the song with Taylor singing out the title line one final time in an incredibly high falsetto voice, the audience went crazy. This was the boys' first standing ovation of the many they would receive no doubt, before these performances were over.

The audience's appreciation expressed through their robust applause lasted so long that the boys had to let it run its course before Trevor again addressed the audience.

"Thank you so much, thank you all, you're most kind."

"Yeah Tre, in fact I think they might be—like maybe—every kind." I could not believe my little Taylor, man had he come out of his shell—big time.

"Alright bro, can it. What 'ya say we give the folks a little 'listen' on the keyboards Tay?"

"Sure Tre."

As I watched their banter now, I was totally impressed. It seems that as 'tight' as Taylor's timing was becoming, I couldn't ignore how well Trevor was beautifully playing Taylor's straight man as well. Every time I stared over at Larry to acknowledge an exceptional line coming out of either of the twins, there he was, grinning from ear to ear. I even got a wink out of him this time. As Trevor announced:

"Ladies and Gents; here's Elton John's Funeral for a Friend for your pleasure."

The boys began the piece with Taylor's wonderful effects on his new keyboard, as Trevor's haunting organ solo began followed by Taylor's horns which were far more fuller than ever before. Trevor began his piano solo now, while the audience already seemed mesmerized by their incredible 'two-piece' sound. As Taylor went into his synthesized guitar solo a few moments later, the reaction from the audience was no less dramatic.

By the time the boys got to the vocals two thirds through their tune, this audience was air drumming on their tabletops to the music, while taping their feet . . . totally engrossed into it. Trevor's lead vocal was great, while Taylor's harmony—was spot on. I noticed some people were up on their feet dancing, standing in one spot, as others just chose to sing along or listen.

When the boys had finished the song, the audience's response was nearly identical to the prior visit's performance of this classic. The audience was on their feet as they applauded like thunder . . . we all were, it was that infectious.

"Thank you everyone. Taylor attempted to get out several times before the audience finally subsided with their applause, so he continued.

"Didn't Tre do some great work on his keyboard and vocals?" The audience again went nuts with applause as Trevor took a bow before the boys' high-fived one another.

"Hey, you weren't so bad there yourself, little bro?"

"Thanks Tre." Taylor took his own bow now, to much applause too.

"Listen Tay, turnabout is fair play. I'll bet our audience would like to hear one from you now. All right everyone, here's my 'baby' brother doing his best Davey Jones impersonation with Daydream Believer. Since I know he can't sing 'and' play at the same time, I'll handle the piano for him . . . alright bro?"

"Sure Tre, 'handle' yours all you want . . . just don't touch mine!"

I was a little concerned that comment might have crossed a little line in the 'corporate' sand. Only time and management's eventual critique would tell. Meanwhile Trevor began his piano track, as Taylor laid out his very 'British' and charming vocal, purposely toning down his big voice to make it more angelic than projecting it outwards.

With Trevor harmonizing, the song went over incredibly well. The audience must have agreed as they showed it in their abundant applause along with a standing ovation. This song was never one that I personally would think of for causing a standing ovation, if you take my meaning. Then again, Taylor did come over so angelic on his lyric, I was sure that the ovation was definitely started by the younger females in the audience.

As the boys moved professionally and tightly through their set, their talent on the keyboards, their big voices, as well as their wonderful banter with one another, more and more took the audience into their 'embrace'. Like their last performance here, the crowds were now overflowing to well outside the Quad's Terraces.

Yet, by the time they were on their final two songs, the entire audience inside the Terrace, simply remained standing on their feet, I think from the energy level emanating out of the audience and the boys. Clearly this was Scoot's genius at work. He was no fool after all; he knew exactly how to build excitement and frenzy with the order of their songs.

Scoot had decided that 'I'm Still Standing' would be announced as their final song. His decision made sense, as the tune's driving beat and rhythm, was a perfect tune to end their set. Yet when Taylor made the announcement moments later, he was harshly admonished by the audience immediately, first with boo's, then pleading of no, one more . . . anything it seems to convince the boys to continue on with a longer set.

My sons nailed the Elton John classic solidly. When they had finished it, they walked forward to take their first 'twin-bow' of their performance as they yelled out thanks while waving to the cheering crowds along with throwing kisses too.

The audience inside the Terrace had now been on their feet for some fifteen minutes.

What became amazing to me was taking a panoramic scan with my movie camera of the entire area. The surrounding area outside of the Terrace had to have more than three to four times the amount of the audience inside the terrace, now totally entranced into their applause for the boys' performance.

Many guests in the outer area could only see the backs of the boys, but that did not seem to matter to them, because they could still hear them play.

The first time Trevor heard the applause coming from behind him, he peered around the stage's edge to see them. He pointed it out to Taylor, so now the boys ran to the stage's edges where they peered out to these crowds while they started waving . . . much to the audience's delight and applause.

I thought to myself that none of this could be getting lost on our T-M 'partners'. Our entourage was ecstatic, as was I of course. The applause was deadening as the stage began to lower. Then, seconds later, it reversed itself, to begin moving back up, which initiated an incredible roar out of the audience along with the applause and yells for 'more', catcalls, and the like.

In the short time the stage had been going down, the boys had donned their 'black and white look' with black 50's style collarless sports coats, matching black shirts but with bright white hats and wide white neckties, completing the gangster look. The boys did another twin-bow as the yelling for more had now increased to a fevered pitch. Taylor finally held up his hands to quiet the crowd down, before he began to speak.

"My God Toonland, what a bloody blinder you are." Taylor yelled out to the audience, naturally, few of them understood the British slang, but continued clapping and yelling just the same.

"Ladies and Gentleman, and all our younger mates out there, we thank you for your warm kindness. Tre and I are so glad you have enjoyed yourselves in the time we have had together. You have been most gracious. By the by, have you noticed that anytime we have to use a real big word like gracious—I'm the twin who has to do the talking?"

Once again Taylor had them busting up at his brother's expense. But then Taylor really floored me, along with the rest of the audience no doubt, by walking over to his brother, as he said to Trevor with half the park watching:

"Actually, I love you bro, and I don't ever want to sing with anyone else."

Trevor was still stunned as Taylor grabbed hold of him as the boys then hugged deeply, which only further heightened the audience's endearment to both of them, expressed through their applause now.

Trevor then addressed the audience.

"Thank you bro, I feel the same way . . . and thank you Toonland . . . to all of you out there too—really. We would love to play all night, but after all—Tay was supposed to be in bed twenty minutes ago!

This time Trevor got the last laugh, or so he thought at the time.

"You've all been so 'gracious' . . . Taylor, I think it would be nice to do one more song for our wonderful audience, but maybe a nice soft one to really close this evening out on a nice feeling—what do you say Tay?"

"I say—let me hear you spell 'gracious' in front of all these folks so they know I wasn't lying?"

"Dang it, Tay—stop it . . . and it's G R A C I O U S, so there!"

"Fine, fine Tre, but if it's past my bed time, it's past your 'play' time, so you'd better forget about Bettie—would you like me to see if good old Dopey the Dog would be willing to 'tuck' you in?"

"Cute bro—but how about one more tune?

"Sure Tre. Mr. Light man, can you give us that street light back and lower the lights please?"

The request was instantly done of course, as Taylor then finished his comments.

"Mates, we have a new CD coming out in around eight weeks for the Verandas Foundation, which we hope you will all consider purchasing to help us in our crusade to raise some much needed money for some wonderful people that need all of our help.

"And you know, for once, I think Tre has the right idea for a closing song on the softer side, so here is our very first tune for our new label—Tornado. It's called 'My Prayer' . . . we sing it a Capella, here it is, and again; thank you so much for all of your kindness."

The boys waited for the audience to become silent which took some time. Once it was essentially quiet, they then approached their mics where they closed their eyes as the prerecorded vocal 'do-wop' tract began followed by Taylor's commanding vocal.

Taylor's haunting lead left no one unmoved in the audience. This time however, we got the full effect of that along with the full back up vocals, Tay's enhanced new synthesizer, even the costumes, and the added stage lighting contributed to the wonderful way this song came over to the audience. You could only sum it up as perfectly staged and presented . . . just as Mom had produced it and predicted.

So when Taylor hit his final crescendo of the song, we were almost expecting the gasp en mass we all heard. It was amazing, as well as how the boys performed it—that made this tune such a stone-dead killer, as this audience went certifiably nuts with their ovation!

As befitting a sellout performance at the Metropolitan Opera, the audience's reaction, with their tremendous applause, remained unabated even as Teddy and Bettie walked up to the boys on the stage close to three minutes later, carrying beautiful bouquets of roses for each of them. Apparently, everyone in the audience thought this was a wonderful gesture by all the extra applause we were hearing now.

After several subsequent twin-bows, then thrown kisses from the boys, the stage began to lower as the boys continued waving along with Teddy and Bettie, until it was totally below view.

The applause then continued for another minute or so, as people remained transfixed—hopeful for yet another encore. When the announcer made his 'we hope you enjoyed' comments, before announcing the times of the boys' other performances, only then did people get up in mass to leave inside the Terrace, even as they began to disburse outside the Terrace.

We had told the boys that it might take a few minutes to get down to the bunker below the stage . . . which it certainly did. I took this opportunity to speak to Larry, who deserved a lot of the credit for the boys' stage presence and banter.

"Lar-man, I know that was you out there with the boys' routine, so I just want you to know that you're not only my personal speechwriter, but its official now . . . you're the boys' gag writer as well."

"Thanks HB, it was fun,—besides, Tay and Tre learn real fast, don't they?"

"Yes Lar, I would most certainly say they do. How long were you three working on that stuff?"

"Since Thursday at Hebrew HB, beats the hell out of listening to the boring old Hebrew, I can tell you that."

"Yes Lar, I guess I can concede your point, however, if you don't learn the Hebrew, you can't have a Bar Mitzvah . . . but you need that Bar Mitzvah in order to become a real man Lar, don't you?"

"Who says you do HB, hell I'm already sprouting sixteen hairs now—and I ain't had my Bar Mitzvah yet?"

"Sixteen, you say, my—that is impressive. Nevertheless Lar, your Bar Mitzvah is much more than its tie-in to puberty. I can see you and I will have to have a further conversation on this at another time, but right now, let's get down to your best mates—shall we?"

"Sure HB, whatever you say, after all, you're picking up the 'check'—not me."

"Well said Lar-man . . . but you're right—I am, so let's go."

Larry and I caught up with our entourage as they made their way to the downstairs entrance. By the time we were close to the boys, mostly T-M folks had surrounded them, while Mom, Dad, and Austin were the closest to the twins from our group. Larry and I could only wave to them, as there was no way to get any closer until those around us gave us a pathway, which didn't seem a priority for any of them, at that moment. After waiting patiently as we tried to move closer for around ninety seconds to no avail, did I finally speak up.

Instantly now, we had our pathway, so we got right up to the boys, as we exchanged hugs with our entire entourage. I then thought it was only fitting that I say something to the large assembled group to congratulate the boys' stage success.

"Can I say a few words please everyone?"

The room instantly quieted down as I began, but not before Larry threw me 'the look' . . . that look said it all: I will be counting your words old man, so get to the point quick.

"Everyone, I just want to say that I don't think there's a prouder father anywhere on this planet tonight—than I. I would also like to introduce to all of you, the boys' personal comedy coach, Mr. Lawrence 'Lar-man' Levison." I put my arm around Larry's shoulder, while everyone clapped as he just beamed with pride.

"Thanks HB, but the credit really goes to the guys, because they're the ones who had to say it all."

It was at that moment that I felt an arm on my shoulder as I turned to find Jared, whom I had not, realized had made it to the underground until that moment. He had been seated with all the press during the performance, so I had assumed he was still with them.

"Marc, I'm so totally jazzed right now, that I can't begin to tell you, I'm so proud of the boys' accomplishment tonight on that stage. Marc, in all the years our Future World Quad has been opened, we have never had a reaction like that. Or audiences even close to the size we just experienced upstairs. The boys were so phenomenal; I can't even imagine what they'd do in a normal concert venue, but we're certainly going to find out soon enough."

"Thanks Jared, coming from you, I'll take that as the supreme compliment."

"Don't thank me Marc, thank those boys of yours. You won't believe the reactions I've heard from the press, they were overwhelmed . . . every comment was unbelievably positive!"

"Really, that's great."

At that moment, a woman who had been speaking to the boys came up to Jared and I. She looked at Jared and asked:

"Jar, would you please make the introductions?" Actually I couldn't wait myself, as she was a total knock out.

"Sure Donnie, I would be delighted. Marc Morgan, say hello to the Executive Vice President of Toon Media Entertainment—and my boss, Ms. Donovan Sage—Donnie to her many friends."

"It is my extreme pleasure to meet you Mr. Morgan; I have become a great fan of the boys in recent weeks, ever since I watched the video of their last performance here. Now after seeing them live, I must confess I was bowled over with their talent, my God, how they overwhelm an audience. Are they truly only eleven?"

"Thank you Donovan, but yes, they're really only eleven, but please call me Marc . . . so may I call you Donnie?"

"I would be insulted, if you didn't Marc."

"Great . . . but while I'm at it, I want to personally thank you for sending Jared to us; he's been truly wonderful to work with."

She looked at Jared for a moment before then looking back at me. She jokingly quipped now:

"Yes; we think highly of him 'now', ourselves."

I figured this was the least I could do to make amends for how I had privately thought of him for those few weeks. I could see that Jared too was touched at my gesture on his behalf.

"Thank you Marc, but that isn't necessary. Our negotiation was certainly a most pleasurable experience for everyone concerned, at least I think."

"Most definitely Jared, it was really more enjoyment than I've had in my own business in a long time."

Donovan then added:

"Marc, I can't even imagine where the boys will be two months from now, let alone, a few years. This is going to be explosive, so let me warn you right now."

"Yes, I get that feeling too Donnie, but the boys really do have their heads set straight on their shoulders, so that's the best way to start in my opinion."

"Yes, and you and your late wife should be proud of how you two raised them, as it certainly shows. I've heard from many on my staff that they are an absolute delight to work with, but what manners too."

"Yes thank you Donnie, yet really my wife deserves the credit for that . . . not I. But I'm certainly most proud of them Donnie, so thank you on behalf of both of us."

"I only heard about her passing recently from Jared, so please forgive my comment if I wasn't sensitive to your recent loss."

"No, you were most kind. Again, thank you for your kind words."

At this point, Scoot joined our conversation.

"Hey there Donnie, so what do you think of our twin tornados?"

"Scott, let's just say I finally understand your resignation . . . I was honestly blown away." We all had a nice laugh with Donovan's crack.

Mom and Dad joined us as we immediately introduced them to Jared's boss. Mom obviously was not going to let this opportunity slip by either.

She immediately kissed Jared hello before turning to Donovan to speak:

"You know Ms. Sage, in great part; it is this man who is responsible for this entire night. I hope you appreciate him, because I know—we certainly do."

"Mrs. Morgan, believe me, I do." Jared could not help himself now, he was beaming with pride.

"Listen, I hate to be the party pooper here, especially when I'm the one getting the pat on the back at the moment, but we do have to go to greet the press in the admin building for a press conference. They aren't known for their patience as you all know.

"Now here's the drill on this, they'll want to ask the twins tons of questions so; Marilyn, or gentlemen, any of you cut it off when you feel they've pitched enough, alright?"

"Sure thing Jar, but who exactly is going to handle the T-M side of the equation?"

"I will Scott, Marc why not invite your entire group as well."

Naturally our group wanted to go too, so we all started to move out of the bunker and into the park. This was a big mistake! We had not gone more than a hundred feet when a group of teens saw us, then immediately ran over to us screaming for autographs. Our security detail tried to keep them barricaded, but Trevor immediately spoke right up.

"Dad, I'm not going a foot further until we've signed our fans' autographs!"

"Yeah Dad, me too, these are our fans."

"Jared, can we blow another two minutes?"

"Sure we can, besides I think the boys are right. I'm proud of them for recognizing this time-honored obligation of celebrity Marc . . . they've certainly got character."

The kids all got their autographs while the boys both got kisses or hugs from the girls present . . . this pleased Trevor no end, as we all know. We finally got to the exit into the backstage area where we hopped on golf carts to get us to the admin building.

When we arrived at the admin building, we walked a maze of hallways until we came to a meeting room used specifically for the press, I was told.

Walking inside, we immediately heard cameras clicking away with flashes. The room was packed with reporters and there were plenty of videographers as well as Jared approached the podium.

"Hello everyone, we're so sorry it took a bit getting over here, but the boys had a little 'fan' encounter in route. Boys, come on over here with me . . . you too Marc, Marilyn and Scott."

We joined Jared at the podium as he introduced all of us to the press.

The press had their questions ready, and Jared I noticed, gazed over the room apparently to seek out certain representatives. Obviously he wanted to set a tone or something, so he knew who to go to . . . or perhaps whom to avoid for a while.

"Joy, what's your question please?"

"Hello boys; are you ever intending on doing any original material or perhaps some of your own songwriting?"

"Miss, we don't know right now, do you think we should?" Trevor asked her right back. I think that 'Joy' was a little taken aback at having her question answered with another straight away to her, but she answered it anyway.

"Boys, if you two can write songs half as well as you play, sing, and captivate an audience; you will own this industry before you graduate high school."

"Thank you Miss." Came from Taylor at the compliment.

Jared then picked another reporter.

"Bob, I see you hiding back there, what's your question for our two new stars?"

"Thanks Jared, I'd like to know what's in the boys' future specifically with T-M?"

"Excellent question Bob—with a protracted answer, so I'll just say, anything and everything. The boys will continue a few more engagements here and in Asheville, before they move on to larger venues. A TV series for our Broadcast network is in the planning stages. Music videos as well as in-depth specials will be the focus of our cable networks commencing next week. We're looking at a full-length feature movie to be in the pre-production stage by summer's end, while the boys will be in the recording studio quite a bit in between. They have launched their own recording label 'Tornado' under our umbrella, as you already know from your press kits."

Taylor noticed Larry miming to him and eventually picked up on his message. Tay then seized on the comedic opportunity it presented, so he opened his little 'pisk' right up.

"Say Jared, do you suppose that once in a while, we might get to go to sleep too?" This busted the entire room up.

Trevor then recognized Marna standing in the rear row so he tugged on Jared's arm to ask him to call on her next.

"Marna Baron, you get the next question." Fortunately, Jared apparently knew her.

"Thanks Jared. As you know, I spent a fair amount of time with the boys already, but there was one question I forgot to ask them, so here it is—boys, who is your own personal favorite singer—is it Elton?"

Trevor looked at Taylor, who whispered back into his brother's ear, as they then just nodded to one another, before Taylor finally spoke.

"Hi Marna, hi Nancy, it's so nice to see you both again, but thank you both for your great article, it was fab. To answer your question though, our favorite singer hasn't worked in years . . . I think they call that—a has-been, but we can still tell you from personal experience; he hasn't lost any of his talent . . . our Dad, Marna, he's our personal favorite."

The press were still laughing at the crack while I was blushing a little at the tender compliment, so I snuck in a quick thank you.

"Gerry, what's your question for the twins?" Jared kept the dialogue moving.

"I guess my question—now is, why isn't 'Mr.' Morgan singing with his sons if he's so talented too?"

"Marc, would you care to answer that?"

"Sure Jared. Gerry, the boys' comment touched me deeply. I am most honored and flattered by their compliment; however I want them to do this for themselves. This is their dream . . . it's their reality now; so I don't want to interfere in that."

The press conference carried on another twenty minutes, when Mom motioned to Jared she thought it was enough on the boys, so Jared ended it with three final questions being fielded.

After the conference ended, many of the press corps came up to us where they said some truly wonderful, glowing compliments about the boys' performance, I was literally taken aback. As you can imagine, the press by its very nature, usually keeps their positive comments infrequent and rare.

By this time, we were right at five minutes before eight, so all the kids now started mentioning their grumbling stomachs. Jared once again came to the rescue.

"Marc, let's get everyone out for a little dinner, shall we?"

"Sure Jared, where do you suggest?"

"Marc, it's wholly up to you all. I can tell you that if you want some peace and quiet, the employee dining rooms are always best. If, on the other hand, you don't mind being out in the open inside the park with plenty of security, I recommend the remote location of the Thunderbird Ranch BBQ?"

"How does the BBQ place sound to all of you youngins?"

The kids immediately greeted this question to the affirmative, so that was settled in short order.

An argument broke out however, between Beth and her girls, as Beth announced they were going home for the evening. The girls were so upset, I appealed to Beth personally.

"Now Cuddles, I'm surprised at you, how can you do this to my nieces?"

"Marc, I'm truthfully not feeling well, I thought it would be smart to call it a night."

"Jesus Beth, I'm so sorry to hear that. Why—not let me keep them with us then, won't that make it easier on you? We'll just make room for them with the folks. Let's not spoil their wonderful time."

"Marc, you're worse than them with their pleading. Okay, but are you sure it won't be an imposition on everyone?"

"Only if you say 'no'—Cuddles."

"Alright . . . but stop calling me Cuddles, Marc. Only my Scotty gets to call me that, remember Marcus—you're the stinker."

"Fine, no more Cuddles, but I get the girls for the night—deal?"

"Deal Marc, but what am I going to do about their night gowns?"

"Don't worry; I'll arrange some extra large t-shirts as a substitute, fair enough?"

"Yes, that will suffice." I now turned to my nieces.

"Embeth, Halley, we've decided you two will spend the night in Grammy and Gramp's suite, that is, if you want too?"

The girls both yelled yes to us, so it was all settled, as I was rewarded with huge hugs along with some sloppy kisses from both my nieces. We then all made our way over to Thunderbird Ranch BBQ via the backstage area as far as we could go, after both Scoot and Beth left us for the evening along with Bill.

When we arrived at the BBQ, which really was nothing more than a large chuck wagon with surrounding tables all outdoors. It was largely empty being late already.

We made our way through the chuck wagons, where both Gracie and Reg seemed the most intrigued with this form of food service. Naturally it originated in the drive west by settlers in America's bygone pioneering era.

When we were all seated, eating a fine selection of BBQ specialties, the table talk turned to our resident stand up, Mr. Levison.

"Dang, these ribs are real good, but too darn messy; does anyone have like a bazillion extra napkins?"

Mom passed down a nice size stack as the rest of us ate as we chuckled. Then Jared asked:

"Larry, by the way, are you planning on any more material for the boys' concerts tomorrow?"

"Now that's an interesting question Jared—you see that all depends on you . . . naturally."

"On me, Larry—why?"

"Let's just say it depends upon how much Toon-Media—is paying me of course. Tonight was just my free complimentary appetizer. Naturally Jar—if you want the main dish—it'll cost ya."

"Oh my word Larry, I never realized—you were in the union?"

"Union, smunion, Morison—hell, I need a new bike!"

"Alright Larry, here's my offer, so, take it or leave it. You continue to help the boys with their material for this weekend—then I'll send you out a bike next week, now does that seem fair?"

"Yeah, that works for me Jar, but what about all of my mates here? You know, it's no fun riding all alone, so I guess you'd better include one for each of us, don't you think?"

"Wow Larry, you drive a hard bargain."

"Hey Morison, my Dad runs a bank—any questions?"

"Okay Larry, I know when I'm licked, bikes all around, but—you had better believe I'll be counting the new jokes tomorrow and Sunday."

"No sweat Mr. Morison, you can count on me and the guys."

At that moment, a group of guests had walked over from their table to ours as their father addressed me now.

"Sir, I wonder if it would be an imposition if I were to ask your sons to take a photograph with my girls and their friend."

"Not at all sir, I'm sure the boys would be delighted to, right guys?"

"Sure sir, we'd be honored. Hi, I'm Tre and this little guy out past his bedtime, is my younger brother Tay." Tre winked over to Larry.

The boys then met the entire family who were visiting from Modesto. The father took several shots, before I offered to handle his camera, so that he got into a few with his family along with the boys.

Once this was finished, Tay then asked the oldest girl of around thirteen if she wanted an autograph, which she replied she would very much. The three girls; Karina, Erin, and Joanna, were thrilled. So now, a round of autographs went to all the kids as the family thanked us then went on their way. Jared then commented.

"You know guys, I think what I like most about you two already is—you both have big voices, huge hearts—but very small heads. Take my advice boys, don't ever lose that quality."

"Thank you Jared, we'll try to remember that, won't we guys?"

"Yes Dad, big hearts, small heads; got it . . . pass me the BBQ sauce please." Taylor returned.

"Listen guys, here's the plan for tomorrow. Around 10 am, we will all meet up at the Tour Garden where you will join our Cable channel crew who will be getting some footage of you guys at play on some rides. They also mentioned wanting you both to give them a guided tour of your planes. Afterwards, your guide Sharon will escort you to wherever you care to go, along with security, until one pm, when you are required at make up for the 2 pm concert . . . I hope that all of this meets with your approval?"

"Sure Jared, but our guide has always been Hilary, can't she help us again?"

"Oh, I'm sorry Tre, that's right, don't worry; we'll do our best to make sure you have Hilary.

"Now Larry, this schedule doesn't give you a whole heck of a lot of time to get the boys some more material, but I know you'll try, won't you son?"

"Sure JM, just leave it to me, they'll have two or more new lines for 2 pm or I'll give you the bikes back!"

"Great Larry, but if you can't, you can't."

"You let me worry about it JM, I create material best when I'm under some real pressure, just ask my mom . . ."

. . . "Yeah—he had pressure alright—right at 29,000 feet—he started blowing his trumpet." Taylor added as he started all of the kids off laughing . . . and a couple adults too.

Jared, tried desperately to be diplomatic now over Taylor's crack, so he turned his attention back to the young 'tooter' as it were.

"Okay Larry, whatever you say. You had better get it done then—young man!"

"That's better JM, trust me—and don't get me started on your trumpet solos—Taylor."

"I'd say you already 'got started' at 29,000—Lar?"

"By the way, since you're calling me JM, Larry, I was wondering why you always refer to Marc as HB?" Jared continued to try to run interference between the two boys' inappropriate conversation.

"If I told you the answer to that one JM, I'd have to kill you afterwards. But if I did tell you—HB would kill me afterwards—see my predicament JM?"

"Fine, sorry for asking." Yet Jared was still busting over our young Mr. Gleason.

"Don't sweat it JM."

"Thank you Larry, I guess I can relax now, right?"

"Sure. Kick your shoes off JM, I mean as long as your feet don't stink, that is?"

"Look's who's talking about letting out a stink Trev, bloody hell."

Taylor was not letting up on his best mate. I knew he was just practicing for the stage . . . but since it was at Larry's expense—that made it a treat for all of us naturally.

I decided to change the subject myself; to rescue Jared before this went any further.

"So; who wants to join me on a ride or two before we call it a night?"

"We would love . . . Reg and I haven't been on a single one yet."

"You know Grace; you're most definitely correct—so shame on us. Tell you what; you and Reg pick our first ride."

"Honestly Marc, we wouldn't know where to begin."

"Speak for yourself Grace dear; I know exactly where I'd like to go first."

"Where, Reg?"

"Marc, I've heard the boys talk over and over again about how that Ghostly's Mansion attraction reminds them of your Verandas . . . so why not start there?"

"Excellent suggestion Reg, but I wouldn't say too much about the comparisons around 'you know who'. I then pointed to our Toon-Media guest." Jared laughed at my crack.

"Gee Marc, I'm afraid it's a little late don't you think, I mean; how many restaurants do you have already?"

"Near 350 Jared, so I guess you make a fair point."

After we cleared our tables, we headed over to Reg's pick, Ghostly's Mansion. Jared walked us right inside, which turned out to be a good thing. The line of guests outside had several folks that had obviously seen the performance. They were about to rush us I surmised for autographs, as several camera flashes were already going off.

We did the ride twice at Gracie's insistence, as she really loved it. Then I suggested since we were so close, we should do the Bahaman Buccaneer, which everyone agreed too. This one was a favorite of my folks as it was for me, so we did it twice as well. The boys ended up signing around half a dozen autographs in that big boat making all of those new fans- happy in the process.

As our boat was nearing the exit of the ride the second time around, a group of girls around eleven to fourteen started screaming for the boys from the line on the dock. The boys smiled, then waved hello to them . . . damn if it didn't look, as if a couple of these girls were about to faint. What were we getting into, I thought pensively to myself? It was at this moment that Dad piped up.

"Wow Marc, you certainly never had that problem when you were the boys' age."

"Gee thanks Dad,—I love you too."

"I'm sorry son, I didn't really mean for it to sound like it did."

"Okay Pops, you're forgiven then—for now!" I then heard Trevor's plea:

"Dad, we gotta do Wrong-way Murphy's now, we just gotta?"

"Alright Trev, we're here, so that's fine, but if we have to wait long inside that building like last time, we're only going through once."

"Okay. Jared, can you get us in further through the line inside the building?"

"Tre, you just leave everything to me." Jared then led us all up through the ride's exit until we stopped at the handicapped elevator at the launching point of the ride. We took that up and were practically at the front of the line. Wow I thought to myself, I could really get used to this . . . as my Dad now said out loud:

"Now I could get used to this, son."

I couldn't help myself as I laughed at how the two of us thought sometimes.

When I explained my laughter to Dad, he wasn't surprised at all.

"Listen Marc, like Mom always says, the apple doesn't fall far from the tree."

"Yep, I guess you're right Pop."

"Did you have any doubt?"

"I did!" Mom of course now interjected as we all laughed.

We boarded our 'SUV' for Wrong-way Murphy's Adventures for our serene little jaunt.

When we exited after three rides in succession, we were made aware of a sizable throng of teenage girls ahead of us that apparently were holding back for us to exit as well. Security suspected that they were from some youth group by their matching t-shirts. Meanwhile, did they ever swarm us when we got out of the actual building. They were screaming loudly, along with yelling the boys' names, clamoring for them to sign their autographs. The enormity of the camera flashes alone was blinding. The boys were fine with the attention, but as for myself, it was getting 'old'—quickly now. We then obliged them with autographs along with photos with the boys, before they would let us leave.

We left as soon as the boys finished, but they followed us whispering and giggling the whole time, trailing behind us. We made our way to the Secrets of the Amazon, which we had to do for Mom. After all of these years, she still held it high on her personal lists of favorites.

We completed our little cruise on the Amazon, and then exited as fast as possible into the backstage area behind the Bird Sanctuary, as the throng of girls was still fast on our heels yet again.

Now finally free of these admirers, we called it a night. We made our way out of the park, and then quickly went to the resort's Towers.

I have to tell you, I was more than a little relieved to be in the privacy of our suite at this point. The boys however, could have cared less. They were already hard at work with Larry, who was sounding them out on some ideas for new material using Austin, Embeth, and Halley as the audience. If more than one of the mates laughed—Larry seemed satisfied.

We were all going to hit the hay around ten-thirty. I had to secure the T-shirts for the girls, so I did so by running down to the gift shop for them. Upon my return, I sent all the kids to bed in their respective suites.

I woke up our group at eight-forty-five so that we could all quickly shower and dress for the morning.

After a quick breakfast, we waited for our security detail to arrive. We then made our way to the Tour Center to pick up Hilary hopefully, along with Scoot and the film crew. Beth was in bed at home according to Scoot, sick—as a frigging dog.

The film crew seemed genuinely excited to meet the guys in person, as they simply instructed all the kids to do whatever they normally would do . . . paying no attention to their filming, as much as possible.

Hilary and the boys did as requested; they hit all of their favorite rides, accompanied by their four mates naturally, while the adults did the rides without all the limelight of the film crew. The crew followed along on many of the rides to capture all of the excitement close up with the kids. After an hour of this, we then left the park for a tour of the planes at Long Beach Airport.

The morning went by quickly as you can imagine, so, soon, we were having lunch inside the Door at Forty-Four.

The boys immediately pinned down Rudy, who of course agreed to their request to have another go at the Harpsichord . . . and why wouldn't he?

After they ordered their lunch from our server, they immediately asked to be excused to go play it.

"Sure guys have at it, but one of us should be with you for a little back up."

"HB, are you forgetting the four linemen they call security that's just outside this room, they look like they just ate a whole cow for lunch . . . raw?"

"You know Lar-man, I always knew there was an excellent reason I've kept you around." God, how that kid could make me laugh . . . but he was right, besides.

"Thanks HB; I feel the same way about you."

I called in our lead security person to ask him to escort all the kids over to the Harpsichord. With this accomplished, the adults were able to have a kid-free room for over twenty minutes.

"Loverly" as Gracie put it so succinctly after they had departed.

As we sat there munching down our salads, we could hear them playing . . . it sounded wonderful. The boys were playing Chopin at that moment which sounded so nice on the Harpsichord. Mom then commented.

"You know Scott, listening to the boys playing the classics, has me thinking . . ."

. . . "Oh God Marilyn . . . not again!" My Dad now threw in for a quick shot at my Mom.

"Thank you Mal, I knew I could count on you for a crack like that. But seriously, I don't know, but it just seems to me that with their roots in classical music, we should try to incorporate it more into their performances somehow. After all, most rockers out there can't touch the genre, but our two are naturals at it. Besides, Miranda I'm sure, would much appreciate that, what do you think Scott . . . Malcolm—you keep still?"

"That's an interesting thought Marilyn, besides being an excellent suggestion; perhaps we should investigate that with some of the songwriters too?"

"Yes, I think that's the right approach myself. Maybe something can be composed bringing the two elements together like Funeral for a Friend so beautifully does, that would instinctively fit the boys' style and talents."

"Okay Marilyn, I'll look into it further."

"Marc what do you think?"

"Mom, I think that's a great idea. I know while it's been done before, not too many of the rockers out there can do the actual classical portions themselves; typically it's an orchestra backing them up. Since the boys can do it themselves, that should say something to an audience naturally. I really like the idea actually."

Reg now commented:

"As for me, I think it's the only 'true' music to reach one's soul, so I most wholeheartedly concur Marc."

"Thank you Reg; have you any particular piece or composer in mind you'd suggest then?"

"No, not particularly Marc. I really don't see how the boys can miss with any of them really, particularly Chopin, Rachmaninov, or Mozart. I've listened to them play wonderfully since they were around seven or eight, so I don't think it matters who they choose to play, it will sound truly marvelous— just listen to them right now."

Reg was right, they sounded incredible on the harpsichord at that moment. I then posed a question to the assembled adults:

"Listen, does anyone have a guess as to how many guests, who watch the next performance at two p.m., might return to come back for the eight pm show as well?"

"Yeah I do Marc—I believe nearly half of them. You mark my words son; the eight pm show will be SRO all the way out to The 500 Speedway track." Dad announced matter-of-factly.

"Come on Dad; give me a break that seems a little optimistic don't you think, I mean that's a far way's back from the Quad?"

"Maybe so son, but remember the Future World Quad is a small area. The surrounding area will be swamped by this evening, believe me. What we had last night was nothing, just you watch. Don't forget son, many of these guests are on two-to-five-day passes; so we'll definitely see a lot of repeaters from last night, at both of today's concerts.

"Jesus, Scoot, if Dad's right, it could be an issue doing the same sets, don't you think?"

"Relax bud, who said anything about repeating sets? Each set is different with only three carryovers—didn't I already tell you that?"

"I don't think so Scoot . . . if you did, I must not have been paying attention."

"Well they are bud, Marilyn insisted . . ."

. . . "That's right Marc, I did. One I didn't want any repeat guests to hear all the same tunes again; secondly I want to see how all of the songs play over individually so I know which ones hit the audience the hardest. They only repeat Funeral, Still Standing, and of course; My Prayer."

At that moment, we had to stop to join the applause for the boys, as they finished their piece on the Harpsichord. Moments later, we heard Rudy on the PA.

"Ladies and gentlemen, boys and girls, please give another warm hand to our Harpsichordists this afternoon—Tay 'n' Tre Morgan, who will be singing and performing a more timely selection of music at two pm and eight pm at the Future World Quad for your entertainment. I understand that their show last night, attracted over 17,000 guests who all came away marvelously impressed with these eleven-year-old twins from Las Vegas."

Again we heard clapping, yet as in their prior visit, much more robustly, as it kept getting louder as the entourage of kids made their way closer to our private dining room, no doubt. As the kids all walked in, we gave the boys our own round of applause and hugs.

"How'd we do Daddy?"

"T-man, you guys were just wonderful, simply stellar. In fact we were just talking about incorporating a little classical into each of your sets to give your audiences something to hear a little worldlier out of you two."

"Cool, I think that's a great idea too, but if we do, we'd prefer some real pianos after this weekend Daddy . . . not our keyboards."

"Oh. Well, that seems logical T-man—Scoot can you speak to Jared or Stacy about it?"

"Sure thing Marc, I'm sure they'll love the idea too."

"So listen kids, you had better eat up because you're food's getting cold . . . we'll have to get a move on in a few too."

"Okay HB, you don't have to tell me twice, when it comes to eating."

Larry started shoveling his food away.

"Uncle Marc, can we spend the night again with Grandma Marilyn and Gramps?"

"Sure Halley, if it's all right with your Father? With your Mom still sick, I think it's a good idea personally—don't you Scoot?"

"Yeah bud, I do indeed, Beth was again praying to the toilet God this morning, so I don't want the girls to get it, so yes; I agree if you're sure it's not an imposition."

"Not at all Scott, it will be our pleasure." Dad assured him.

"Thanks for saying yes Daddy."

"Your welcome Em, but you mind your manners with everyone, okay?"

"Of course they will Scott, they're wonderful girls, and I just loved having them, didn't you Grace?"

"Most definitely. They're loverly Scott, really." Grace added.

After finishing our wonderful meal, we were compelled to rush in order to be on time for the boys' make up artists. So we moved at a big clip to get to the golf carts in the back lot area. Despite our efforts, we were four minutes late arriving to make up. As the boys were being made up, Scoot and I posed a question as a follow up to our luncheon conversation with them.

"Guys, do you have something on the classical side that's short enough to hold the younger members of the audience's attention, but will leave everyone in awe?

The boys were trying to think this over, while not being able to talk much with the make up artists still doing their work at a feverish pace now. Finally, Trevor spoke up.

"Yes Dad, there is . . . Tay, don't know, what do you think—how about doing our dueling bees?"

"Yeah Tre, that's brill, it would be wicked—awesome in fact, especially if we give it our full Monty on the dueling."

"Perfect boys, you mean I will finally get to hear the dueling bees?"

"Sure Daddy, it's about time, don't you think?"

"Yes I do think—Taylor, with all of your rehearsing, I've been waiting for it after all."

Scoot was lost over this whole exchange when he asked:

"Boys, the 'dueling bees', please fill me in?" So Trevor did.

"Sure Uncle Scott, that's just what we call it, we use to do it as warm up practice of our scales so we could limber up our fingers . . . it's the Flight of the Bumble Bee. You see Uncle Scott; we do it dueling back and forth, overlapping one another, so we get going real fast; even faster than it's written. We're finished in around a minute, maybe a little more or less."

"Really, what do you think Marilyn?"

"Sounds perfect Scott, boys will it sound presentable on the keyboards though?"

"Yes, sure Grammy, just not as full and clear as on our Bluthners (pianos)." Taylor offered.

"So Scott, what do you think?"

"I say we listen to it, once the boys are finished with make up before we decide if the sound is rich enough. If it is, then yes, I say we add it in around three from the top."

"Don't worry Uncle Scott, it will sound plenty rich, plus we know it backwards and sideways. We really get into it, the dueling I mean, so the audience will probably go bonkers for it—we used too."

"Okay Trev, you don't have to sell me on it, I'm not worried about you two—I'm just concerned that your equipment will do you and 'it', the justice it deserves?"

"Maybe you don't understand us Uncle Scott. We have done it on the keyboards lots of times before; we use it as an exercise whenever we'd been off the keys for a few days, that's the only reason you haven't heard it already. We haven't been off the keys for weeks now!"

"Are you trying to tell us something with that comment, Tre?"

"No Dad, we aren't unhappy or complaining. It's just that we only do it when we need to limber up or we're out of shape. Natch, with all our rehearsing, we haven't been, that's all I meant by it."

"Fine son, sorry for the confusion . . . well Scoot—what say you?"

"All right, pardon me for even bringing the sound issue up. Add it in at three on the song list—I'll speak to the techs about some suitable lighting effects."

"Okay boys, I'm going to take everyone up top now to our seats, so any last minute concerns or questions?"

"Yeah Dad, let Larry stay down here a little longer, we want to go over some of our lines again."

"Sure. Larry, do you want a security escort to get you back up top, or are you okay on your own?"

"Security just for me—yeah, I can dig that? Send him round in another ten minutes, that should give the mates and I enough time, don't you think?"

"Whatever you say Lar . . . you're the boss."

"Thanks HB, but if I'm the boss, where the hell is my secretary—cuz all this writing's killing me."

I ignored Larry's final crack before I took everyone topside for our first surprise of the day. The Terrace was packed like sardines . . . packed to the gills. We had no problem finding our tables, as they were the only ones unoccupied in a sea of packed-in guests.

In the time it took us to walk over to our reserved tables, at least four parties had tried to occupy them, but security was not having any of it. In fact, the security guard was a little bit brusque with us naturally, when we first arrived.

Before I could even introduce myself, our guard said:

"I'm sorry sir; these tables are reserved for special guests".

"Yes, they are officer . . . we're your party."

"Oh I'm so sorry; this has become a little bit strained in the last few minutes. May I have your name sir?"

"Morgan, officer."

"Great . . . we have a winner. Look, we have been expecting your party as you can see?"

"Fine officer it looks great, we appreciate your help."

We sat down to make ourselves comfortable as a man sitting the next table over, turned to me, before quipping?

"Are you some big shot from Toon-Media bub?"

"No, can't say that I am sir, I'm just the 'schlep' who supplies this entire park—with their toilet paper—that carries a lot of weigh around here though, pardon my pun. Yep, seventeen hundred rolls every day, that's a huge responsibility, believe me. One missed shipment during the day, and this whole place turns to crap everywhere, believe me."

"Are you pulling my chain buddy?"

"Sir, what would make you say that—of course I'm pulling your chain." I then chuckled.

"So what do you do that you get your own personal table without waiting? My kids have had me sitting here saving this sorry table for over two damn hours, just to hear a couple of damn brothers sing. They tell me that these two can sing and play like nobody's business—but—do you see my kids anywhere?"

"I can't say that I do, but I'm sure they'll make it in time to hear my two damn kids sing."

"Oh Christ, sorry about the 'damn' crack. I will say this; my three told me they heard your two last night, so they insisted that we all had to see them today. Damn if they didn't say they were incredible . . . but believe me bub—my three are true 'critics'."

"Thank you sir . . . you know, I don't think I caught your name?"

"Kineret bub, Dr. Stephen Kineret . . . and yours?"

"Marc Morgan, nice to meet you doctor."

"Likewise Marc, my wife Leinaala will be thrilled to meet you, she'll be here in a moment with our food, we're visiting from Northern California, come here every year like clockwork." I then proceeded to introduce Stephen to the rest of our entourage.

"Are these two guys (pointing to Austin and Larry) yours as well Marc?"

Larry had just returned himself in the middle of all this, thanks to his security escort.

"Nope, Austin and Larry are both good friends of my sons. Actually, Larry here writes the boys' comedy material, while Austin's currently been serving as my co-pilot aboard my corporate jet."

"You're kidding me—right?"

"No Stephen, I'm most serious."

"How old are you Larry?"

"I'm twelve Stephen, but if you want any additional information on me, you'll have to go through my agent here—Austin, when he's not too busy flying Marc's jet."

"Okay Marc, I see your point. Well nice meeting all of you, I think I'll just wait on the wife, before I say anything else—I'll regret later."

"Good idea Steve." Larry quipped, as Stephen turned around to try to disappear into his chair.

As it got closer to two pee, Dad commented that he would make an ice cream run for everyone to kill the time. He left with Em and Halley to help him carry them over.

In the short time they were gone; we were amazed as the crowd outside the Quad was increasing considerably, even as we watched. Given the music had yet to start, these were obviously guests making an informed decision to hear the boys specifically.

"I told you son, the show's not even going yet, but look at that group surrounding this place now."

"Okay Dad, don't gloat, but they're still a huge distance away from the 500 Speedway tract."

"Yeah son, you're right, but that's only because the boys aren't on yet. Besides, I said by tonight's show—remember?"

"Okay Dad, I agree."

We enjoyed our ice cream sandwiches as we made small talk until we heard the announcer's voice.

"Ladies and Gentlemen, boys and girls. Toonland is pleased to welcome back their fabulous new musical stars; Tay 'n' Tre . . . The Morgans!"

The audience went nuts, many jumped up on their feet applauding, even as the stage had not moved an inch yet.

"See Marc—there's your repeaters son, a good twenty percent of the audience."

"Yep Pop, I guess they are, why else would they be on their feet already?"

"HB, it sure isn't cuz they plan to break wind at 29,000 feet?" As Larry now picked up the torch on the trumpet gag.

We were all up on our feet as well, as we heard the opening riff to 'Crocodile Rock'. Tay would be on organ on his synthesizer, while Tre would hold up the piano solo—brilliantly.

Unlike Elton's version, the boys immediately came out in harmony. Elton saves this for his final verse. My two were going directly for the audience's jugular right out of the gate . . . it was working big time.

Some inside the Quad's audience were trying to dance or clap in rhythm, but most just listened. The 'one' advantage to being out on the outside of the Quad, was the issue of space. Tons of both kids and adults had the room to dance to the music. Yet they were losing that open space quickly now, as other passersby simply stopped dead in their tracks to listen as well. At that moment, Dad threw a devious grin my way.

The boys ended the song with its signature falsetto la-la-la, done with comedic body language and aplomb that the boys threw in with great affect.

The audience just loved it all. Their applause along with a standing ovation was sustained for nearly a minute.

"Good afternoon Toonland, 'ow are you?"

This came out of Trevor with his still intact British accent that this audience seemed to be swooning over now.

"Its bloody brill to be here with all of you, but it's nice to see some of you from yesterday too, thank you for honoring us again . . . hey, don't you love those multi-day passes—they're brill? By the by, I'm Tre, but while I keep waffling on anyway, that's my little brother Tay over there—talking to his synthesizer. What the bloody he . . ."

. . . "Relax Tre—I'm not talking to it, I'm fixing it, so give me a tick."

"Really bro?"

"Yeah, I think I've almost got it now, so give me a tick . . . don't toss your bits and mess up your kecks Tre."

"Okay folks, while he's goofing around with his 'tick', I'd like to tell you a little bit 'bout us."

At that moment, a girl's voice yelled out in the distance:

"I love you Tre."

This brought out general laughter, along with another young lady as well:

"Me too, Tre." She yelled out.

"Thank you ladies, but I'm much too young, so call me in a few years— dang it bro, what am I saying?"

"Nothing—as usual Tre." Taylor threw in, but his brother chose to ignore it.

"So; about me and Tay. We're eleven, and we've been stuck with one another for all of that time, at least as far back as I can remember. You know, having a twin isn't all its cracked up to be, believe me . . . sometimes I wish that he'd just toss off."

"Oh, I don't know bro. I think you're lucky enough having me around to look after you?"

"Gee, I'm glad you see it that way Tay, but that's my whole point. You're 'always' there."

"Fine Tre, look—if you want to take your own dang bath yourself—just say the word."

"Taylor Shane Morgan, that's not something the folks need to know about us, do they?"

"Heck Tre—they're entitled to know we're clean—aren't they?" Larry 'fifteen', Jared 'love'.

"Folks, please excuse my brother's crudeness . . ."

The same female I believe from before, interrupted Trevor as she now yelled out:

. . . "I'll take a bath with you anytime Tre."

"Tay, have you got that thing fixed already, cuz I want to stop talking and start singing?"

"Good Tre—cuz we'd all appreciate that too—bro. Tay retorted. And yeah Tre, the synthesizer is fixed, so—let's get it on."

"All right . . . you got it Marvin. Ladies and gentlemen, kids of all sizes, here's one from my 'clean' brother Tay. This is his version and tribute to one of our personal favorite groups; Little Anthony and the Imperials. Here is the fifties classic; Since I Don't Have You . . . . but girls, you'd better be careful, cuz he does it real purdy too. Take it away Tay!"

Taylor jumped right in, as he had his 'key' down perfect in mimicking Little Anthony's trademark soprano along with his pauses and emphases. His keyboard work was right on as well, as this tune had music tracks up the kazoo. There was a violin lead, drums, keyboards, you name it. His soprano falsetto in particular was impressive, especially as the song ended. Trevor did a nice job with augmenting the prerecorded back up vocal harmonies with his own live back up as well.

When T-man was finished, the girls were all screaming as everyone else was clapping madly too, while those from the terrace were on their feet.

You know, I really had to remember to compliment Scoot on his music selections. He chose the tunes among the boys' favorites, wisely. He always seemed to favor the higher pitched singers, at least for the ballads. That really worked well for the boys' ranges along with their still maturing—yet big voices. Indirectly, it made the boys' voices naturally sound more mature.

Taylor took a bow as he also made sure to wave to the many screaming girls, before then speaking to the crowd.

"Thank you all so much, thank you. Well, as you know, I'm the 'clean' one, for telling you all about the bathtub thing . . . I mean what's the big deal anyway? After all, we do some of our best harmony practice in the loo.

"Right now, we'd like to do something for you, that we've been doing since we were like five years old . . . we were still learning to play the piano. But in our house, that meant 'only' classical music for the longest time, well—at least until we were seven."

That confession had its desired effect on the audience as it forestalled Tay being able to continue for a few moments, as they responded.

"So this piece is special to us, because mostly, it seems we practiced it for years to perfect it in our own way. It is classified an orchestral interlude, but became most famous as part of an Opera. Tre and I have always used it as exercise instead, every time we needed to limber up our fingers to play. Over the long time we've been playing it, we started doing it together, where eventually, we started treating it like a duel between us. You know something like in dueling Banjos, but with pianos instead, so we renamed it the dueling bees. For those of you who know it by its given name, here is Flight of the Bumble Bee, by Nikolai Rimsky-Korsakov."

As the audience applauded politely, I realized we may have made a mistake already in offering something this classical in this type of venue—they seemed so 'under whelmed' with Taylor's introduction. Oh well, it was too late now.

Meanwhile, the boys set themselves properly on their stools in front of their keyboards, before simultaneously cracking their hands and fingers, then beginning the piece—their dueling bees.

Taylor went first. I swear to God, I never realized that an eleven-year-old could play so fast . . . it was overwhelming. Then Trevor just jumped in right over him, as he began his part of the movement. Again, it was unbelievable—with his finger work—even faster! Then just like that, Taylor jumped back in. In the end, it was finished with the two boys doing the final portion together in a flourish.

It couldn't have been much more than a minute long, the boys were right, it was fast—but so incredible too.

Apparently, no one went as crazy or more—certifiably nuts—than the audience—they were now on their feet yet again. Their shocked reaction was deadening. As the boys ended the tune, they came up to take another of their twin bows, before turning around to run to the back of their stage where they popped their heads out the rear panel to wave to the outfield crowd, much to their delight too. The standing ovation meanwhile, continued for another near minute.

But then, as if by magic, the rear panels of the stage began lowering into oblivion below the fog-covered stage, which now began to revolve slowly clockwise . . . it, was truly something to see as it all transformed.

The rest of the performance followed the same trend as yesterday's. The boys kept putting on the steam with each additional new song with more and more excitement along with an increasing energy in their selections until they were at: I'm Still Standing. That tune had the same affect on the audience, as the day before.

The audience was singing right along with the chorus, while doing a chain-wave with their arms over their heads. Dad, at that moment, knocked me with his arm as he pointed out to the outside crowds. Damn if the crowd wasn't now all the way back to the 500 Speedway attraction, with this being the 2 p.m. show! It was a mass of people doing a chain-wave . . . but it was certainly an infectious atmosphere.

Taylor then spoke to the hyper crowd, while still adjusting to a theatre-in-the-round setting somewhat. He'd walk clockwise a moment, but then seemed to stop momentarily before beginning to walk again.

"Thank you everyone, we're Tay 'n' Tre . . . and we love you Toonland. Thank you. We hope to see you next time at eight pee. Here's our closing tune, My Prayer."

The lighting affects were lost during daylight, so the boys left their costumes alone per mom's instructions. They simply waited now for the audience to quiet down, which took nearly a half minute. The boys then began the song that was quickly becoming their signature tune. It was exactly what you would want for your cover track tune anyway—right?

As usual, even without the 'gingerbread lighting affects' it had lost none of its appeal. When Taylor hit his crescendo, I immediately saw a repeat of yesterday's reaction of the deep gasps of air as people were just overwhelmed with the power of his crescendo.

The boys simply owned this audience, it was definitely clear now.

It was not any fluke, or a one-time thing. They were connecting with each audience, so they had definitely made the transition to pros—truly now . . . even I had to admit it.

The boys got up from being on their knees in prayer, and took their bows again to all of the various sections of the audience, including those clapping from lines and rides as the stage began to lower to tumultuous applause. I could not have been more pleased for them, or for us.

After people heard the announcer's remarks, they all started to disperse, just as Stephen Kineret at the next table, tapped my shoulder.

"Yes Stephen?"

"Marc, those are some two boys you've got, damn man, I told you my three were true critics."

"Thank you Stephen, did you think it was worth the wait the kids put you through?"

"Are you kidding, I might just sit here now, for the next show Marc. My God man, they are something else.

"Thanks Stephen, I'm touched that you enjoyed them so much. Do you think your kids would enjoy meeting them downstairs?"

"Would they? Hell . . . I would!"

I had to chuckle, yet felt touched by his obvious sincerity in the statement too.

"Stephen, if you, along with your wife and girls would like to follow us, I would be delighted to introduce you and your family to the boys."

"Lead the way Marc, but thank you my friend, this is going to be the highlight of our trip, right this minute meeting your sons . . . believe me."

"Thank you Stephen, I appreciate that, I know the boys will too, so let's go."

Stephen quickly explained to his wife and three girls what was about to transpire as his older girl who I took to be probably twelve, started to faint, right on the spot. I am not kidding, she started to go down, but thankfully her mother caught her. She would have been on the ground, had it not been for her mother's quick reaction.

After they had cleared her out of her fog, while composing her, we then made our way downstairs with our security detail. The young lady was shaking all the way downstairs as she kept repeating loudly:

"I can do this, I know I can do this."

Heading into the boys' dressing room adjoining the make up room, we found our two rockers sitting on their sofa, covered in a fair amount of sweat while downing bottled water.

While they immediately got up to greet all of us first, and then met the Kineret family—I was instantly troubled because I knew instinctively, that they were not speaking to one another.

Somehow I could always pick up on when they 'disconnected', if you will. It was so rare of an event that when it happened; I never reacted to it well. I really didn't know why exactly, after all, brothers are always fighting I would suppose. Yet these two were so close being twins, it always troubled me when I saw it . . . so now was no exception.

But I could also tell something else—right at that moment . . . that was, Mr. Tre Morgan was definitely attracted to our pretty 'fainter' whose name actually was Lii. She along with her sisters, Lani and Malu, were all tall and darling. Just like my boys, they were also very personable. I guess that made for an instant attraction in Trevor's mind, especially for Lii. He walked over to her while everyone else was talking about the performance.

"So, is your name Lii, did I pronounce that right?"

"You were close, take the name Lee, but then just add an extra letter 'e' after you say Lee, so it becomes Lee . . . e, see? Are you Tre?"

"Natch, that's me, so did you like the concert?"

"Did I, well—yeah! It was like truly awesome."

"Good. So do you have a boyfriend?"

"No—why?"

"Oh, I don't know. I mean like you're really pretty, so I just thought you would have a squeeze, ya know—a boyfriend."

"Oh."

"So Lii, your name's really pretty, is it Swedish, you kinda look Swedish?

"No, it isn't Swedish, it's Samoan . . . our Mom is Samoan."

"Wow that's cool, so where is Samoan, anyway?"

"Tre—it's Samoa, and that's a chain of islands past Hawaii in the South Pacific."

"Oh, cool, we have a home in Hawaii, but I've never been to it."

"That's awesome Tre. You know, I read that article about you guys, so I know about the weird way you met your Dad."

"Great, then I don't have to try to explain it all, so that's brill."

I was checking out this whole discourse from a father's perspective, so at present, I felt it was going fine.

"So how about you Tre—have you got a squeeze?"

"No—Natch—I'm too stinking busy—taking baths with my bloody brother." He had belted it out so loud; I was convinced they could probably hear it on Americana Avenue. Well, at least I knew I wasn't crazy. I immediately looked at Taylor, who I could see, was about to break into tears.

I did what I knew was needed most at that moment, I asked everyone to let us get the boys going as we all now said our good byes to the Kinerets.

The Kinerets departed with autographed photos along with the first merchandising item from T-M Merchandising, a metal picture pin of the boys wearing their infamous Teddy Toon hats. I then cleared the room of everyone else as well, as I asked them to meet us topside.

When it was just the three of us, the temperature really went up big time.

"I can't bloody hell believe you did that to me Taylor. God I'm so miffed at you I can't even talk." Trevor then literally screamed in disgust into the air looking at the ceiling.

"I'm sorry Trev, it was just a little comedy . . . I didn't even think about it, it just sort of slipped out. You know, this is all new to me too." He was now officially turning on the faucets to his floodgates.

"Alright—damn it, that's enough from the both of you. On the sofa, right now!"

The two combatants took their respective seats at each end of the six-foot sofa.

"Okay, now that's better. Trevor, you will concisely and politely explain your position first, so that we can then hear Taylor's explanation."

"Dad, what can I say—he's a bloody 'idiot'? Who would ever say something so personal, embarrassing, and humiliating, that had even the slightest amount of a brain—who Dad?"

"Okay Trevor, is that your issue in essence?"

"Yeah, isn't that enough?"

"Yes Trev, from your perspective it is, I'm sure."

"Thank you Dad, I'm glad you agree."

"Now wait—just a cotton-picking-minute there—Sparky. I never said I agreed with anything. I'm acknowledging that I can see it from your perspective though."

"Well that's the same thing Dad, isn't it?"

"No son, it isn't, I can assure you. Now Taylor, might we have your explanation."

"Daddy, it's like I said, I feel horrible about it now. I didn't want to hurt Tre intentionally, I'd never do that—I love him . . . I love you Tre." He was outright bawling buckets now.

"Don't know, but that was a brill way of showing it bro!"

"Look, it just sort of came out of me, but besides, didn't I have just as much to be sorry for afterwards?"

"Okay. So now we have our issue from Trevor, with an explanation from Taylor . . . do you want to hear my opinion now?"

"Yes."

"Fine—leave it in the act!"

"Dad—are you going stupid too—now?"

Did my eleven-year-old actually just say that to me? I said to myself as I instinctively and immediately gave Trevor a nice slap right across his cheek, while I added in an angry . . . albeit—loud, voice:

"Do not ever take that tone with me again young man, unless you'd like a further demonstration of my hand's talents across your backside next time. Are we clear, Trevor Sean Morgan?"

Trevor was now crying himself, more out of embarrassment than pain . . . I hoped. Nonetheless, he got out the desired response:

"Yes sir, I'm sorry—please forgive me Daddy." His 'Daddy' acknowledgement told me he had indeed gotten the message.

"You're forgiven son. Now as I was saying, I'd leave it in the act. No one believes its true anyway Trevor; they assumed it was a gag . . . it was nothing more than that son. Trev, people, including a younger audience, are used to that kind of gag in a stage show. You're blowing this way out of proportion in the process, Trevor."

"You really think so Daddy?"

"Yes Taylor, I do, but there's something else. I know that you are truly sorry for what happened out there. That ought to be enough for your brother to get off his high horse to forgive you. You know, he's not exactly exempt from making these kinds of little faux'pas remarks himself, is he?" As I stared down Trevor sternly . . . yet again.

"No I guess not Dad; I've said a few, but bloody hell, not in front of twenty thousand strangers."

"Trevor that may be true, but just so you know—this little tidbit of information will not make you any happier either, but the number was closer to twenty-five thousand people. Yet that shouldn't matter Trev, should it?

"Trevor, your brother unintentionally erred in what he said, but he apologized for it. Since when, is that not enough to forgive someone in our family, young man?

"Son, let me point something else out to you. I can prove that Taylor's joke wasn't even embarrassing, or damaging to your 'rep' in the least. Listen son, young Lii fainted out on the Quad—the moment she learned she was going to be meeting you . . . so was she worried about what Taylor said earlier—I think not?"

"She did Dad, for real?"

"Yes son, she did."

"Okay Dad, I guess your right. Taylor, I accept your apology, and I forgive you. Dang it, I guess I still love you too."

He walked over to his brother to embrace him, which of course started Taylor off on a fresh gallon of tears . . . he really was the more sensitive twin at times like this.

"Thanks bro, I really am sorry."

"I know Tay, I can see that, but Dad, I still don't want that gag in the act. I refuse."

"Okay Trevor, it's yours and Taylor's decision to make, not mine or Grammy's or Scoot's. I recommend you keep it in, or at least a version of it, why not try working it over with Larry a little then?"

"Alright Dad, I guess we can discuss that with Larry, okay Tay?"

"Yeah, but thanks for forgiving me Trev."

"Heck Tay, you know I can't ever stay mad at you for long anyway."

"Yeah, it's like that for me too Trev," which it really was.

"Good, now that we're all friends again, I also want to comment on something much more significant than this disagreement itself. I want to tell you both how proud I am of you.

"As professionals, you obviously realized how important it was to not allow this argument to become obvious during your performance? I would have never known you two were fighting from your stage demeanor. That was an important test in your turning pro, boys . . . which you both passed with flying colors—not everyone can do that."

"Great . . . at least something good came out of it." Trevor acknowledged.

"Fine, now let's get topside to join our group—shall we?"

"Okay Dad." I heard.

We began to pick up their stuff in their dressing room that they wanted to take along, when I realized that I had better take Trevor over to the make up room first. His cheek remained crimson, so I didn't want him further embarrassed by his punishment—literally at my hand.

"Trevor, come with me for a moment, Tay can you get all the stuff upstairs with some help from a security escort? Remember, there is to be no going up on your own. Trevor and I will be right up son."

"Okay Daddy—good luck bro."

"What did I do now Dad?"

"Nothing honey, you're fine—I guess Taylor's just a little bit paranoid is all. I simply realized that I gave you a nice slap there, so your cheek is quite flushed now. I want to give it some of that powder stuff that the girls use on you guys. It should adequately reduce the redness, that's all."

"Oh, blimey, I guess I just survived my first real punishment from you Dad."

As I started lightly powdering his cheek, I responded as I worked along with his makeup.

"Yes, but I don't ever want to have to do that again—ever. Jesus, you boys mean the world to me; as I love you with all my heart. I also respect both of you so much along with what you're trying to do with your crusade.

"Trevor, respect's important. It must always be returned properly from son to father, or else what happened before—will certainly happen again . . . you crossed a line there son.

"Even as you two get older, you must always remember to speak to me, as well as all of your elders for that matter, with proper respect, or believe me, you won't be happy with my reaction . . . ever!"

"I understand Dad, but you know that I really love you—with all of my heart?"

Yes son, of course I do." I instantly stopped my 'cover up' work long enough to embrace my son with an added kiss thrown in, for his tender, heartfelt, words.

"I mean it Dad, I've, I mean—we've, got the greatest Dad in the world—you!

I was a little bit choked up myself now, as I commented:

"You know Trevor; a year ago, I didn't even know that you or Taylor existed. Yet right now, with what you just said, I don't think that matters one bit—I have always loved you both, even when your existence was merely in my dreams as a younger man.

"You see Trev, I always knew I wanted children, in fact your Mum and I had intended on having four. So, maybe I got two of those in the equation, but what a pair of wonderful boys I got. God I love you so much son."

We embraced again, but this time I think, both of us had a nice little cry to boot.

Once we had composed ourselves, with my handy work complete as the cheek appeared 'ok', we went upstairs, arm-in-arm—proud father and son.

We joined our group topside, to find Taylor mobbed now with fans seeking autographs. I immediately suggested to Trevor that he lend his bro a hand, which certainly added to the excitement for the fans as we walked over. Tre joined his brother as I then went over to our entourage.

"What took you two so long—was there a problem?"

"Mom, nothing that a few tears along with a little make up couldn't fix."

"Do you want to enlighten me dear?"

"Not now Mom . . . maybe later."

"Alright, but we'll certainly be discussing it sometime today I hope?"

"Sure, no problem."

"So kids (I was addressing the younger foursome) what's next on our ride agenda?"

"Gee HB, are you actually asking us?"

"Sure I am Lar, you're all a part of our group family here, so why wouldn't I?"

"Oh, I don't know, I just thought that Tay and Tre got to pick the rides?"

"Why Lar, last I checked, they weren't the only kids here with an opinion on which rides to do first—so what's it going to be?"

"Uncle Marc, while we're here in Future World, can we do Mars Attacks Again and Along the Milky Way, Halley and I would like to go there?"

"How does that sit with you and Larry, Austin?"

"It's fine with me Marc, what do you think Larry?"

"Fine with me Austin, now all we have to do is to wait for our mates to finish with their fans so we can get going."

"Well said Lar-man, because it's those fans that make all of this fun possible in a way—isn't it?"

"Yeah, yeah I suppose, but sometimes it's just too much for me."

"How so Lar?"

"Jeeze HB, it's just kind of crazy for me to think of my mates this way, cuz when we're together, we're just three regular guys. I mean, none of us make a big deal about it or nothing—hell they hardly even talk about it. Why can't everyone else, just act that 'cool' around them too?"

"Larry, I can't answer that, other than to say that it's simply part of the phenomenon of celebrity . . . it's just the way things will be for the foreseeable future. Sorry pal, but we all have to adjust to it. But I'm glad to see that you four don't treat them any different, because you all know they hate that—right?"

"Yes Uncle Marc, we sure do, cuz they told us so."

"You're right Em, but that's the way we should all treat the situation, alright?" I received a round of yeses from our assembled diminutive entourage as the adults rejoined us now, too.

Once the boys had finished their autographs, we quickly avoided any further crowds by going through the back lot with security.

Our security team took us directly inside the Mars Attacks Again building through the back lot, which made it much easier—until the boys appeared through a door for our maybe twelve steps into the roller coaster.

Once recognized, the twins elicited mass screams, followed by applause, from many of the waiting guests in the area. The boys took it all in stride by simply choosing to return to their 'regular guys' mode after a quick wave a few times before then ignoring it any further.

Reg and Gracie loved this ride so much; they asked if we could go again. God how they were laughing and yelling throughout our second go-round.

We all agreed to do Along the Milky Way next, where once again; our group used the back lot area to get inside the ride with our security detail.

With this ride however, Reg and Gracie were not so inclined to request a second go. Grace actually looked green as she exited, so Reg forced her to sit down for a few minutes before we moved on. Once she recovered, the kids all decided on the attraction next door.

Afterwards, Mom suggested we all return to the hotel for a little breather, to which the kids of course replied that the adults were more than welcome to do that—themselves.

After our entourage was lessened by our most 'senior' components, it was just Scoot and me with our gaggle of kids. This suited us fine, as we were having a ball ourselves on the rides.

I think throughout the day though, Scoot and I were mostly watching Austin's excitement as this was only his second visit to Toonland. He was only four at the time of his first visit, so this was his first 'real' cognitive visit. There is just something wonderful, watching a youngster constantly in awe of his surroundings.

From Future World, we opted to pick up the Toonland Railroad at the Future World Station to get us over to The Louisiana Purchase, where the newest sections of the park were.

Getting on the train proved not so smart as the boys were instantly surrounded with more of their new fans seeking autographs. The boys were happy to oblige, but this made it necessary for us to go around the entire park twice to give them the time to complete the task.

The boys had not one word of complaint—as in my boys, because I was certainly not including Larry . . . as he was most vocal in his feelings by this time.

"Christ HB, we have to find a way to cool this signing autographs' crap because I'm getting tired of it?"

"You're getting tired of it Lar? Imagine how the boys must feel with all this attention—and all the writing . . . you don't see them making a fuss, do you?"

"No, but its part of their job, as for me, I want some action on these rides. I don't want to wait until I'm as old as you—to get there either!"

I was busting up, as was Scoot, but I tried to humble my young surrogate son a little too.

"My Lar, now that would be terrible—wouldn't it?"

"You're damn straight HB."

"You know Lar; it would be appreciated, if you could hold your more worldly expressions to yourself, instead of babbling them around Austin and the girls?"

"Oh . . . sorry HB, I didn't mean to, it just sort of comes out sometimes, you should hear dad, he's worse than me."

"Well Lar, actually as you'll recall, I have had a little taste of his commentary myself, so I know what you're saying, but that's different, he wasn't twelve at the time."

"Okay HB, I'll shut up, but I don't like it—this waiting I mean."

"You know Lar; I do understand that, so we will try to work around this issue a little bit more for the rest of our stay, fair enough?"

"Thanks HB, you're the best . . . besides, poor Austin's never going to get on all of these rides he hasn't tried, if we don't."

"Yes Larry, that's true as well. Austin, are you having a bad time with all of this?"

"Are you kidding me Marc, I'll make this trip with you and the guys anytime. This is so cool, being with rock stars plus seeing everything there is here."

I looked at Larry to speak, but before I could even get a single word out, he already had read my mind.

"Okay, okay, I get the message HB, but try to do something, please?"

"Sure Lar, you can count on me." I immediately called over our lead security detail officer.

"Joe, what do you suggest we do, to get the kids in and out of the west side of the park without more of these autograph sessions?"

"Leave it to me Mr. Morgan; I'll get it all fixed up. I'll have the kids through every single attraction from Calico Mining Railway to Mt. Splashdown, with everything that's in between within fifty minutes!"

"Really Joe, is that even possible?"

"Sure it is, just watch me Mr. Morgan."

"Joe, for the twentieth time, would you please call me Marc?"

"Sorry Marc, it's just not in our protocol to do that, but I'll try to remember."

"Thanks Joe."

"No problem Marc."

True to his word, Joe arranged a golf cart caravan through the back lots behind the Louisiana Purchase train station, where he succeeded in having us all over the western regions of the park, while we hit every single attraction except The Huck Finn, which was avoided for obvious reasons, within forty-seven minutes . . . Scoot clocked it.

By the time we had finished our quick tour of attractions on the western side, I was hearing some rumblings about stomachs . . . they wanted to eat again. Kids just never seem to get enough, even with all the crap they had been snacking on over the last two and a half hours.

"Joe, what's your suggestion on where to eat?"

"Marc, anywhere's fine, but 'anywhere' inside, will bring the crowds, so it's up to you all?"

"Since the boys are officially employees now, I think it's time for them to experience Scott's and my old hangout."

"What's that Marc?"

"The Zone, Joe."

"Oh, yeah, I keep forgetting you're an old employee yourself."

"Dad, what's 'the Zone'?"

"Trevor, that's one of the employee restaurants here within the Louisiana Purchase. Uncle Scoot and I used to spend much of our lunch hours there when we worked here together—the food's great, but it's an exciting little joint to hang out in too."

"Oh. You mean even the employees have their own restaurants here?"

"Yes of course Trev, there's like five thousand employees working here on most days, they have to eat somewhere, don't they?"

"God, Dad, I never even thought about that, that's amazing."

"Well, if you say so Trev, but you have to realize this place is like a City within a City actually. They have their own police, firefighters, even a small hospital!"

"Really Daddy?"

"Yes Taylor."

"Wow." Austin offered."

So we all headed over via golf carts to the T.L.P. Main Kitchen, where yours truly spent much of his days while working there. I blew the kids away by entering the kitchen through a back door behind the pillaged village of the Bahaman Buccaneer, so the kids went crazy with this chosen route into one of the largest commercial kitchens in the world.

Walking through the enormous facility, I naturally recognized all of the various stations, as I flashed back to my own early days there. Scoot and I were hearing all types of 'wows' from the kids as we made our way through, so I gave them all a little tour as we walked along.

Nevertheless, as we were walking by the small administrative offices off the main kitchen floor, I froze solid—right in my tracts. I absolutely couldn't believe it. There in the Executive Chef's office—sat my very first boss, as well as being—my beloved mentor, Raul Mendez. I assumed he was long since retired—or worse.

Rex, as he was known by all, had not only taken me under his wing, but he was a fine person along with being a friend to everyone in general.

I stopped right in front of his door as I just stared into the doorway waiting for him to look up from his paperwork to see me standing there. When he finally did, his reaction was no less stunned than mine, once he recognized me, that is.

"My word, as I live and breathe—after all of these years . . . look who comes marching back to Papa—the local boy who made good. But look at the skinny bastard now—how the hell are you Marc?"

Rex immediately stood to walk over to me as I put out my hand . . . but apparently it wasn't my hand he wanted. A moment later, I was in a deep and touching hug with my old mentor and dear friend.

It was clear to all—that there were two grown men standing side by side, all broke up, both trying to make it appear as if none of this was happening or embarrassing.

"Hello Rex, it's nice to see you looking so well, yourself." This was about all I could get out now.

"Please son, come in and sit a spell with me?"

"Rex, I'm afraid with this handful of hungry kids here, I'll have a mutiny if I don't get them into the Zone—can you join us there instead?"

"Sure, just give me a minute or two to check the hotline and then I'll be right in. God, I can't believe how wonderful it is to see you again, but you look fantastic without that weight you were carrying before".

"Thanks boss."

"Boss? Now stop throwing the bull son."

"Rex, I realize you're much too modest to accept what I'm about to say . . . yet I know you'll understand that it comes from the heart. Every chef as you know all too well has someone in the business that influences them the most or leaves that indelible mark upon them throughout their professional career. You have been that man for me, so I'm forever in your debt . . . I mean that Rex."

Rex immediately seemed taken aback as well as obviously deeply moved. He grabbed me again, but this time along with his hug, I received a discreet peck to my cheek that he concealed from our group that was hanging onto every word, outside the office door now. Through considerably moister eyes now, he whispered back while still hugging me:

"Thank you Marc, I'm humbled by your remarks, yet thrilled for your success. You have always made me proud of you—this now allows me to be proud of myself as well, so I thank you for that son."

I quickly introduced Rex to Scoot, along with all of the kids present, when he then seemed to have an epiphany when he was shaking hands with my identical off spring.

"Wait just a minute Marcus—now don't tell me that these two—are the twins busting all the crowd 'records' over at the Quad this weekend, while also playing the Harpsichord upstairs?"

"Yes Rex, these are them . . . boys, I want you two to know that this is the man responsible for my commercial success as a chef, so I owe him a lot."

"Hey Dad, I thought Grandfather got that honor?"

"Yes Trevor, Grandfather is very much responsible for my success in learning the restaurant business, just as Grammy is responsible for teaching me how to cook and understand it all. But boys, Rex here, is responsible for inspiring me creatively as a chef. He encouraged and nudged me along mentoring me, by taking me under his wing of sorts. You could say Trev, that Rex taught me the difference between being a great chef—over an exceptional one, I owe him big-time, believe me."

"Cool—boy Mr. Mendez, you must be special for Dad to say all that."

"Thank you young man, but your Dad's just being his typical modest self—he had the talent the moment he walked in this place some fifteen years ago. I just set him free to develop that talent . . . which he did, like—a bat out of hell in here."

"You know Marc; I've followed you all these years, so I admit that I take just a little bit of pride when I'm eating one of the omelets at Verandas."

"As you should, after all, I stole the technique from you in the first place."

"Not stole Marc . . . offered, is the proper term. So boys; is all this hubbub I hear about you two—true? I've been told that you two are blowing SRO crowds away at every performance . . . and that upstairs, you've given that Harpsichord as good a workout as it gets when Phyllis Diller honors us with a visit.

Taylor then offered an answer.

"Yes Mr. Mendez, I guess we are—but it's great to see all the guests having a good time listening to us."

"Yes, I'm sure it is. Well listen, you all go into the Zone since you are all so hungry . . . order up anything you want—my treat. I'll come in to join you all in a minute, alright?"

"Sure sir, but thank you for treating us, right guys? All the kids thanked our host before Trevor added:

"And Mr. Mendez, it's a real pleasure meeting you too, sir." Then Trevor shocked the hell out of me . . . along with Rex naturally, by giving him a heartfelt hug . . . my old boss about lost it, right there on the spot . . . Jesus, what a softie.

We walked into the Zone, where all of our kids immediately 'dug' the place's atmosphere with its casual yet lively appearance expressed through its décor.

The twins quickly mentioned how special they felt, seeing tons of other employees like themselves, all dressed in their respective costumes and uniforms, just taking it easy as they ate or conversed.

Yet, as those other employees sitting there, saw our group of juveniles walk in with Scoot and I, within moments it seems, they appeared to derive the correct conclusion of the twins' identity, but in doing so—they now blew us away. Each table began to stand up in place, first one table, followed by another, but always, one table at a time, increasing their applause while in a standing ovation . . . it was so damn touching.

The boys themselves, were so deeply moved by this gesture, they started blushing big time while it looked as if Taylor at least, was going to spill a few over the tribute.

God, they really had floored us all . . . but it was weird for me especially, because there was something familiar about it too . . . a faint memory in the back of my mind that wasn't yet clear, told me that it also made sense.

Somehow, while I was always very proud of my two boys, this unexpected, as well as, spontaneous and sincere expression by their fellow park employees really got to me too. My pride was ten-fold honestly—how was that even possible, I thought?

The boys held up their hands to stop them as they blurted out some thank you's before they quickly took seats at a large table against the wall. I had everyone reading the menu board as I wrote down everyone's order, so that Scoot and I could then walk up to order at the counter in an organized fashion for a party of our size.

With our security detail still in line behind us, we returned to our table—with mountains of food . . . literally.

Our security team knew they could kill two birds with one stone by eating with us. They knew all too well that the other employees would give the boys their space and serenity now-to enjoy their conversations at the table uninterrupted . . . they were correct too.

"Marc, that was a touching ovation for the boys, wasn't it?"

"Yeah pal, it was, but I'm getting old . . . I'm forgetting the significance of it, can you believe that? I guess it really has been too many years for me."

"Relax Marc, let me remind you. Our fellow employees are just showing their appreciation to the boys for all the extra hours they'll be scheduled to work, during the boys' subsequent visits here in the park."

"Right, I remember now. Jesus, how could I have forgotten the keyword around this place anyway—it's all about the turnstile, isn't it?"

"Yes it is Marc, but don't sweat it bud, at least its nice having you back here anyways." Scoot joked.

Good old Scooter, I could always count on him to set me straight . . . at a minimum over the half-forgotten ovation for the boys.

"Dad, I love the food and the Harpsichord at forty-four, but eating here is so much better, we can just be ourselves here—so do you think we can do this more often?"

"Sure T-man, I certainly don't have a problem with that . . . besides, it's all the same food they serve to the guests, so it's not like it's a punishment to eat here, is it?"

"No, the food's great . . . so I like it here too Dad." Trevor now added his two cents into the mix of comments.

"Okay boys, the Zone it is, along with some of the other employee restaurants too. But now that I know that Rex is still working here in this main kitchen, I'm sure the Zone will remain our first choice, besides forty four."

"HB, I don't get it—what were you thinking anyway? You worked here, so you knew about this place all this time . . . yet this is the first time we're here? What's the matter with you anyway?"

"Sorry Lar-man, you know—maybe we should just put you in charge of our entire weekends here?"

"Whoa—that's the first smart thing you've said this whole trip HB"!

"Oh, thank you Lar, I'll keep that one in mind . . . when your Mom asks me how you behaved this trip . . . won't I?"

"Oh Jesus HB, don't do that, I didn't mean nuthin' by it—it was a joke."

"Okay Larry, but let's try to be a little bit more sensitive to the respect you pay your elders . . . alright?"

"Sure HB, I will—sorry."

"You're forgiven; now eat those wings before they get cold."

Larry immediately dug in; convinced he might have been spared his 'hide' from Carol's wrath.

The security detail was now at the table next to us, as I turned to Joe.

"So Joe, what are your suggestions for Bayou Country as well as The Louisiana Purchase?

"Don't worry Marc, I've got them covered too, the only variable is how many times the kids want to ride Wrong-way Murphy's and the Bahaman Buccaneer." This immediately elicited a response from Taylor.

"Joe, if there's no such thing as a limit, I vote for five times on Wrong-way Murphy's, plus at least twice on the Buccaneer, what do the rest of you guys think?"

Embeth was the first to respond.

"Tay, I don't know if I can handle five times on Wrong-way Murphy's, it might make me sick after eating all this food."

Immediately, those words were not lost on Larry.

"Em—be sure you don't sit next to me, okay?"

Austin found this subtle crack of Larry's so funny; but he quickly got in trouble with the milk he was drinking at that moment—as his laughter sort of made him choke. Sure enough, he was soon blowing the milk right out through his nose—it was truly a Kodak, moment.

"Nice one Austin, but let's see what you can do with this Gatorade being slimy green and all?"

This got Trevor instantly miffed at his best mate.

"Larry, cool it. Here we are—having a feed, with poor Austin just laughing at your own stupid joke . . . so you decide to reward him with a bloody rub like that? Have you gone bloody crackers mate—what's the matter with you? You better apologize to our mate now . . . aay?"

"Sorry Austin . . . sorry Tre, you're right, I screwed up."

"No problem Larry . . . sometimes you're just so funny I can't help it."

"Thanks Austin, I think you're cool too . . . especially like when you fart when you think no one's looking."

Austin instantly blushed; while Larry was laughing alone . . . yet again.

"Larry! Did everything Trevor just said to you, go in—one ear, while out the other? Damn it, now apologize to Austin again, while you keep your 'wind' comments to yourself please—for everyone's benefit." I added testily.

"God, sorry again guys, but you too Austin . . . I guess I don't know my own mouth sometimes . . . you know, it's not easy doing stand up constantly."

Scoot then responded to Larry's rationale.

"No Larry, it's not—so why not give it a rest before you run out of funny things to say . . . hell, I fear you might be scraping the bottom of the barrel already . . . don't you?"

"God, could that really happen Scott—for real?"

"I don't know Lar, but if they keep running downhill like your last few, I'd say—yes. You had better keep still for a bit and—recharge, don't you think?"

"Yeah, I guess." Larry added in an uncharacteristically sullen voice.

This got all of us chuckling, including our security team, so I guess we all then went quiet ourselves to return to finishing our meals, even as we saw Rex walk in to join us now.

"So boys, I've only got one question for you two, and then I'll leave you to your dinner. What's it really like—living with the world's most infamous practical joker?"

At hearing Rex's words, I immediately slumped down into my chair another few inches—knowing all too well where this was leading already— the Silence of the Pheasants!

"You mean you know about Dad's jokes Mr. Mendez?"

"Know about them—yes . . . sadly, you could say that—but are you Tre or Tay? But by the way children, feel free to call me Rex."

"I'm Taylor, but can we call you 'Uncle' Rex then? Daddy must really respect you to say what he did before. He doesn't say things like that to that many people."

"I would be honored Taylor, but it's only if you want too."

"I can't speak for Trevor, as I've done too much of that already today, but as for me, yes, I'd like to call you Uncle Rex." I immediately chuckled at that one, believe me.

"Me too, Uncle Rex," came from Trevor now.

"And me three, came from Larry."

"Oh heck, me four."

After this came from Austin, the girls didn't want to be left out either, so Rex was immediately loaded with six new nieces and nephews . . . not bad for a man with no family to speak of. Again he was touched big time by the kids' gestures.

"So Uncle Rex, you really know about Dad's little jokes?"

"Yes Taylor—too well, I'm afraid."

Trevor now added his own two cents.

"So I guess he got you sometime too, huh Uncle Rex?"

"Most definitely Trevor." At this point, I started shaking my head from side to side as I began laughing, just reliving the whole episode once again in my mind.

"So—tell us about it already Uncle Rex?" This came from Larry of course.

"Sure, but I have to think back on the circumstances. Marc, could you refresh me on the opening details, you know I'm getting older son?"

"Rex—if I must, but somehow I feel like I'm planning my own funeral with this, you know what I'm sayin'?"

"Go ahead son . . . get it started for me. I'll remember the specifics that way."

"Okay Rex, you win, but only this one time. As I recall, we were going to have some special guests up at forty four, close to the hearts of Trevor and Taylor I might add . . . along with their Mum too."

"Who were they Dad, these guests, I mean?"

"Yes Tay—none other than Prince Charles, Princess Diana, as well as the royal Princes."

"Wow—you mean you really cooked dinner for our Royal family?"

"Sure boys, several of them over my years here . . . including the Queen Mother along with your Queen too."

"Wow. How come you never told us that before, Dad?"

"I don't know Tre; you know I don't like to drop names, besides it's nothing unusual for the door at forty-four . . . we always had nobility eating there."

"Yes, but this is different Dad—this is our Royal family!"

"Okay, forgive me for not telling you before, fair enough?"

"Sure thing Dad, so what actually happened?"

"Honestly son, I'm trying to get to that, if you guys will give me a chance?"

"Okay, sorry Daddy, please continue, we'll shut up, won't we Tre?"

"Yep. Go ahead Dad, tell the story."

"Alright, now let's see, well as I was saying, we were going to be having the Royals for dinner that week, so Uncle Rex here was an absolute wreck . . . which was nothing new for him, by the way. He always got like that when any 'Royals' or major celebrities were scheduled . . . or is that an unfair statement, Uncle Rex?"

"No . . . that's putting it mildly Marc . . . I was beside myself with nerves, kids."

"So anyway, all week, Uncle Rex was running around the kitchen, constantly worrying about everything being perfect in his plans. In particular of course, the menu had to be stellar . . . so he sought out suggestions from me along with a few others. Eventually, he and I sat down over coffee one afternoon about three days before the big event, to plan the menu. In fact, right here in this restaurant—wasn't it Rex?"

"Yes Marc, but stop stalling—keep going."

"Fine Rex. Kids, your Uncle Rex, had a soft spot for my presentation of 'Pheasant under Glass', so he asked me to prepare that as the main entrée. I of course immediately agreed to Uncle Rex's request.

"You see, at that moment, a prank had also instantly flashed into my mind's eye, just thinking about that particular main dish, along with Rex's ridiculous nerves over having royal guests. I realized I could pull a beauty on—good old Uncle Rex without much effort that would forever teach him to stay nice and calm with any or all royal guests in the future.

"But then Uncle Rex added to his own 'downfall' by telling me that he wanted to assist me in preparing the meal . . . I relished that thought naturally, as I quickly agreed to accept his offer of help. You see, I knew all too well, that Uncle Rex helping me would afford the perfect set up along with the proper environment for the gag to work out. From that point forward gang, there was no turning back.

"Now kids, that's the general set up, so I think I'll leave Uncle Rex to take it from here—alright Rex?"

"Yes Marc, it's all coming back now—but painfully so!"

"Okay—where to start? Hum, yes—that's it. Alright children, so there we are in forty-four's kitchen, with our plans all set for prepping all afternoon for the special dinner menu we had planned together. Your father had suggested doing his preparations downstairs in this kitchen outside the door here, so we would have plenty of room to work on the meal. I didn't argue, but boy—I should have known better to smell the rat roasting—right at that moment, as they say.

"At any rate, we were getting close to dinner now when Marc came upstairs to inform me that everything was ready at his end. He said he had the Pheasant finished, purporting that it was sitting on a cart, covered with a tablecloth to keep any grease or dust from getting on the glass dome that covered the entrée. Like a naïve fool at that time, I completely bought into that story—but worse—I felt relieved actually.

"You see, everything had gone perfectly through the first three courses already, so I was quickly calming down . . . but how short-lived that turned out to be, as you'll see. Well, then the time came to get the Pheasant under Glass reheated to raise the fragrance of Marc's wonderful truffles and cognac reduction, and then finally into the butler's pantry for serving.

"Naturally, I asked Marc to get the entrée . . . but he replied that at that very moment—he needed to use the restroom before he did anything else . . .

which I was stupid enough to believe. Marc therefore suggested that I retrieve it while he insisted that he would rejoin me as soon as he could."

"Oh boy Uncle Rex, yep—that's Dad for you . . . right Tay" Came out of Trevor.

"It sure is bro."

"At any rate gang, I had been such an absolute wreck that whole day up until only fifteen minutes before, that I was now too relieved to sense my own dread as I continued to unwind even a bit more.

"So I glibly excused your father to fulfill his request for a bathroom break, while I left to go downstairs for the Pheasant under Glass myself. I was of course careful not to touch or move the cover—or bump into anything, as I knew it could ruin the delicate presentation of the dish . . . naturally we needed it perfect prior to reheating it in the oven.

"So I carefully made my way to the service elevator pushing the cart along. I took the elevator up to the forty-four kitchen, where I gingerly got out with the cart. I walked into the finishing kitchen, where the servers were standing by to assist us. They would wheel it through the butler's pantry and eventually into the Royal Family to serve it, once the dish was reheated.

"I remember having some small talk with the servers about how delightful the Royal Family was. I then said something to the affect of; well I guess here goes, let's get it in the oven, shall we?

"So at that moment, I removed the tablecloth only to find eight—'live' and very—upset, baby Pheasants staring at me. There they were, giving me the evil eye through a glass dome . . . yet it was the distinct Silence of these Pheasants that surprised me most. You see children, their beaks were all moving at around forty miles an hour!

"It seems that Marc had drilled the dome so structurally sound around the cover's base, that they could breathe . . . so therefore, taunt me unendingly, but for whatever reason, the thick dome seemed to muffle all of their sounds. Looking back on it now children—years later, it was all—too funny for words!"

Rex was right. Everyone at our long table was busting up so hard now; that it was extending into many of the surrounding employees tables too so they were listening in now as well. Rex had to stop long enough, for everyone to recover before he could continue finishing the story . . . but through his own ample laughter—Rex did so.

"So there I was, in the kitchen with the eight live Pheasant, but then I went nuts in a panic . . . I was going totally out of my mind now. You see, at that moment, I somehow assumed we were lost without a main entrée for the Royal family's dinner.

"I was so hysterical it seems; that my two servers had to seriously calm me down as I called your father every expletive I could find . . . every single one! The servers suggested I go out to the Royal family first to explain there would be a slight delay. Pulling myself together, which wasn't easy at that time, I prepared myself to do just that.

"I walked out to their private dining room through the butler's pantry, and I knocked on their door softly, before entering. There, I found your father! He was smiling at me . . . while serving the real Pheasant under Glass to the Royal family.

"Honestly children, I was so shook up, yet so relieved, that all I could think to say at that moment was—please forgive me—I'm looking for the Berman Bar Mitzvah, as I backed myself right back into the pantry and got out of there. Naturally, I then proceeded to walk straight into my office. I slammed the door shut, took out my pad, and then and there, wrote your father up for his little prank—in a nine-page report. Well, that's the story, boys and girls, in all its glory."

The better part of the room was hysterical still and now applauding. I then threw my arm around Rex's shoulder as I said to him:

"Boss, you know, I only did it out of love." This brought forth even more laughter and merriment.

When our group had finally calmed down, little Halley asked Rex:

"So were you mad at Uncle Marc for a long time Uncle Rex?"

"Mad? Halley that would be putting it mildly. I had him in my office, the minute he finished as I let him have it for over an hour, reading and screaming to him from my report. I was so spent when I finally had enough yelling, that I stopped right there, as I looked at him in total disbelief. I asked him, so—what do you have to say for yourself, Mr. Morgan? And do you know what he had the nerve to say to me kids—after all of my ranting?"

"No what, Uncle Rex?" This came from Trevor.

"Your father looked at me as straight-faced as he could—then asked me:

"Now seriously Rex—didn't you honestly think it was funny?"

"So gang, I just lost it all over again at that question. I was so enraged by that point; I had to sit down just to think. I then informed Marc he was suspended for the week. I also threatened him. I told him I would have to 'rethink' his position in the restaurant when he returned—if he returned at all."

"Wow, you were mad, weren't you Uncle Rex?"

"Yes Taylor, I was mad at that moment, but by the time the week was up, I couldn't stop laughing over the whole mess. You see, in the end, your father had been right—it was funny . . . but more importantly, serving the many royals we catered to, never bothered me again in the future . . . not once!

"Yet every time I saw your father in the kitchen his first day back, I flashed back on it again so I just had to laugh . . . as he was running around like a little scared chipmunk himself—which made me laugh even harder. But believe it or not, we never spoke of it again—until today I guess. And that's the story—the end!"

"Wow, that's a cool story Uncle Rex." Austin offered.

Then Rex remembered something more as he added:

"But I do recall that from that day forward, I always referred to Marc around the kitchen as, 'the little stinker' . . . you see, that name most certainly fit his behavior at the time, and I can assure you all."

"Yet it certainly still does Rex." This lovely zinger came from Scoot.

Everyone laughed anew at the moniker along with Scoot's crack. Yet to this very day, I still refer to myself as the little stinker, whenever I pull a nice gag off.

Before we all knew it, Rex had to excuse himself to return to his office, but not before receiving hugs and kisses from his assorted nieces, nephews— besides me. As we were leaving, I gave him my telephone numbers as I asked him to stay in touch since I would be seeing him regularly again with the boys' schedule here at the park . . . both things seemed to please him to no end.

Meanwhile, Joe and his crew got us around this area of the park as promised, so that when we had finished our rides, we had just enough time to get the boys back to the Quad underground for make up and their costume changes.

When we finally arrived at the Future World back lot area, we had scant time to do anything more than to walk through the gate and into the park towards the entrance to the stage . . . what we encountered going through that gate was truly a site to see. As we came into the park for our brief, two-hundred and fourteen-foot walk over to the bunker entrance, our security detail was joined with another, four times the first detail's size . . . and for good reason.

Immediately they surrounded us tight in formation in the shape of a mason's trowel—as the entire area was a full sea of guests simply standing around, waiting for the show to start. I could not even begin to estimate the size of it but it had to be at least forty thousand guests if it was—one. I was simply shocked, utterly and completely shocked now.

Scoot, always being the one for a little flippancy, whispered into my ear as we walked slowly towards the underground entrance:

"How much—did you say you wagered your father again?"

I said something under my breath to Scoot's crack, as we carefully made our way through the crowd. I now had my arms around both boys, holding them tight. I think for the very first time, the boys were somewhat scared by this crowd size too. They were surrounded with our large security detail on all sides, yet they were still frightened.

"Dad, this is too much, I can't believe it."

"Believe it Trev; this is all for you and Taylor, so I'd suggest you two thank all these adoring fans, the moment you get on that stage this evening."

"We will Daddy, but that's if we make it to the door 'for' the stage." I could tell that Taylor was not making jokes; he was a little bit overwhelmed as well as scared.

"Don't you fret Honey; I've got both of you tight . . . so no one's going to hurt either one of you."

"Thanks Daddy, that does make me feel better."

Our security formation continued slowly through the crowd. People close to our path began screaming, yelling, clapping, crying, or otherwise carrying on anytime they caught a glimpse of our group as they saw us pass them . . . not to mention the thousands of camera flashes.

Finally we were at our entrance door—and safety. It was at this point that I saw that Trevor had been holding Austin's hand apparently the whole time. Little Austin had been walking directly behind us.

Once the boys were in their make up chairs, they seemed to calm down somewhat with my reassuring as I then immediately thought to call the folks. They were still lounging at the resort so I felt compelled to warn them to leave extra time after speaking with Joe the head of our security detail.

Dad answered the phone when I dialed their suite.

"Hey Dad, how's your break going from all of this?"

"Hi son, fine, we were just leaving for the Transporter, what's up?"

"Dad, you'll see for yourself in a few minutes, that's all I'll admit to at this moment."

My Dad immediately started laughing.

"Let me just guess then. I'm assuming that it's a little bit crowded over there—am I warm?"

"I'll put it this way Dad; I was just informed by Joe, that apparently, they called in full security forces as well as recalled the T-M Channel's film crew to capture this all on film. You'll remember that they were only going to shoot the two pm show—right?"

"Yeah, so they're calling them back?"

"Yes Dad, they are. You see, there has to be at least forty thousand people waiting here right now. It's a bona fide record for not only this venue, but for any of their Parks worldwide, according to Joe . . . management's going nuts throughout the entire organization."

"Really, now that is good news son. Jesus, how the hell are we going to get into that area then?"

"Gee Dad, why do you think I'm calling you for Christ's sake?"

"Oh. So what's the plan son?"

"Just get to the Tour Center, it's all been arranged with security from there. God, I wish Bill was back from Laguna to see all of this, he'd be blown away—you know him."

"Yes Marc. Look, we'll get to the Tour Center, but tell my boys that Grammy and I love them—very much, alright?"

"You know Dad, by this time; I think they have a pretty good idea of that, don't you think?" That was clearly not the right way to answer his request.

"Listen smart ass, as their Gramps, it's my prerogative to say it, any and every time I want to—you get me, son?"

"Sure Dad, Jesus, sorry. I was only trying to make a joke."

"We don't joke about our love and pride for one another Marc, you know that."

"Yes sir, I do know that—forgive me?"

"You're forgiven, but I love you too."

"Thanks Dad, me too."

"Okay son, we'll see you—when we see you."

"Got it Dad, see ya soon."

"You got it son." As he hung up.

At that moment, speak of the devil, but in walked the film crew from the T-M Channel. Stacy was leading the way.

"Hi Marc. So, did you ever imagine all of this, from their one little 'test' here last month?"

"No Stacy, I can honestly say I would have never imagined anything like this, its unreal, isn't it?"

"Listen Marc, its real all right, so this crew is back to capture it for prosperity, I can assure you. Marc, with over a half-dozen park and corporate records being broken simultaneously, this is a first for us. We would like to capture this for archival purposes plus all of the excitement accompanying it. We also want to use this time for an additional interview of the twins from the one earlier, while they toured the planes."

"Sure, I'm curious myself how they're feeling right now, because I can tell you, their intense walk over to the bunker was anything but comfortable."

"Yes, I can only imagine what runs through a child's mind at a time like that, you know?"

"Yeah, I think we all were thinking about something like that . . . I mean for them, you know? My word, you should have seen Austin, he wouldn't let go of Trevor's hand . . . when was the last time you saw two boys their ages—holding hands?"

"Wow, I see your point, but listen I can help you out though. There's another way out of here totally underground, but we normally never need to use it anymore, until the boys, I should say. It will take some time, but I'll get security started on unlocking all of those doors along the way—for your exit after the concert—okay?"

"God Stacy, you're a life saver . . . thanks girlfriend."

"No problem Marc . . . but don't let Larry hear you calling me that! Now let's go get those interviews. I'm just a little bit curious myself as to what they'll say to all of this." We both got a nice laugh over her crack.

We took the crew into the make up room where they immediately set up to get their interviews.

While this was going on, Stacy added something more to our conversation.

"By the way Marc, just between us, your comments to Donovan regarding Morison—didn't go unnoticed . . . in light of all of this, the scuttlebutt in the office is that she's promoting him to a VP on Monday."

"You're kidding—really? Well I'm glad Stacy, I sincerely am. Jared turned out to be the biggest surprise of my life professionally speaking. You talk about a first impression setting you down the wrong path about someone, he'd be the poster child . . . I know you remember how he turned us all off at our first meeting last month."

"Yes I know, how can I not remember that as I witnessed it all. Yet he can be an a-hole sometimes Marc, that's the whole weird part of it. It's just that he took to the boys so thoroughly, on top of both of yours and Marilyn's motives. Obviously, he found it so unusual or refreshing, that he allowed his true human side out for a change. I'm actually kind of proud of him over this; it may be a breakthrough of sorts for him. Personally, I've never seen him happier, that's certain—he always wears a smile now, every time you see the guy—he's got this huge, goofy grin all over his puss . . . which used to be so dour always . . . they've transformed him into a real human being Marc, that's what your twins did to Jared . . . I think I should thank them for that too."

"That's nice of you to say Stace, but whatever it is, I'm pleased and delighted to also hear of this promotion for him, as Mom will be—we'll be the first ones to congratulate him if it happens, I can assure you. But—what about you Stacy, you're the one who really started all of this, where does your promotion come in, dear lady?"

"Who knows Marc; I haven't heard a word, not a peep, but who do you think laid the seeds and got that video of them to Donnie in the first place?"

"I know only too well Stacy; but thank you for confirming our suspicions. We will never forget your help, believe me."

"I do appreciate your kind words Marc, but all the same, I'm the one who feels honored to have been of help to the boys and you all."

"Thanks Stace."

At that moment, the video crew was ready so they quieted all of the kids and us down so they could begin. The videographers panned the room before the interviewer; Candy, from our earlier interview, began her opening comments.

"I'm here backstage and underground of the Future World Quad inside Toonland, in the make up room with Tay 'n' Tre . . . The Morgans. Toon Media's newest singing stars. As you can see on your television screen, outside of this building, over forty-five thousand Toonland guests wait impatiently for the twin eleven-year-olds' arrival on the Quad's Transforming Stage. Normally, this area accommodates on the Quad itself, two thousand guests comfortably."

At that moment, Scoot and I could see on the cameraman's monitor, Candy talking on half the screen with the other half devoted to film taken minutes before outside of an excited and hyper audience. There was waving and carrying on for the film crew as they panned the crowd behind the Quad area. Girls were screaming we love Tay 'n' Tre, while the remaining crowds were enthusiastic to say the least. Candy continued with her opening, as we watched in amazement.

"These twins are originally from England, but now reside in Las Vegas with their father, restaurateur Marcus Morgan of Verandas fame . . . yet neither are they ordinary eleven-year-old boys.

"They began playing the piano at five and branched out into singing as well at the ripe old age of—seven! Now nearly twelve; they are not only first-class musicians, but phenomenal singers on top of that. Offering up stellar versions of hits from some of Rock's classic artists like Elton John, the Who, and fifties legends like the Platters and Jackie Wilson, their music is anything but ordinary.

"If all of this isn't extraordinary enough, they personally spearheaded a national fundraising crusade that currently has raised more than five million dollars for charity, even as—they donate 60% of their own earnings, to their own charity foundations!

"So here's a little of my interview earlier this morning with the boys aboard the two Lear jets that bear their names honorably."

The camera's screen now switched to footage from earlier in the day at the airport inside number II-Trevor . . . with the real Trevor and Taylor.

"Tay, how does your plane differ from Tre's—their interiors appear to be identical?"

"Well Miss, they are identical—all except the names on their noses, and their different license numbers."

"How does it feel to have your own plane Tay?"

"Gee Miss, they aren't really ours. They just belong to Dad's business . . . but in case anyone's curious, they are Lear Sixty models, so they're really brill to fly in."

"You know Tay, I was just about to ask that, so yes . . . thank you. Do either of you ever want to try flying them yourselves, one day?"

Trevor immediately jumped in with a little 'less' than his normal modesty:

"Actually Miss, I already fly them all the time, with Dad—I mean."

"Wow Tre, really, that must be so exciting?"

"It is Miss; I especially like to listen to Dad talk on the radio while he gives me the controls. He talks kind of weird, so it's funny."

"Are you hoping to become a licensed pilot some day yourself then, Tre?"

"Yes Miss. Dad and I have already talked about it; he says he'll get me started so that I can become licensed to fly—before I can even drive a car, so natch, I can't wait."

"I'm sure you can't Tre . . . thank you again boys, for this wonderful tour—this is Candy Simpson reporting for the T-M Channel."

Candy's picture live, now filled the camera's screen, so we knew we were back to her current interview.

"And now, I'm here in this little make up room, to find out what's on these two budding superstars' minds, as they prepare to greet forty-five thousand—or more, of their new fans. You see, that number is expected to continue climbing to over fifty-thousand by the time they start their performance this evening."

Turning to Taylor, Candy asked:

"So Tay how does this reaction from your new fans make you feel . . . to see all these people react so well to your music?"

"Well Candy, don't know. I'm bloody bonkers over it . . . but so honored too—we both are. You see, we had no idea that our music would be liked, you know—this much. We just started out trying to raise that money for our Dad's foundation and their work—now look at what's happened . . . it's all crazy. But before I wake up from this dream Candy, I just want to say thank you Toonland, right now. We really love all of these people waiting outside for us, they are supporting us so much, that it means a lot to both of us Candy."

"So Tay, does this feel like a dream to you?"

"Sure Candy, in a way it does . . . but now it's a dream come true too, but a dream—all the same. Jeeze Candy, I'm an eleven-and-a-half, year-old-kid. Two months ago, if you had told me I'd be singing to this many people tonight, I would have laughed like a bloody old sod waffling on over nothing forever. This is all just too much, but it is a dream come true for both Tre and me."

"So, has this been hard on you and Tre, with all of these changes?"

"No, not really, we're okay . . . I guess Dad sees to that—believe me."

"Is your Dad strict with you two by the way?"

"When he has to be, sure Candy . . . usually though, he's pretty fair, but he's no ordinary Dad anyway."

"He's not?"

"No Candy, he can't be. I mean every kid we know, says their Dad's the greatest Dad in the world, and sure that's cool—really it is. I mean, every kid's Dad should be number one—right? But, I got to say, they haven't seen nothin'—until they've met our Dad . . . right Tre?"

Candy immediately jumped her mic over to Trevor who was now finished with his make up, so he was free to speak as well.

"Right Tay, Dad's certainly the best."

"Tre, what makes him so special to you and Tay then, those are some pretty big claims after all?" Candy was chuckling to lighten the accusatory nature of her statement.

"Jeeze Candy, just about everything really. Like what we talked about before, teaching me how to fly and everything—hey, I'm bloody eleven; I'm not an adult you know . . . did your Dad teach you to fly when you were my age?"

"No he hasn't Tre, you are correct there . . . is your Dad looking for other students to teach?" As they both chuckled briefly before Trevor continued.

"But look Candy; take what happened, just a couple of weeks ago. Candy, my best mate in England, Toby, was busted up terrible from an accident at St. Moritz, where he went skiing. He got so bloody hurt; he had to be moved by charter plane from Switzerland back to England—but that whole time, he was in a bad coma.

"Dad thought that maybe, I could get him to wake up, cuz he had been calling out to me while in his coma. Dad said if I went to see him—to talk to him some, maybe he'd wake up for us. So dad decided to fly us home to London, just to see him.

"And you know what; he flew us all night long to get us there as soon as it was possible. But when we arrived there, instead of getting some sleep first, he immediately took Tay and I over to the hospital to see Toby. Now Candy, you know he had to be pretty tired after all of that flying—but he didn't say a word . . . he just took us. Now what Dad do you know—Candy, that would do that—just for his kid?"

"Wow Tre, that is some father you've got . . . but how is Toby now, did your Dad's idea work at all?"

"Well Candy, when we got there, he was still in his coma bad so we couldn't get him to wake up, even after I talked to him. Then Dad got an idea and started using this reversal psycho stuff on him . . . then Toby wouldn't let go of my hand. Then finally, Tobe just sort of woke up when his Mum asked him to let go of my hand or open his eyes, which was amazing when he opened them. He's doing real well now, but he's still in the hospital. His leg's still busted up bad; he even had to have three surgeries."

"My word that is something Tre, no wonder your Dad's so cool in your book."

"He's the best Candy . . . just like all those nice people outside waiting for us right now, they're the best for coming back each time Candy."

"So that's it folks, now let's just wait to see what treats, the boys have in store for all of us. Stay tuned to the T-M Channel, we'll be right back with more."

Candy got the cut sign as she put down her mic. After thanking the boys for their patience, she casually walked up to me with a big grin smile all over her face . . . something was coming, I was sure of it.

"Mr. Morgan, 'should' you be looking for a more mature daughter to adopt next—I'm readily available . . . but I'd love to learn to fly—Dad?" We both laughed.

"Thank you Candy, but two is enough right now, yet I'll keep it in mind."

"I just have to ask you Mr. Morgan, what motivated you to fly all the way to England to see Toby?"

"Necessity Candy—it truly is, the mother of invention. I knew from Toby's mother that he was calling out to Tre in his coma. I've read a fair amount about comas due to my position as a board member of Las Vegas' largest Hospice Care facility. Given what I've read, I believed that my son's presence would potentially create some kind of reaction in Toby's state of consciousness.

"All things considered Candy, any reaction, even if it wasn't the one we were hoping for; anything would be an improvement I thought. Thankfully it all worked out, but not at first, just like Tre said. God; that kid was really stubborn to wake up at first."

"Amazing. Well Mr. Morgan, I've got to get out there for the performance . . . but my offer still stands anytime."

"Thank you Candy, that's sweet, but thank you for both of your great interviews today."

"My pleasure sir, so long."

"Bye Candy."

We were right at 7:40 pm now, so I thought it might be best to give the boys a little extra moral support for their humongous audience outside, as I joined them in their dressing room now. I could offer up a little pep talk this way, if one was required at all, while they changed into their costumes.

"So guys, how you hanging with all of this? Hey—thank you by the way for those undeserved remarks about me to Candy. I certainly don't warrant two wonderful kids like you two . . . that's the truth of it?"

"Poppycock Daddy, stop being like that . . . we meant every word, we love you too—so there." Then I was rewarded with both of the boys sticking their tongues out at me.

"Okay Taylor, I love you both too, so much it hurts. Right now though, I'm only concerned that you two feel all right with the size of our audience tonight . . . isn't this crazy?"

"Sure we are . . . why wouldn't we? You know Dad, you should try it again sometime yourself; but for us, this is what we've hoped for-since we started. Bringing as much joy and happiness to as many people as possible . . . just like Mummy said to Grammy.

"You know Daddy, Trev, and I believe this is what we're supposed to do, so we're sure of it now. The more in the audience means, the better it makes us feel inside, so we're happy too—aren't we Tre?"

"Yeah Tay, I'm so ready and bloody excited, I've got to use the loo right now though. I don't want to get too keyed up and ruin my britches, so excuse me for a tick." As Trevor went into the restroom, I realized—so much for my worries as their paranoid father.

"Okay T-man, then I guess I'll just wish you guys to break your legs along with some of those young ladies hearts outside. I'll get out of your hair; we need extra time anyway just to get to our seats. I also understand they removed the tables to make more room on the Quad itself."

"Really, that's good Dad." Taylor added.

Moments later, T-1 emerged with the happiest grin on his face I can remember since our hospital visit to Toby.

"Okay my twin Rockers, knock them dead, but remember I'll be that special Dad out front rooting you both on. Is there anything you guys need before I go topside?"

"No—we'll see you later Dadio, but can we see Larry and Austin for a moment?"

"Of course."

I got up to call out their dressing room door for their mates to hurry in, which they did. I hugged the boys, as I swatted their bums for good luck as was my custom as their father, before I left them to their two close friends.

Three minutes later, Scoot, the girls, the two mates and I, made our way upstairs to our seats.

Sure enough, it was clear the crowd had to be over fifty-thousand now. Park security was forced to set up those tensa-belt barrier fences, just so—those not stopping for the performance could still get to their ultimate destinations. Just the same, the whole area around the Quad was a zoo of people, many of them adults, which surprised me more than anything else. I even pointed it out to Scoot who was not surprised in the least.

"Damn bud, what made you think only kids would love the boys' music? After all, think about the music they're playing . . . think about who enjoyed that music years ago, the first or last time the songs came out."

"Oh yeah, I guess you're right Scoot, but it's just a little surprising to me is all."

"Okay, well—now it's not, alright?"

"Yep."

Security got us safely to our seats; where I then had to shake myself awake just to realize I wasn't dreaming. Again sitting next to me yet again—were Stephen and Leinaala Kineret with their three girls.

"My God Stephen—you weren't kidding . . . were you?"

"Marc, what can I say, Leina and I loved the show as much as the girls. There was no way we were going to miss another opportunity to see them. Lii wants you to give Tre her cell number, so she insisted herself that we hang here. Leina and I kept taking turns with the girls so that neither of us totally missed out on the rides, so we're happy enough."

Turning to Lii I said:

"Sorry young lady, but I refuse to take that phone number from you—as Tre would never forgive me . . . I suppose you'll just have to give it to him yourself after the performance, fair enough?"

"Oh thank you Mr. Morgan, I was hoping you'd say that."

"I guess that makes two of us. I shouldn't be the one to share this with you, but Tre will be thrilled to see you again I'm sure, but that's our little secret—right Lii?"

"Sure Mr. Morgan, you won't get a peep out of me. I really like him for sure, so I'm just glad he likes me. I mean—he actually spoke to me before, can you believe it? He was actually talking to me—just like a normal person would!"

I tried not to chuckle, so I just cleared my throat to regain my composure before answering her.

"Yes I know dear, but I think you really made an impression on him as well."

"Cool, do you really think so?"

"Yep, I do."

"Wow."

Moments later, I saw our group here joining us now, including Jared. Reg stood to scan the crowd before he then sat back down as he commented:

"Marc, to think that for six years, I had their music all to myself and Marie—our downstairs maid as we ran around dusting the furniture. It's absolutely mind boggling, don't you agree?"

"Yes Reg, I can see how you'd say that, but I agree, it is mind boggling in a way for me too naturally."

"Certainly it is Love—now how many people are here, is there an estimate?"

"Jared here—tells me it's over fifty-thousand Gracie. It's a record for any Toon-Media performance event staged anywhere within their parks worldwide."

"My, my—isn't this loverly?"

"Yes Grace it most certainly is." Jared now added himself.

"So Grace did you and Reg have a pleasant afternoon then?"

"Oh yes love—that was loverly too." Moreover, they both were immediately blushing for all of us to see.

I heard Mom laugh so I immediately gave her the evil eye to be quiet. For a change, it worked! No doubt because Jared was there too.

Right at one minute past eight by my watch, the announcer came on the PA system but for once, there even seemed to be sincere enthusiasm in his voice.

"Ladies and gentlemen, boys and girls, welcome to Toonland's Future World Quad. You are all a part of creating and therefore witnessing Toon-Media history tonight. At eleven-years-of-age, these young brothers are breaking a forty-five-year-old park record among many—as this is the largest audience ever assembled in any Toon-Media Theme Park—worldwide for a single performance.

"Now here's the reason you've all been waiting so patiently—please welcome back to the Quad stage, the two newest stars in the Toon-Media family. Ladies and gentleman, boys and girls, here are—Tay 'n' Tre . . . The Morgan's!"

The audience was immediately on its feet going nuts, while the first note of music had not even been played yet. It was incredible. I looked over at Stephen Kineret, when I about died as I saw the excitement on his face. Hell, he was even more excited than I seemed to be now—yet these were my kids.

I thought to myself, this was such an odd phenomenon. Was I just too jaded or used to it already—did I just expect it?

At that moment, with the stage still underground, I heard the boys in beautiful a Capella harmony over the sound system. They began their first song with Trevor I believe, taking lead vocal.

"Is this the real life, is this just fantasy, caught in a landslide".

It was Bohemian Rhapsody by Queen, as I noticed that the stage had not moved an inch yet. Jesus, they were really stringing this audience out for all it was worth. I suppose management wanted them begging before the boys would magically appear.

Personally, I had no idea honestly, or any knowledge if it had been intentional or not. Then again, Jared didn't seem to know either, so what does that tell you. It told me that even money would confirm it was either Scooter or Mom's idea.

Yet no matter who thought of it—the delay was working. The affect it had on the audience was amazing all the same; they were becoming frenzied and tumultuous now.

When the first notes on their keyboards came through, the stage finally began rising as the applause now grew explosive as the boys continued this Freddie Mercury classic rock standard.

This was the first time though; I could distinguish our 'Verandas vocalists' on one of the boys' tunes other than My Prayer. As it must have been for Queen themselves, for this tune to go over, additional vocalists would have to be there to perform the operatic chorus'—my guys were great, but alone on those chorus'—the Mormon Tabernacle Choir—they weren't!

I swore old Scoot had not said a thing to me about them doing Bohemian Rhapsody. Hell it didn't matter, because the song went over tremendously well. The audience was singing right along with each chorus of the song—it was wonderful.

When this classic heavy piece ended, it was much to the talents of Trevor on his vocals along with Taylor on his synthesizer. Taylor worked overtime in fact, particularly with guitar and percussion tracks while Trevor's ending with those final words of 'anyway the wind blows', was simply angelic.

The audience was on their feet as another Trevor and Taylor Morgan 'spectacular' was clearly in the offing. Taking their bows moments later, Taylor then addressed the group.

"Hey there everyone, thank you, thank you all so much. So I hear, all of you have set a record today—how's that make you feel Toonland?" As Taylor, and then Trevor held their mics out to capture the audience's applause and screams.

It was a good thing that the engineering department had greatly increased their sound system for this performance. One would need to hear it from a fair distance away in the outfield if you will, along with compensating for substantial applause too.

The boys' took advantage of their new stage set up with one of them always circling the full audience between each song. This way, no one felt slighted, especially the boys . . . apparently they were really digging the view too with their gigantic 'theatre in the round' set working, so they were going crazy with that too. Thousands of people had glow sticks waving, making it a hyper, yet genuine, party scene.

"So how'd you all like my bro's impersonation of Mr. Mercury? Bloody brill wasn't it?"

More applause awaited Taylor's remarks as Trevor took another bow. Then Trevor repeated the process to acknowledge Taylor's contribution before he continued.

"Thanks everyone. For our next song, Tay and I would like to do one of our favorites . . . it is also one of the first song's we learned. Actually, weren't you still in diapers Tay?"

There was howling laughter at Trevor's crack, as he then continued.

"Here is Elton John's, Mona Lisa's and Mad Hatters." The audience clapped but then quieted down as the boys began the tune.

Taylor's vocal to Trevor's piano lead was a nice balance, while Taylor's mandolin work on his keyboard was truly melodious. Trevor took the piano lead to a stronger element than in Elton's original, which really came across quite well too. Yet, most of all, their pitch-perfect harmonies on the chorus, really put this tune over. Many of the audience were hearing this more obscure EJ tune for their first time. Nonetheless, they seemed to adore it by their generous applause at its conclusion. Taylor then addressed his brother directly:

"Hey, your piano work was good there Tre, I mean, all things considered."

Still more applause erupted from the audience as Tre took a bow before addressing his brother's parting crack.

"What do you mean, all things considered Tay—just what does that mean?"

"Gee Tre; blimey, do I really have to spell it out for you?"

"Spell—what out Tay? I'm not bloody following you here."

"Well then Tre; let's just forget it—it really doesn't matter."

"Yes it does Tay. Whatever you're talking about, matters to me a whole lot, especially since it seems to be about me—so where is this going Tay?"

"Okay Tre, fine. All things considered—we 'both' know that I'm the stronger of us on the keyboards." Taylor was laughing big time now.

"Yeah, right Tay—sure you are—I can play bloody circles around you—and you know it."

"Oh certainly—you can Tre . . . circles—yes, music—no!"

The audience was now really starting to laugh at Larry's little acceleration of a fight between the boys, even if it was all staged of course. But of course, none of us really knew where it was all heading either.

"Fine Tay, we'll just see about this, won't we folks. But by the by, little bro, you 'were' in diapers when we began to learn Mona Lisa's and Mad Hatters. Heck bro, I seem to remember—you even carried your own 'poop' aboard—shall we say, to 'hit the fan' for every time you messed it up on the piano!"

The audience was busting up now including our table. Yet nothing came close to Stephen Kineret's reaction. He honestly could not contain his laughter. It had me thinking—was he a Doctor of Proctology?

"Yes Tre, but at least mine was 'in' my diaper. We won't mention where 'yours' was, will we Tre. God—you had that whole period of confusion over what was really Play Doh . . . and you know—what wasn't—remember bro?"

Poor Stephen was choking now . . . while turning crimson.

"Fine Mister Smarty pants—I mean—diapers. Here's what were going to do Tay. Let's see you play the 'dueling bees' faster than me—I challenge you to a real duel Tay."

Taylor let out a loud raspberry burble with his lips, much to the enjoyment of the audience, but then followed up with another crack.

"Whew—Tre, dang it—you got me bloody shaking."

"Knock it off smarty diapers, we both know, you're scared, cuz you know I've always been able to play it faster."

"Fine bro; have at it—we're all waiting for you to be faster than me."

Trevor said nothing, but prepared for the duel instead.

Trevor sat on his stool, gained his concentration, before beginning the Flight of the Bubble Bee. Then he was off . . . he was so damn fast, I could not believe it—no one could. When Trevor finished less than a minute later, the audience was screaming and whistling now, while on their feet once again. Trevor took a quick bow, as he smirked from one cheek to the other as he gloated at his brother's expense. He now addressed his audience.

"Thank you everyone, now let's just see how fast Mister Smarty diapers does, shall we?"

"Certainly Tre, I'd be delighted to, however I will need a little help. You see bro; I know all your little dirty tricks—Trevor Sean Morgan, everyone of them in fact. You'll just try to flub me up to make me screw up by making some funny face or something else. I'm not going to fall for that trick this time, I can tell you that—right now."

"Now bro, I'm surprised at you, I really am. Do you honestly think I would do that to 'you', my own baby brother—in front of all our fans?"

"I can answer you in one word bro—yes! But don't you worry Tre, I've got it all worked out already."

"You have—how bro?"

"Simple Tre, if I can't see you, you can't mess me up, so I'm going to play the piece—blindfolded!"

The audience let out a mass 'gasp' as Taylor said the words, including our group of course . . . this was news to us big time.

"Oh this, I've got to see bro—you're joking right?"

"Tre, speak for yourself about seeing things, because as for me, I won't be able to. Are all of you ready out there?"

The audience answered with their tremendous applause, catcalls, and yelling. Taylor then proceeded to adjust himself on his stool, as he removed his bandana from around his neck. He quickly folded it down into a strap-length blindfold. The look of seriousness on Taylor's face now, spoke volumes as he tied the blindfold around his head.

"Okay Tre, come over here to check it out . . . I don't want you complaining later on that I was cheating."

"Gee Tay, what a nice thing to say about your older brother."

"Stop stalling Tre, but the way you talk, you'd think that you potty trained yourself in those four stinking minutes you keep bringing up!

"So listen Tre, I don't want any doubt left in anyone's mind about this. After all bro, we all know there's nothing much left in your mind, is there? Oh and gang, please don't ever try this at home without your parents help. And Tre, don't you ever try this in the loo—okay." This brought out more hysterical laughter at Tre's expense.

"Cute bro. Okay, it's on and it's tight."

"Good, now be quiet Tre, so I can concentrate-in fact I'd appreciate it if everyone could help me out by doing that now."

The audience instantly obliged Taylor's request with their dead silence. Actually, it was more like sitting on pins and needles anyway. That included our entourage as well I can assure you . . . Jared was almost hysterical now.

Moreover, Taylor did concentrate at that moment. He first rechecked his position on his stool, then acclimated himself to the keyboard as he found his starting key on the piano. A scant moment later, he just cut loose like nobody's 'get-out'.

Although not as fast as Trevor to be sure, yet for being blind-sighted, it was still fast. It was amazing really—as it was absolutely flawless! He finished in sixty-six seconds to literally an uncontained uproar from the audience that could be heard all the way to Las Vegas, I have no doubt.

Taylor immediately stood, removed his blindfold, as he began taking his bow. I really should say—bows—as in several. Taylor then waited through over two-and-a-half—minutes of sustained, thundering applause. He then made several 'I'm the Man' gestures over towards his brother, while smiling and eating up the applause from the very impressed audience.

Trevor himself gave up now as he began applauding his brother as well. Tre walked over to high-five Taylor, before hugging him deeply. The audience ate it all up . . . including all of us in the Morgan and company clan. We were all in shock even as some of our adults were near tears.

Finally the applause lessened, as Taylor now spoke to his brother on the mic.

"Ah—Tre?"

"Yes Tay."

"Should I rest my bloody case now?" Again, the audience went wild with laughter and applause.

Trevor was not one to 'miss' getting the last laugh in, when he could. He quickly walked up to his mic as he queried the audience:

"Hey gang, did I ever mention I'm four minutes older than Tay?"

The audience busted up to this crack so much that we again had to wait the noise out. It also made us realize how large the repeat audience was—as this crack originated at the prior evening's concert.

Finally, the boys were able to go on with their set . . . but what a set it was.

After a few more tunes, Taylor took over his mic again.

"We can't thank you enough for making this a wonderful time for us—we love you Toonland!"

The audience was still on their feet inside the Terrace—while the fifty-thousand—some-odd outside, had no choice obviously.

"Thank you everyone, thanks lots. This is our final performance today, and we're so honored to have all of you here with us. But what Tre and I would like to know is how many of you were here earlier? Raise your hands—and no cheating."

I could not believe it, gauging by all the hands we could see now. Knowing the two pm attendance was approximately 27,000, we were sure most of them were back for this one. Scoot and I in particular, were floored, there had to be nearly 25,000 hands raised now, it appeared to be nearly half the present audience there. And of course, there was our 'Stephen Kineret' barometer as well.

Taylor then continued his comments.

"God, Tre, look at that, isn't it great?"

"Yeah Tay, it's fantastic, but hey everybody, you can put your hands down. We've got a good idea now that many of you are back. Thank you so much for being here again . . . but speaking of being 'back'—here's: Back in the USSR by the Beatles . . . 1-2-3-4 . . ." And they were off again running, this time with a monster Beatle hit.

The audience was clapping right along; glow sticks were swaying, while arms were swaying along too which was amazing. The boys' version was good, but I clearly saw more advantages in the original version. Just the same, the audience was digging it, while going to town with their applause when it was over.

The boys followed their tried-and-true pattern going through the latter half of their set, constantly building on their ability to raise the energy as they built further excitement with each subsequent tune.

"Thank you so much everyone, we've got to call it for the night soon. You see, it's past Tre's bath time. Oh did I mention—he's finally bathing alone now." The audience was howling again.

Then Taylor continued his remarks.

"But before we go, we'll leave you with two more, with all of our love and thanks for coming. Here are two of our favorite ballads from the fifties, In the Still of the Night, followed by My Prayer. We'll do them both a Capella, and back to back, so we all have to get quiet again." The little pisher actually shushed them into silence now.

The twins made their costume change on stage into their all black motif, as the lights lowered. The silhouette appeared of the trusses on the street corner with the spots flooding the boys in light as they began snapping their fingers. You could have heard a pin drop out in that crowd, they were that silent.

The audience was now taking in their beautiful harmony—enjoying that, along with the music itself. When that tune ended, Taylor seamlessly went right into his opening line to My Prayer . . . since there was no break in the music, there was no applause generated either.

The twins both had this song down so well, particularly the harmony with their pre-recorded back up vocals with #1's singers. Each time they did the song now, they added some new inflection or nuance that complimented the tune nicely. I could only wonder how developed it would be, by the time they could record it the following month.

After the song was over, the applause as was becoming the norm—was deadening. The boys walked with the rotating stage to all four corners of their stage and did their twin bows. The audience it seemed could not get enough tonight, but who could really blame them. They kept yelling for more, or one more, or 'no'. None of this surprised me as Trevor now began speaking . . . then I heard:

"Thank you everyone, thank you . . . do you want one more then?" He yelled out. What were they doing I thought to myself? I looked to Scoot and Mom for some guidance, but they just shrugged their shoulders right along with me. It did not matter anyway, because from the audience's reaction, they were going to get one more song for the night even though the boys were right at one-hour and two-minutes on stage now.

"Thank you, thanks so much. Listen; after this one though, we really have to split—it's my bath time after all." As he started laughing at himself, which the crowd loved.

"Okay . . . so bro, what are we going to do for our friends out here before I get out the Mr. Bubble?"

"Gee I don't know Tre, why don't you think of something we haven't done this weekend yet?"

Trevor then asked the audience:

"So what works for you guys—you want something soft or something that rocks? Show us with your applause—are you all ready? Okay, who wants something soft?" The applause was deadening.

"Okay, now—who wants something that rocks?" The applause was nearly as loud, but not quite.

This surprised all three of us 'mavens' of music. We thought for sure it would have been the other way around, so it was a telling message. The crowds loved the boys rocking away, but they went certifiably bonkers for their ballads.

"Okay Tre, there's your answer, so now what do we play for bloody sake?"

"You know Tay, I can tell you what I'd like to do, and I'm sure you'll like my choice too, but there's only one problem in us doing it now."

"What's that Tre?"

"Well Tay, we would really need Dad up here, in order to do it."

"Oh—okay Tre, so why don't we just get Dad up here with us?"

As the audience began clapping, I was caught going in two distinct directions. I was both turning furious along with beet red—while hopelessly searching for the closest exit route—like I could make it anyway.

"So-what do you guys think?"

Trevor yelled out to the crowd, while I planned to do my own yelling later on myself, I can assure you. Meanwhile, the audience was signaling—my doom, with their applause.

Clearly, I had been submarined by somebody, but for whatever reason at that distinct moment, I turned to the good doctor next to me for moral support . . . and there he was, cheering me on—what a help he was . . . not!

I looked at Scoot now, who was just busting. Mom and Dad and Jared were no better, then it hit me—they were certainly all in on the gag, I was sure of it now. Even Larry! Now I knew I was screwed—payback is definitely a bitch . . . the Master of Gags and Mirth was about to be dethroned!

"Come on Dad; get your bum up here." Trevor now yelled out over the applause.

Damn it all to hell, I knew I wasn't going to get out of it, so while they were still clapping, I got up to make my way towards the stage, which of course started the audience clapping louder as I slowly made progress up the aisle to the stage. While I was still making my way up there, Taylor jumped into the fruckus too.

"Everyone, this is our Dad, Marc Morgan, and Dad, this is—everyone else."

This of course, brought out another good round of laughter as I slowly got up on the stage with the assistance of the security team. I walked over to my boys, to a nice sustained round of applause.

"I can't believe you two are doing this to me, you know it's singing in the shower for me—but nothing else. Listen guys, if I had my preference, I'd still be sitting out there, like I was, just enjoying the show . . . but no—you two have to make a spectacle out of me by dragging me up here. I can't believe you did this to your own father . . . how could you?

Naturally, I had decided that I was would play the wounded soldier to the hilt for this little 'caper' of theirs.

"Honestly Dad, you know we can't sing Mummy's song without you?" Trevor added as his justification . . . and it was hard to argue his point besides that.

"Fine, but when this is all over, you two have some serious 'splainin' to do!" I said it in my best Ricky Ricardo voice. This got all the I Love Lucy fans in the audience going nuts from my impression.

"Come on Dad, be cool—you don't want to embarrass us in front of our entire audience, do you?"

"You know Tre—yes—yes I do, very much so son.

Hell I was a hit now . . . ah revenge is sweet indeed!

"Okay, let's do this; I'm getting older—by the minute." I added.

"Dad, you know we need your lead vocal for this one, but you don't have to handle the keyboards, if you really don't want to?"

"You know son, since I'm here, I really don't care who handles the ivories, just get me the heck out of here before—before I soil myself!"

Taylor now spoke.

"Okay ladies and gentlemen, boys and girls, now that we have dad up here . . ."

. . . "And against my will, I might point out!" I yelled out over him, before he could continue.

"As I was saying before that 'big wind' blew through here, we are now ready to do this special song in honor of our Mum, Miranda Morgan."

"Mum died last October, so we miss her terribly every day. This song is for you Mum, from all of us—your Morgan men."

The audience applauded graciously, but through their obvious condolences.

With that cue from Taylor, I began playing the opening bars of A Lady Like You. This time though, I was rewarded with a beautiful surprise. The boys were singing harmony to my lead right out of the gate which was so beautiful. Even as I played and sang, I was overwhelmed with its heightened beauty now.

The audience had to be enjoying it too, as there was total silence out there as we sang. Our tender three part harmony by the ending line to the song brought the inside Terrace crowd to their feet while the entire crowd went wild with applause. The boys both grabbed my arms as they made me get up to take a bow with them, which I thought was special.

At that moment as the applause subsided, Trevor then spoke to his brother, but more so to the hyper crowd.

"You know Tay; the only problem with us singing with Dad is no one could hear him with us singing all that harmony. I mean, after all, his voice isn't so bad on its own, is it?"

"Yeah Tre, you're right, it isn't—but I think we can fix that easily bro."

"How Tay?" Trevor asked.

"Yes—how Tay, because I'm now officially retired . . . moreover—I'm leaving!"

I said it just as I started to get back up on my feet again, with the entire audience howling from my interruption.

"Cool it Dad, you aren't going anywhere—now sit down!"

Don't ask me why, but I followed the stupid orders of my insubordinate son at that instant, by sitting back down. Who's in charge here, I quickly asked myself silently. I was sitting there, back at the keyboards again, shaking my head from side to side. While I had my suspicions, I was dumbfounded of what they had up their sleeves next . . . where was this going, I had to ask myself now. I wasn't buying into any of it, I can assure you . . . but what could I do about it anyway?

"You're not going anywhere Dad, until you give our audience another song, mostly on your own—right everyone?"

"Tay, you know son, I just want to remind you—that these are real 'career' choices you're making out here tonight."

"Dad, you're going to play and sing for our audience—so that's—that, now stop waffling on . . . don't be a wuss."

"Oh, Taylor Shane Morgan—you are asking for it big time."

"No Dad—the audience is asking for it, not us.

"Fine. One more song—then I'm finished forever!"

"Okay Dad, fair enough. Believe me, after one song from you Dadio, you will be finished—forever." This came from Trevor.

"Oh, so now you're asking for it too—aren't you Trevor? Fine, since I'm such a 'wuss' I'm doing a nice slow, old one—like me, or maybe you'd like me to do a little classical, would that satisfy you?"

"Good Dad, that's smart, after all we wouldn't want you to 'hurt' yourself up here doing any real rock and roll, so have at it."

"Thank you Tre, but you two are already 'in so deep' in my book, I wouldn't push it any further. You are both already so far past merely grounded, you're, 'buried' up to your necks!"

"Alright Dad, sing a song already, will ya?"

"Fine Tay."

"Ladies and gentlemen, honestly, they're both usually respectful kids. I can only pray that they'll live to see their Bar Mitzvahs in one piece next year.

"Now, what to do—what to do? Alright, here's one for all us old-timers out there. But what the heck, I will pick up the tempo a little, so are there any Elvis fans out there?"

What a stupid question that was. The audience immediately went nuts to the affirmative so I knew immediately what I wanted to do.

Truth be told, I did quite a fair impersonation of Elvis's younger vocal range. It all began when I had to perform nightly at my restaurant myself, during my company's infancy. I discovered I had a latent talent—I was a singing mimic of sorts. Like the many musicians that I had learned to impersonate over the years, I had Elvis' inflections and nuances down cold . . . I knew I could put this tune over, while giving the crowd an excellent effort. Best of all, I was pretty sure that the boys had no idea I could do any of this as this all began after I returned to the states, so Miranda was out of this loop.

I also realized that my sons were entitled to be one-upped now and then by their old man—at least once in their careers . . . and not just a little bit either. Hell, I am the stinker, aren't I?

"Boys, how many Elvis songs do you guys know?"

"Gee Dad, don't know, is this a quiz?"

"You know Tay, just keep that up—you'll soon be grounded and buried so long; you just might be sprouting roots before I get through with you."

"Okay Dad, I guess you're serious, so which Elvis song are you thinking of doing . . . natch we know a lot of them?" My younger son added.

"So, do you guys know the one Operatic song in Elvis' list of number one hits?"

"Sure Dad, you mean Surrender—don't you? God, I love that one—hey wait a minute, were talking real Opera here Dad, are you sure you can handle that crescendo—I mean—at your age?

"Alright Dad, do you want us to handle the instruments for you along with the backup vocals or what?"

"Sure Tay, if you and Tre would like?"

"Heck Dad, we're here anyway, might as well. Anyway, with this tune, it's your funeral, not ours—right Tre?"

"Now Dad, you be sure to tell us if were playing it too fast for you to keep up at your age." Tre then added along with an obnoxious laugh.

"Boys, we'll let the audience decide that, but thank you Tre—for those wonderfully kind words."

"Okay ladies and gentlemen, boys and girls, for your listening pleasure, here is one of my very favorite Elvis Presley tunes. It's one of his best in my opinion; I'm told that it originated as an Italian Operatic Movement. Here is, 'Surrender'—for your listening pleasure.

Taylor opened with his synthesized guitar lead along with all the percussion including Calypso, as I played the piano lead while singing away to this great Presley hit.

Taylor was doing an excellent job on the synthesizer while I was putting in all the energy I could muster, along with every ounce of Elvis inflection I could produce.

The audience really ate it up. I couldn't believe it, but when I hit that wonderful crescendo, while stretching it out—I received an immediate standing ovation from the Quad before the song actually ended—that really shocked me.

Naturally the boys were both just a little bit stunned at the 'old man' now themselves, I can share that with you honestly. Yet they had been greatly influential in helping me put the song over so well in their own right. Their Jordanaires-style back up vocals alone, were incredible. Yet the boys wanted none of my limelight apparently, so it was especially sweet when they backed up after our bows together, so that I would enjoy the final appreciation from the audience solely.

Then it was over. Taylor's comments finally released me from my imprisonment on that stage.

"Thank you everyone, good night. See you tomorrow at two pee for our last show, thanks again." Taylor had to yell out to get through the tremendous

applause. Just then the stage started transforming as it began dropping . . .
I was finally alone with them now, so I was free to take out my wrath on
them, ground them until the next millennium—or just scream bloody hell
at them!

So what did I do the moment that stage was finally down and the sound
system was off? I did what any person in my situation would do. I simply asked
the most important question on my mind at that moment:

"So guys, was I okay out there?"

"Jeeze Dad, listen to that applause still going on up there—that was for
you too, you were great, really. How come you never told us you could do
Elvis so well?"

"Gee Trev—you never asked me."

"Dad, that's so weak, it's pathetic, but God, you were unbelievable, really
Daddy, I wish I could stretch my crescendos out that long, dang I'm proud
of you."

"Gee thanks Taylor. Okay, now what in hell were you two thinking with
all of that anyway?"

"'Hey Dad, don't blame us. It was Grammy, she told us to do it!"

"You're kidding me Trevor . . . Grammy?"

"Yes Dad, Nan wanted you to know what it was like to experience that
many people in an audience listening to you, so this was her way of doing it.
Grammy wanted you to experience it—the way we do."

"Oh. Well I guess that at least makes some sense."

"You aren't really angry at us, are you Daddy?"

"No guys, I'm not mad at you now. Grammy on the other hand, is an
altogether different story."

"Cool, so will you play with us again tomorrow?" Taylor added.

"No way Jose. Like I said before, I'm officially retired from show
business."

"Okay Dad, we understand, but it sure was grand having you up there
with us tonight."

"Well guys, I think I enjoyed it too. My God, did I just sing to fifty
thousand people—oh no, I better go change my slacks? Seriously guys, thank
you for including me." At least I had the boys laughing at my cracks.

"Don't thank us Dad—thank Grammy."

"Okay, I'll do that first chance I get—after I murder her of course." We
were all laughing now.

I joined the boys in their dressing room where we waited several minutes
for our entourage to appear. I would be making a beeline straight to my mother
when she arrived—naturally. I didn't have to wait long, as miraculously she
appeared with Dad and Scoot, along with the Kinerets moments later.

I walked up to them, quickly pulled Mom aside as I simply said:

"Well Mom, nice going—you're priceless I swear."

"Thank you dear, I hope you enjoyed yourself. By the way, your Elvis was absolutely delightful as always."

"Mom?"

"Yes Markie?"

"If you even think of something like this again, please—don't!"

"Why not dear, after all, don't your sons' talents fall right from you and Miranda's tree?"

"That may be so Mom, but please don't do it again without my expressed permission while I'm in a damn sober state!"

"Fine dear, suit yourself."

"Good".

"Alright."

"Okay."

"Enough!" Mom immediately walked over to the boys for hugs and kisses along with congratulations.

"Son?"

"Yeah Dad—what's up?"

"You know son, I can't remember the last time I heard you do Elvis, you should do him more often, you were truly sensational tonight—did you know ahead of time you were in such good voice?"

"Well no Dad—but thanks, hell, I could just kill mom sometimes, I swear."

"Marc, as I recall, the largest audience your choir ever performed for was around 6,000 people, does that sound correct?"

"Yeah, why do you ask Dad?"

"Oh, no particular reason. It's just that you just sang to over fifty-thousand people while receiving a standing ovation for your excellent effort to boot. Doesn't that count for something in your Mother's logic?"

"Touché Dad, I guess I owe her an apology, don't I?"

"Touché yourself, Marc."

Just then, Stacy walked in with a photographer. She immediately asked to speak, quieting everyone down.

"Folks, we would like to shoot some shots of everyone to commemorate this historic night. According to our computerized estimates, this performance was enjoyed by over fifty-five thousand of our one hundred-seven thousand guests in the park today. That is an all time Toonland record broken after nearly 45 years. It's also a record for any T-M park anywhere in the world, congratulations boys!" Everyone applauded as the boys smiled proudly, while the photographer shot away.

"Once our photographer is done, I'll escort all of you through a different route to the back lot where you'll be met by Hilary so the kids can do some more rides if you'd like.

"Now, one last word—Marc, just say yes, and we'll amend the contract right now to add your name right on in?"

"Is this a conspiracy Stacy? No thank you girlfriend, I'm sticking to my day job!"

Then Larry answered Stacy's question about hitting more rides just as brazen as I had answered my question from her.

"Yeah, we like rides girlfriend, so bring them on." Larry quipped.

"Oh, so I'm back in your good graces then, Lawrence?"

"Sure . . . if it gets me on a ride that much faster."

"Oh, I see then—so I'm only good—for a 'ride'?" Stacy giggled at her own crack, the significance of which seemed totally lost on Larry for a change.

"Gee Stacy, everyone has their job here—isn't yours making ours—easier? Rides are a part of that, aren't they?"

"Well Lawrence, I'm crushed, absolutely devastated. Here I was going to invite you home to meet Mother tomorrow after the boys' performance."

"Meet—your mother? Why would I want to do that Stacy? Haven't I got enough problems with my own mother?"

We were all hysterical with their conversation.

Once the pictures were shot however, we slowly said our good byes to the Kinerets. We then made our way through some dark and dank hallways until we finally came out directly into the back lot.

Hilary was there waiting, but she immediately ran up to the boys where she hugged them tightly.

"Guys, you were so incredible, I simply can't believe it. You know, I worked swing-shift today so I missed your two pm show, but after being a part of tonight's, I can assure you I won't miss tomorrow's that's for sure."

"Thanks Hilary, we're glad you liked it."

"Taylor, I didn't like it, I absolutely loved it. I can't believe how you two have developed since the contest last year, it's amazing. No wonder you two are emptying the rest of the park."

"We are? Gee thanks Hilary."

"Yes you are Tre, and you're most welcome. By the way, who was that older person you two had up there—he wasn't so bad himself?

"Oh Hilary, don't be silly, that was just Dad."

"Oh. So, now that we've had the chance to discuss your awesome performance, where does everyone care to start tonight on ride rotation?"

"I think that the honor of first ride should go to Austin, if no one has a problem with that." Taylor spoke right up.

No one objected within the diminutive entourage, so Austin offered up his choice.

"I'd like to drive those cars around that big track, how does that sound?"

"Great Austin, you can count me in." Came from Embeth, followed by all the other kids within seconds.

"Okay then gang, let's go. We'll come out right there so no one will disturb you. Joe and his detail will see to that."

"Good Hilary, cuz I for one have some driving to do—right into whoever is unlucky enough to be in front of me." Larry added.

"Well I guess it's all settled Lar. You'll be taking the lead car, won't you?"

"No HB—please, why are you being such a party poop?"

"Don't worry Lar; I'll take the car behind you so no one else can touch you."

"You will, you promise HB?"

"Sure Lar, I promise no one—absolutely no one, will touch you!"

"Okay HB, as long as you've promised, I'm all right with it."

"Good, now let's get a move on."

We followed our security team along with Hilary, over to the 500 Speedway track where we got directly into the final portion of the queue for cars. We had Larry in the lead car with me behind, followed by the nine cars our party occupied. The boys waved to the many screaming young ladies in the line as we left, which was enjoyable to watch. The reception the boys got will not soon be forgotten by that ride's staff, I can assure you.

It delighted me to no end, that Larry's car was a real dog. It kept bogging down right out of the gate. About half way through the course, his car crapped out yet again so this time I gave in to my vices whereby I rammed him so hard he went at least four extra feet from the impact. He was totally in shock as he looked back at me. I just threw up my arms as if in shock myself, as if to say, I don't have any idea how that happened. Later, just as the end of the ride approached, I got another opportunity, so I again walloped him soundly.

This time he made a fist and he shook it at me angrily.

When we got out of the cars, he ran right over to me—peeved big time.

"You promised HB, you promised!"

"Yes Lar, I most certainly did pal. I promised no one would touch 'you'—I never said anything about your car—did I?"

"That's no fair HB; you used the words against me. You really are a stinker, just like Uncle Rex said."

"Gee, thanks Lar."

As I laughed much to Larry's chagrin. In fact everyone was laughing now at Larry's expense. Oh my—payback is a bitch, isn't it?

Larry was peeved at me for the remainder of the evening. The only time he was even civil to me was when he wanted something to eat of course. Only then was he willing to speak to me.

Right at 11:30, we said our goodnights to Hilary as we began heading back to the Resort escorted by security.

We all felt wiped out, so everyone immediately wanted to hit the sheets.

When I entered the living room of our suite, I saw Bill mixing himself a drink.

He had just returned from his friends' house in Laguna.

"So how did it go today with the boys?"

"Unbelievable Billy boy, simply unbelievable."

"Did they get a nice turnout?"

"Yeah, not bad." I chuckled at that one, believe me.

"Good. Can I pour you one?"

"Yep, you bet."

Bill poured me a drink. As we sat down, I filled him in on the entire day's events.

"Wow. Good for them, good for them. How did you like being up there with the both of them?"

"Oh, I survived . . . that is—everything but my pants!"

"Yeah, right, that will be the day when anything could ever make you do something like that."

"I don't know Bill; I have to tell you, that was one big crowd of people out there tonight. Hell, my sons could have cared less, to them, the more the better."

"That's good pal—because I have a feeling that their crowds will be exploding from here on in—don't you?"

"I guess you're right, I just hope we can deal with all this celebrity stuff once it really starts rolling."

"Jesus Marc, don't you mean—now that it's rolling? Boy you're in denial, aren't you pal?"

"Am I?"

"Hell yes—my friend. My two nephews are like a barreling locomotive now. Nothing's going to stop them from plowing down that old steel track, mark my words buddy boy."

"Okay—if you say so."

"I say so Marc."

"Let's hit the hay Bill."

"Fine with me."

Just then, my room phone rang.

"Marc; I hope I didn't wake you?"

"No Jar, I was close, but no. What's up though?"

"Christ Marc, can you believe it? One out of every two guests in this park today saw the boys perform at least once. That's simply amazing. I am so proud of them!"

"Yep Jar, it really was something, wasn't it?"

"Yes Marc, but look, I just called to tell you there will be a little surprise for the boys on our Cable Channel tomorrow morning exactly at 9:08 am.

"We got a lot of great film, so we want to drop a tease to gauge viewer's responses. By the way fella, I see why the boys tapped you as their personal favorite singer. Jesus Marc, seriously—killer job on the impersonation of the 'King'. Man I couldn't believe it when you hit that high note, matter of fact I swore I could feel it—in my groin." We were both going to town laughing with that one.

"Thank ya very much. But don't you start on me too. But as far as the TV tomorrow morning, I think I'll surprise them by not saying a word about it. I'll just nonchalantly snap on their TV around 9:05 as a proxy for their alarm clock."

"Good God, I wish I could be there to see their faces tomorrow morning—they're going to love what we're putting on."

"So—why don't you Jar? Join us for breakfast here in the suite at eight-thirty."

"Marc, hey, thank you. That's a great idea, I humbly accept with pleasure."

"Great, then we'll see you at eight-thirty, but what can I order you for breakfast?"

"Whatever the boys are ordering is fine by me, Marc. In their honor, I'm going with their instincts on breakfast."

"Fine, see you in the morning Jar, but if you're going with their normal breakfast, you had better bring your appetite. I live with two bottomless pits you see—just so you know."

"Okay that's fine, now get some sleep!"

"I will, good night Mr. Morison."

"Same to ya, Mr. Morgan."

We hung up as I instantly started speculating on what we were going to see in the morning. Little Markie, 'the stinker' was deciding on whether he wanted to come out and play!

My mind became a torrent of thoughts, conniving, and devious thoughts! Yet at the next moment, I said to myself, no! This was too important to the twins to make any kind of light of it . . . so maybe I would just compromise by simply making it fun for them?

I think I fell asleep in mid-thought, I was that tired. I don't even remember saying good night to Bill.

I awoke at eight am, on a Sunday no less. I ordered the breakfast from everyone's written instructions. I knew better than to preorder it the prior evening. I hopped in the shower for a long enough time to feel more relaxed as I got out. Finally I felt as if I had some sleep that recharged me. Bill however was still in dreamland with nothing short of an earthquake apparently going to wake his sorry ass up at that moment.

I dressed, and then went in to look on the unsuspecting foursome. Peeking inside their room, they were all still dead to the world in deep slumber.

Right at eight-thirty, there was a knock at the door. Jared greeted me as I opened the door—with his own soon to be patented 'grin'.

"What a great morning I'm having Marc, how's yours been so far?"

"Not too shabby Jar—just had a nice shower so I do feel more awake now."

We rehashed the previous day in all its glory before exactly at two minutes past nine, creeping into the boys' bedroom. There, I turned on the TV to the T-M Channel on a moderate volume, while we waited on the boys to react to the sound from our improvised alarm clock.

Unfortunately for them, not one of them opened his eyes to see us standing between their beds—before 'it' happened.

It all started with the sounds coming from their TV I suppose. The noise was definitely taking its toll on their slumber. As they all started to stir, they began to 'come around'—so inevitably, one of them sounded reverie from his own horn section. This immediately ignited a domino affect with a full-blown competition amongst the bedded participants in between mass giggles.

Yet with this full cornucopia of farts permeating the air, there they all laid still—with their eyes closed, trying to feign sleep I suppose.

Once this large amount of pungent fragrances filled the air around them, they really started laughing from the two beds. They finally opened their eyes, still carrying on, staring us right in the face—then the serious laughter ensued . . . naturally!

Taylor managed to speak first.

"Jeeze Dad, don't you know how to knock? Serves you right for not knocking." As he laughed some more.

"Yes it does Taylor, so I apologize, but you guys just looked so funny. You were all mixed together, so we just couldn't resist waking you all up.

"But whoever hit that high 'D' a little bit ago gets 'first chair' in the Trumpet Section of the Crop Dusters of America Symphony Orchestra."

The foursome was really going to town laughing with that little quip, as I quickly ran to open their sliding glass window—it certainly was called for.

"I did it Marc; I'm your 'first chair', whatever that means?"

"Well Austin that was a nice richness of sound you had, first chair means you are the lead trumpeter with all other trumpeters falling in behind you . . ."

Larry immediately jumped in now to finish my statement to Austin.

. . . "Listen HB, if you want to stand next to him, suit yourself. As for me, I'm standing clear of him." Austin then answered me while ignoring Larry's crack altogether.

"Gee Marc, if you think I play a 'mean' horn—you should hear Dad after he eats Italian!"

"Austin, I think that's too much information for this group, trust me."

"Okay Marc, sorry."

"Don't apologize Austin, you were just being honest. There's nothing wrong with that."

"Okay Marc."

At that moment, Larry yelled out.

"Hey what the heck—hey quiet everyone? I think there's something coming on about the guys." As he quickly put the volume up some.

Two young teen girls were on the monitor having a conversation as I smiled wilily over at Jared.

"Sarah, I say Tay's cuter than Tre."

"No way. Tre's the cutest—Crystal."

"Well, I guess you can all decide for yourselves who's cuter, cuz here's the first music video of T-M's newest recording stars on their own Tornado label, they're Tay 'n' Tre . . . the Morgans. Then stay tuned afterwards gang for exclusive interviews and clips from their incredible live performance just last night, right here from Toonland. Unbelievably, the boys have broken a forty-five-year-old-record for the park's largest concert audience ever!"

The monitor then switched to the film shot at the two pm performance, shown in the Music Video format. It was the boys doing Crocodile Rock, while the four boys here in front of us, were all silent on the floor of their bedroom—watching every 'pixel' on that screen.

It was all playing over extremely well, given it was being recorded live.

The T-M Channel engineers had done an admirable job of patching and mixing the music for later broadcast or recording. The video ended with the crowd going nuts.

Then our two young ladies were back on the screen.

"See I told you Sarah, Tay's cuter."

"Yeah, like we look any different." The real Taylor now commented.

"Okay guys, let's just listen." I said.

The boys returned their attention to the two young girls on the screen.

"Anyway, while we keep arguing over who's cuter, Tay or Tre; here are some more clips from their awesome record-breaking performances yesterday."

The piece then went through several short vignettes of particular songs and banter between the boys on stage. When they came to the blindfold, the engineers made sure that the entire set up was included as well as the entire segment all the way through to the end. The way this played over caught the drama of the audience's reactions, while doing the difficult piece so well.

It was a brilliant piece of footage for merely promoting the boys, I knew it instantly . . . Taylor for the first time I'd seen him, lost his modesty watching it.

"Dang, I was a bit of all right, wasn't I Tre?" Which of course Trevor only agreed after much sarcasm and joking around with his brother

Then we saw Candy with her entire interview again, which also went over well in my opinion. After this segment, the final clip was our tribute together last night for Miranda. Again, the editor did it extreme justice by catching the set up so the footage got its full affect.

"So there you have them, guys. In case you didn't hear, Tay 'n' Tre are eleven and they live in sunny Las Vegas. They are originally from merry old England . . . but don't you just love those accents of theirs? Be watching for more in-depth looks and specials on this dynamite duo in the weeks ahead. And hey, if you live in Southern Cal like us, and you have the afternoon free today, the boys are on one more time this afternoon at two pm. Then you can make up your own mind on who's cuter—I say it's Tay."

"No Crystal, its Tre." The screen then faded into commercials.

"Wow!"

"Yes son, that's putting it succinctly Trev."

"Dad, don't you think it was good, I did, I thought we looked pretty cool?"

"Yep Trev old boy, it was good . . . but you two can thank Jared here, for it. It will also be a great help in getting you two going I can assure you."

"Thanks Jared." Jar heard from the boys in their famous stereo. He then added:

"No problem boys, my pleasure. But Marc, I'd say they were a fair ways along already."

"You know Jar, Bill said the near same thing to me last night. The poor fool thinks I'm in denial."

"Well Marc, maybe you are a little."

"You know Jar, I didn't think so yesterday. Yet with the two of you bringing it up though, I actually think you're both talking me into believing it."

"Marc, either you are, or you aren't, I don't really think there's a gray area in my opinion."

"Okay—then I choose to believe I'm not Jar. I realize they're lives as we've known them are irreversibly changed now. I just hope it's for the better, not worse."

"See, now there you go Marc, you really 'aren't' in denial. Good!"

"Dad, what exactly does being in denial mean?"

"T-1, that simply means a person, chooses to not accept the reality of something that's plainly happened already or been said. Something that is just obvious to everyone else. He or she denies the fact exists on a conscious level, even though it does exist."

"Oh."

Just then, Bill finally stumbled into the boys' bedroom yelling:

"Hey, where is everybody?"

He was standing there yawning in his long johns, so he was certainly a site. He was a picture that could launch a thousand Blackmail notes I can assure you. Then he saw Jared sitting there admiring his modest attire, that really put him at a loss as to what to do.

We were all laughing so hard, Jared almost missed the ring on his walkie-talkie.

Picking up the cell phone-like device, he listened to his caller. We could make out bits and pieces. He was advised that in the last five minutes, the park's switchboards had been inundated with calls. There were inquiries of the concert times, along with ticket prices for the concert, which was free. There were even some requests for admission tickets paid by credit card over the phone.

Jared hung up, before turning his attention over to me.

"You don't know how happy I am you're not in denial Marc. This news would surely send you into la la land."

"What?" This response came more from all of us simultaneously, than from just me.

"It seems that our telephones are jammed with calls at the moment, all about getting here for the two pm concert, boys."

"Jesus, I can't believe this, it's just incredible."

"Believe it—Marc, but stay with me please, don't slip over into la la land just yet."

"Oh I'll stay with you Jared, but did you yourself, expect this kind of reaction?"

"Marc, I've learned over the years, to never count on anything, one-way or the other. I did however; purposely add that final concert remark as a gauge of the boys' drawing power after a mere cable channel preview. Nevertheless, who can say why a screaming public, instantly embraces one performer, or performers, when another—is not. One thing's for sure however, and that is this, attendance records at a performance do not lie. No one has ever matched the boys' reception by our guests. I would venture it would take Elton John dropping in for a set to outdo their numbers."

"Okay Jared, so what does this do to the two pm concert, if anything?"

"Bill, for one thing, I wouldn't want to be on security detail from about twelve-thirty on in Future World . . . any more than I would want to be responsible for picking out your sleeping attire."

As we all were screaming with Jared's hilarity at Bill's expense, I had to wait to throw in my own two-cents while purposely ignoring Bill's look of embarrassment.

"I would agree with that Jar, those poor guys, and gals get a mouthful from the frustrated guests, don't they?"

"You know it Marc—they're heartless at times, simply awful."

"Say, who's hungry, cuz that knock on the door is our breakfast?"

"Oh, I guess I could eat something."

Larry of course was the first to reply to the question as he self-servingly opened the door for room service. Meanwhile, the rest of us heard:

"Yeah Lar, eating something like maybe . . . a Buick." This nice little crack came surprisingly out of Austin. Meek little Austin—well no longer apparently! We were all busting up big time as well.

"Okay guys, let's all get along, we have a big day ahead of us. What with the final performance at two, along with our flight back to LV this afternoon?"

"Marc, I don't believe you ought to think that fast forward at the moment."

"Jesus Jared, what's that supposed to mean?"

"Simple Marc, if these phone calls translate into a major increase at our turnstiles, we would need to rethink things—that's all. We might all really need to consider adding another evening performance or forestalling the two pm show. A lot of people might not get into the park in enough time to make it to the Quad with these crowds. Then we'll have some upset guests. Guests that will tear our security and staff apart, if they've missed the last show, especially after paying over thirty-five dollars to get in for essentially no other reason than seeing the boys perform."

"Now Jar, I don't want to seem insensitive, but we had an understanding on the boys' schedule. After all, tomorrow is a school day."

"I more than understand how you feel Marc, so I'll of course honor everyone's wishes on this issue. Ask yourself this though, what time do the boys normally bed down on Sunday nights? If it's nine pm or later, I still think you could keep to that schedule, heck the flight's only like forty minutes, right?"

"You know Jar, you could be right. If the concert ended at seven, so that we can get to Long Beach by seven-thirty, we could make it anyway. After all, the boys didn't want to leave right away, as it was."

"Good. I promise if you consider doing this favor, should it become prudent, we'll escort you out of here and over to the airport before seven-thirty, as long as the boys are off that stage by seven."

"Fair enough Jar, if it comes to a second show, I'll support whatever the others decide."

"Thank you Marc, that's most understanding of you."

"No sweat Jar, believe me I can understand your point . . . the last thing I would want is for your guests to be peeved over something like this. I don't want it to reflect negatively on the boys under any circumstances."

"Great, but let's just see how things shape up, maybe we're worried about nothing. I can always push the two pm performance back fifteen, or so minutes anyway."

"Okay, now let's all chow down".

We all made our way into the main living room. The room service attendants were still setting up the three tables. We excused Bill so that he could slip into something else . . . more stylish. In the meantime, we set the tables into a circle so we could have table conversations within earshot. I called the girls next door to come for their breakfast too.

When Bill re-entered the main living room just as we all found our spots by our individual meals . . . everyone dug in.

"Dad, I think that if Jared's right, we shouldn't disappoint our fans, after all they're rushing down here on a count of us."

"Yes Trevor, I'll keep that in mind for your vote on the subject. Taylor, what say you?"

"I agree Dad; I wouldn't want to upset our fans either."

"Okay T-man, I read you."

"There you have it Jar, if you need to arrange it, the boys are in. That's all that really matters . . . but I agree with you that they'll be home early enough anyway. Scott and Mom wouldn't go against the boys' wishes on this, I can assure you."

"Great Marc, but let's not panic yet."

"Right, I remember."

We had a delightful breakfast. Afterwards, Jared and I talked shop, while the rest of our group showered and changed into their clothes for the first part of our day. I realized while in an animated conversation with Jared, that he and I were quickly becoming friendly and comfortable. I had a sizable respect for him now, mainly for his sincerity in respecting the boys' wishes. I think he had a likewise respect for me. Our conversation after breakfast simply bore this out.

"Marc, I hope the boys don't think I'm pushing them into this extra performance if it becomes necessary."

"Not at all Jar. The boys' seem to understand your logic, as do I, but frankly, we'd be the last ones to want to peeve off our own fans, wouldn't we?"

"Well, I just have some guilt, that's all; I really don't like even suggesting something like this to them, but I really think its for the best if it comes down to a choice of doing it, or having a whole hell of a lot of angry fans."

"Don't worry about the guilt Jar, don't forget . . . we're Jewish . . . we invented the concept . . . believe me."

Jared laughed heartily before adding:

"You know, my mother's mom was Jewish, so I guess I get it from her then?"

"Most definitely Jared, you see, if you mother's Jewish, even if your father's not, your considered Jewish under Jewish law, so if we're speaking of your mom's mom, that would make sense . . . see?"

"Yes I do Marc. I remember celebrating Chanukah as a child plus some of the other holidays and rituals as well, but as I grew, they seemed to fade away."

"You know Jar, if you enjoyed them, that's too bad, because Judaism is a wonderful faith . . . besides; saving twenty-five percent off retail everywhere you shop—isn't a bad thing either, is it?" We were both cracking up at my remark.

"Damn Marc, I never thought of it like that."

"Gee Jar, maybe you should, you know, it's never too late to get in touch with your roots . . . while saving a bundle in the process."

As we continued to laugh, Jared's walkie-talkie went off again. This time I recognized the voice—it was Donovan calling.

Here is how that conversation went.

"Hi Jared, its Donovan."

"Hey Donnie, what can I do for you?"

"Jared, have you heard?"

"If you mean about the switchboards—yes."

"So what do you think?"

"Donnie, if it becomes a real factor at the turnstiles, I say we add another show . . . we don't want a sizeable number of T 'n' T fans fuming at us, do we?"

"Good call Jared, that was my sentiment exactly . . . but do you think the Morgans would consider it?"

"Yes Donnie, I already took the liberty of asking them—just in case. They understand, but only if it's absolutely necessary. After all, these guys have sung their hearts out for our guests all weekend, so I for one, think that they've worked hard enough already Donnie."

"I agree Jared—that's a sound argument. We ought to know for sure in around another two hours based on credit card sales over the phone, so I'll call you back then, or do you just want to handle this yourself?"

"Whatever works for you boss, I'm comfortable making the call, believe me."

"I'm sure that you are, Jared . . . okay, then it's in your court, I'll stand by whatever decision you make."

"Thanks Donnie, I appreciate your support."

"Well Jared, if I can't trust my Vice President of A&R, who can I trust?"

"What? Did I just hear the words Vice President attached to my name . . . are you playing with my head boss?"

"No Jared, of course not . . . congratulations, you deserve the promotion. It's all been set since Friday; I just had to wait for the final paperwork from LA naturally."

"My God, I can't believe this!"

"Why not Jared, you single-handedly landed what should undoubtedly prove to be the studio's most successful singing act in its history."

"Hey Donnie, don't get me wrong, I'm not complaining, I just can't believe it, that's all."

"Fine Jared . . . listen you can start believing it as of tomorrow, as I won't even tell you the salary now . . . we wouldn't want you spending it before you get home, now would we?"

"Cute Donnie, but I don't know what to say."

"Don't worry about it Jared, you've earned it."

"Listen; back to business Donnie, I'll call you when I know which direction this is going."

"Fine, speak to you then . . . Mr. Vice President."

"God, that's sound so good Donnie, I'm still in shock."

"Save the shock for your paycheck Jared . . . life's too short."

"Okay boss, talk to you soon."

After Jared hung up, I had picked up enough to know what had transpired, so I walked over to T-M's VP of A&R, giving him a hearty hug of congrats, along with my handshake.

"Jesus Marc, do you believe that, a Vice Presidency?"

"Yeah Jar; I believe it, as I've known about it for nearly twenty-four hours."

"You did?"

"Yep, but I wasn't going to say anything until it was official, so congrats Jar, you deserve it."

"God, thanks Marc, but somehow I don't think this would all be happening without the boys and yours and Marilyn's kind words in front of Donovan?"

"Maybe . . . but maybe not Jar. Just the same, our words were sincere, so who cares?"

"Thanks Marc, I can't begin to tell you how much I appreciate what all of you have done for me, especially the twins. You know it's crazy, but they've given me a new reason to be excited when I wake up each morning as I drive into the office . . . isn't that weird?

"I don't want to seem maudlin Marc, hell, I hardly even know you yet, but your two boys are already so special to me, you know—in my heart . . . can you understand what I mean?"

"Sure I can Jared, but that's what makes all of this, such a pleasure for all of us too."

Our conversation was abruptly ended by the sound of young boys laughing, as they emerged from their sanctuary all dressed and eager to depart for the park. Once Bill emerged as well, I called Mom and crew in the other suite, where they finally answered on the fourth ring.

"Hello."

"Oh, hey Dad, what's shaking?"

"Gee I wouldn't know son, I haven't been in the bathroom for some time now."

"Cute Dad, are you guys ready to join us in the park?"

"Definitely not Marc, we're laying low for now. We have decided to get over there around one-thirty, but not a moment before. We've agreed that we're all going to stay here to relax some—around the Bridge table, while we still remember how to play. Honestly son, accompanying six kids over three days inside a theme park does have its limits son, if you take my meaning?"

"I guess I can understand that Dad, so we'll see you at one-thirty then, all right?"

"Yes son, that will be fine, please arrange everything like yesterday, we'll get to the Tour Center to meet security right at one-thirty, fair enough?"

"Sure thing Dad, I'll get everything arranged and see you all then."

"Fine, adios son—see you."

"Bye Pops."

I hung up as I then told the boys the game plan before calling Scoot on his cell."

"Scoot?"

"Morning Marc, how's your day starting off?"

"Fine, how about yours, how did you like the boys on the T-M Channel?"

"Fabulous Marc, when Stacey told me last night all of the film they had already, I was thrilled, but now having seen it, I thought their execution was flawless".

"Me too Scoot; so where exactly are you at this moment?"

Driving bud, Beth's somewhat better now, so we're both in route in the Cobra, this is my first chance at driving it . . . wow what an incredible automobile."

"Yep Scoot, it certainly is, so what's your ETA?"

"Honestly, in this thing, I'm sure to shave three minutes from our trip if Beth would only lighten up on me."

"Okay, tell you what. How about meeting us at the Tour Center, we're picking up security and Hilary there?"

"Cool, see you in a few then."

"Great".

I hung up the phone, while we all proceeded to leave the suite for the lobby once the girls returned from changing. It was now necessary with the boys' celebrity, to avoid the Transporter, as we could not predict what would happen once we would get off the train in Future World.

So I called security from the lobby, whereby four minutes later, our private shuttle pulled up. In that short four minutes though, my sons signed over 15 autographs in the Toonland Towers lobby!

"Good morning Joe, I'm afraid you're stuck with us for another day."

"Are you kidding Marc, your detail is a pleasure, just ask any of our team."

"Thanks Joe, at least that's a comfort; we'd hate to be a burden to you all."

"So what's on tap first thing this morning?"

"Other than stopping to meet Scott Davis and Hilary at the Tour Center, I really don't know beyond that . . . I was just thinking that same thing to myself. But you know what I discovered Joe?"

"No Marc, what?"

"'I' realized, that not once since arriving here, have I had the opportunity to pick any of our first attractions—so today is my lucky day Joe, because I'm going to call it, whether these hoodlums like it or not."

"That's cool Dad, you choose, we don't mind at all."

"Thanks T-1 . . . like you really had a choice?"

"Okay Daddy, even if we didn't, we'd be honored to have you pick our first ride anyway."

"Wow, thank you T-man, that's sweet of you . . . but most intelligent as well, given your stunt last night—pulling me up on that stage."

"Hey HB, we're not schmucks—we know the hand that feeds us." Larry immediately commented.

"Thank you Lar, for adding that most sincere of sentiments."

"Your welcome HB, so what's it going to be, then?"

"Well Lar, I was thinking that we haven't paid much attention to my old personal favorite from when I was your age, so I'd like to start the morning off there, with Toboggan Alley. I can remember when that was all there was for thrill rides here."

"Cool Dad, I'm up for that."

"Me too, Uncle Marc."

"Good Em, so once we meet up your folks and Hilary at the Tour Center, that's where we'll go first."

We did just that.

Several minutes later, when Hilary brought us up to the front of the line at Toboggan Alley, all hell broke loose again with screams, crying, pleading yells—you name it.

The next thing I knew, we were passing a very stunning woman, along with a young teen boy, who appeared to be around the boys' age. When they were passed at the front of the line by part of our party, she now appeared puzzled or annoyed by what had transpired. So she turned towards me, looked at me with her beautiful face and friendly eyes, while asking:

"Excuse me sir, I was wondering why all these kids are screaming for all these kids of yours?"

For a moment time stopped. In that split second, she touched me somewhere inside . . . I think she just tugged at my heartstrings. Before I could reply though, her own young escort answered her.

"Mom, those two twins are the Morgan brothers I told you about from last night . . . they're incredible Mom, and their Dad—this man, was totally cool too . . . you should see him do Elvis, Mom, he was awesome."

"Oh, thanks Ricky, at least I've got the picture now."

"No prob Mom, but please don't embarrass me, these guys are too cool, I would really dig getting their autographs."

After hearing the kid's compliment and commentary, I naturally was in love with him, if for no other reason that he, being young and hip, thought I sounded 'awesome' despite being an old fart. After all, this 'was' the supreme compliment a teenager could ever pay any adult singer in similar circumstances in the new millennium—wasn't it? Therefore, I jumped right into their conversation.

"Thank you . . . Ricky is it? I'm Marc Morgan. You know son, I would be delighted to arrange some autographs for you right this very moment, how does that sound?"

"Would I—well yeah—sure Marc . . . and thanks."

"Okay Ricky, give me a moment."

The boys were deep into conversation with the girls at that moment so they had tuned me and everyone else out . . . they were oblivious to what had transpired until I asked them to sign an autograph.

"Sure Dad, but for who?"

"Young Ricky behind me here—he'd like it."

"Okay, Cool. Hey, hi Ricky, I'm Tay, this is Tre, and these are our mates."

"Hi guys . . . and this is my mom, Sam. This is so cool of you, thanks dudes." As we all said hello to one another . . . I was smitten already!

"No problem, so you saw which show?"

"Both of them, I only got on three rides the whole day after one o'clock!"

"Gee, that's too bad, but if you had a good time, I guess it was worth it."

"You know it dude, I was going to try to get Mom here to hold us seats for the show today, but so far I haven't convinced her . . . she just wants to do her stupid shopping."

I immediately jumped in at this point.

"You know Ricky; you can't blame your Mom after all. You know, your tastes in music and her's aren't too likely to jell, are they?"

"That's the thing Marc; she loves the guys' music, if she'd only stop to listen to it."

"Okay Ricky, I follow where you're going. Sam may I reserve a seat for you and Ricky for the two pm show then?"

"That's most kind . . . Mr. Morgan."

"Yes, but please call me Marc . . . may I call you Samantha?"

"Marc, that is most kind of you, please call me Samantha or Sam, and we would be delighted to accept your invitation." I then took the opportunity of introducing Bill, Scooter, and Beth to Samantha before continuing.

"Good, so when you see us at the Quad, just walk over to us where we'll have two extra seats reserved for you and Ricky, fair enough?"

"Again Marc that is most kind of you."

"It's our pleasure." We were now told to get a move on, as we started to board our toboggans. I was a little disappointed actually, I was so much enjoying just looking at this truly beautiful woman, let alone speaking to her.

When we met Hilary and our security detail at the ride's exit, I immediately told Joe to add two more seats to the two pm performance. He then got on his radio to have it arranged.

As we completed this, Ricky and his mom were now off the attraction as well, so I now told them it was all set up and to meet us as planned.

"Gee, that's wonderful, thanks again Mr. Morgan . . . I mean Marc, the only thing better would be hanging with Tay and Tre between now and then." Ricky got up the nerve to comment.

"So, why don't you then Ricky, we'd love to have you hang with us— wouldn't we gang?" Trevor offered this answer while the sextet was all nodding to the affirmative.

"You sure it wouldn't be any trouble?"

"Are you kidding Ricky, no trouble at all, as long as your Mum doesn't mind?"

"God, you Brits talk so different . . . 'Mum' sounds so weird to me."

"Blimey Ricky, 'Mom' doesn't exactly bloody cut it for us either, so I guess we're even?" Taylor added as he then had all the kids laughing with him.

"Samantha, why don't you just join all of us, we can always use another chaperone?"

"Marc, that's most kind of all of you, but if you wouldn't mind a rain check till the concert, if you can manage without me, I could use to take this time to finish my shopping from yesterday?"

"That's fine Samantha, you do that. If you get done before twelve-fifteen though, just find any security guard and have him radio to Joe here, so that we can meet up with you later for our last rides."

"I'll catch up with all of you later then—bye." And she was gone . . . much to my utter disappointment.

While we walked under the close guard of our detail, all the kids and Ricky exchanged the usual teen questions—where do you live, favorite video games, favorite musical performers, what's your school like, hobbies, sports, and so forth?

By the time we had passed the Transporter station, we had learned from Ricky that he lived in Heavenly Valley in Lake Tahoe, where Samantha managed a restaurant with an attached grocery store in the village, while Ricky attended school when he wasn't too busy skiing the slopes and giving lessons.

He was also working up to join onto the junior safety patrol when he hit fourteen, which was three years away. As it turned out, he was exactly a week younger than the boys were, so they had that in common as well.

We spent the rest of our morning and afternoon doing Wonderland. Before we knew it, we were right at one, twenty-five, so we had to make our way to the bunker for make up.

"Boys, do you need any of us downstairs with you, or should we just say our 'break a legs' now, to let you go with Joe? That way we'll get our seats to wait for Samantha?"

"Dad, we're okay on our own . . . really!" Trevor boldly conveyed.

"Okay then, so we'll wish you good luck now, and to break a leg or two . . . or some hearts. We'll see you both in the dressing room after the show, alright?"

"Cool Dad, but can Ricky and our mates all come down with us to talk to us while we do our make up?"

"God, you have to put on make up Tre?"

"Sure Ricky, its part of what you have to do."

"Okay, but I wouldn't be able to stand that myself."

"It's not so bad Ricky, once you get used to the brushes, cuz they tickle sometimes."

"Really Taylor?"

"Yeah."

So we sent all the kids with Joe and his detail, while Scoot, Beth, Bill, and I found our seats upstairs as we waited on the rest of our party. I soon saw Samantha looking around for us, so I flagged her over.

"Did you get some serious shopping in Sammy . . . I'm sorry, do you dislike Sammy?"

"No Marc, not at all . . . but yes, I did get some great shopping in without Ricky distracting me. If there is one thing we Jewish girls are good at, it's shopping. I get it from my Mother actually; she was the queen of shoppers.

"My poor Father always used to joke to my Mother that he wanted to be buried under the front door of Macys so he would be sure to see her three times a week!" We all busted over her joke.

"You're Jewish, Sam . . . so are the boys and I?"

"Really? With those two boys of yours with blond hair, blue eyes, and high cheek bones, you must have married a shiksa?"

"Well, yes and no Sam, you see, Miranda was born Protestant, but she converted to Judaism."

"Same difference, I knew those two were too fair-featured to be pure bloods."

"Do you disapprove of conversion then, Sammy?"

"No Marc, not at all. It's just that every Jewish kid I know in Lake Tahoe, but believe me—they're few and far between to begin with, come from a similar parental situation."

"Oh."

"Are you divorced Marc, or is your wife merely elsewhere today?"

"I'm a widower Samantha; the boys' Mother passed away just this past October."

"Oh, now I'm the one's who's sorry . . . was it sudden?"

"Honestly, that's somewhat of a complicated question Sam. You see, yes, for me it was quite sudden, shocking, and painful . . . but for Miranda, it was the end of an eleven-year struggle she never shared with me."

"She never told you Marc?"

"No Samantha, she didn't, nor the fact that I had two sons. You see, we were separated all that time as well."

"My word, this has to be some story."

"It is, but it's much too long and sad to bore you."

"I understand Marc, besides I hate people that pry into other persons' situations and lives."

"You're certainly not prying Sam, it's merely so complicated and convoluted. It's much easier to read about it in the latest issue of Teen Pop . . . nearly all of it is in there."

"Oh, well Ricky has a subscription for that magazine; I'll save you the pain of rehashing it by reading it in there, then."

"Great. I appreciate you sparing me the twenty minutes, along with the pain."

"No problem Marc, but if you ever need an open 'ear', I'm a great listener?"

"You mean—besides being a great looker?"

"Oh Marc stop it, I'm not at all anything to look at anymore. It's been all down hill since I hit thirty last year."

"Okay Sammy, but I hate to argue with a beautiful woman."

"Stop it Marc, you're embarrassing me, I'm not beautiful at all. Pretty—possibly—a beauty; no."

"Fine, suit yourself. Say Bill, how would you size up Sam's looks on a scale from one to ten?"

"Marc, that's easy. She's a rather charming—ten . . . and yes, she's delightful too!"

"Thank you Bill. Now Scoot, I realize the love of your life is just to your right, but could you elaborate on Samantha's looks, up to the point that Beth gives you the dirty eye?"

"Marcus, allow me to interject if you will, as Scott will only regret everything he says in my presence . . . anyway. Samantha is one of the most attractive and beautiful women I've had the pleasure to meet."

"Thanks Beth. Well Sam, I rest my case."

"Am I blushing Marc, because I swear I can feel it?"

"Sam, maybe just a little, but I wouldn't have said it if it wasn't so, ask anyone who knows me, I don't throw the bull."

"You've got to be kidding Marc? You throw bull from here to next Sunday!"

"Christ almighty—thank you Bill. What I meant to say to this lovely lady, is that I never throw the bull about a woman's looks . . . now is that accurate—Bill?"

"Oh, come to think of it, no Marc, you don't."

"See."

"My, thank you just the same Marc, for your compliment."

"You're most welcome Sam."

At that moment, I was just about to see if there was a Mr. 'Samantha,' when I saw the rest of our group walking over to our seats. I immediately introduced Sammy to my folks along with 'the lovebirds'.

With everyone seated now, we resumed our conversation, but not before Mom inadvertently threw her own 'coals' into the fire, instinctively knowing something was afoot with Samantha's presence at our table.

"My word Marc, however, did you of all people, meet such an enchantingly beautiful woman as Samantha?" I immediately laughed.

"Mom, thank you for so clearly stating the obvious. Sam here seems to think that's she not so much to look at—so we were just having a discussion on precisely that subject."

"Son, don't thank me, I'm merely stating a fact. Samantha, you are a most attractive woman—believe me I know more than a few."

"Thank you Mrs. Morgan, that's most kind of you."

"Marilyn dear, please, it's just Marilyn—and Mr. Excitement here goes by Malcolm, Mal, or Gramps."

"Okay Marilyn, thank you . . . hi Mal." Sam finished her greetings to the folks.

"Hello yourself there Sam, my—I must agree with my son dear, you are stunning."

"So are you here with any family dear?"

"Yes Marilyn, my son Ricky, he's eleven."

"Do you have other children dear?"

"Yes Marilyn. I have a little girl—Marisa who's just turned four."

There was dead silence at that moment.

"My Samantha, that's certainly ironic. Tell me, is Ricky your son's full name or is it short for Richard or Rick?"

"Richard, Marilyn . . . why?"

The Morgans were never 'too keen' on thinking coincidence meant—nothing! As Mom continued the interrogation.

"Well my dear, it just so happens that Marc's late mother-in-law, happened to be Marisa Richards, that's all."

"My, that is a coincidence."

"Yes . . . or maybe fate?"

"Fate, Marilyn?"

"Mom cool it, are you trying to scare this lovely lady away?"

"No son, I'm sorry—so are you married, my dear?"

"Yes Marilyn, but sadly my husband is seriously ill . . . as he has diabetes. Last fall he suffered a seizure and has been comatose ever since. I had a tough miscarriage last fall which I don't think he ever recovered from the stress of it all.

"This has been the first opportunity I have had to get Ricky away by himself, from the sadness of it all, as well as for me too. My husband is a wonderful man, a great father and a truly wonderful husband. I only pray he pulls through by waking up, but it doesn't look good, so poor Ricky is just going through a horrible time right now, that's why I thought to bring him here. He's fragile at the moment, but adores Toonland, so I thought it would do us both some good."

"Oh, I'm so sorry for your hardship Samantha, though I'm afraid we've had our own share of losses ourselves, as of late."

"Yes I heard, I'm so sorry for all of you too, really I am. I even mentioned to Marc that I'm a good listener, after all, I know the pain all too well, I'm afraid."

"Yes, I can see that you do."

"Samantha do you live here in California?"

"No Malcolm, but on the northeastern border, you see we live in South Lake Tahoe. Brian had a consulting business in the lumber industry so Tahoe served as a perfect home base for all of his clients. Once his illness worsened, I was forced to close it and liquidate its assets, all but his mistress."

"My, that's open minded of you Samantha." As my dad laughed just to make sure everyone knew he wasn't serious.

"Thank you Malcolm, but actually Brian's mistress is his plane . . . and as long as there is air in his lungs, I will not sell her."

"Really dear, Marc's a pilot too."

"Wow, all these coincidences, it's a little freaky, but anyway, now I'm managing a store and restaurant to try to make ends meet. Our situation has been most trying, I can assure you all. It's funny as I'm quite a private person, and while I hardly know you, I feel comfortable—telling you anything.

"I'm ashamed to admit for example, that I had to put Marisa with my in-laws, so that I could work and augment the income from our investments."

"Really Sam, I'm sorry for all your troubles, truly—but perhaps I can help you out with that, as we have another coincidence."

"Really, what now Marc?"

"Let me just ask you a few questions first, starting with—how much management experience do you have on the restaurant end and beyond your current position?"

"Gee, I don't know, I would guess between all my restaurant experiences about eight years between the times before and after Brian and I married, why?"

"Sam, I'll tell you everything in a minute, but let me finish these few questions, okay?"

"Sure".

"How many employees are you managing, both full and part time?"

"Twenty seven."

"Okay, so far so good. What's your annualized income for the entire operation you manage?"

"I can share with you that between the restaurant and the store, we are in the 2.5 to 5 mil bracket."

"Okay, that's great. Now how many of your employees have 'turned' in the last year or since you began managing?"

"For starters, I termed one myself, but none of the others have left."

"Why did you terminate that employee?"

"She was rude to customers, even after counseling her twice. When the behavior continued, I felt it was for the best to terminate her."

"Fine. Do you have any experience in musical theatre in your background per chance?"

"Yes in high school, I did a couple of musicals plus three . . . no four plays."

"Okay. Now what are they paying you, if you don't mind me asking?"

"Thirty-six thousand, plus bonus."

"Have you earned bonus?"

"Yes Marc, every quarter including my first."

"Okay Sammy, I've certainly heard enough. Sam, you probably haven't connected my name, but I'm the owner of Verandas."

"Really, no you're right, I didn't connect the name. Well here's another coincidence for you then, because Bri and I spent our last anniversary in your North Shore restaurant . . . not two weeks later, he had the seizure."

"I'm really so sorry for you Sam, I truly am. I hope with all my heart, that Brian makes a full recovery soon."

"Thank you Marc, that's most kind."

"Anyway, did you happen to see our new location under construction on the South Shore?"

"Yes of course, why do you ask?"

"Simply said, we're going to need three lead managers that's why, perhaps you'd like to join our family?"

"Marc, Verandas is a huge undertaking, what makes you think I'm qualified for it?"

"Your answers were above 90% of our hiring matrix Sam, that's all it takes honestly. Tomorrow, I want you to call my assistant Robbie, he'll have you do a courtesy interview with our HR on April 21st when they fly into Tahoe, but the job's yours if you want it, once everything checks out, of course."

"My God Marc, are you kidding?"

"Believe me Samantha, when it comes to Verandas, my son never kids."

"Thanks Dad, but I think I can field the questions myself, if it's all the same to you."

"Sure son, I didn't mean to overstep my bounds?"

"Dad, now you can forgive me. I wasn't implying you were overstepping anything, I just thought I was conducting the interview here."

We both laughed, as Samantha seemed to remain in shock a little.

"Tell me Marc, does the job come with any benefits, because mine doesn't?"

"Yes Samantha of course." I answered to the affirmative as Sam perked right up with my statement.

"Wonderful. You know, thank God Bri has always been a good financial planner, while also being a successful timber broker, I believe he has us smartly invested, otherwise we would already be homeless, which I'm sure would be a first for a nice Jewish family in Lake Tahoe, the few that they have."

"Oh, I didn't realize you were Jewish Samantha . . . did Marc tell you we are as well?"

"Yes he did, but believe me, we're a rare 'sighting' in Tahoe."

"So I can gather—how do you handle the high holy days there?"

"We drive into Reno; otherwise we would have nothing to fall back on."

"Well have you ever considered moving to Las Vegas, you can find a Jew on every corner there?"

"Doing what Marilyn; holding up a sign to the passing cars that reads 'I work for wholesale'?" Sam had us all busting up something fierce with her crack. After I stopped laughing at the joke, I added:

"My God Sam, you're such a funny lady—but Mom, I'd hardly call one hundred thousand Jews out of a million-plus people 'one at every corner'?"

"You know dear, compared to Tahoe I would, I understand they don't even have a single discount store there yet."

"That's true Marilyn, but worse than that—they're still flying in bagels every morning as there isn't a local bakery that can bake a decent one to this day."

"Shocking." My mother responded.

"Now Mom, stop with the stereotypes . . . that's my job after all. Besides, you know all too well that plenty of our Gentile friends like to 'grind' just like we do?"

"Yes Marc, they do like to, but how many of them actually succeed at it?

Hell, they hear one little 'no' and they actually accept that, can you believe it?" We all had a nice laugh at that one too. Gracie then jumped in.

"I don't care what all of you say about yourselves—or we Gentiles, all I know is, Marc is one of the most generous men I've ever met . . . there's not a parsimonious bone in his body."

"Thank you Gracie, but would you mind not saying that so loud in front of Dad, I fear it might give him heart failure.

"You see Sammy, among his many talents—Dad not only has the first nickel he ever earned, but he has it framed like a dollar you see hanging in a retail store . . . this was after the coin spent seventeen years in his pocket to boot!"

We were all laughing again now, as my father simply slumped in his chair.

As we took our minds off our conversation for a moment, Scoot took the opportunity of surveying the area.

"Damn Marc, we're packed again." I looked around before concurring with Scoot, but then added:

"Yeah, but guess what Scoot, Jar should be here within ten minutes to tell us whether or not the boys will be doing another show at six o'clock . . ."

. . . "And you were alright with that dear?" Mom never let me finish my comment to Scooter.

"Yep Mom, after Jar explained the boys would still make their bedtimes, I decided it should be the boys' decision. The twins said they're a go if it's necessary to do another, so I called Carol and Lisa to make sure they were all cool with it too, which they are."

"Okay, but I'm just a little bit surprised at your willingness?"

"Mom, I really didn't see how we had much choice. This is all being caused by that raucous on the T-M Cable Channel this morning, telling the viewers the boys were doing one more show today at two pm. Within ten minutes of that segment on TV, the switchboard was on fire with calls from across Southern California."

"You don't say son?"

"Yes Dad, I do say. You see, Jared was concerned that these people in route might not make it into the park in enough time for the single show. With all the crowds, they might get upset and potentially turn hostile, so this is the smartest solution. That's also why were at eighteen minutes past two, while the show has still not started. They are delaying it twenty minutes to allow more time."

Before our conversation could go any great distance further, we heard the familiar sound of the Toonland announcer.

"Ladies and Gentlemen, boys and girls, Toonland is proud to welcome back to the Quad stage, our record-breaking new singing stars. Please put your hands together to help us welcome back, Tay 'n' Tre . . . the Morgans."

At that moment, we heard the opening riff to 'Funeral for a Friend.' As before, the crew was definitely holding the stage back to build the momentum . . . they need not have bothered as the crowd inside the Quad was on their feet, along with the surrounding crowds applauding wholesale.

As the wind 'effect' on the synthesizer began fading into the church bells, the powerful organ lead began with Trevor at the helm. Now the stage began to rise while the audience increased their applause. As the heavier dirge commenced, the audience silenced themselves to simply listen to the music intently.

Samantha whispered to me at that moment:

"I can't believe all this sound is coming from two musicians and instruments?"

"Actually Samantha, Taylor's wielding a synthesizer within his keyboard, that's the reason for their fullness of sound." I replied.

Then Trevor's strong piano lead shot right in along with Taylor's percussion and horns on the synthesizer. The boys were giving the tune the 'full Monty' while the audience was again mesmerized like the audiences before, no doubt with a lot of repeaters.

The final third of the song was as strong as ever, as this audience began singing along with the chorus on the first go round. The second time around on the chorus, Taylor and Trevor simply held out their mics to the audience for them to take over which they did with much self-satisfaction expressed through their applause. As the boys' concluded the song with the final verse of no words, merely the sliding scale of 'oh', the audience broke into a chain wave. Both the boys, along with their audience were just digging it all. When they finished, they were rewarded with thunderous applause in the Quad, which had remained standing throughout the entire tune anyway.

Trevor then spoke to the huge crowd, which was easily as large as the evening before.

"Hello Toonland . . . 'ow are you? The audience then answered with more applause.

"You know people—we all know who we are, but we don't know your names, so, on the count of three, everyone please yell out your name, okay?" The audience was laughing at Trevor's intentional absurdity. Yet as he counted out to three, everyone yelled out their names, including our entire group— now how stupid was that? Then more laughter along with applause followed this foolish, yet unoriginal—but cute—'bit'.

"That's better gang, now we know all of you, right Tay?"

"Oh yeah bro, absolutely . . . not"

"Now Tay, are you doubting my sincerity?"

"No Tre, just your certainty, that's the oldest stage gag in the book."

Taylor was on one of his rolls now, so where it would stop, nobody knew?

"Tay, are you going to be doing this stuff to me the entire show?"

"That all depends Tre—on whether you've learned to keep your mouth shut yet?" More laughter ensued now.

"Dang Tay, heads you win, tails I lose . . . blimey, you never play the straight man, so I'm always the butt of your jokes."

"Honestly Tre, if you could just keep your 'head' straight from your 'butt', maybe you wouldn't always end up in that situation?" The audience was hysterical at Taylor's play on Trevor's own words.

"Now stop it Tay, you're confusing me."

"And—I rest my case bro." The audience was going bonkers now.

"Listen everyone, maybe I'd better introduce this next song, while my brother decides what I just said to him, okay?" The laughter was still coming on strong.

Taylor then laughed a little himself, before continuing with his introduction.

"As you know, this is our final day here at Toonland; so far we've done a lot of groups' songs plus many tunes by some of the classic singers of the fifties and sixties.

"This next one though, is from a group we haven't played here yet, even though they're one of Tre's and my faves. So we can't close out our visit here, without at least one tune from them. Here is 'How Can You Mend A Broken Heart' by the brill—brothers Gibb, better known as the BeeGees!" The audience was applauding again.

The boys went right into this classic tune from the early seventies and they performed it wonderfully. The audience was really digging it big time with the boys perfectly duplicating the BeeGees wonderful but unique, baroque harmonies and inflections. When the boys had it finished, another standing ovation followed, as Trevor again took to his mic.

"Thank you everyone, thank you so much. I just want to say right now that I don't plan on talking to Tay anymore now than I have to, cuz he's just a pill that's too bitter to swallow . . . so if you see me going out of my way to not talk to him, you'll understand."

"Thank you Tre, for explaining that to our audience. Do you feel better now—did your 'pill' help?" The crowds were busting up yet again, while poor Tre was just crushed (for their benefit, I might add).

Trevor was purposely silent now, which only egged Taylor on more—naturally.

"Alright everyone, while my brother sits there behind his keyboard like the beaten little twin—that he is, I think it's time for another tune, don't you 'Tre'?"

"Tay, I'm not saying anything more to you, as long as I do that, I can't possibly put my foot in my mouth with you . . . will I?"

"Oh sure you can Tre—it's early yet."

"Taylor Shane Morgan, cool it now, or believe me, I'll get Dad up here again to tell you himself."

"Bro, after dragging Dad up here and forcing him into singing last night, you've got as much chance of getting him up here again voluntarily, as you do of starting to shave by this summer.

"Listen, let's stop fighting, so we can sing something Tre, these people want some music . . . right everyone? Thunderous applause along with catcalls, etc, followed.

"See what I mean Tre, our guests want a tune now, so I'll tell you what, why don't you take lead on this next one?"

"Fine, but what are we doing next Tay, cuz you've got me so bloody upset, I forgot?"

Taylor immediately addressed the crowds:

"You see folks, I bet you thought that being twins, we'd both got equal amounts of everything—wouldn't you?"

The audience was off once more at poor Trevor's expense. Even our group was busting up at the cost of Trevor's dignity, even if it was all staged.

"Bloody hell Tay—you're really pushing my buttons now."

"Yeah, well which one—switches on your brain then bro?" God, was Larry ever earning that bike from Jared!

"Taylor!"

"Yes bro?"

"Not another word—or I swear . . ."

. . . "Well yes Tre, you do 'swear' jolly good—I must say that. Look Tre, may I simply suggest that you peek at our list of songs for this set, you know—on that piece of paper lying right—right here on top of your keyboard in front of you?"

"Dang it Tay . . . please, let's just do this bloody song already . . . and that song is, Making Love out of Nothing At All."

Trevor immediately went into the beautiful piano intro and then began singing the lyrics with just the slightest amount of reverb from the soundman, while Taylor then joined in on the harmonies. Their clarity on the lyrics adding to their prerecorded backup vocals, made the song just as dramatic and moving as the original from Australia's Air Supply.

As the momentum on the musical score grew, so did the intensity of Trevor's vocals, also like in the original. It was obvious he truly loved singing this tune; as there was so much feeling in his voice. That played over so well as he built towards his crescendo.

Meanwhile, Tay had all the sound effects going on his synthesizer, with his percussion and guitar riff going over the strongest. The audience was not sitting idly by either. Every time the boys came to the chorus of 'Out of Nothing At All', the crowd all sang along with the boys beautiful harmony—it was captivating and infectious, truly.

When the boys ended the tune, the Quad audience was once again on their feet—going bonkers. They sustained their applause for well over a minute.

"Marc, that one's certainly a keeper, I can tell you that." Mom commented.

"Yes Marilyn, but not only that, did you notice how intense Trevor's vocal was?" Scoot then added.

"Yes I did Scott—is it one of his favorites?"

"I'm not sure Marilyn, but they never seem to avoid rehearsing that one much, so that says something right there, doesn't it?"

"Yes it does Scoot." I threw in.

At that moment, Trevor now addressed their audience.

"Thanks everyone, glad to see you love that one as much as we do. Now in order to keep my brother quiet, I'd like him to go right into our next tune. Do we have any Bonnie Tyler fans out there?" The audience acknowledged yes with their applause, so Trevor then continued.

"Good—just as I thought, so here is Tay now, with what I think is one of the best songs that he sings. Here is, Total Eclipse of The Heart." The audience was applauding feverishly now, as this was a truly giant hit on the charts currently.

Taylor began the piano lead, with Trevor offering up the initial back up vocal lines to his brother's sweet vocal. True, Taylor was not Bonnie Tyler, but boy did he have the feeling for this song, along with his big, clear, alto voice that shined all the way through. Taylor nailed the tune in his own right, right down to the inflected gravel in his voice.

Trevor was definitely right about Taylor's talents with this tune, it was his best effort other than My Prayer in my opinion.

The audience was once again in a chain wave out in the 'outfield' behind the terrace, when Trevor hit the high final lines in a tender soprano falsetto singing: 'turn around bright eyes', as the song ended with the audience going certifiably nuts. Taylor took a bow as he then offered a comment.

"Thank you everyone, hey how about that brother of mine on those beautiful back ups and falsettos?" The audience reacted of course with that much more applause to the already huge response they were giving the boys.

At that moment, in between the audience's roaring applause and Taylor waiting to speak, Jared walked over to our group to take his chair. I looked at him and quipped:

"Gee Jar, did you decide to avoid the long lines and hit some of the bigger rides while the guys have emptied your park?"

"Cute Marc—but no. I've been in the switchboard center this whole time, helping to determine what we ought to do . . . but we're now decided, if you have any interest in the outcome?"

"Oh, sorry—sure, what's the verdict?"

"Honestly Marc, the guys can leave anytime after this one—but still— we'd honestly be relieved if they would consider doing the extra show. You see, we're almost convinced that everyone made it here by pushing the performance back those twenty or so minutes. However, our numbers here at the Quad are as best as we can estimate. We're concerned that we may be off by six hundred or so guests from the tally of our calls. As such, we would all feel much better if the boys are still willing to do it. I'll also be sure to thank the boys for another last-minute, four-thousand estimated guests we've already added during this timeframe."

"Marc, the boys have just added over one-hundred and twenty-five thousand dollars—just to our turnstiles—that's not exactly chump change my friend. In fact, we've also decided to double pay the boys for the extra performance."

"Now that's music to my ears, Jared."

"Thank you Marilyn, I thought you'd like that—but there's more. We're also matching that amount in a donation to the boys' foundations."

With those few words, Jared had managed to silence Mom right there on the spot. She could barely mouth out a thank you to Jared, she was so overwhelmed. For his part, Jared seemed touched by the unintended outbreak of her emotions too.

I then introduced Jared to Samantha.

As our table conversation was proceeding, the audience had finally calmed down so that Taylor could begin to speak to the huge crowd, now verified at just slightly fewer than fifty-seven thousand guests, according to Jared.

"Thank you all, thanks so much. We'd like to slow things down a tick now and do a nice ballad for you, anyone have a problem with that?" The audience started yelling to convey their delight at the idea.

"Good, cuz we were going to do it anyway." Taylor and Trevor both laughed at themselves before high-fiving each other in the process.

"Ladies and Gents, and you kids out there like us, in the history of Rock and Roll, only a handful of singers ever sang better than this man. In a career that covered more than thirty years until his untimely death, few could do a tune—better than—one of our top faves—Mr. Jackie Wilson."

Robust applause followed Taylor's remarks as he continued with his comments and tribute.

"In honor of Jackie, we would like to offer you our version of his classic; 'To Be Loved'."

Taylor began his music track of violins on the synthesizer as Trevor then began his moving vocal complete with many of Jackie Wilson's inflections and nuances. I immediately noticed some couples attempting to slow dance out in the 'outfield' to the moving tune. It was interesting to watch as there were so many now, yet each couple seemed squeezed into one person's space, so that those guests around them not dancing were not forced out of room by those dancing around them.

When it was over, the boys received a tremendous amount of applause with their standing ovation, particularly from the many dancers in the 'outfield'.

"Thanks everyone. Tay and I would like to say—how much we appreciate your kindness in coming back for all of these performances. We've had a bloody-right time, so we hope you all will come back when we return here in June, I know both of us can't wait—right Tay?"

"You know it bro, but in the meantime, we just want to remind everyone that our first CD which is for the Verandas Foundation will be out in around two months, so please look for it at our Minis Dessert Courts at any of the Verandas restaurants in the entire country after June 10th . . ."

. . . "Yeah bro, but tell them the good news about that." Trevor interrupted his brother.

"Sure bro. Gang, being that all the profits raised go to the Verandas Foundation, which does great work around the world—we're pleased to tell you that our crusade has already raised more than five-million-dollars thanks to all of our Verandas customers help."

After an abundant response, the boys continued with the remainder of their set, building energy and momentum as always.

Returning to the final two tunes from their first performance, Taylor announced 'I'm Still Standing.' The crowds were already on their feet now as they began going nuts. Once the song began, they were immediately singing right along with the boys.

It was clear that much of this audience had seen the boys at least once already, if not several times. This audience knew all too well that the boys were on their final tunes now of their final scheduled performance; so their level of excitement was only lessened by their desire for the boys to play all day, undoubtedly . . . it was now that Scoot chose to inform me, that he and Mom had okayed having the boys do up to two additional songs.

"Jesus Scoot, when were you and Mom going to tell me that?"

"I guess right about now—bud?"

"Gee, thanks for the update Scoot."

"No problem."

As the boys finished the song, the audience applauded tremendously as they transitioned into 'stadium' clapping in rhythm—to push the boys for more. They knew the end was coming, so they were refusing to accept that, I can assure you . . . they wanted more—much more.

"Marc, the boys are truly remarkable, you must be so proud of them." Samantha whispered to me now.

"Yes, I am Sam, but thank you for your kind words."

"Hey, I'm speaking the God's honest truth; those boys of yours are super-talented . . . but let me share with you that I know this, as my own kid isn't so bad himself."

We were then cut short on further conversation as Taylor began speaking to the audience.

"Thank you Toonland . . . thank you. Since this is our final day, we're going to do a couple more, but then, that's it, cuz Tre and I want to get on some rides ourselves. And I just bet some of you young misses would like to know which ride we're hitting first—wouldn't you? Well—we ain't telling.

"So Tay, what are we going to do now that we're adding a couple?" Trevor jumped in to ask his brother.

"You know Tre; let's start with the Beatles . . . In My Life, cool?"

"Cool Tay."

The boys went right into this Beatles classic with their own blend of harmony along with a lovely piano solo that Trevor did beautifully, while Taylor handled the guitar lead on his synthesizer and harpsichord too. When it was over, the boys were thanked with tremendous applause.

"Thanks everyone. Okay bro, so what now, it's your turn to pick one?"

"I don't know Tay, what would you think about doing something on just our keyboards?"

"Wicked Tre, sure, how about a little dueling Bogey Wogey . . . can you get your head around that?"

"Sure Tay, sounds fine to me, how about 'Sweet Georgia Brown' in fact?

"Wicked Tre . . . lets?"

The audience quieted down as the boys sat down again at their keyboards. They then did some of their telepathy momentarily, before then starting right into their duel of Bogey Wogey and swing . . . sort of in a combination of Louie Prima and Cab Calloway.

It was up and bouncy—with a strong Boogey Wogey influence pushing it 'over-the-top'. The boys would alternate solos—each trying to upstage the other with their many talents on their 'boards'. It was incredible, with the audience not only digging the music, but they were really getting into the energy and challenge the boys put into their dueling performance of it.

The boys kept right on increasing the tempo on the piece so that it was being played so fast now, it was almost impossible to comprehend how someone could play that fast—but they were! To be sure, they were giving it the full Monty.

They were now in a high-speed frenzy on those keyboards. I actually heard several gasps coming from the stunned audience all around us.

As they finally ended the piece in a flurry on their boards, they yelled out while singing one single line of lyric of the song . . . 'Sweet Georgia Brown'.

The applause became literally deadening. It was such a level of magnitude; your ears more-or-less went numb. It was after all, an incredible piece to perform, but played so well, that the audience was now attempting to express their appreciation and enjoyment of the boys' effort with it. Finally, Taylor got them quiet enough so he could speak.

"Thank you everyone—that was fun." As the audience erupted again.

"Well, all good things must come to an end . . ."

Taylor was immediately admonished with yells of 'no' and 'more' and 'one more,' before he could continue.

"Look everyone, you've all been wonderful—so we love all of you for your support and love . . . but we need to hit those rides . . . and so do you. Here's our title track from our new CD. Most of you have already heard it, but we love doing it for you. We're pretty sure that you guys love it too . . . so here is 'My Prayer' and we leave you with this along with all our thanks and love, we'll see you soon."

The boys went right into their a Capella do-wops and prerecorded four-part harmony, as Taylor began his opening bars that he had so obviously mastered. The audience was silent as always, until that final crescendo which of course brought out the 'gasps' from the current class of first-timers. For those guests, Taylor had hit his final line more powerfully than ever before. This ended the song leaving the audience stunned from his haunting version of this classic, as always.

The boys took their twin bows at all four corners of the revolving stage now to tumultuous applause, screams, pleas, and everything else in between. The audience was still screaming as the stage finally started going down.

Within moments of reaching the twins in their dressing room, my two troopers agreed to the additional show. Frankly, I think they would have been disappointed if it hadn't been needed.

But what a final show it was. The boys seemed to catch their second wind or maybe just some added adrenalin, but they were hot.

At the end of the performance, they must have thrown kisses for over two minutes straight—when all of a sudden, out walked Teddy and Bettie, as they made their way across the stage, while waving to the crowds—Teddy was carrying a box.

Once on stage next to the boys, Teddy then spoke.

"Boys, we wanted to come up here to acknowledge your unbelievable, fantastic, record-breaking performances. Tay and Tre, on behalf of your new family here at Toon Media, I'm thrilled . . . I mean, I should say that—Bettie and I are both so very honored to be here with you. Since your performances here these last three days have been enjoyed by more than two-hundred-thousand guests . . . which is merely one of the records you two have broken this weekend, we feel that you boys should have these."

Teddy then opened the box to reveal the two golden keys the company had already presented once at the airport in their private ceremony.

Teddy now held the keys up for the audience to see while they applauded before he began to read the inscription.

"Boys, these keys now read: To Tay 'n' Tre . . . the Morgans: Your wonderful music fills our hearts, while your infectious spirit lifts us to new heights, as your deep love for one another—inspires us all. Commemorating your record-breaking official debut performances, April 14—16th, 2000. Here—are the keys to Toonland and all of Toondom." The audience was once again on their feet.

Taylor and Trevor, now hearing the added inscription, were both touched as they took their keys from Teddy and Bettie, who received a peck on the cheek from both boys, as they then shook Teddy's hand, while the stage began to lower to thundering applause.

Closing Moments

▼

The Party's Over

The performances were finally over. It was amazing in a way, but each of us had survived. Yet none of us left Long Beach that day, the same as we had arrived the prior Friday.

All of us I think had learned something about why the boys were so important and special to us individually.

For Mom and Dad, surely it was the absolute pride any grandparent feels for their own. But in the case of my folks, it was that much sweeter seeing how the boys could so dramatically make others happy while affecting them so deeply too through their music.

For Reg and Gracie, it was the utter joy of seeing the boys having had all those years of study and practice, before taking it truly to such a professional expression on that stage. These sweet, yet fragile boys, still in mourning over their own losses, had put all of that aside to make so many new fans happy.

For Bill, I think it was simply his happiness from seeing that the twins had made me whole again and happy after so many unfulfilled and empty years . . . being their newly ordained proud Uncle, it filled a void in his life too.

For Scoot and Jared, who had only recently come into their lives and vice-versa, the boys' success meant something too. For Scoot, it meant knowing that he was greatly responsible for helping the boys reach their full potential—

along with being the greatest believer in their talents. For Jared, it was an affirmation that he still had much to offer professionally; to both his employer and those he was now privileged to represent as liaison to his company.

And for Larry—well for him—it meant a new bike.

Yet for me, it was many things—pride, love, fear and hope among them. Nevertheless, as I think back to really only a half a year before, my life now seemed to be that of another person entirely.

For the first time in my life, I knew what it felt like to have two someone's totally dependent on me. To know the angst of whether something I decided for their benefit—fit their plans, my late wife's, or mine.

Moreover, to come to terms with deeply buried memories and regrets that I knew all too well, were not in my best interest to harbor—but could now—finally set free.

I also knew that in all of these wondrous changes, there was truly only one special person to thank, for all of these wonderful blessings . . . and so I thanked my precious late-wife.

Yet most importantly, I learned that these two boys were the most important concerns in my life now . . . they were the key to my sustained happiness. They held the highest, most priceless value, now and forever more. I loved them, I needed them, I would nurture them—and I would raise them.

My two sons were truly—The Blessings of The Father.

The End of Book Three

FINAL QUESTIONS

Will the boys find total happiness with their success?

Will Marc ever find the right woman who will bring with her—true love for him again?

Will Mar and Mal find their Golden Years in Las Vegas . . . Golden?

And is it likely that the new car will ever be for—Robbie?

Lastly—will someone ever succeed in shutting Larry up . . . and can we all wait to find out?

The boys will be back—watch for the next installment of the continuing saga of the Morgan family in—Blessings of The Father—Book Four—The Missing Piece.

Thank you friend for your read.

Mitch Reed

Please add me as a friend on facebook under Mitch Reed.

All email questions/comments welcomed on all social mediums, including at mitchreed@hotmail.com . . . *but you must put 'blessings' in your subject line on all correspondence to all sites, to identify you as a book fan.*